J K Davidson

A COLD WIND
FROM THE NORTH

AUSTIN MACAULEY PUBLISHERS™

LONDON • CAMBRIDGE • NEW YORK • SHARJAH

A CIP catalogue record for this title is available from the British
Library.

ISBN 9781398437074 (Paperback)
ISBN 9781398437081 (ePub e-book)

www.austinmacauley.com

First Published 2021
Austin Macauley Publishers Ltd
1 Canada Square
Canary Wharf
London
E14 5AA

Pronunciation and Language

British

The languages spoken at the time of this story were British and Ænglisc. We have no written record of British, but we do know that it was one parent of modern Welsh (the other being Latin). So I have asked modern Welsh and English to stand in for them. Welsh is strongly phonetic: what you see is what you get, most of the time. Quite unlike English which, being a tatterdemalion ragbag of a language, sets up more traps than the average rat-catcher. And of course there are regional accent and usage differences, in Wales just as much as anywhere.

Vowels

A sounds like a cross between the English bark and back.
E sounds like the English best.
I sounds like the English EE, as in the English between.
O tends to be short like the English god or boss.
U is pronounced like an English I, as in still or will, so Rhun is pronounced Rin.
W is an English OO sound as in moon, but short.
Y in Welsh is (mostly) pronounced like a short UH sound in RP English – a bit like the ER in Butter or Mugger, but short. Only when it appears at the end of a name does it acquire the English Y sound.
AE in Welsh is pronounced like the I in Mine.
EI sounds as a cross between the English care and lake.

They are written as separate characters, Welsh does not use diphthongs.

Consonants

Firstly: the Welsh alphabet has no J, K, Q, V, X or Z. It adds DD, FF, and one or two others we do not need to worry about here.

C is always hard like K.

CH is always a soft semi-gutteral for which there is no English equivalent. NOT like the CH in church, more like the Scots word Lo<u>ch</u>. And I don't mean 'lock', as most English people would pronounce it.

LL is well known to be impossible to pronounce unless you are born to it. There is absolutely no English equivalent – the nearest a Saesneg can get is the Scots soft CH (as above) followed by an L, but it is not gutteral.

D is D. DD is a hard TH, like Bro<u>th</u>er.

TH is a soft TH as in Bro<u>th.</u>

F sounds V in English, FF sounds the English F.

And don't forget to roll the Rs.

NOTE: There are no direct equivalents to Yes and No in modern Welsh; a question would be met with a negation of that question: "I will not; or, "I do not" for example; but modern Welsh does borrow, and slightly modify, Yes and No from the English, and so have I.

Tad and Mam are the Welsh for father and mother. Dad and Mum are Anglicisations thereof.

Saxon (English)

I have used the ancient spelling Ænglisc. The bulk of the new population were Ænglisc; the Saxons mostly occupying only those regions which, in some cases, still bear their name: Essex, Middlesex, Sussex and Wessex.

Æ is a diphthong, it is neither an A nor an E but something of both. It is subtle but not difficult.

People

Names underlined are historic characters and places, with some of whom, or which, I may have taken some liberties.

Rhun: a young man with much to learn.
Meical: his devoted friend.
Cwyfan: Rhun's father. A chieftain of Magonsæte.
Angharad: Rhun's mother, of patrician descent.
Gethin: family retainer who suffers Rhun gamely.
Ysgyrran: a big lad, finding his feet.
Cynrig: a romantic and no mean archer.
Eryl: as good with a sword as he is with a scythe.
Einion: captive of war, by no means as slow as he looks.
Ithwalh: the Saxon, deadly with a bow.
Llif: a fine bowman in the making.
Tecwyn: the runt but deadly with a sling.
Peleg: a sad loss.
Carwenna: Peleg's mother, an unsettling presence.
Talhaiarn: Meical's father, the village blacksmith.
Brother Cledwyn: a holy pragmatist.
Ecrig: a significant influence.
Cadwallon: king in Gwynedd.
Penda: Mercian noble – tipped to be king.
Merewalh: king in Magonsæte.
Edwin: king in Northumbria, with expansionist ideas.
Teifion: a friend in a dark place.
Balthazar: a man chancing his arm.
Qaseem: his muleteer.
Canthrig Bwt: a monster out of Welsh folklore, though possibly not contemporary.
Cathan: an unwelcome presence.
Afalach: apparently whatever he wants to be.
Dyfnwal: a wandering healer, according to himself.
Brynach: a holy man.
Elaeth: king in Lleyn.
Aelwen: Elaeth's queen.
Gwenifer: their daughter.
Afaon: Cynrig's father.
Gwrtheyrn: also known as Vortigern.
Myrddyn Emrys: also known as Merlin.

And some incidentals.

Places

Magonsæte: middle part of the Welsh border with England.
Wrœcensæte: northern part of the border. You can still visit the ruins of Wroxeter.
Ercyng: southern part of the border, now Archenfield.
Lenteurde: now Leintwardine.
River Lent: now River Teme.
Afon Hafren: River Severn.
Teifion's village: now Caersws. More or less. Once a Roman way-station.
Dinas Emrys: a ruin in Gwynedd.
Yr Wyddfa: still Yr Wyddfa – Snowdon.
Brynach's **Holy Place:** St Cybi's Well, a truly numinous place.
Trwyn Du: Penmon Priory, a ruin in Anglesey.
Tre'r Cyri: a massive hillfort in Lleyn.
Ynys Môn/Mona: Anglesey.
Ynys Manau: Isle of Man.

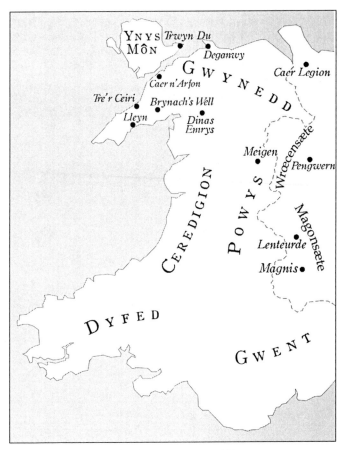

Rhun's Country c. 625 AD

This story is based in history. I am not an historian, but I have done my best, and I apologise to those who know better, for any errors I may have made. Likewise I apologise to my Welsh readers for any howlers I may have committed with their language, culture and history.

"Once it is grown, a bird cannot fall;
falling is, at worst, merely an unplanned descent."

Anon (to me)

Prologue

The storm had been building all day.

The air had grown thick and stuffy. The trees swayed sluggishly, stirred by small stifling breaths starkly different to what was threatened. High towers of cloud had built, darkening the day before its time.

A man toiled up the path through the woods. His clothing stuck clammily to him, and he gasped for breath in the close air.

As he left the trees, at last the storm broke into the waning light, and it boiled and raged, throwing its anger about freely, hammering blows onto the hills as if they were guilty of some outrage. Yet dry so far, holding the rain in reserve, perhaps, in case the noise of its fury should prove not impressive enough.

The man cast about; peering into the half-light of the exposed hill-top he wiped the sweat from his eyes. A jagged flash was followed at once by a mighty clap of thunder. It exploded into the gloom, as if in its madness it sought to rend the earth itself. And in that searing instant, he saw what he had come for.

A spectral figure, wild and wind-blown, stood silhouetted against the sky, his long robes thrashing about him as if they were possessed by demons. But he stood firm, immovable, defying the forces that would throw him down. Arms outstretched, he held his long staff up into the storm, as if he might challenge the very power of nature.

Our man strode up the slope and stopped.

'So it begins?' he shouted into the gale.

'It begins.'

'The Blessed Friend succeeds the Noble Peace – tcha! – I think not.'

'*Na*, there will be blood and death aplenty.'

They stood side by side and stared out into the storm.

And then the rain came.

And the two figures moved into the shelter of the trees, and dissolved into the shadows.

Chapter 1

Rhun ap Cwyfan ap Erthig rode quietly, following the track towards the river crossing. He rode easily, confident of himself and his mount, at home in this place. He could quote his ancestors all the way back to Macsen Wledig, but two generations were enough. They said who he was and that was all he asked of them. His own person could say the rest.

This was his fifteenth summer; he could at last begin to call himself a man. Recent months had been a turmoil of growing, all awkwardness and aching limbs, but it had settled now. He had yet to fill out, but at least he had stopped shooting upwards. His voice had also settled down, for the most part, and he was beginning to feel he belonged in this new adult form: well made and tall like his father. His most striking features were his fair hair and his clear blue eyes, both unusual among his people. He got them from his mother's side, so she said. She was dark herself but she claimed they came from her Frankish ancestry and for all he knew she was right. Yet combined with his height they made him a very much more imposing figure than he knew. And nothing so far had happened, worse than the usual scrapes of boyhood, to dent his youthful confidence.

He was hot and thirsty. At least under the trees it had been shady. Now that he was out in the open, the sun caught him fully, adding to the discomfort of his coarse-woven shirt, sweaty and soiled from the long day's hunting. High above, small clouds moved languidly across the sky; down here the air was still. The bird on his wrist fidgeted in the heat. He flicked his horse into a canter in search of any sort of a breeze.

They splashed across the stream where it widened to form the shallow crossing place, sending up a storm of spray, and the small brown fish darting to safety in the deeper water above the weir. This crossing was old even when his people first came here, used by travellers since it had been made in the golden age when the Empire still ruled these lands and built roads the better to control them.

He urged the horse across the narrow strip of flood-wash, up the steep bank on the far side and drew him to a stop on the crest. He twisted in the saddle and looked back to the river.

'Come along Gethin, do. We shall be late.'

'Yes, yes. I'm coming, aren't I?'

Rhun grinned. His companion bounced across the water on the back of his solid cob, clinging onto rein and saddle with one hand, the catch grasped in the other.

'Gods! I'll never make a horseman. Not as long as I live.'

Rhun turned back and looked ahead. For the last half-mile or so they had been out of the trees, crossing the fields his people had reclaimed and cleared three generations ago when they fled the great plague which had killed Maelgwn Gwynedd, their king, and so many of his people. They had struck east and south out of the high hills to forge a new home in this disputed country on the edge of things. They had found the ruins of an old town, a way-station on the old Roman road, a relic of times remembered now only in song.

Most was gone of the ancient works, but there were still signs if you knew where to look. Bits of wall and paving here and there, and the parts Rhun's people had reused. The strong place around his father's hall was built out of the ruins. Poised as they were between Powys and the new Ænglisc kingdom of Mercia to the east, they had been ignored by both, and had flourished. From the holding of one family had grown a village with several dozen houses, many boasting two storeys, and a scattering of serf hovels clinging like fungi and tumbling down towards the river. Beyond the fields were scattered the outlying farms of those who looked to Rhun's father for protection in times of danger.

The land rose gently from this side of the river. He could

see the smoke of the cook-fires, and the glow of warm gold as the last of the sun caught the thatched roofs of the taller houses. Now, away from the chatter of the river, he could hear the cattle lowing and the evening bustle as all was settled after the day. And it seemed too much. That was not the soft grumbling of the evening milking. The cattle were disturbed and surely the bustle was livelier than was usual.

Rhun kicked his horse into a canter. 'Something's not right, Gethin – catch me up when you can!' Horse and rider, attached only by the grip of his knees, flowed as if they were one thing, the urgency passing freely from boy to horse. He heard a great shout go up and the harsh ringing clash of steel on steel. Attack! He urged his horse to greater speed. Not Ænglisc, surely – his people had been at peace with their Mercian neighbours for as long as he could remember. But if not Ænglisc then Britons – but from where? Direct attack was not the way of the usual raiders from the hill country. He urged his horse to greater effort, scattering anything in his way as he hammered up the broad street, people staring out in fear from the shops and workshops as he passed. Deftly he moved the reins to his left hand and drew the long sword from the scabbard fixed to the saddle by his knee. And then he was on them. A seething mass of men, armed to the teeth, some with a long sword like his own, all with shield and spear.

He took in the scene with a single glance. In the same instant he drew sharply on the reins, heaving the horse into a sliding, scrabbling halt. By a hair's breadth he missed careering into the backs of the crowd. His horse stopped but he carried on, crashing to the ground, a tangle of stunned boy, sword and angry hawk.

'Gods, boy! What are you doing?'

The crowd parted and let through a man very clearly in charge. Tall, dark and angry. 'We have important guests and you come piling in as if to murder them all?'

'I'm sorry father, I ... I thought you were under attack.'

'So you were going to beat them off single-handed, were you? Idiot boy – sort yourself out and get inside. Look at you

– you're a disgrace.' He turned back to the crowd. 'I am sorry, my lords, he is young…'

He let the remark hang in the air. Suddenly, a man laughed and the tension drained out of the moment. His father moved away, drawing the bulk of the crowd with him.

Scarlet with embarrassment, Rhun scrambled to his feet, trying the while to soothe his irate hawk; so long as he kept a hold of the jesses, the bird could not escape, but it was doing its best. Just as well, for it turned the shock of his arrival into an entertainment. Several men began to offer advice, and a small discussion broke out among them as to what best to do with a bird in these circumstances. Rhun grabbed the chance to recover his sword and his horse, and gather his hawk and his wits.

'Excuse me – please.' He slunk away, utterly crushed, back the way he had come, the men's laughter ringing round his pride.

As he led his horse away from the crowd, Gethin rode up to meet him.

'Well – you *will* rush in without thinking – how often have I told you?'

'He called me an idiot – in front of all those people! He didn't have to humiliate me!'

'Humiliate, is it? Climb down, boy! Thank the gods you saw your error in time, you'd likely be dead otherwise.'

Rhun glared at him.

'Look, Rhun – you're an untried boy, like it or not. For all I've taught you, you've little skill in arms, and they were seasoned fighting men. Are you mad?'

'You'll never think I'm ready!'

'Now you're being stupid as well as reckless. Well – I'm for the kitchen with this lot – I'll see you when you've calmed down.'

Rhun looked up at him, still seething. Gethin. Part body servant, part tutor. It was Gethin's task to train Rhun for manhood – to bear arms and, in due time, to take his place beside his father. But Gethin was also his friend. And he was right. Rhun kicked at a turf as if to blame it.

'*Na*. I know. Look – I'm sorry, but it all seemed so clear...'

'That's better! You've some sense, it seems. But clear or not, best not test the depth of the stream with both feet, eh?'

'*Na*,' Rhun said quietly.

'Come on then, cheer up. You didn't drown this time. Let's get ourselves in, you've not much time.'

An hour later Rhun made his way to the hall, a quite different figure from that he had been earlier. Clean now. His hair was combed severely into some sort of control, and he wore a fine undyed shirt trimmed with green ribbon, and soft leather breeches.

Now he was no longer a boy he was expected to attend table alongside his father, and tonight would be a feast in honour of their guests. All the freemen would be there and his father would count it a great occasion. Rhun was dreading it. Embarrassment was new to him and not something he wanted to repeat. But there was no way out of it: he would have to sit and risk their laughter and hope to avoid further attention.

Twitching aside the heavy curtain he walked into the great room, unusually bright this evening with oil lamps and a rare wealth of candles; not just the usual stinking tallow this evening, some were even of beeswax, but all adding to the heat and light of the long pit-fire. Around three sides were set benches and tables facing into the centre. Above his head the room towered into smoky-timbered dimness; beneath his feet fresh rushes were strewn onto the packed earth. If tonight was up to form they would have to be changed in the morning, he thought absently. Every bench was filled with people. Guests and hosts all jumbled up, except at the high table where sat his father and his visitor, surrounded by the great men of their houses, and an empty chair waiting for him. He breathed a small sigh of relief – at least it was not right beside his father. And he need not have worried: no one noticed him amid the noise and bustle. He saw Gethin laughing with friends but he didn't even try to catch Gethin's eye. He gathered himself and made his way forward, his reluctance mixed evenly with his curiosity to learn who this guest might be.

As he approached, his father's voice rose above the hubbub.

'Ah, Rhun my boy, come. My lord, here is my son – you met him earlier you'll recall. Rhun, meet my lord Cadwallon, Brenin Gwynedd.'

Rhun stopped, acutely aware of every eye on him. The man turned. They examined each other. *So this is the King of Gwynedd,* Rhun thought – *well, you'd never know it from his clothes.* Rhun wore a heavy brooch with pride, his only piece of gold, but this man wore no finery, no gold, no crown. He bore no outward sign of nobility. And yet, Rhun had to concede, no one would doubt his authority or misjudge his power. Cloud-grey eyes devoid of expression held Rhun. They seemed to pierce him to his very soul and he felt naked and small before that hard gaze; a thing of no account and yet one being judged. It can only have lasted a second or so but it felt like eternity. And then the man smiled and the tension was gone, run away like oil off a hot skillet.

'Rhun, is it? A royal name indeed. My grandfather bore it and you do honour to it and to him. I hope your father is proud of you – it was a brave thing you did today even if in error. I value courage.' He held Rhun's eyes a moment longer then turned away and spoke to his host. 'Though, in truth, I usually prefer it with at least some sense of caution!' The two men laughed and the talk moved on, and he was released. Dazed, Rhun slipped into his seat, happy to use his mother as a shield between himself and his father. She patted his hand in her usual absent manner. She loved him, of course, but more as a symbol than a real thing. They had not been close since he ceased to be a child, and though she clearly felt she should give him some support, she had little notion of what would serve.

'It was a good thing you did, my boy, but do take care, won't you?' she said, and felt that was enough. He fumbled for his knife, keeping his head down, hiding in silence. His favourite dog stuck its nose into his lap. Its foot caught his own and he winced as the claw dug into his skin, letting out a small cry quickly smothered. 'Ow! Saeth! – mind yourself, you great lump,' he muttered. But not in anger, it was a welcome diversion to fill the waiting before the food arrived. Anything but face that crowd, for all the King's words, and the dog gave him the perfect excuse to duck his head without inviting comment. But when the food did arrive Rhun tucked in gratefully. He was ravenous after the day's hunting.

'You got away with it, then.'

Rhun started. It was the man on his left who had spoken. He steeled himself for whatever was to come, and turned. The man was watching him closely. 'I'm sorry – I am Penda. I am here with Cadwallon's party,' he said.

He was young. A few years older than Rhun, maybe four or five, but no more; dark, solid and tough. He had a quiet confidence and an air of authority well beyond his years. Rhun liked him immediately. His fear of ridicule was suddenly forgotten.

He put down his knife and grasped the proffered hand. 'I'm Rhun ap Cwyfan.'

'Yes, I know – you are famous today.' There was laughter in his voice but it bore no mockery. 'And you have earned approval from the king. That is good – he is not much given to words of praise.' He sounded strange as he spoke, as if the language was foreign to him, well known yet not his own, but he had a way about him that made him easy to talk with. So much so that Rhun found himself speaking as if to an old friend.

'I was expecting a roasting. I'm not sure my father will forgive me as quickly.'

'*Na*, courage is always good to see.'

'But I just dashed in. He was right, it was plain stupid. Gethin told me but I didn't listen.'

'Gethin sounds sensible – who is he?'

'Oh, he keeps an eye on me for my father. That's him down yonder with the big laugh.'

'Well you should listen to him. You get cowardice for life, but you can learn not to be stupid.'

'Tell me about your lord. I've never met him, at least, not properly. What brings him to Magonsæte?'

Rhun had been a child the last time he had seen Cadwallon, far too young to be brought out and shown off. Despite that, it was an occasion burned on his memory. And it was a memory of evil. Oh, not of Cadwallon, who had been only young himself, but of the one with whom he had come. Edwin of Deira, an Ænglisc king in exile from the north. He would never forget Edwin. It had been the first time he had seen an act of deliberate cruelty. A shameful, spiteful act against one who could not defend himself. While others saw only his ready smile and glib confidence, with the eyes of a child Rhun had seen Edwin for what he truly was. And the more spiteful for having been observed.

'Oh, Cadwallon is not my lord, I just follow him for the time being. On loan, you might say.' Penda laughed, and as he did, he seemed suddenly lit from within. It warmed the otherwise serious face. 'No. I'm not of Gwynedd, I am Ænglisc in case you hadn't guessed – from Mercia. My people have land there, but I am a guest of my lord Cadwallon. It keeps me out of the way.'

Rhun was not sure what to say. Out of the way of what? Or of whom? Here his people lived amicably alongside Ænglisc settlers. They were nothing new; many had been here for as long as his own people, longer. There were several families in the village and as things stood there was enough land for all among these hills. For sure there was no quarrel about occupying these old ruins: many Ænglisc feared and avoided all things Roman. Puzzling. But he put the thought aside, remembering his duty as host.

'I speak your tongue well, if it would be easier.'

'That is very gracious of you, Rhun, but I have not lived at the court of Gwynedd without learning the language – though I fear my accent will never be good. Yours is a hard tongue for an Ængel to master.'

Then he seemed to come to a decision.

'As for why we are here...' He looked Rhun over, as if appraising his quality, as one might with a sheep or a cow at market. Rhun felt the gaze and to his surprise he found himself wanting to appear grown up and capable in the eyes of this strange young Ængel. He sat up and squared his shoulders.

'How much do you know of Northumbria?'

'Northumbria? Not much, except that it's a kingdom somewhere in the north. Oh, far away I believe.'

'A kingdom in the north it is indeed, and far away it may be, but not far enough, I fear. Æthelfrith made it in our fathers' time and it nearly destroyed us – it is a long story but, put briefly, he started by consuming his neighbours and moved on from there. His closest neighbour was a land called Deira which had a new king just come to his throne – Edwin – still just a boy really. Well, by the skin of his teeth he escaped and fled into exile, ending up in Gwynedd. But as long as he lived, Æthelfrith saw him as a threat, so at last he came looking for him – it was years ago now, I was only a boy myself at the time. Our people formed an alliance to fight him off. Cadfan – that was Cadwallon's father you know – Selyf of Powys, my own lord Cearl, they were all there. There was a big battle up at Chester – Cær Legion as you call it – and it was a massacre. He nearly destroyed us. Gwynedd and Mercia survived but Powys was smashed and has still not recovered. Æthelfrith had the whole region in his grasp and he would have overrun it, but by some chance he was called away back north and never came again. And then he died, a year or two past, and now Edwin is king in his place and it seems he has similar ambitions, possibly greater. Alas, it seems Cearl will not help, but perhaps his borderers will. Cadwallon has been in Wrœcensæte at Pengwern to see if Elisedd is ready to fight should the need arise. We are visiting you on our way to Lene to ask your new king Merewalh the same question.'

'Fight? But Edwin – he is a friend of your lord's, isn't he? I remember him – he came here with Cadwallon when I was little.'

'Friend? Hah!' Penda looked bitter. 'He lived among us when he fled from Æthelfrith, but I'm afraid his ambitions override any friendships – he has friends only as long as he needs them, that one. They say he is much loved at home, but then he is no fool after all, so perhaps he has given them good cause. Oh yes, it'll be war, and soon I'm thinking.' He looked into the fire for a long moment, his mind wandering far away. Suddenly he shivered despite the heat and was back again. He clapped Rhun on the back. 'But I am spoiling your food! Don't you worry, young Rhun, your people and mine have stood side by side in battle before now, and won. We honour our friendships.'

Penda took a deep draft from his horn, as if in toast. They were interrupted by the arrival of more food, and all talk ended for a while.

Rhun looked around as he ate. The people were happy, talking, laughing. There was no sign of unrest or apprehension, no premonition of war. He realized that Penda had done him an honour – he was among the first to know.

Again Penda's voice cut across his thoughts.

'But tell me, how did you manage to keep hold of your bird? This hunting with birds – it is an art few of my people know.'

Rhun had learned the skills of hawking as a child. His people had always known them so far as he was aware. Rhun loved the sport and Penda got the full blast of the enthusiast. It had been a genuine enquiry, but Penda still found himself more interested in the teller than the tale. He listened with only half an ear as he watched this newly formed young man. He had not been wrong. Here was someone without side, someone who kept no part of himself hidden. Penda felt sure that if this boy gave his word it would be honoured above all risk or danger. *This is one I would have as a friend – I pity the man who makes an enemy of him. He would love and hate with equal passion. We are very alike*, Penda thought ruefully. *But he is untried – how will this shining thing do in the face of darkness, I wonder?*

His thoughts were broken by a loud shout. Rhun fell

silent. It seemed there was to be entertainment. Cwyfan's place was neither big nor important. It rarely saw much entertainment that was not home-made, but on this night they were lucky. Also on his way to Merewalh's new court at Lene, a bard was staying some while so that he should not arrive unprepared. He had refused to perform so far, keeping himself to himself, but clearly he thought the King of Gwynedd was worth the effort. People sat back with full cups and full bellies, prepared to be amazed or be frightened or just made to laugh. Rhun was no musician, his skills lay with making and doing, but he loved to listen, and a bard was a rare and precious thing. This one was ordinary enough at first glance, but Rhun saw now that his face was lined and tanned as if from much travel in hotter lands than these. He took his seat by the fire and his harp from the small boy who was his servant. He plucked a few notes and all who heard were at once in his thrall. His voice was rich and strong, filling the room, and it seemed that he was no court bard, bound only to sing of lofty things, instead he held them spellbound with tales of adventure and love and high deeds.

Rhun was aroused and lulled in turn, enraptured throughout. As the last notes faded too soon into silence they were answered by a great cry of applause. The people were on their feet clapping, calling for more and telling each other how good he had been, comforted and gladdened by his skill.

But he was an old hand at this game; always leave them wanting more, it was an axiom of his trade. Yet he stood and was honoured to receive the gifts of thanks from Cwyfan. And, as if it had been a sign, house-slaves appeared and began to clear the tables and benches, and the party broke up, some to their homes and some to the guest houses.

'It has been good to talk with you, Rhun ap Cwyfan,' said Penda. 'We must not let this acquaintance wither. Perhaps we shall meet again in the morning and you can introduce me to your hawk?'

'Gladly,' said Rhun.

As they parted he thought – *I gave him my full name and*

he has used it, yet he has never given me his own. I wonder why.

But he was not to sleep just yet. As he left the hall his father met him.

'Come, Rhun, we must talk.'

Now I'm for it, he thought, *now comes the roasting.* He loved his father and honoured him but he was new to adulthood and was unsure of his ground. His earlier nervousness returned. Cwyfan was forthright and just, but he had high expectations of his son and Rhun knew he should look for no soft treatment. He deserved none. He had made a fool of himself and should expect the consequences. But part of him still felt it unjust, as if he should be forgiven by right of childhood, still uncertain of what was trivial and what was enormity. Cwyfan drew him away from the mill at the door. This was unusual: his father was also a spontaneous man – he did not hold his dressings-down in secret.

Night had fallen, still warm but clear, the sky ablaze with stars, and the fresh air was good after the smoky atmosphere of the hall. They crossed the compound, heading for the chapel.

The chapel was modest, just big enough to hold such of them as were Christian. Only the floor was stone; the rest, like the hall, was timber, yet it was solid and well made: a simple building, plain and unadorned. The only concessions to furnishing were the altar and a few simple seats placed against the walls, put there that the elderly and infirm might worship in some comfort. The place was deserted and deep in quiet. A lone candle burned on the altar casting small light but deep shadow; sweet beeswax, not like the acrid rush lights he was used to. Cwyfan used it to light another which he took to one side.

'Come boy, sit.'

Rhun perched uncomfortably on the edge of the bench.

'Oh, relax – you're not here for punishment. What you did today was a fine thing and I'm proud of you. No, we have more important things to discuss, and this place is at least private. What I have to tell you is not a secret but it would be helpful if not too many people knew of it just yet.'

Rhun was immediately intrigued. He settled into his seat, trying to look intelligent and awake.

'I saw you were talking a lot with young Penda while we were at table. What did you make of him?'

'I liked him. Who is he? I mean, I know he is Ænglisc – his accent would have told me that if he hadn't himself – but what is he to do with Cadwallon?'

'What else did he tell you?'

'He said he was from Mercia but, apart from that, almost nothing. He said he was a guest at the court of Gwynedd. Not of his own will I thought, though he didn't say so – is he in exile? He is surely no prisoner.'

Cwyfan sat and looked into the flame for a while. He seemed to be gathering his thoughts. Rhun said nothing.

'Did he say anything else?'

'He told me to expect war from Edwin of Northumbria, but he didn't say how he knew. He told me something of a big battle at Cær Legion, years ago before I was born, but that was all. Were you there father?'

'I was, with my own father. It was a terrible day, I would as soon not remember. And I fear Penda is right. That Edwin is hungry for territory and power. He has ambition and that is dangerous to all. He came here once – you'll not remember I expect, you were only small.'

'*Na*, I remember him. He was a cruel man.'

'Why do you say cruel? Dishonourable, duplicitous, yes – they call him Edwin Two Face – but I hadn't heard that he was cruel. His own people love him, I'm told.'

'I had a little cat. He killed it.' Rhun whispered it, almost afraid to remember. 'He was teasing it and it bit his hand. He wrung its neck and threw it away like a piece of rubbish.'

Cwyfan was astonished.

'What?'

'I didn't tell anyone. He didn't think he had been seen but when he saw me watching – the way he looked at me – I was frightened. It has stayed with me, I don't know why. It seems such a small thing now.'

Cwyfan was at a loss; what was the boy blathering about?

'Never mind that – we were speaking of fighting – of war! Be sure, boy, if Edwin comes to trouble us here we will fight him, of that you can be certain.'

He paused to make sure this had sunk in.

'Which is what I want to talk to you about – leave such childish things and pay attention. Edwin's ambitions already threaten Cadwallon. They were friends once, it is true but that now means nothing it seems. *Na*, Edwin has got it into his head that he should be Gwledig, and not just among the Ænglisc but the whole of Prydein and that includes all of us. Cadwallon is Brenin in Gwynedd as you know, but Edwin was Cadfan's foster son and is the older. That is his claim and not unreasonable, you might think, but it is a delusion – it is for the kindred to choose who will lead, it is not a right.'

Cwyfan fell silent awhile. Then he sighed and continued.

'But that means nothing either. It seems he will have it at any cost. He has annexed the lands of the Lune, north above Mersey – way beyond Wrœcensæte, and now we have news that he is in Ynys Manaw. Cadwallon is concerned for the safety of Gwynedd – and if he falls so may we all. The men of Powys will help, of course, at least those of Pengwern and Wrœcensæte, but they are much diminished since Cær Legion, and the hill folk are far too busy squabbling amongst themselves, when they are not stealing our cattle.' He paused. 'Now, Rhun, I want you to know that if I am called to war, you will assume command here, so forget about cats and listen.'

'But father, I want to go with you!'

'I'm sure you do, but no argument. I will not take us both to possible death and leave this place undefended. You may still be beardless but you are no longer a boy. You are my only son so you get the land, as is the law, and I'm thinking – though nothing is certain in this world – if the elders are put to it there is no one else they would choose to lead the people. *Na* – you are grown up now, you will stay here. Be worthy!'

Rhun held his breath to keep his tongue still. He knew his father. Better to say nothing.

'But I am sorry, I did not answer your question. No, Penda is not in exile, yet there is more to your new friend than you might think. Do not be fooled by his youth, though he has a few years on you I think – he is already tested in battle and not found wanting. Perhaps too much so since it seems that his king prefers him out of the way. But Cearl is old and if I am any judge Penda will take the crown when he goes. And it is in my mind that he will make a better job of it than has Cearl. It is well he liked you – look to him if you are in need.'

'Penda will be king in Mercia? I didn't know.' Rhun was surprised. Penda had given no hint of it.

'*Ie*, it is certain I am thinking. There are those who would wish it otherwise and he may not be of the blood but he is a leader, make no doubt.'

Rhun didn't. From the little he had learned at dinner, he was well able to believe it. Perhaps, somehow, that explained why Penda hadn't given his father's name when he introduced himself, but it was still odd.

'But king or not, you may be sure he will not want Edwin as overlord. Well, we are not yet come to such a pass and maybe we shall not. You may rest easy for now.' He stretched his long arms and yawned. 'Indeed it is time we were both at rest. Come, your mother will be wondering what I have done with you.'

He blew out their candle and they left the chapel to its shadows, and the lone altar-flame to burn its quiet midnight vigil.

Chapter 2

The sun rose on a courtyard busy with the preparations for departure. Though still early, already the air was warming for another hot day. There was much to do, for it was a fair way to Lene and a party this size would move slowly and might well have to spend a night on the way if they ran into trouble. Even using the old Roman road was no guarantee of speed, so much of it was in decay. No one expected trouble, tucked as they were into the shadow of Mercia, but there was still some difficult country to get through and the party would need provision for the unexpected. With nothing to do but get in the way, Rhun took refuge in the mews.

The place was quiet and only dimly lit from the heavily slatted windows, made more to allow air into the place than light. The birds sat quietly on their perches, not long settled from their breakfast. Rhun didn't disturb them but made his way to the little workshop at the back with its own much larger window looking out over the water meadow and the hills to the west. Even this early, with the shutters down it let in all the light needed, but this place would stay cool until noon when the sun got round. On a bench were scattered an assortment of tools, bits of leather, feathers and all the odd things which a craftsman collects for his work.

And there Penda found him.

'Good morning. You too are keeping out of the way, I see,' he said.

'Oh, excuse me, my lord, I must just tie this off,' Rhun mumbled. Busy with his work, he did not see the look of surprise on his visitor's face. Penda stood quietly and watched the boy's deft fingers as he teased the makings of something into place, holding a loose end in his teeth.

At last he looked up. 'There, that's done.'

'Why "my lord"? I did not tell you anything but my name.'

'Oh, I'm sorry, my lord, my father told me something of you last night.'

'Well, whatever he said, I am not your lord, nor anyone's lord as things stand. I told you my name and you should use it. How can I make you a friend if we are to stand on ceremony? So tell me, what is that thing you have just made?'

'Oh, this is a lure. We use it for getting the bird back after it has flown – see, we tie a bit of meat in here. They get in a bit of a mess after a while. It's not very good, I'm afraid. Gethin makes a much better one, but he is busy helping with the preparations. I suppose you saw?'

'Yes, they swarm like ants, we're much safer here for an hour or so. Will you show me your hawk?'

Rhun put down his new lure. He acknowledged the attempt to sidetrack him, but his curiosity was strong. He looked at Penda. Not of the blood, his father had said, so what did that mean? Dare he ask? But 'friend' Penda had said, so, as a friend, he took the risk. 'If you will tell me how things stand that mean you are not anyone's lord?'

Penda smiled. *I was not wrong last night about this boy,* he thought. *He is not afraid to be bold. I was right to trust him.*

'Ah, that question. Well, young Rhun, it is not so hard to grasp, and certainly no secret. The truth is that I am not quite as Ænglisc as my people would like. My mother was a Wealas woman – I'm sorry, that is not a kind name, I should say she was a Briton – and any lands I hold have come from her. That is bad enough; but worse, I fear, is that I cannot trace my ancestors back to Woden like a good Ængliscman should, because I do not know where to start. Except that he was Ænglisc, I know nothing of my father. Oh, our peoples have married each other for generations and nobody really minds it now, but when you combine that with an unknown father, well – you see the problem, perhaps. I am master in my own home, of course, but I must work extra hard to gain the respect of those who should be my equals.'

'But you are a great commander. My father told me.'

'He does me over-much honour – I would not use the word "great", but then nor should any man of himself. It is true that I have had some success recently against Cynegil's people in the south, but that does not make me great. Perhaps it only makes me lucky.'

Rhun made no reply for a moment. He had his answer. Then he grinned widely and said, 'Come and meet my hawk. She's forgiven me by now, I hope.'

Cadwallon's party rode out within the hour, setting their faces south. Penda had made a last farewell. Leaning down from the saddle he had said quietly, 'Remember, young Rhun, I would be your friend not your lord. Do not forget that when we meet again.'

Rhun stood with his father at the gate and watched them ride out over the river crossing. So far the day was fine but things had changed since dawn, and if the clouds building in the west brought the rain they threatened, the broken places would turn to sticky, clinging mud, and they would have hard going.

'Will they come back this way, father?"

'It is not likely. Merewalh is the last one to consult. Cadwallon will return by a speedier route.'

The year waned and no news came from the north or south. If Cadwallon's visit to Merewalh had produced the result he had hoped for, they were not to know. Life returned to normal.

It was a good harvest and the people celebrated in their various ways, but then the serious work of preparing for winter kept everyone hard at it and Rhun had little time to think of abstract things like wars in far away places, nor the people who fought them. Then at Michaelmas the first snow came, and though it didn't last, it foretold hard times ahead. With the cold come this early there was a real danger that wolves would not be far behind it. The defences made by the Romans around the camp to guard the crossing place were still substantial, though the breastwork had gone long,

long ago. The bank was still high but it was old, and failing in places where rabbits and even badgers had dug their tunnels, and every year it got worse. Rhun and his father worked alongside the men, mending the fences and rebuilding the bank where it had collapsed. And just in time, for it seemed that they had only just finished when the snow came in earnest. The work on the farm was brought to a halt but there was never a shortage of things to do. For Rhun, at least, the snow meant he could concentrate on his training. Practise at arms, practise at law, practise at all the things he would need to know if he was to be chosen after his father. He thought often then of Penda and of how things were with him. For such a brief encounter, it had made a very deep impression, and now he felt alone in a way he had not before.

The days shortened. The turn of the year drew nearer. Rhun came in from the fields, marrow cold as darkness fell. They hadn't seen the sun for days. The constant chill blowing down from the north was merciless, and the sky hung low like an old grey blanket, filled with the threat of yet more snow. He passed the forge on his way up the street. The heat and glow beckoned.

The blacksmith was not there, but his son was busy at something behind the forge. 'Hello, Meical,' Rhun said. The blacksmith's son was almost his age, they had known each other since they could walk. The village boys had always tangled together as children, scrapping amongst themselves, bouncing from love to hate and back again, as children do, but as they had grown the differences in their status had begun to show and their relationships had altered subtly. Yet Rhun still looked on them as friends, and Meical more than most. He supposed the same was true for the other boy. Seeing Meical now at work, he realized that he had never given it any thought. They had known each other in an easy, uncomplicated way, and not looked further.

'Rhun – good. Give me a hand here, would you?' Meical was bent over the bellows. 'You're good at this sort of thing. I'm trying to fix this – my father has a big job on with old

Clydai's plough. They're off to fetch it now.' He showed Rhun the hole where years of work had finally worn the leather thin. It had dried, and cracked along a fold.

'Let's see,' Rhun said. Together they examined the problem. 'Well, you're going to need a patch and I suppose it had better be hide – can't do this with thin stuff. I've got some over in the workshop. Give me a moment and I'll fetch it. We're going to have to unpin it at the top but with luck we can fix it before your father gets in.'

But, when he got back Meical's father had already come in. The broken plough sat forlorn in front of the forge. 'He shouldn't have asked you – I left him the job to do.'

'I'd like to help. Honestly – it's no problem.'

The blacksmith sighed. He stood back. 'Call me when it's done,' he said and went out the back.

'Is it all right?' Rhun asked in a whisper.

Meical looked up, a strange expression on his face. He seemed in doubt as to what to say.

'Yes. Yes, it is really,' he said. He hesitated and then went on, 'He would be happier if I was more like you – you know – good at things.'

Rhun was lost for words. It had never occurred to him that all boys were not like him. Surely everyone could do things like this. It never struck him that Meical had asked his opinion because he didn't know himself. To cover his confusion he took refuge in the work.

'Look, you hold this as flat as you can while I get some stitches in,' he said, and the embarrassing moment passed. The work was soon done. Meical called his father. He looked at the bellows and grunted his approval.

'I'd better go,' said Rhun.

'I thank you for your help,' the blacksmith said. His voice held a strange tone which puzzled Rhun, but he said nothing.

That evening he asked Gethin. 'You know everyone,' he said, 'what's wrong between Talhaiarn and Meical?'

'Ah, that one.' He took a pull from the horn of ale he was drinking. 'Well, it's not so hard to see. Every man needs a son to pass his skills onto, for what else is your own training? But I fear Talhaiarn feels he doesn't have the right sort of son. Young Meical takes after his mother, I reckon. He can't see his way into the work. He's willing enough but, well – if you don't get it, then you don't.'

'What of his mother? She died a long time ago, didn't she?'

Gethin sat back, his gaze in the fire.

'Oh, many years now.' He lowered his voice. 'Of course, they do say she didn't die but went back to her people, that she was of the Twylwth Teg and was summoned home, but that's just talk. Mind you, she was a wild one – when she were young. All the young men fancied her, but she wouldn't have 'em. When Talhaiarn tamed her he reckoned he'd got a good bargain. She was forever full of song and fancies, was canny in her way, and there you have it. There's the problem. He reckons young Meical takes after her. He can't seem able to get at the work. Head elsewhere, like. Talhaiarn don't say as much but I know he believes it. Oh, he loves the boy well enough but he's no use to him. Meical is very handy around the place but he needs an apprentice, see, and no time now to grow another. For sure, there's none in the village that can be spared.'

'But I thought the Færy Folk couldn't stand the touch of iron,' said Rhun.

'Well there you have it, see.'

Rhun shivered. The Twylwth Teg, the Good Folk, Færy. You didn't speak of them but everyone knew who they were. Everyone had heard the stories. Everyone knew someone who knew someone who had met one on a dark night, or some such. He had never seen any himself, of course. But now it seemed he might actually know one – be friends, even. He found the idea strangely exciting.

'Na,' he said, 'He can't be. Not Meical. He's too – too ordinary. Isn't he?'

He took to spending time in the forge. It was a refuge from the cold, of course, but he was intrigued by the blacksmith and his work. Rhun could make things from wood and leather, and make them well; he understood the skill of making, yet the working of metal was a powerful magic which Rhun did not understand, and he was fascinated. And this story of Meical's mother just added to the appeal.

Then came a day when Cwyfan called him to the armoury. The weapons needed regular attention. There had always been raids from across the western hills, raids for cattle and goods, but there had been none now for several years; the preparations for winter had brought their usual distraction and the weapon store had been neglected. Now, with even the vaguest threat of real war, they needed a thorough going over. Rhun was delighted that his father had asked him: another mark of adulthood. They inspected all the stored weapons, and set aside those which needed attention. By and large the metal work was in good condition; greased and wrapped, it had not suffered. Mostly it was perishables that had, like bow strings and the slingshot leather so loved by rats in need of a snack and drawn by the goose grease, but there was a good lot of arrows in need of new fletchings and a number which either needed re-pointing or had lost their heads altogether. This was metalwork on a fine level.

Rhun took a bundle down to the forge. 'We need to fix these,' he said.

The smith set down the thing he had been working on. It had been a hinge, as Rhun would recall forever, as he would all the events of that day.

'Arrow-heads is it? This is a skill all warriors need,' said Talhaiarn. 'Perhaps you would like to learn the way of it?'

Strange question, he thought. 'I should think I do,' he said.

Meical took to the bellows and fired up the forge, and then joined Rhun to watch over his shoulder. He didn't question that his father would teach Rhun first. Though a blacksmith's son should know the skill just as well, Rhun would be the warrior, not he.

'Now, this is not heavy work like plough shares, this needs

a light touch.' Talhaiarn's voice was solemn, with a hint of the craftsman not expecting much from his audience.

Together the two boys watched as Talhaiarn took an arrowhead in his tongs and thrust it into the heart of the fire. They watched it for a while until it glowed red, then white, in the coals, and then he took it and gently remade the tip where it had broken off, using only the lightest hammer. Then he plunged it into the water bucket to harden the work.

'Here, have a go yourself,' Talhaiarn said, taking up a second arrowhead. Rhun never really understood why, but instead of taking the piece, he passed it to Meical. Perhaps it was a test – did Meical really take after his mother? He knew it was silly – he had seen Meical handling metal often enough, but perhaps working it would be different?

Meical looked at him, with a strange expression on his face. He took a gulp of air and turned to his father, 'Could we watch you do another one first? I – I'd like to be sure.'

Talhaiarn said nothing, but the room brimmed with his unspoken words. He mended another one. Then he handed the next to his son. His face said it all: there was no need of talk.

Rhun held his breath and watched closely as Meical took hold of the tongs. The air crackled with the tension, but the only sounds were the slight hiss of the flame and the small rustlings of unseen things in the dark corners of the forge.

Meical held the tongs and thrust the arrowhead into the white heart of the fire, just as he had seen his father do. He watched it anxiously, not daring to take his eyes off it. Rhun watched Meical every bit as anxiously. Would he melt? Turn to stone? Either seemed horribly possible. But Meical gripped the iron tongs and it seemed not. They watched together as the metal heated. After a while it looked right. He took it out and tried to remember what his father had done. He took a few tentative taps, and suddenly it seemed to him that he was taken over by a force greater than himself. Something beyond his control seemed to command his hands and, as he watched, amazed, they made a new arrowhead just as his father had done.

He looked up, his excitement glowing enough to match the forge. 'Give me another,' he said, his voice small and tight.

In silence his father handed him a second arrow, not sure he believed what he had just seen. He glanced at Rhun who caught the hint and took to the bellows without question. The fire spat and glared. Meical made another. And another. He stood with an idiotic grin on his face, his eyes shining, dancing in the firelight. 'I can do it,' he said simply. 'I can do it!'

No one spoke. It did not need words. Meical had found his way into his father's world. It had not been spectacular, but a great thing had happened, and, in truth, Rhun was more relieved than disappointed.

Chapter 3

The turn of the year came amid much jollity and good cheer. The womenfolk had made their usual efforts and both the chapel and the hall were hung deep with holly and ivy. Many attended the service in Brother Cledwyn's chapel, others made their own arrangements, though they did it quietly out of deference to the priest. But even of those who were Christian, plenty saw no reason to ignore the old gods just because Brother Cledwyn claimed they did not exist.

'I can't say I really approve of all this greenery about the place,' he said, 'but it keeps the waverers happy.' The bishop would not approve either, but he was far away and Cledwyn was a kindly man, not so pious that he could not understand the frailties of others.

It was approaching Candlemas when a lone rider came, tired and mud-bespattered, hammering down the old road from the north where, far away beyond the horizon, the big hills, still snow-capped, leaned down to hug it close. Lambing time was upon them and the people were busy in the folds. No one could be spared from the lambing. Sheep are not generally very bright and there were many ewes that found themselves in difficulties. Rhun was down by the river trying to persuade one that the water was not a good place to give birth, when he heard the distant sound of a horn followed by the beat of iron-shod hooves ringing on the still hard ground.

'Horses!' he shouted. 'Horses coming.' The sheep complained bitterly and fought with him, but he managed to drag her to safety. Once free, he climbed onto a stack of hurdles set by to make pens, straining to see across the great meadow.

'*Na*, one horse alone, if I'm any judge.'

Few travelled at this time of the year and he wondered at a man travelling alone, for to be alone was to be in peril even in summer. To do so this early in the year his need must be great.

'Come on, Gethin, we must greet him.' He ran to the north gate and met the man as he reined in hard at the barrier.

'Is this the place of Cwyfan ap Erthig?'

'It is, sir, and you are welcome.'

'Thank the gods! Is he within?'

'He is, sir, let me take you to him. Gethin, will you take our visitor's horse to the stable and find someone to tend to him?'

Gethin said nothing but nodded and led the horse across the yard to the stables.

The rider watched him go.

'You will be Cwyfan's boy. Rhun, is it?'

'You know of me sir?' Rhun was astonished. And secretly delighted.

'My lord Cadwallon speaks highly of you.' He smiled. *You could scarcely be anyone else,* he thought, *unless Cwyfan has more like you.* But he kept the thought to himself. 'Indeed I am glad it is you who met me, otherwise I should have had to seek you out. My lord bids me remind you of the need for circumspection. I have no idea what he meant by it, but I suppose you do?'

Rhun looked flustered but was relieved of his confusion by his father's shout from across the compound.

'Will you stand there all day, boy? Bring our guest in.'

The man grinned at Rhun as if in conspiracy. He nodded to no one in particular and walked across to the hall door.

'I am Pedrog ap Peleg of Ynys Môn: I come from my Lord Cadwallon with urgent news.'

'Welcome and come on in, Pedrog ap Peleg – you too, Rhun, you should join these councils now you are in training.'

The hall was warm, hot after the bitter cold outside, and quiet except for the noises from the kitchen where refreshments for this sudden guest were hurriedly being assembled.

Cwyfan held out a goblet of wine. 'Food will be with us shortly, but please, tell us quickly why you have come.'

Pedrog took off his gloves, drew a chair up to the fire and collapsed into it. He took the goblet and drained it in one go. He set it down and looked Cwyfan in the eye. 'My lord, Ynys Manaw has fallen, fell last autumn, and now a ship has been sighted off the coast of Ynys Môn. Cadwallon calls on all his friends to aid him. He will be sore pressed if Edwin comes in force. I have been sent to Magonsæte to gather as much help as I can find. And you, my Lord, are on the way. Others have gone to Pengwern, some even into western Powys, though we have little hope of help from there.'

'I can field twenty good men in arms, and doubtless Merewalh many more were he here. Alas, he is away in the east chasing a new wife. But even if he should return tomorrow, how can any of us hope to reach Ynys Môn in time? It is days away.'

'That is ill news. I had hoped for greater numbers. But, as to time, it is urgent but not, I think, critical. Edwin is not come yet, nor will he, we judge, this early in the year. Yet, when I left a lone ship had been sighted way up at Holy Island, an early spy we suppose. That was four nights ago.'

'Four nights – you have ridden like the wind!'

'It is so, but a man alone can travel more speedily than a host, and I have ridden hard. Assuming he does mean to attack Gwynedd, Edwin will not be in a position to threaten my lord directly for a good while yet, and we are not wholly without strength! Yet my lord begs that you attend him as soon as you can – you could try taking the valley of the Dyfrdwy, but Llyn Ogwen is a perilous pass and I would not try it at this time of the year. *Na*, best go north – there is still much risk of snow in the high mountains, but with luck you could reach the fords of Menai by the fifth day. It is the road Elisedd of Powys will take from Pengwern, and perhaps you may join him.'

Cwyfan was on his feet.

'Very well, we will do as you suggest and pray God we arrive in time. I'm sorry I cannot bring more but I must not leave this place undefended – since Elisedd moved his court to Pengwern, western Powys has made an unquiet neighbour, and will be the more so if we strip our lands of fighting men.' He clapped his hands in an unconscious gesture of urgency. 'Come, we must prepare, there is not a moment to be lost. Rhun, I must go and set people about it: will you stay and see to the needs of our guest? And find your mother, you will have your own preparations to make if you are to do here with twenty men short.'

'But father, my place is with you!'

Cwyfan stopped at the door.

'And what makes you think that?' he barked. 'Have you forgotten what we spoke of last year?'

It was true. In his excitement, Rhun had indeed forgotten. Now, like a cold slap, he remembered that strange night in the chapel.

'But...'

'No buts – I told you I would not risk us both and I meant it. Now do as you are told. I have much to do and no time to argue.'

There was an embarrassed silence for a moment after he had gone. Pedrog broke it. 'I have heard nothing but good of you so far: will you now go against that reputation?'

Rhun looked furious, but he rallied.

'Of course not,' he replied with a brittle edge to his voice. 'But because I must, not because I wish to.'

'That is understood. But look, we all have our separate tasks, and we must do them with a glad heart or risk dishonour. Perhaps I should remind you again of my lord Cadwallon's message, since it clearly made sense to you. Be circumspect. We cannot always do what is in our hearts.'

Within the hour, freshly mounted, Pedrog had gone, hoping, he said, to meet up with his fellows in the north and rejoin Cadwallon now he knew a trip to Lene would be pointless. Rhun and his mother stood in the hall discussing what needed to be done. She was a strong and capable woman, not given to panic. She knew that once the war party was organized and away, there would be little to do out of the ordinary. The farms were well run and only twenty of the free men would be going. There would still be plenty of people left to do the work, and the women could help. She would, of course, consult Rhun at every turn, though she could manage it all perfectly well without him. She may not have been the most perceptive of women but she knew that she must not undermine his new authority.

'The people will be worried. Once your father is gone, you should go to the outlying folk and give them this news. But be gentle – reassure them that all will carry on as normal and let them see that you are in charge.'

For herself, she kept her own counsel. Not since the days of Æthelfrith, before Rhun was born, had the threat of war come to these quiet woods and meadows, and then Lenteurde had been far enough south to escape it. Of course there had been perils enough – wolves in winter, the occasional cattle raid – but this was full-scale war, and on a scale such that it might engulf them all. She had grown complacent. They had all grown complacent. Now she had to face the idea that she might never see her man again, and the thought chilled her. But she would not look away from it, she would face it and deal with what came. And part of that was to make sure of Rhun.

But it was a hard parting. No sooner had Pedrog left, it seemed, then Cwyfan was ready to follow. His twenty free men in arms, all mounted, each with provisions for the four days it might take, and each armed with shield and spear, as had been their way since the golden days when his people still counted themselves as Romans.

Rhun stood with his mother and watched them ride away.

'So, Mother, I will do as you suggest and ride around the people. I shall take Gethin.'

'*Na*, I shall need Gethin here, you must find another or go alone.'

He found Meical in the forge bedding down the fire for the night. He had not meant to ask him, but now he found there was no one else he wanted. They say that if you save a man's life you become responsible for it. Rhun had not intended any such thing, but after the incident with the arrowheads Meical had become almost doglike in his devotion.

'Is your father here?' he asked.

'He is – he's out the back. Why?'

'Look, Meical, my mother has asked me to ride around the outlying farms – you know, reassure them and all that. Can you get a way for a while and come with me?'

'You don't have to ask! I can be the first member of your war band.'

'What war band?'

'Well, now your father's gone you'll be in charge – you'll need a war band.'

'But there's Gethin and the other men – they'll be more than enough.'

'Of course they will – but you've still got to have a war band – all leaders have a war band!'

A leader? he thought. *Of course – why not.* 'All right!' he said. '*Na*, it's a grand idea – and you're really with me?'

'Try to stop me!'

'D'you think your dad'll let you?'

Meical's face fell. His father – there was always his father. He sighed. 'I don't know – glad to before, I expect, but I'm useful to him now.'

Rhun placed his hands on Meical's shoulders and looked into his eyes. 'You stay here. I'll do this alone.' He squared his own shoulders and went through to where the family lived. He found Talhaiarn holding the baby as they both watched Meical's elder sister stirring a pot on the fire. A baby, perhaps now also to be without a father if the war went ill. The smith was singing a little song to lull his grandchild. The family seemed complete even without Meical's mother. And for sure they were all human.

'Rhun, welcome. Come in, come in.'

Meical's sister turned. 'Hello, Rhun,' she said, 'what brings you here?'

Rhun swallowed hard. 'It's this business of the war. I must ride out to the farms and tell them the news. Few of them will have heard, it has all happened so quickly.' He paused, 'I'd like it if Meical could come with me.' There, he has said it, the worst he could get was a refusal. 'Do you think you could spare him for a few days?'

Talhaiarn looked long at him, his face unreadable, his big hands playing absently with the child. At last he stirred. 'I'm thinking it would be hard for me to say no,' he said. Then he broke into a smile. '*Na, na*, we'll manage alright. Let him go.'

Rhun went back into the forge. Meical was standing awkwardly by the fire, now covered in a layer of ash to keep it warm until morning.

'Was it alright?' he asked.

'It was – I only told him we were going away for a day or so. Best we keep quiet about the war band for now.'

In those first few weeks the war was constantly on his mind. Often, when the day's work was done, he would stand at the north gate looking up the old road. Longing to hear news, fearful of what that news might be. How was his father faring? How went the war with Edwin of Northumberland? When would they get news? But no one came.

There was no news, never any news.

Chapter 4

The boy watched the squall as it crossed the valley towards him. He grunted a small curse. He was about to get wet again, yet the curse was more out of habit than any real concern. The rain had not been heavy, yet it had already got in everywhere and, in any case, there was nothing he could do to prevent it. A thin trickle had found its way down his spine to the small of his back where it had gathered slowly into a puddle. Though he knew it would do no good, he squeezed himself further into the lee of the rock and resumed his steady watch.

Three days now and nothing had happened. No one had come, no one had gone. He was stiff and cold but nothing would persuade him to leave until he had found what he had come for. He had heard and seen nothing except the small things that crept among the grass, the birds, and the occasional small animal scuffling amongst the trees below him, almost bare now after the autumn gales. A small herd of deer had spent the previous day browsing the hillside, a mother and this year's young he guessed, and he had spotted a fox questing along the valley floor. He had watched that fox every day and now he thought he had worked out where it lived. He had heard the vixen in the night but seen no youngsters. *They'll have gone this late in the year,* he supposed. *Foxes don't form herds like deer.* But he wasn't here to watch for foxes or deer, he was here to watch for men. And he had heard or seen no sign of any. They would come, of that he was in little doubt, but he must know for sure.

Rhun had sent them out to discover the raiders' base, and he was sure that he had found it. The place was deserted, yet it was not abandoned. There was a small huddle of mean huts, roughly wattled and thatched with reeds from the river, beside some makeshift pens standing empty. This place was made by men to gather stock, but where were they? And who were they? It would be no good if they just turned out to be locals. And they may well be, he thought. The steading was long established, yet there was something about this place which spoke of raiders and he could not, would not, return with a guess, no matter how well founded. He had been fine for the first day or so, enjoying the freedom, the solitude, but last night the weather had turned and he had woken wet and cold. Although the worst of the rain had passed, now his discomfort almost outweighed his sense of duty. And to make matters worse, his small store of food was running out. Like it or not, he would have to leave tonight or starve.

And then he heard a sound. Not an animal or a bird this time, but the clink of metal. A sound such as only men make. And the sound of cloven hooves. He shrank into the scant cover of his rocky hilltop, his eyes darting about to catch the slightest movement. Below him was a small enclosed valley, open only on its southern side where its narrow entrance hung above the greater valley below. Through this gap came a mixed herd of cattle, a pig or two and some horses, driven by a small, ragged body of men. They kept carefully within the cover of the trees, where they would be invisible from below. An ill-assorted bunch, wild and unkempt. Not all in rags, but all armed and wary. Not locals, then. One of the better-dressed men spoke quietly and they waited while he opened a rough gate in the stockade. Well disciplined: none but he had said a word. He must be their leader. And no fool. This was well controlled and well thought out. They filed in, quietly, and the rough fence was closed behind them; made from fresh-cut trees, it was sturdy enough, and would look more like a thicket when seen from the main track, way down by the river.

The boy willed himself to wait until all had settled. He scanned the hillside in case he had missed a lookout, but saw no one. When he was satisfied, he eased himself back from the crest until he was safe from sight. Then he picked himself up and ran.

A lone buzzard rose from a patch of scrub, disturbed by his passing. Once up, it sent out its mewling cry, perhaps in thanks that the boy might startle its next meal into fatal motion. Had it been looking for things other than dinner, it would have noticed, even through the veiling rags of rain, several other boys moving across the hills, separately but all heading for the same place. Only one had the news which Rhun sought, but all were making their way back to Lenteurde to report.

Eight boys in all, nine with himself. Rhun's nascent war-band. That is how they thought of themselves, though no one had said it out loud. Not yet. Farm boys, village boys, any who were willing and looked likely. Even one or two who didn't. Meical's idea had struck a chord, as if they had been looking for just such a thing. Ysgyrran, Peleg, Llif, Ithwalh the fletcher's son, one of several Ænglisc families in the village, and the younger boys: Cynrig, Eryl and little Tecwyn. They were all he could find who were not tied or too busy.

He had taken them to Gethin.

'A war band, is it?' he asked as he looked them over. 'And what sort of a war do you expect to win with this lot?'

Rhun squared his shoulders, keenly aware of all their eyes on him.

'Besides, I doubt your father meant you to go to war.'

'Perhaps not, but he does expect me to look after this place while he is gone. He told me so.'

'Aye, well, you have me and we have men aplenty for that.'

Rhun flushed red. How could Gethin do this? But with an effort he checked himself and spoke as quietly as he could. He would not allow Gethin to embarrass him in front of the others.

'These can better be spared.'

Gethin stood, hands on hips, and chewed his lip.

'I dare say you are right.'

'So – will you teach them to fight?'

Gethin sighed, lightly.

'As much as I can,' he said.

That very day he had gathered them together. By the

end they were exhausted. Muscles unused to such work ached and complained. Further, it was clear that none of the younger boys could use the long sword. Rhun remembered his visit to the armoury, forgotten 'til then with all that had happened since. The next evening he produced a heavy bundle and let it unroll onto the ground.

'Here – these will do better. What do you think, Gethin?'

'It was well thought.' Gethin looked around. 'I'm thinking that only one or two of you could stand up to fight with swords proper. It may well be that these are better suited. It would please your mother's people to know they were back in use.'

'But what are they?'

'Roman swords – from long ago. It was with weapons like these that the legions conquered the world.'

The boys had picked them up in wonder. They pulled them from their leather scabbards and marvelled at the steel, fresh and clean and unchanged by time.

'I have my own, of course, but I thought they might be better for Cynrig, Eryl and Tecwyn.'

'True, but remember – the Romans fought as one, rank after rank of them all backing each other. How else do you think they did so well? I have it in mind that if you all use the same weapon you can use the same tactic. That might surprise some.' He smiled.

Rhun's eyes shone at the vision of himself leading his men in a phalanx and cutting down the enemy left and right.

Until Gethin pricked the bubble.

'They were made for stabbing, these were, not for slashing, so don't you think it'll be easy to use them against a long-sword. The Romans also had big shields – you'll have none. Best keep your long-swords, those of you who can use them. So, come along – look lively.'

And he had explained, and demonstrated and cursed and encouraged in equal measure and they had all worked hard at it, even when the first glow had gone; when it had become a discipline and not a game. And not only with the gladius but their own favourite weapons. Each evening after the work of the day was done, Gethin put them through their paces. Spear, sword, bow and sling. All hard skills, all necessary. Rhun's talents lay with sword and spear, as did several of the others, and most were at least familiar with the tools of the hunt – bow and slingshot. Between them they could use all the weapons they could lay their hands on, and they rejoiced in them. But they were still just boys. They would have thought themselves invulnerable in any case.

They had been at it for about a week when Rhun first noticed Einion standing in the shadows, watching. Einion: a captive of war since a child, he was now come of age, as had Rhun, but not to the glory of manhood – he was just a slave. Aware of this, Cadfan had bidden Rhun to keep half an eye on the boy, but Einion had committed no offence, no act of rebellion. It was supposed that he had swallowed his pride and settled down. But the slave boy was there again the following evening. Keeping back, watching. On the third day Rhun had decided he must do something. It was becoming annoying. But he hadn't wanted to make a fuss so had walked quietly over while the others were too busy to notice.

'Why do you watch us?'

'It does no harm. Why shouldn't I?'

'Have you no work to do?'

'I might have. Would you give me some?'

'You cannot think to join us?'

'Why not? My father was a warrior like yours. Am I not good enough?'

'My father would never permit it!'

'Would *you*?'

Rhun was taken aback. Faced with the question, he realized he didn't have an answer.

'Why did you not speak up after your father died?'

'What good would it have done?'

'They might have freed you; it would have been the custom.'

'As you say, your father would never permit it.'

'But you could have said something.'

'Like what? They know I should be a warrior – instead,

your father captured mine and there was my future gone. Well, he's dead and well out of it, but here I am – still a slave. But I won't plead – I wouldn't give them the satisfaction. Or you.'

Rhun could find nothing to say. Einion glared at him. He spat on the ground and walked away.

Rhun knew he should have stopped him. Should have reprimanded him at least. But now it came to it he found he could not. Annoyed with himself, he had gone back to the others.

Gethin had spoken of it later. 'Why don't you ask him to join you?'

'But he's a slave – besides, my father would never let me.'

'I'm not so sure – other bondmen train in arms. It's not so strange.'

'Well – I don't know. I don't know him at all really...' He tailed off.

'But?' prompted Gethin.

Rhun made sure no one else was listening but Gethin knew him too well to equivocate. 'Well – look, I didn't ever really notice him 'til the council meeting – you know – that one when my father wouldn't free him. But I have since then. He's done nothing wrong but – well, he always seems so sure, strong somehow. He unnerves me. I don't know how I would cope with him close up.'

'Oh, better than you think, I'd say! Why not give him a chance? And yourself. I reckon he could be more than useful. Remember – the decision is yours while your father is away.'

'I suppose it is.' But his father had not felt quite so far away until that moment.

The next evening Einion had come again. The boys had worked at sword practice for about half an hour, Rhun and Ysgyrran practicing together. Rhun worked the fight over towards where Einion was standing. Seizing the moment, he tossed him his sword. 'Here, see what you can do!'

Einion's reaction was instantaneous. He caught it and immediately Ysgyrran engaged with him. It was an unfair match – Ysgyrran was practised, Einion had never held a sword in his life – but, total novice or not, he gave a good account of himself for a few minutes until Ysgyrran disarmed him with a trick.

'Will you join us?' said Rhun.

Einion had stood, panting. He had flicked the hair out of his eyes and looked hard at Rhun.

'Why do you use these funny little swords?'

Rhun glanced around. 'They suit some of us better,' he said.

'Not me.'

'You could get used to one if you wanted. Will you join us?'

Einion looked from one to the other, his clear contempt mixed awkwardly with surprise.

'Why would I?' he said, and he had walked away.

'He'd be dangerous, that one, if he knew how to fight,' said Ysgyrran. 'And you'd be a fool to teach him.'

Rhun watched him go. 'He hates us,' he said simply.

'You sound surprised. *Na*, don't expect to see him again,' said Ysgyrran. 'He'll not risk another embarrassment.'

But he did come. And the next day, and the day after that. And then it seemed as if he had always been there.

Rhun had gathered them together one Sunday after mass, about a month after his father had ridden away to war.

'You know about these raiders, I suppose?'

Nine heads had nodded. A few murmurs. Tales of raiders had been trickling in for a week or more. A farm attacked and burned here, livestock taken there, nothing too close as yet but enough to cause concern, and somehow more than usual. If the tales were true, something about these attacks was out of the ordinary run of cross-border skirmishes.

'Well, don't you see? This is it! This is what we have been waiting for,' he said urgently, as if to convince himself as well. 'We must find these men – stories and rumours are useless. We must find out who they are and where they are hiding. They must have a base somewhere. All the stories are coming in from the west, so my guess is they're up in the hill country where they can be secret. Most likely that's where they come from, anyway.'

He had paused and watched their faces. He could see doubt and little else.

'Look, we must know. I want you to take enough supplies for three days and spread out. We must find them – and quickly. Merewalh may not have heard of this yet, and he must be told if his borders are threatened.' *And if they come this way we need to know well before they get here,* he thought, but he kept that to himself.

No one had said anything. Rhun had looked at each in turn, had seen the doubt in their eyes.

'What's the matter with you all? What have we been training for if not for this? We are all the sons of free men. And, by God! we would have gone with our fathers to war if they'd have let us! Well, now it seems war has come to us. Maybe to our very door – would you rather wait until it does? You are a war band – were you expecting to fight wolves only? Well, wolfsheads have come instead. So, we may be few, but we are not puny and it may be up to us to defend our people. So – we must know how many they are and if they are looking this way.'

And suddenly they had believed him. All doubt gone. Suddenly they believed they really could take on a raiding war band and win. They were under his spell. They had gathered round Rhun like moths to a flame, in need of light in their darkness, and with Gethin's help he had knocked them into a well-disciplined little force. In his heart, Rhun knew the truth – it is all very well to train, to fight mock battles with each other, yet they were untried. Not one of them had ever fought in earnest. Not one believed in his own mortality. But now, what had started as an urge just to do something, anything that might be useful, had turned deadly serious, in the way that such things do.

Then he had turned away, and missed the look in Einion's eye.

Tecwyn was not the first back but he made the biggest

entrance. Filled up with his news, he was shouting it to the world as he came, scattering the sheep in the long meadow. Little Tecwyn: under-grown and scrawny, he would never be big nor called pretty. He was too small to hold a sword, even the old Roman ones, but his skill with a slingshot more than compensated for the lack, and he had a way with him which could charm the leaves off the trees, and a huge grin to match. And he was bursting with his cleverness.

'I found it, I found it. Rhun – I found it!'

They gathered round him as he splashed through the gate.

'It's up river from here,' he said, panting. 'Before the valley narrows. About two hours.'

It had been an anxious few days for Rhun. He had realized early that he could not go himself, but he had had to force himself to stay, convince himself that it was the right thing to do. Yet however sure he was, he had been wound up tight worrying about what they might find, if anything, or that it would all be too late. Or that they would all be captured. Or worse. Now that they were home and with the news he had hoped for, he was weak with relief.

'Oh, well done,' he said. 'Come on, we must tell my mother at once. Someone find Gethin!'

Tecwyn stood with his back to the long fire and steamed as he told his tale. The mud on his stick-like legs baked hard and, with no hair to hold it, fell amongst the rushes as he moved.

'It is well hidden, my lady, I only found it because I came over the hills hoping to get a long view.'

'Do you know this place, Gethin?' she asked.

'I do, my lady, I have a cousin who lives up that way. It has been used to keep stock, off and on. It has water in good supply, and it'd be an easy place to defend. They have chosen well.'

'They have heard that our men are gone to war, I make no doubt, and hope for easy pickings. They are too close – we must send for help. Elisedd is gone to war with Cadwallon. No – it must be Merewalh. He will defend us.'

Rhun stood with his arms clasped to his chest, a fierce frown on his face. He knew one thing: if you pick up a weapon you must be prepared to use it. His father had told him so often enough. Well so be it, he had made his weapon, his little army – he must not back away now. He could have wished for more time, more people, wished that they were stronger – at least older – but such was not in his hands.

He tried his best to sound grown-up, yet it came out in a bit of a rush, with his voice on the edge of cracking. 'We may not have the time, Mother. They are only two hours away if they choose to look this way. And if the tales are true they may not be the only gang – what if Merewalh is gone to deal with others further south? He may not be able to reach us before they strike. We must deal with this ourselves. You can do it, can't you Gethin? You've enough men and you'd have us as well. Together we'd be strong enough. I'm sure of it. We can take on a dozen men.'

His mother burst in. 'Don't be ridiculous! It was not to make mad gestures that your father left you in charge. It was very clever of you to find where these people are, but a handful of men cannot defend this place alone, and as for you boys – I won't hear of it.'

You boys, Rhun thought bitterly. But no – he wouldn't plead – that would indeed be the act of a boy.

'No, Mother, and we shouldn't try! We don't have to wait here to be attacked. We must take the fight to them. That way, if we should lose, they'll not know from where we came, and you'll be no worse off. Even if we can just delay them, it would give Merewalh time to get here. But we won't lose.'

His mother stared at him. She shivered and shook her head violently. 'We won't lose, indeed – how can you expect to win? Rhun, you are only boys, you cannot face men like these.'

'Not in open battle, no. But what if we could ambush them in their own place – take them by surprise?' He was making this up as he went along, his mind galloping ahead. He had no idea how he might do it, but he could worry about that later. 'Look, Mother – Gethin is master at arms, he has good men here, not many but they're good men, and we may be boys, but – well, we are not stupid boys,' he added rather lamely, an afterthought he was not quite sure he believed himself.

Gethin stepped in. 'It is a good idea, my lady. In principle, at least. As Rhun says, we have enough men in reserve. We can leave some here and still outnumber them two to one, assuming Tecwyn can count. I know the place: I think I can see a way it might work. We can sort out the details this evening. Meanwhile, we can send a man to Lene and hope that Merewalh gets here soon, but anything would be better than waiting here to be trapped.'

He turned to the small cloud of steam that was Tecwyn, 'Well, Tecwyn – can you count?'

The boy bristled, like a little skinny boar. 'I've got ten fingers, haven't I? There was one for each.'

Rhun's mother gripped the arms of her chair, her knuckles white.

'I will not lose you as well as your father! I will not!'

Rhun looked at her, his face set. He did not want to defy her but he knew that he must. His heart was hammering. He was fully aware that most likely he was committing himself and his friends to violent and swift deaths. But he would not be seen to falter. Not in front of the others. And, in truth, not in front of her.

'Mother, you may lose everything otherwise,' he said quietly.

She stared at him, almost unseeing. For a tense moment the debate hung in the balance. Then she sagged. In that moment of silence something had changed. Perhaps it was his tone, perhaps his certainty, perhaps her own doubt. Suddenly she was no longer the resourceful matriarch, but a worried mother at a loss.

'Very well, we will follow your lead, Rhun. For the time being. Now, do go and get out of those wet things, all of you.'

The boys poured out into the dull grey afternoon, chattering like a flock of starlings.

'I can count to ten times ten if I use my toes.'

'How does that work then?'

'It's easy – Brother Cledwyn showed me.'

Angharad watched them go.

'Stay a moment, Gethin.'

'My lady?'

'What should we do? Please, tell me what we should do. Oh, I know the boy has done well with his little army, he is brave like his father, but they are still children. He cannot fight these men. You must agree? We must send to Mere-walh immediately.'

'Indeed we must, my lady, as Rhun himself suggested, but I also agree with Rhun that we risk his arriving too late. A man's main advantage is his strength, and we may not have much, but surprise and numbers may well level the balance, even tip it in our favour. Much of this raider's strength lies in our fear of him. With your permission, I will hear Rhun's plan and if it is good it would be a shame to rob him of his glory. I know him – I fear that if you try to take this away from him you may lose him anyway. Besides, I have a few ideas of my own. My lord Cwyfan left us enough men who can bear arms, and more we can use in a pinch. They are children as you say, but there's not one who would not have gone to Ynys Môn with their fathers. If they couldn't it was not for the lack of courage.'

Angharad sighed. 'That is all true. Alas, I do not know my son as well as I should. I know he is brave but – is he capable? *You* I have every confidence in, but him? – I just don't know.' She paused. Then she seemed to make up her mind. 'Very well, let it be so, but send to Merewalh – he must be told in any case.'

Suddenly she grasped Gethin's hand, her fear loud in her voice.

'And Gethin, look after him – I could not bear to lose them both.'

'You have lost neither, my lady. Do not hasten fate.'

The day after Tecwyn's return dawned bright and dry, the rain driven off in the night by a new wind, blowing up warm from the south. A good strong drying wind, and much needed if their plan was to succeed. It was only because of this change that Gethin had agreed. They had spent the night discussing the possibilities and assembling the bones of a plan which depended much on dry weather. Now that it had set fair – all the old ones said so – he had given Rhun the nod.

Now, as the day waned, they were in position. Rhun lay flat out on the cropped turf, his friends strung out similarly along the ridge. The ground beneath him was still cool, keeping a memory of the rain, but all day the sun and wind had done their work; it was dry enough. Now with the evening a small wind was drawn down into the valley with the retreating heat. A useful wind: it got the animals used to their smell.

All was quiet down in the little hidden valley. The stolen livestock had been fed and settled and the men had gone indoors to prepare for the night. He could see none of them, not even any on guard. Of course, just because he couldn't see one didn't mean there was no guard. Still, it was too late now to alter things so he put it out of his mind. At any moment the men below the gate would attack. They would douse the fence in oil and set it ablaze. Gethin was well prepared. He had oil, fire and a couple of dozen men with him and should be able to keep the enemy busy for the critical moments. True, not all were fighters, but all were strong and all, bondmen included, carried a good weapon of some sort.

From his position by Tecwyn's rock, Rhun could see the whole of the valley. He examined the terrain one more time. Never too often, Gethin had said. Below him the slope dropped steeply for a couple of hundred feet, and then flattened out at the bottom into a small level area where he could see the penned beasts, and the rough huts the usual occupants had thrown up for shelter. Across the valley, the slope was smothered by a thick growth of trees and scrub, difficult to get through in daylight, impossible in darkness. This and the steepness had made the men complacent. They would not expect an attack from behind. Silently Rhun thanked God that the bad weather had broken so early. The night was dry, even the grass under him was more chill than damp. There would be no moon for several hours. Strung out along the hill crest, his little army lay poised. He looked along the line. All quiet. Any nervousness seemed under strict control. Nothing must give them away.

The plan was simple. While Gethin was drawing the enemy to the gate, the boys would make their way down the steep slope to get behind them. If the hidden valley had been good for a secret hideaway, it was also a trap now its secret was revealed. Gethin would feign retreat, just far enough to offer hope of escape. At the same time Rhun would fire the huts while Ysgyrran led the others to stampede the cattle. Caught between the two, Rhun hoped that the raiders, confused and uncertain of the force attacking them, would make a break for the open. It would be a trick, and like all good tricks, it depended on illusion and, above all, surprise. He lay motionless, scarcely daring to breathe. The timing was critical – it was vital none of his little band moved too soon or made any noise. Sound travels far and clear at night. His plan depended on the noise of the first attack covering their descent.

And it almost worked.

Suddenly fire broke out by the gate and a great shout went up. As the outlaws stumbled from their huts, a rain of rocks and turfs fell among them amidst a great pall of acrid smoke. Groping for their weapons, they rushed to defend their camp as the fire spread out on each side of the rough gate, springing from branch to branch and gathering strength as it went. Without a word, Rhun leaped up and started down the hill, trusting his companions to follow. There was not a scrap of cover and the hillside was riddled with rabbit holes. He picked his way down with desperate haste, praying that anyone who stumbled would do it in silence even if they broke a leg. But no one did break a leg. His feet slithered on the grass from the steepness. It seemed to take forever, but suddenly he was at the bottom. He stood absolutely still, holding his breath. Had any one heard? It seemed not.

He could hear the tell-tale sounds of slithering feet and grunts from those still on their way, but the noise from the gate covered any noise he and his companions could make. The only thing louder in his ears was the sound of his own blood pounding. He grabbed Ysgyrran by the sleeve and pointed a route around the back of the pens. Then without a word he set out, going straight ahead. It was darker down here. The fire was dimmed by its own smoke and there was scarcely enough light to see his hands, but almost at once the fence loomed and he grabbed at it with relief. The cattle were already alarmed; it would not take much to panic them into a stampede. Leaving that to those whose task it was, he worked his way around the pens to the huts. So far so good. Silently he poured his own small supply of oil onto the thatch of the nearest hut, scrabbling at it with his fingers to find the dry stuff deep inside, making sure the oil penetrated and didn't just run off onto the ground. Crouching down, he took out his little fire-pot and blew onto the grey coals. Flying ash stung his eyes but nothing happened. Please God it hasn't gone out! It seemed an age, but at last they sparked into life. At once he thrust in a handful of dry grass and straw and passed the flames onto the hut itself. For another agonising moment again nothing happened. His hand shook as he held his brand to the thatch, willing it to catch. His mind knew nothing but the moment, no room for fear, running on the rush of adrenalin. It was taking too long – too long.

A great bellowing and crashing started up behind him as the others whipped the cattle into panic and drove them through the crude fence. The loose structure was smashed to splinters as the cattle burst through. As if in response, his fire caught. The thatch erupted, the flames fanned by the evening breeze, sending Rhun staggering back, his arms held up to cover his eyes. The cattle had been well on course for the gate but this new terror scattered them. The boys fanned out in a desperate effort to head them back to the gate and send them crashing into the backs of the outlaws. It was all going to go wrong – it seemed obvious now. He must have been mad to think it would work.

The heat was vast. Rhun stood like a spectre, the remains of his brand in one hand, his sword in the other. Tears born of sheer madness ran down his smoke-blackened face. Tears of anxiety and frustration. And then, without warning, a man stood before him – a sudden apparition with a naked sword in its hand and vicious rage in its eyes. What? – This was certainly not in the plan. Rhun was rooted to the spot. By the skin of his teeth he thrust up his guard and parried a blow which would have killed him instantly had it gone home. But he was far from ready and the force of it knocked him backwards. He staggered, frantic to keep up his guard, and fell flat on his back.

'So they send boys against me, do they?' It was not a question but an expression of disgust. The man's blade flicked out, stabbing downwards. Rhun squirmed, his body arching on instinct, and the sword missed by a hair's breadth. He rolled over and scrambled to his feet, the skin of his back crawling in anticipation of the next blow, his mind wild with the vision of himself a bloody corpse. But it didn't come. As he turned, he saw that the man, in his fury, had thrust his sword so hard into the turf that only now was he recovering it. They stood facing each other. Rhun's chest heaved as he fought for breath. His head pounded as his heart pumped the blood through his temples. His whole body was wound up as never before. Boom, boom, boom. So loud. It was deafening. He had never felt more alive, nor so close to death.

The man was dribbling spittle through broken teeth. It ran and hung in strings from his ragged beard. Above the beard his face was a map of past encounters, scarred and ravaged, now made the more ugly by rage and frustration.

'Ach, you little filth – you can squirm, but can you fight? Eh? Can you fight?' His sword flashed down. Rhun threw up his arm and caught the blade on his own. A screaming of metal on metal that set the teeth on edge. It was like being hit with a hammer. Rhun staggered again, bringing himself to guard. His attacker stood poised and eyed him through half-closed lids. He shifted his weight back and forth, stepping lightly for such a heavy man. His eyes flickered and he sprang again, his sword sweeping in a tight undercut which should have taken Rhun's hand off at the wrist. But Rhun's body jumped, long before his head could form the order, and the sword just caught him a nick as it passed, glancing only, but enough to open the flesh of his arm and send his own sword clattering into the dark. He slipped and fell to the ground again, gasping for breath as the wind was knocked from him. Blood poured from his arm. His hand was useless. Now it must come. The man stood over him and slowly raised his sword. The light from the flames danced on the blade and was reflected in his eyes, making him look more wildly savage than ever. His voice came as a rasp, 'Well boy, this is the last time you challenge me.'

In the same instant, his face changed from gloating madness into a mask of horror. A sword appeared, as if by magic, straight out of his chest in a burst of blood. It sprayed out, straight into Rhun's eyes, soaking his hair and the front of his shirt. Sticky and bittersweet. The man stood for the longest moment, his eyes wide in disbelief, and then he collapsed as though his strings had been cut.

'Well he was right in that, at least,' said a gruff voice out of the dark.

Rhun propped himself on an elbow. He scrubbed at his face with his sleeve. Then his face cracked into a broad grin. The sheer relief turned it into a cackle of laughter broken by the effort to regain his breath.

'Gethin! Am I glad to see you!'

'I promised your mother.' Then he seemed to see the blood for the first time. 'Are you all right? Did he get you?'

'He did. I think my sword arm is bad, but this is all *his* blood.'

Gethin squatted down. He took Rhun's hand in his and carefully turned it over. He dabbed at the place gently with his own sleeve. The cut had missed the artery by a hair's breadth. It was just a flesh wound. Messy but not fatal.

'You'll do fine. You were lucky, he was too angry to be careful. But it's too early to celebrate – it's not over yet.'

But it was. As they ran to the gate, it became clear that the fight was at an end. Rhun's struggle had been seen. With the loss of their leader and their profits run off into the night, the raiders had scattered. And now came the reckoning.

'Have we lost anyone, d'you think?' asked Rhun.

'Let's see.'

They walked down to where the others were standing, leaning on each other, quite spent, all their strength drained.

'Are we all here?' he asked.

'Peleg is dead,' said a voice out of the dark. Einion stepped forward into the dim light of the fires, dying now as the dead stuff burned out. 'That much I know for sure – he was right beside me,' he said.

'Peleg! Dead? He can't be!' No no – not dead. Surely, not dead.

'I killed the man who did it.' Einion did not boast, it was a statement only. Rhun could well believe it. Big Einion, sixteen years and nearly six feet of muscle and resentment. He had no need of boasting.

'Where is he? Show me.'

Rhun looked down at the bloodied figure, lying broken and ugly. And clearly dead. He who had been so fine in life.

Peleg. Gone. The reality of what they had done broke over Rhun like a summer storm. His heart clutched with a bitter regret. His glory made a sham by this death. He felt sick. His little force had done a wonderful thing, and a brave thing. With scant training and far less experience, they had routed a band of battle-hardened men. But it had been more by good luck than good judgement, and Rhun felt a wave of nausea at the thought that his plan could so easily have killed them all.

He struggled to find words.

'Thank you, Einion – that was well done.'

Einion stared at him.

'I liked Peleg.'

It felt like a slap, but Rhun had not the strength to think about it just then. Besides, perhaps he'd earned it.

Chapter 5

It was a subdued group that came back to the village, bearing among them a burden on an old hurdle drawn by a liberated ox. Many walked awkwardly, favouring this limb or that. Most wore at least one hastily improvised bandage. Yet, though they made no clamour, their heads were high. With them came a small herd of cattle, several pigs and some plough oxen. And one man, stumbling, his arms lashed to a pole set across his shoulders, his legs in a long hobble. Enough to walk, not enough to run. In front walked Rhun. A new Rhun, suddenly grown from boy into man and already recovering from his sadness after the fight. His face was grim but, to one who knew him, behind it glowed an immense pride, a happiness marred only by the burden they bore. He would have to tell Peleg's mother. Only he could do it, it was not a job he could give to another. Yet even that could not quench his inner fire.

But he was tired. It seemed a lifetime since they had set out. They had spent yesterday going round the farm-steads talking to the people and, burdened as they were, it had taken them a whole day to get back and the time had dragged. Still, they had been gone only two days yet those two days were quite time enough for Angharad's message to have reached Merewalh and been answered. As they came though the gate, they were greeted by a small band of men in arms. Real warriors, these – not boys and farmers.

'Ah, it is the boy who fell off his horse!'

Rhun's cheeks flamed. He stopped, his ragged army stumbling to a halt behind him. Before him stood a bluff, stocky man in the prime of life, his dark hair just beginning to show a frosting at the temples. A strong face, from which shrewd eyes looked out and missed nothing.

'Who are you, stranger? Why do you mock me in my own place?'

'Peace, young Rhun. I am Guthlac of Lene and I meant no mock. I am come at the behest of your mother who feared that you may have taken on more that you could deal with. Alas, we could not get here sooner.' He looked them over. 'But it seems that she was wrong. You are back and you have a captive. These are not the signs of defeat.'

Rhun stood in silence. To his surprise he found himself grateful. Relieved. Someone else could take charge of the prisoner and deal with the aftermath. He would have enough trouble dealing with Peleg's mother.

'No, we did not lose. They are scattered and their leader is dead.' He said it with no emphasis, concealing his pride. He looked up and held Guthlac with his gaze. Somehow he knew that this man would understand just how big that brief statement was.

'Dead – that is news indeed. And you killed him?'

Rhun braced himself. He did not want to reveal how closely he had come to his own death, but he would not lie. '*Na*. He died fighting with me, but it was Gethin who killed him.'

Guthlac did not miss a beat.

'Well, between you, you may have saved us a deal of trouble. These raids from Powys are growing. They are becoming a worry.'

'He was not from Powys,' said Rhun.

'Not!'

'*Na*, he spoke in Ænglisc.'

Guthlac nodded. 'Ænglisc? – this is a story I'd like to hear in due time. Well, he'll cause no more trouble, it seems. What of the others?'

'This one's from Powys for sure,' said Gethin. He looked grimly at the captive. 'No doubt we can find out who was with him.'

Guthlac merely nodded. 'Well, enough for now. Come, we must not keep you standing here. Here is your gracious mother in person.'

Rhun's mother had appeared in the doorway to Cwyfan's hall, waiting. Silent, but eloquently so.

He allowed her a brief embrace. Thank God they had taken the time to clean up – the last thing he needed right now was his mother fussing over the stains of another man's blood.

'You look exhausted, Rhun. Come inside, there is refreshment within.' But he would not allow her even that.

'*Na*, I must seek Carwenna. Peleg died in the fight and I must tell her before anything. I will join you as soon as I can.'

Carwenna was not hard to find. As Rhun turned out of the gate and down into the village, he saw her walking up the street, heedless of the mire in the gutter, a shawl gathered close around her, defensively, as if she knew what was to come. Heedless too of the little knots of people gathered here and there, stopped in their daily business around the open shop fronts. Word of Rhun's success had spread speedily among the village folk, but they had heard nothing about Peleg's death. They were ignorant of this private drama, yet her passing drew their gaze like a lodestone. Rhun watched them, seeing many as if for the first time. These were his people. The ordinary people. Who grew things and made things and bought things, and ate and drank and lived, safe in the belief that men like himself would protect them. How close he had been to disaster. He stood and waited, a lump knotting his throat.

She stopped before him. A wisp of hair blew across her face. Her eyes anxious, accusing. 'He is dead, then,' she said. She made it a statement. 'How?'

In a terrible flash Rhun realized he did not know. He had not even asked the question. Of course she would want to know. Anyone would want to know. But he could not tell her. He had not been there. He looked at her pale, drawn face and knew he could not dissemble, could not lie to her.

'I was not by him when he died. I am sorry for it, for there might have been something I could have done. But, Carwenna, you must know that he was courageous and bold, and know also that I valued him highly. His loss sits heavily on my heart.'

She hugged her shawl closer. 'I saw it,' she whispered. 'In the night, I saw it.' Her son. Her eldest. Scarcely become a man, whatever other men might say. She looked up, her voice sharp now, 'He was only fourteen! Why, why did you have to take boys?'

She held him with her eyes. He willed himself not to look away. 'How could I not?' he said wearily. And in that moment the transformation was complete. No more a boy talking to his elders, he had become a man talking to his equals. 'It was better to take the fight to the enemy than let them come here to threaten us all. We all knew the risk, Peleg as much as any of us. D'you think I could have left him behind? But he did not die in vain and he will not pass unmarked.' At the last moment his voice failed him, cracking into a boy's treble. His cheeks burned.

She stared at him. He felt defenceless in that gaze but he would not appear weak. Like Peleg, he must endure the trials of adulthood. Yet it was a bitter test.

'*Na*, you are not to blame,' she said at last. 'You are truly your father's son.' And with that she turned away.

'Einion was with him when he died. Shall I send him to you?'

'Do that,' she said, and as her voice blew away on the wind, 'thank you.'

In the Hall refreshments had been laid out for the visitors, as yet untouched. When Rhun walked in, he found a great bustle was underway as the household set about tending the wounded, food and guests momentarily forgotten.

'How is she?' Gethin asked quietly.

'She will recover, she has other sons. Sons enough to till her strips.' He turned, sharply. 'But look, Gethin, we must not let him slip away unmarked. He was of the old faith in his heart, I know it – and it's no secret his mother is. What must we do to honour him properly? That won't offend Brother Cledwyn,' he added darkly.

Gethin looked at him and smiled. 'Let me think on it. But now you must look to the others. And to your own mother.'

Once the wounded had been seen to, the company settled to food and drink. It may not have been a big victory but Angharad would not have it pass unmarked for her boy's sake. His first blood spilled, his first test passed.

And it seemed that Guthlac had more to say. 'My lady, your messenger was one among many. There are rumours of raids up and down the border. We know that Powys has heard of our situation here: they know that the better half of our fighting men are away in the north. If they have put aside their quarrels and set their sights on our lands here, then we are all in danger. Greater danger than we think, perhaps. We may learn more from Rhun's prisoner – why it was that they were led by an Ænglisc man, for one thing. But I must congratulate you on your son, madam – Rhun here has done something worthy of his forefathers.' He clapped Rhun on the shoulder and raised his voice to fill the whole room. 'I say he shall no longer be known as the one who fell off his horse but as the one who rid his country of a vicious beast.' A ragged cheer went up and Rhun found himself redder in the face than he had ever been. He looked desperately to Gethin but saw no help there.

He gathered his wits. *No good being embarrassed,* he thought. That would help no one.

'It wasn't just me, it was all of us. They all deserve your thanks at least as much as I do. Still, I thank you for your words: it will indeed be a better thing to be remembered for. But now, may I ask a favour of you? Would you take this man we caught off our hands and deal with him as should be done?'

'But he is yours, Rhun, yours to do with as you wish. By law you may keep him as your slave. You have won the right. And you are head man now, unless – until your father returns.'

He stopped, embarrassed in turn. Rhun glanced at his mother but it seemed she had not noticed the slip.

'I know that,' he said, 'but I have no need of a slave, no

wish for one really. Besides, it may be that he knows things that Merewalh should hear.' He swallowed – this was going to be hard but it had to be said, 'and I fear we are not the ones to get them out of him.'

'Bravely said. Very well, I will take him with me as you ask. But I shall make sure that the king does not forget this. Now, madam, we must sleep and be away at dawn. I do not believe you will be troubled for a while, and not by this gang now that they are leaderless, but I will leave a few people here should they try anything. Indeed, I hope they may – it would do no harm to catch or kill a few more of them.'

After eating what he could, Rhun walked out into the dark. He was impressed by Guthlac. The man made it all seem so easy. Would he himself ever have such command? Such confidence? He shivered as he remembered how close he had come to death. He had thought he could fight, but that Ænglisc man had been so very much stronger and better than he had ever dreamed. The attack had seemed so simple when they had planned it. Uncertain, yes, but easy enough. They had thought it exciting, never dangerous. And perhaps there lay the truth – real courage came from facing the unknown, knowing that it might kill you. But he had not known it, could not imagine his own death. So was that courageous? Or merely foolhardy. And he had risked more than himself, and it had killed one of his best, and that was unforgivable. A tear picked its way down the side of his nose. He tasted it on his tongue and it seemed to him the savour of defeat.

'Did you mean that?'

A figure had appeared quietly at his side.

'Einion?'

Einion stood in silence.

'Did I mean what?'

'What you said about not wanting a slave.'

Rhun thought back. 'Yes,' he said firmly, 'I did. In all honesty I cannot find it in my heart to own another man.'

Einion showed a flash of anger. 'I wish your father had felt the same. Or am I not a man?'

Rhun was lost. How to answer this?

'I told Carwenna that you were with Peleg when he died. Will you speak to her?'

Einion sighed. 'I will. I know her.'

'And listen, Einion – I want you to know that if it was up to me you would be free. Even if you hadn't earned it!'

'Easy to say,' the bitterness strong in his voice.

'Look, you are one of my companions. I asked you, you came. To my shame I had not thought how hard that might be for you, or even that you could scarcely say no. But now I give you that choice – will you stay?'

Einion looked hard at him, as if weighing up the measure of Rhun's sincerity. *He actually believes it,* he thought, *he really thinks he is some sort of war leader. He's got the confidence, I'll give him that. Perhaps he is.* 'I will,' he said at length, 'for the time being.'

It was Meical who found them. He glanced at Einion before laying a hand gently on Rhun's shoulder.

'They are missing you at the feast. Will you not come in?'

The village was not rich, Peleg's people in particular. In the fresh light of morning they laid his body out in a simple shroud, waiting for the priest to conduct it to the Church. His mother stood, stone-faced, clutching her younger sons to herself as if in defiance. *You shall not take them too,* she seemed to say. Rhun had begged his own mother for some good candles from her store for his friends to carry, knowing that Peleg's family could not afford them. He had insisted that he, at least, be amongst those who carried the body.

This was the burial of a humble man. Here were no great ceremonials, but the power of this simple procession was palpable. None saw it who had not known Peleg, and none who had not liked him. His life had barely started, yet already he would lie among the dead, alongside so many others who had given their lives for the village in one way or another over the years. But he would not be forgotten.

In the chapel they laid him on his bier, his hands crossed in lieu of the crucifix none could afford to pay for, his feet towards the east, towards Jerusalem the centre of all things Christian, ready for the walk into the unknown. Perhaps into God's embrace, perhaps to the mead-halls of his fathers, who really knew? A single candle burned, as was the custom. Brother Cledwyn began the ceremony, a simple vespers for the dead. There would be no psalm and response, no chorus of voices lifted in praise of the fallen. He was on his own, he could do no more. The village understood and were content.

As the priest's last words faded there was a movement at the back of the chapel. Cynrig pushed forward and in silence placed a makeshift cross onto Peleg's folded arms. It was a crude thing, made of sticks bound with a strip of willow bark.

Cynrig looked up, hollow-eyed. 'It is the best I could do,' he whispered. 'He was my friend.'

The priest looked at him. *Little Cynrig, more poet than warrior – must be thirteen by now,* he supposed. *So young. How fast he has had to grow.*

'It was well done,' he said gently.

The following morning Rhun awoke filled with a new urgency. They had escorted Peleg to the burial ground, and now he must make sure none of the others followed for the lack of training. The fight with the raiders had shown Rhun how much he – how much they all – had to learn, and they must start now while Guthlac's soldiers were still here.

He found Gethin in the hall eating his breakfast. There was a surprising amount of good meat left from the victory feast and Rhun took a knuckle of mutton and a flask of ale and joined him. But how to broach this? They ate in silence until Gethin could stand it no longer. 'All right, Rhun, what is it? Something's on your mind. Spit it out.'

'We need to learn better how to fight. I thought we might ask Ecgrig to help.' Rhun had not meant to be so abrupt – would Gethin be angry? Now it had come out in a rush. But Gethin took it in his stride.

'Guthlac's sergeant? Well, you could do worse. I have taught you all I can that's for sure.'

'D'you think he'll do it?'

'I can see no reason why not. Guthlac and his men are not overstretched. We will ask him – but afterwards there is something we have to do together.' Rhun waited, but Gethin said nothing more.

Guthlac agreed readily. '*Na*, Gethin is right, we can do no more than stay here and guard the door for a while. Now that my lord Merewalh has taken the field in force there is little work for us here. My men could do with the exercise and if we can't get your band of young ruffians up to the mark then no one can,' he said. He called over to his sergeant. 'Ho, Ecgrig, these boys want you to teach them how to fight – will you do it?'

Ecgrig was a solid man, no taller than Rhun but built like a wall. Serious but likeable: twenty years of fighting had left him scarred in his body but not in his mind. 'Aye,' he said, 'I will that.' And so it was agreed they should start that evening when those boys who had to work would be free to join them. 'Better they all start together,' he said.

'So, what was this other matter, Gethin?' Rhun asked as they turned to leave.

'This morning there are more important things than work, even than war. Not that this will take long. Go gather your friends who are not Christian and join me at the south gate. Quietly, mind.'

Peleg. Of course.

'*Na*,' said Rhun, 'I will bring them all, Christian or not. He was a good companion.'

They left Ecgrig to his duties. He was Ænglisc and of their faith; it made no odds to him.

It was Rhun's mother who was the Christian, like so many of the womenfolk. The new faith had not yet taken firm hold among the people of the deep country, particularly in those places where Rome's touch had been light. The church in Prydein was strong, but even before the fall of Britannia it was the noble and the educated who had taken it up in earnest. Many of the simple folk still felt it wise to hedge their bets. Carwenna and others of Peleg's family joined

Rhun and Gethin and the companions, and they made their way quietly out of the village. No one spoke. There was nothing to be said.

They left the river to their right and took a path which led them east and a little south. Out among the farm-strips, those who knew what was afoot stopped in their work and made signs to help the little procession on its way. Some nodded to their fellows, put down their tools and joined behind. No words were spoken: there was no need for secrecy, but neither was there any call to offend. And it was not hard to offend some Christians.

Once beyond the strips, the land rose. Gethin led them into the trees, and they toiled up a steep, narrow valley. Tall oak, ash and holly with a tangle of underbrush, the woods closed in around them, cloaking the small procession with their shadow, but Gethin never faltered. He followed a path no one else could see, but he followed it without hesitation.

After a climb of about half a mile the woods came to an end, forming a great circle a hundred paces wide around the hilltop. The hill rose another twenty feet or so but it was bare of all but grass and the sharp herbs that like such places. From here it was not steep and soon they came to the very crest and stood on its flattened dome, forming a circle of their own around a low grey rock.

This place was known to them all, but today it seemed unfamiliar, strange even. Beside the rock stood a man they did not know. A stranger, awaiting them. Dark hair greying at the temples, deep-set eyes either side of a great beak of a nose, in a nut-brown face deeply lined. A commanding face. He was dressed in a long robe of woven stuff, dark, all deep greens and greys. Across his shoulders was a light cloak of fine skins held by a golden brooch of intricate and ancient design, rich and beautiful. He had a torc of twisted golden wire around his neck, with bracelets of similar work on his arms. At his feet a circle of turf had been cleared, wherein a low fire burned. As they gathered around him, he stirred it with the foot of a long staff of dark wood, subtly carved and worked with silver.

Rhun glanced around at the gathering. They were standing in a tight semi-circle, keeping a small but respectful distance from the flames. None looked about to flee, but the Christians among them, Cynrig, Eryl, Llif, looked as uncomfortable as he felt himself.

The man stood in silence, it seemed, for an eternity. Then he held a hand out over the flames and barked a command. A thick, aromatic smoke arose as if in obedience. It swirled around them and the world seemed to darken, for all it was still morning. Rhun became aware of a low, wordless chant. A sound that seemed to have been part of him since time began but one which he heard for the first time only now. He stood transfixed, suspended, no longer aware of his fellows. And then the voice changed or another voice started, Rhun was never sure which. Words this time but in no language known to him.

And it seemed as if Peleg stood before him again. A new Peleg, clean and bright. No longer scarred by wounds and death, still the youth of fourteen summers, fresh and strong, ready to go. And Rhun thought that he spoke. 'Do not grieve Rhun, you gave me more than you can know. Now we must both move on, and you have much work to do. Farewell.' Rhun's heart leaped. He held out his arms to embrace his friend but Peleg faded and was gone.

The smoke cleared, the morning sunlight returned, and the songs of birds. Rhun looked again at the strange man and found him gone also. In his place was a quite ordinary person, dressed the same – but now his clothes looked simple, unadorned, his staff a plain stick. And Rhun realized with a jolt that he did know this man, had seen him often when his wanderings brought him to Lenteurde. He was the healer, the eye man, the man who mended bones and fixed your back when it was stiff. In his life Rhun had never known a *derwydd*, but he knew that he beheld one now. He knew of them, who did not? He knew that they had been once a great force in the land, but long long ago. It was like meeting a figure out of legend. What glamour had been on him that he had not seen this earlier? He shivered slightly. Probably best not to ask, he thought. But he knew that he would: as soon as he could get Gethin on his own he would find out what had just happened.

It was over. The small group stirred as the spell was broken. They shook themselves, dusting down their clothes as if to rid themselves of something. They looked at each other as if surprised to see them. But no one said a word. In silence they gathered themselves and made their way back, down from this perilous place, leaving the wanderer to himself.

As they entered the trees Rhun looked back. The man had gone.

So too had the fire.

They returned to the village and to their ordinary lives and Ecgrig was true to his word. When the day's work was done, they found him waiting for them in the courtyard.

'Now then young Rhun, are you and your lads ready?'

Ecgrig was a little puzzled at first by the short Roman swords the boys carried, but he recognized their value. 'I can see these will take some special training – so be prepared for some hard work.'

True to his word, he proved to be every bit as hard a master as Gethin, more so, and they knew now what skills they lacked. For the next two hours he drove them hard. Bruises taken, blood drawn, they fought on until they were exhausted.

It was dark and getting late before Rhun had a chance to get Gethin on his own.

'What happened up there, Gethin? – I saw Peleg!'

'I'm glad that you did. As did I – as did all, I should think. It may have worried some but – have they said anything?'

'*Na*. Nothing.' Rhun paused. 'Look – that man on the hill this afternoon – I know him – I've seen him often, but never like that. Was it a dream? Surely he's just a travelling healer?'

'Just a travelling healer, is it?' Gethin laughed, and made a sign against ill luck. 'It's true, he is just a travelling healer, most of the time and to most eyes. But what do you suppose that means?'

'Well… I don't know. Is he truly *derwydd* – a druid? I thought they were just stories.'

'You could call him that. It would not be wrong. And they are real enough, even if they do avoid men's gaze in these times. He and his kind are inheritors of ancient knowledge, of healing and much more besides. Carried from the deep past. Such knowledge is not easily come by: they must travel to places unknown to the likes of us, perilous places, secret places. It makes them strange to us.'

Rhun shivered. 'But he is a good man, surely?'

Gethin shrugged. 'Good? Yes I suppose he is. But good and bad are not qualities he would acknowledge, I'm thinking. He is his knowledge. It is part of him, for good or ill.'

Rhun could think of nothing to say. Something from the tales of his childhood had walked out of the past. As large as life. And almost as real.

'Listen, Rhun, you are now the head of this place, as Guthlac said last night. It is no good waiting until your father returns – though I'm sure he will. He took up the new faith for your mother's sake and many in the village are glad. But – well, you know not all are. Many of the folk still believe in the old warriors' gods and are uncertain of this god of peace. I'm not saying there is a problem right now but if there is a conflict, then it is you who must find a way between the old faith and the new that all may follow. If anyone feels frightened or worried by things we saw this afternoon – the Christians in particular – they will look to you for guidance.'

But if any of them did, none said so.

Reports came in from time to time of more skirmishes up and down the borderlands, but none came close enough to trouble them directly. Their days were filled with work. Work in the fields and as much again at arms when the working day was ended. Ecgrig was fair but he pushed them to their limits and beyond. Each day was filled with sweat and effort, first in the fields and then with Ecgrig as he tried to hammer them into the fighters they would have to become if their little force was to be of any use. Yet they would not give up, they would not let Peleg down. And gradually his work yielded results. Their strength grew as their muscles developed to accommodate these new demands. All could shoot with bow and sling, some well, and most could wield a sword with some hope of winning. And they talked of now and of the future. For himself, Rhun let the memory of Peleg's death recede into the back of his mind, where it sat like the scar from an old wound. No longer painful but yet a constant reminder. As did the others, it seemed, for though his name came up from time to time it no longer brought the old fears with it; now he was remembered with humour and affection. No mention was made of what had happened on the hill on that strange morning. They saw nothing of the druid, if that is truly what he had been, and Gethin never spoke of him again.

And then there came news that justified their every effort. Penda returned, the Ænglisc lord who had so impressed Rhun the summer before. He rode in at dusk, quietly, with just a few men at arms in attendance.

Rhun had been in the mews, a place he still went as often as he could. His new falcon had needed a hood and he was busy at the delicate stitching. He had out-grown the merlin he had flown as a boy. She sat quietly now in honourable retirement, flown rarely and then only by his mother. Now he had a proud peregrine, all power and speed, a master of the skies. He had found it newly fledged and brought it home in triumph, a child again in his delight. It had been a battle: many times it drew his blood and it was heavy on his wrist, fully four of his hand-spans tall. But now it was his constant companion when he was not working or practising war. The falconer had helped him and shown him what to do, and now he was as good as anyone with the bird.

'You must give him a name,' the falconer had said.

'I shall call him Ythyr, for he is proud and powerful.'

'That is a good name. He will do well with that name.'

So now, when he rode out with Gethin, it was the

peregrine he took. He still flew the merlin when it was just a venture for the pot, but the peregrine was his pride.

He had been engrossed in the work, intent on catching the last of the light, and had not noticed the new arrival.

'So, I find you where I left you. Have you not been out all these months?'

Rhun jumped and pricked his finger. He turned, sucking the blood, ready with a word as sharp. But he stood stock still, struck dumb, his finger in his mouth. Suddenly he realized how ridiculous this must look and took it out.

'Penda!'

'Ha! Yes, my friend. Come.' He held out his arms, and though they had only met once, it was a meeting as of old friends.

'Where've you come from? Have you ridden far? And has anyone looked after you?'

'Slow down, slow down. My men and I have been welcomed as only your good mother knows how. Indeed it was she who sent me here to find you.'

'It's wonderful to see you. But what brings you here? Is there trouble?'

'Trouble? There is always trouble, but not here yet I think. No, but I have things to tell you – much has happened since our last meeting, and not just to your father and my lord Cadwallon. But are you finished? I don't want to interrupt.'

'You have news of my father? We've heard nothing since he left.'

'News? Aye, I do. News of a great battle and – a defeat, yes, I'm sorry to say. But of your father himself? No, nothing, I'm afraid. Yet, in that there is hope – I have not heard that he is dead either. Cadwallon is reported in Ireland, so let us hope your father is with him. So, come – we will talk of these things later. There will be much to discuss. But now – what of you? I have been hearing great things.'

Rhun nodded dumbly. He stared out into the gathering gloom. His father. Where was he? Oh, please God, where was he?

Chapter 6

'This is good wine,' said Penda. He stared into his glass at the rich red liquid, lit to a glow by the flames. Old thick glass, an heirloom he supposed.

'I'm glad you like it,' said Rhun. 'We still get merchants down from Cilgwri. Especially now that Merewalh has made his court at Lene.'

'Cilgwri? I do not know it.'

'You call it Wirheal, I believe.'

'Ah, yes. Of course.'

They fell into a companionable silence. The arrival of such a guest without warning had set the house a-bustle. What had been prepared as the usual modest family meal was suddenly blown into a full-scale feast of greeting. Angharad had presided, with Rhun at her side, though with Cwyfan away and so many of the freemen with him it was still a small affair, and no one lingered. If his mother was disturbed by the lack of news of her husband, she did not show it.

When the meal was done Rhun and Penda had drawn their chairs to the fire and sat with their wine, lit only by its flickering light, shadows gathered about their shoulders in the quiet darkness.

Penda looked into the flames. Rhun was aching to hear what he had to say but let his friend relax and gather his thoughts. At last Penda looked up and cast his gaze slowly around the hall, taking it all in, missing nothing, as was his way. He sighed contentedly. 'This is good. This is...' he searched for the word '... precious. Do you not agree?'

Rhun was puzzled. This was normal – he had never thought to question it. 'What do you mean?' he asked.

Penda sat up. Suddenly serious, intent. 'I am sorry, you

will be wanting to hear about Cadwallon and your father. You do not want my wandering thoughts. Yet they are not unconnected.' He paused. 'As I said, there has been a great battle. Cadwallon has been defeated. Routed, some say. There is talk that he has fled to Ireland with what remains of his fighting force. Your father among them, I hope. But – that is all we know. The last we heard, Edwin had taken over the strong places on Mona and east along the coast – at least as far as Deganwy. I gather he is still fighting, but westward now. Well, that should keep him pinned down for a while. There are a lot of strong places among those hills. I find it hard to believe that they have all been overcome – that nothing remains. It's my belief, certainly my hope, he has met some stiff resistance, or even that he is under attack himself, though that's a wilder hope. Either way, I'm guessing he'll be digging in for winter. But, well, I don't know. And that is the problem – I don't know anything for certain! I'm supposing he has a big army, but I don't know how big. I have no notion of his intentions, though I fear the worst – I must fear the worst!' He gripped the arms of his chair. 'But by the gods, I need news – to be ignorant is to be vulnerable. I tell you, my friend, if we are to preserve *this*,' he looked around again, 'this precious place, and all places like it, we must have knowledge.'

'Do you really think we are in such danger?'

'I do, and perhaps sooner than we think. And, for me it couldn't come at a worse time.' He leaned forward in his chair, his elbows on his knees, caressing his wine glass absently. 'Rhun, this is between ourselves, but I must tell you that my own future hangs in the balance. Cearl is near death. He has declared me his heir but, as you may guess, there are those amongst our people who will do their utmost to see that I don't inherit. Inheritance is no more automatic amongst us Ænglisc than it is among your own people: a more popular man may be chosen by the council – or at least a more vocal one, and I cannot speak on my own behalf if I am not there. And believe me, Rhun, it is important that they do not win, for if they do I fear for Mercia, for the peace we have between us – Ængel and Briton. They are not like us, Cearl and me, they are hungry for wealth and power and that makes them dangerous.

'If Edwin comes here they will fight him for the spoils like raging dogs. If he does not, you may still have another as bad and one right on your doorstep. I am taking a risk coming here – I cannot be away for long or I may lose all – we may lose all. I am in a bind – I must have information and yet I cannot go into Gwynedd.'

'Is there no one among your people you could send?'

'What – send an Ænglisc man into Gwynedd? I might just get away with it, having the tongue, but anyone else would be dead within a day as things stand.

'And now there is all this unrest along our marches – I do not know what has prompted it but it is growing and I fear what it may provoke amongst our theigns. Merewalh is containing it but I cannot help him. To send a force from Mercia would be to provoke a war too soon. I did think of asking in Pengwern but there is no one there I know and trust enough. Besides, they are grown timorous since Chester – I would still have them as allies but they will not make strong ones just now.'

There was a long pause. The fire crackled in the dim silence.

'I will go,' Rhun said. 'If you think I can do it.'

A log shifted and lit up his face with a yellow glow.

'I will be honest with you, Rhun – I had hoped you would say so, and I believe you can. You and your friends are more than ready, from what I hear, and if all your effort has been for anything, it is surely for work like this.'

Rhun was childishly pleased with the compliment. This was a task far greater than turning a cattle raid. More than just a few villages depended on this. Though Peleg's death still haunted him, any doubts were soon swept aside.

Penda watched him in silence. He waited, toying with his wine, waiting for Rhun to speak.

'So, I will follow my father – you can tell me the way, I hope.'

'Well, your father went by the north road, but I fear that is not the road for you – Edwin will expect attack that way, so it will be well guarded if I'm any judge – as I said, we know he has taken Deganwy. No, you must go more quietly.'

'What other way is there?'

'You must go by Aber Glaslyn and pass under the west shoulder of Yr Wyddfa. The distance is no greater and the country no worse and you will have the mountains between you and him until you are at his door. But you must go soon, for the year grows older. All too soon autumn will be upon us and early snow may close the passes.' He paused, searching for words. 'But I must tell you – that road will take you through the uplands of Powys. The people there are no more fond of you than they are of us now that Elisedd's reach has grown short. They have no love for Edwin either, but it is certainly they who are making this present mischief. It is what they do best, and we still don't know why a raiding band from those parts was led by an Ænglisc man.'

'Do you think it is connected?'

'I don't know. It may be nothing, but – well you must take care.'

Rhun awoke with a start. It was still black night and all was silent. He shook himself trying to clear his mind of the dream which had jolted him awake. He had been with his father, or was it Penda? The battle had been fierce, many had fallen – he was dead himself – no, that couldn't be right, maybe it had been his father. He rubbed his eyes. It had all seemed so clear just a second ago but it was fading fast. A sudden cry from a vixen and the long howl of a farm dog in reply came to him through the open shutters. They resonated with the sense of imminent peril which was all he retained of his nightmare. Had it been a message? If so, it was useless if he could not recall it, even if he could guess its meaning. And now it had gone.

He lay there long, thinking over Penda's situation and the adventure he had talked himself into. Oh yes, he had talked himself into it. Penda had not asked, he would never have put a friend into such a position, but the friend had not needed that courtesy – he had just jumped right in. As always. When would he learn? But Penda was right, he thought. If all their training and their experience, minimal though the latter was, were for anything, surely it was for something like this. The village needed protecting and he should be the one to do it, even from a storm such as this. Even if it meant his death. And if that protection meant leaving the village in the care of Guthlac and his men, so be it. He knew suddenly that this was meant to be. He must follow his fathers and go to war. He could not quite rid himself of the doubt he felt in his inner self, but he fell back into a sleep no longer troubled by midnight fears.

Within two days they were ready. Penda had gone down to Lene: he could not wait. He must warn all his neighbours, he said, with little time to do it, and he had gone the next morning taking with him a special message to Merewalh from Rhun and his mother.

The companions set out at first light. The day was fresh and wind-blown. A new chill was in the dawn with the summer gone, the taller trees showing the first stains of age. Rags of cloud sped across a sky tinted pink by the rising sun. There were but nine of them now with Peleg gone. His loss was still in their minds, but time had dimmed the hurt, and they could scarcely speak for excitement. This was a land-mark in their lives. Let out – *na*, sent out – on their own, and on serious business. Of course Gethin was with them, but he would not be going the whole way so he didn't count. That had been agreed long before. Yet it had not been an easy parting for any of them, least of all for Rhun.

His mother had looked at him, her fear plain in her eyes. 'It is madness – what do you think you can do? You have never been in Gwynedd.' He had heard her words but knew that her protest was different from before. Something had changed. Rhun realized in that moment that she was no longer worried about him, or even the people, but about herself.

'You are our only defence with your father still away.' She shuddered and paused. 'And now I am afraid there is little hope of his return.'

She put her hand to her mouth, biting her knuckles, fearful of having spoken the words. Rhun hated to see her like this. Part of him longed for the days when she was still Angharad the great matriarch, fearless and proud, even though she had had little time for him. She was still his mother. To see her fallen into despair tore at his heart. And yet another part of him grew impatient.

'Mother, this war is bigger than our wants and needs, no matter how pressing. When has it ever been otherwise? None of us can just stand by and do nothing. Even if this place were not in danger, I would have to do this. And don't doubt that we are all under threat from Edwin. He won't stop with Gwynedd. Gethin will be back within a se'night and Merewalh will still protect you – Ecrig and his men will guard you every bit as well as I could.'

But she would not be appeased.

Help had come from an unexpected source. The whole village knew of the plan, almost as soon as it had been made. On the following morning, Peleg's mother had arrived at the hall unlooked-for.

'I have come to tell you that all will be well. I have seen it – do not be afraid,'

'What is this – what are you talking about, Carwenna? Do not think to come to me with your superstition!'

'You may call it so, Angharad, but we who follow the old ways know a thing or two you Christians seem to have forgotten, and I tell you I have seen this.'

'Whatever you have seen – I care not. You have lost your son – how can you now come to me and ask me to lose mine?'

'Why would I not? We must all make sacrifices, I suppose. But, Angharad, be easy: I tell you I know that the future is not as bleak as you imagine.'

'I cannot believe you, I will not believe you. Go home and do not trouble me with your nonsense.'

Carwenna drew her cloak around her, sorrow in her face. She sighed.

'As you wish. It will not alter things – unless you prevent Rhun from doing this.'

Angharad stared at her with blank eyes. At last she gathered herself.

'*Na*, you are right,' she said in a whisper. 'I must not stop him. Besides, I doubt that anything I say could.'

One more thing Rhun did that morning. He spoke to Brother Cledwyn and then called the boys together.

'We must go. We are all agreed. But I will not take any but free men with me.' He turned to Einion. 'Einion, in front of these witnesses I declare you a free man. God knows I owe you that much. I will not be denied this by any man, elder or not. Cledwyn will draw up the document and we will say no more of it. Do you accept it from my hand?'

Einion stood wordless. He seemed confused – almost embarrassed. In silence he took Rhun's proffered hand and solemnly clasped it in agreement.

At dawn they left, their hearts full and their heads high as they walked out through the throng of people lining the street to see them off. The day passed well. They made easy progress, following the Lent along well-trodden ways, through country they had known all their short lives, past the scenes of former glories and adventures, and one in particular. They all looked up at the little hidden valley as they passed, and felt it to be a good omen. In late afternoon they left the river and took a road which led uphill, north-west into higher country. As dusk fell, at last they arrived at the place of Gethin's people. A shallow bowl of a valley near the place where the little river which joined the Lent at Lenteurde had its birth. A small cluster of houses, built round in the old style and deeply thatched, each with its small yard with stack and store. An old sow lay in the shade of the hedge, her litter gathered around her, grown large now but still searching for suckle in an absent sort of way.

She grunted and flicked an ear as the chickens flapped amongst them to be out of the way of the new arrivals. Gethin's people welcomed them and they sat propped against each other on the thick straw which covered the hard clay of the floor, eating a rich bean stew from deep wooden bowls. It had been a long day for those unused to walking so great a distance and most were asleep almost before they lay down, tumbled together in the long bed shared by all.

But Rhun found he could not sleep. Brought up in the hall, he was unused to so many around him. He eased himself quietly from the tangle of bodies on the bed, careful not to disturb them, and picked his way to the door. The moon was up and nearing full, the night cool and serene. He walked to the edge of the small compound and leant on the fence looking out into the moonlight. The land appeared strange, unreal in this mix of dazzling silver and deep, dark shadow. He shivered with a sudden sense of doom. He felt he was looking into the future, into a strange and new land where all his familiar things were gone, where he recognized nothing. A time and a place where he would have to learn all anew. The companions took his leadership for granted. In that moment he wished he could share their confidence.

A small noise behind him made him turn. A familiar form was approaching from the house.

'Gethin, is it you?'

'It is; I couldn't sleep either. So – how're you feeling? Not nervous, I hope.'

He leaned on the fence and together they looked out into the valley, peaceful once again.

'Nervous – well, a bit,' Rhun said after a while.

'Don't you worry – you just keep your head and remember what Cadwallon told you – be circumspect. The gods know I've told you that myself often enough – perhaps you'll listen to him.' Gethin laughed gently, not entirely in humour.

Rhun smiled. He knew the truth behind Gethin's words. It was only a few nights gone that he had accused himself.

'That day – it seems a lifetime ago now.'

'It does indeed – much has happened since then.' He

chuckled, casting his mind back. 'The look on your face! *Na, na* it was nothing to be ashamed of. I say again, much has happened. And look, you'll not be alone. Your little band has grown strong and you will not face peril unsupported. There will be friends along the way as well as enemies. But you must take advantage of your men – use their skills and talents. That Ysgyrran, for example – he's quiet but he's proud – a lot more goes on in his head than he lets show. And Einion, I know he's not easy but all he needs is something to do – find him a task.'

It was just like Gethin to call them men. He had always known the right note to strike.

'You're right, of course. Einion doesn't seem to hate me any more but he does have me worried – how can I know to trust him? He's a year older than me and twice my size!'

'Only trust can beget trust. You find him something to do and he'll be fine. He's a loner or a follower, I reckon – the fact that he's here at all shows he respects you, now he's no slave. Even if he doesn't like you yet.'

The day broke fine. Warm and sun-filled, one of the last flings of the summer. Gethin would not be coming any further. Now they would truly be on their own. While the little army prepared themselves, Rhun sought out Einion and took him to one side.

'I have a favour to ask you. Will you do it?' No point in hedging with Einion.

Einion looked at him, his face unreadable. 'Depends what it is,' he said.

'It's going to need tact.'

There was silence for a moment. Then, 'I can do that.'

'Well, see, it's Tecwyn. You know what he's like – he thinks he's immortal, and since the cattle raid he's certain of it. That's dangerous – and not just for him. And there's Cynrig. Oh, he's brave enough too, but he's got over-much imagination and that saps his confidence.' He paused, trying to read Einion's expression. 'Look after them, will you? Only, for God's sake, don't let them know that you are doing it!'

Einion stared, as if weighing up this request. It seemed to Rhun that he saw a flash of anger, but then Einion just nodded.

Gethin's people gave them dried meat and bread for the journey. He came with them to the gate and set them on their road. 'Now remember – once you get over the hill follow it down and to the north. You'll find a river running west to east – Hafren – follow it upstream. It's not so big up there as it is when it runs south through Mercia, but don't let that fool you – it's still dangerous. Beside it runs the old road the Romans made. Follow it upstream to a place where the river flows from the south and the road crosses westwards. The crossing was still good when I was last there. You should be there in a couple of days at most. On the far side you'll find the ruins of the old Roman place and beyond that a small village – ask there for Teifion, he is a kinsman and will help you on your way.'

'Thank you Gethin – you and all your kin,' said Rhun.

'One more thing. Don't forget what your friend Penda said – you can't trust the men up here to let you through without trouble. Even in normal times, but certainly not with all this fighting going on. Keep out of sight as much as you can, hidden if possible. Avoid all men 'til you cross the river. Even then, be careful who you trust.'

They followed the ridge as it climbed the last slopes westward and took them away from everything they knew. From this day on they would be in strange country. Not one of them had been this far before.

Throughout the morning the fine weather held. From the tops they could see for miles. On all sides long lines of hills ranked, tier upon tier, into the haze of distance. Far off on the horizon rose dark, jagged mountains, still a long way off yet already looming, unimaginably high, unknown and unfriendly. But they were far away. Here, larks rose as they passed, chattering on the wind. Everything was light and air and warm smells. It would take more than distant gloom to quell the joy of their new-found freedom.

But it was not to last. In these hills the weather could change without warning. Iron-grey cloud had been building from the southwest throughout the day. It waited until they had crossed the watershed, and at first it was light, throwing only a few spots at them as they plunged down through bracken and birch into the deep, oak-filled vale of Hafren. But then it came down in earnest. When at length they reached the valley floor, there was the old road, its surface puddled from the ragged drifts of rain. The river flowed in wide meanders but the road was straight and they followed it from the trees, as they had been told, keeping hidden as best they could. The valley wandered northwards for a while and then turned west and south around a low hill, widening as they walked upstream. The land was wild and untilled. They saw a few clusters of huts, here and there down by the water side, and one substantial place which they supposed must be a local lordling, but all looked run down and sad, as if the people had no time or no will to maintain them. The people, indeed, seemed invisible. They had seen no one, heard no dogs. Either there was no work to be done, or there was no one to do it. Though that didn't make them feel any safer.

The need to keep in deep cover made the going slow and it was late on the second day before they came to the crossing place, made long ago by the Legions to carry their road into the great hills beyond. If there was to be trouble they would find it here. Helped by the rain, they were sure they had arrived unseen, but now they had no choice but to expose themselves to whomever might be watching, or wait until nightfall. They lay flat in the undergrowth on the edge of the woods.

They had been going as quietly as they could but as soon as they stopped moving themselves, they heard the sounds of men. Men and horses. Not loud, but close. They could just make out a group camped by the crossing place, out across the water meadows.

The valley floor was flat at this point and the river wide and wandering, splitting into a complex web of smaller, shallow streams. Between them and the main flow was a wilderness of scrub and sodden grazing. The road had fallen into ruin, cut here and there by new channels formed by decades of snow-melt flooding down from the high hills. The crossing looked difficult at any time. Now it looked impossible.

'So, it is guarded, as we feared.'

Ysgyrran lay beside him. 'They don't look very vigilant. See – they're trying to get a fire lit. That'll keep them busy!'

Rhun wiped the film of rain from his eyes. 'Even if we wait 'til dark, they'd have to be blind to miss us,' he murmured.

'They would,' said Ysgyrran, 'but half-light in this weather could hide an army. We can't use the road, but look – we could try a route through those sallows.' He pointed to a line of low, stumpy trees which ran across the valley parallel to the road, cutting across the streams at right angles, and which seemed to offer some cover. 'If we go one at a time, at intervals, they'll never see us. It'll mean a lot of wading but – well – we can't get much wetter.'

Rhun considered this. There was precious little day left. He must decide now or wait out the night on this side. It was possible that the river guard would leave, but they had got their fire going now and he could see no reason why they should. Might as well do it now as ever. 'You must go while we can still see to follow you,' he said. Ysgyrran looked at him, an eyebrow raised. 'Well, it's your idea – you should be the one to try it.'

He grinned and turned to the others. 'Come on – we must go now if we're going to go at all. Ysgyrran will lead, Meical – you follow, then me, then you others one by one. Einion, will you bring up the rear?'

Einion was miles away, staring down to the group of figures at the crossing place. 'Me – sorry – do what?'

'Bring up the rear – make sure no one gets left behind. Would you?' He got a nod. 'Good man. Now come on, let's go. Remember everyone, count to twenty – slowly – before you follow, but don't lose sight of the one in front at any cost.'

'I hope you know what you're doing,' murmured Ysgyrran. 'I wouldn't trust him.'

'I've got to sometime. Now's as good a chance as I'll get.'

Half an hour later Rhun found himself thigh-deep in water, picking his way alongside the sallows as they cut a route through the water meadows, wet and dry in turn. Someone had once made use of these trees, they had all been pollarded for withies. Now, thank God, they grew uncontrolled and gave good cover from the road. Some fifty paces in front of him he could just see Meical, half-walking, half-wading, following Ysgyrran's path. Fifty paces behind he hoped another was following him, but he dared not turn to look in case he lost sight of Meical. As he hoped he had made clear to the others, their safety depended on keeping each other in sight. The rain had eased and the sky had lifted a fraction, but it was getting dark quickly now. Especially at ground level under the trees.

The trees ended. He had reached the final channel. It was wide here but, so far, nowhere had it been deep. Ysgyrran was nowhere in sight but he could just see Meical as he splashed across the shallows on the far side, so he knew it was at least passable. He prayed no one else had seen. He hesitated for a moment, took one last look around and plunged on. Almost at once it was up to his waist and getting deeper. He found himself swimming as much as wading. The current was stronger here and the depth bothered him. Not for himself so much as the younger boys – would Cynrig and Eryl make it alone? And what of little Tecwyn – he'd never make it across this. Wretchedly he stood, uncertain what to do, while the water pressed and rushed around him. Then he turned back and waited by the sallow brake. Almost immediately Cynrig arrived.

'Rhun – why are you waiting?'

'It's too deep for you – we'll need to go together. Is Eryl behind you?'

'He was – yes, look, here he comes now.'

Eryl struggled up to join them, looking half-drowned already.

'The three of us are going to go together: you two hold onto me if it gets too deep.'

'What about Tecwyn?'

Rhun stared desperately into the gloom. The river flowing past his knees pulled at him. He shifted his feet to get a better balance and strained to penetrate the dimness. He looked up into the sky. The brief lull had not lasted. The clouds had closed in again and the rain came down in rods. He waited. At last he saw movement and Llif came into view. Rhun waved his arm, pointing to the two smaller boys. He saw his signal acknowledged, and turned back to the others.

'Einion will take care of him. Come on.' But would he? Should he wait for all the others to catch up? No, Llif and Ithwalh would be fine and Einion would look after Tecwyn, he was sure of it.

With Cynrig and Eryl clinging to his arms, Rhun plunged into the main stream. He had feared the smaller boys might be a hindrance but he found that the three together gave them all an unexpected stability. Still, it was far from easy. The river bed was rocky, uneven and loose in places. The push of the water seemed to grow with every passing moment. They were about halfway across when Rhun heard a small cry, as suddenly cut off, and felt a huge pull on his downstream arm. Eryl had vanished. 'Hold on!' he yelled to Cynrig. He could still feel Eryl's hands gripping his arm. He staggered, trying desperately to keep his footing, fighting against the double pressure of the current and Eryl's dead weight. One foot slipped as he applied more weight to it. It slid half a pace and then stopped, jammed against a rock. Almost sick with fear, he braced himself, and using Cynrig as an anchor, he pulled with all his strength. At last Eryl bobbed up, spluttering and gasping for air.

They stood in mid-stream, clinging to each other, hearts pounding, and gathered their strength. *This is madness,* Rhun thought, *what are we doing?* He felt his skin crawl, and not from cold, as he fought down his fear.

'Are you all right?' he asked after a moment, shouting above the roar of the water.

'Yes. Sorry,' yelled Eryl, his chest heaving as he gulped in lungs-full of air, 'I'm fine. There was a big hole, my foot went right in.'

'Come on, then.'

They staggered on even more cautiously now, testing each step with elaborate care. Yet at last the ground turned to shingle and Rhun realized they were across. He stood on the bank, shivering from cold and fear. Thank God he had waited. He forced away a vision of Eryl washed up miles downstream, a broken and bloated corpse. Holding the two smaller boys by their scruffs, he half stood and ran, stooped, across the turf to a low clump of trees visible only as a patch of greater darkness.

Hands reached out and pulled them into safety. 'That's five across – and here comes Llif.'

Llif staggered up panting for breath. 'I got your signal so I waited for Ithwalh,' he said. 'Good idea, that.' And Rhun saw that Ithwalh followed right behind, his arms above his head clasping a bundle.

'*Duw*, am I glad to be here. Let's not do that again!' He put his bundle down, collapsing onto the ground after it. 'If I'd been on my own I reckon I'd have dropped that lot halfway across – and then what'd we have done for bow strings?'

'Quiet!' hissed Rhun. The noise from the river would cover any sound bar a shout, but he was still scared. That had been too close with Eryl. Where were Tecwyn and Einion? Please God they get through all right. It was nearly fully dark now. The clouds were as black as pitch and the rain veiled everything. He clung to this one comfort – no one could possibly have seen them crossing.

The day seemed to stand still. The sky got darker, but nothing else changed – just the river rushing past as they clung together staring into the rain – none knew how long. At last they saw a shadow, a movement of something darker than the water, which resolved itself into Einion, as if reassembled from a patch of mist, and with Tecwyn clinging to his back.

'You can get off now!' Einon said as they reached the shingle. Relieved of his small burden, he stood up and stretched. 'The water was taller than him in places,' he grunted. 'Didn't want to lose him.'

Rhun grinned. Einion looked at him, his hands in the small of his back, his head held back. For a moment neither moved. Then he too broke into a grin and, as if on cue, they both nodded. It had been a test – they both knew it – but Einion had taken it and had passed. *Thank you, Gethin,* Rhun thought, *you were right, of course.*

They stood quite still, sodden and cold, and listened. Nothing moved. No sound other than the rain and the rush of the river.

'I reckon we've made it. If anyone saw they would be on to us by now. Come on – let's find this village. But be careful, we're still very exposed.'

They cast about, keeping cover where they could, scurrying from one clump of bushes to the next. What at first had been level flood-wash, now rose gently before them, dotted with small clumps of scrubby thorn trees. But they saw no sign of a village.

Tired and dispirited, at last they came to a low bank. They stumbled up its shallow slope and found themselves on the brink of what should have been a dry ditch. It was now a string of long puddles. Across it another bank rose steeply, a few lumps of masonry showing here and there in the dim light, pale like old bones.

'Come on, there may be shelter here,' Rhun said wearily, scant hope in his voice.

They splashed across the ditch and scrambled over the broken walls. They found themselves in an enclosure, all lumps and bumps, overgrown and ruinous. It was just a big open space, lashed with rain, but in one corner a substantial bit of an old wall still stood, its back to the wind and half buried under a heavy growth of ivy, forming a shallow cave. As they approached a pale shadow emerged, speeding towards them. They sprawled in momentary panic, but it was only an owl startled out of its night-time roost. They cowered from it, but even a sign of such ill-luck had lost its power after the fright of the river. They crept inside and huddled together, chilled to the marrow. Rhun longed for a fire but dared not light one so close to the road. Even if he could have got one lit.

'This will have to do – I don't want to blunder about in the dark all night. We'll wait 'til daylight.'

'Should we set a guard?'

Rhun peered out into the dark. 'You can if you like – for myself, I don't think we need one.'

He lay back among the huddle, grateful tonight for the close warmth of other bodies.

Meical was lying close beside him, as he had the night before. 'I thought I'd lost you back there when you weren't behind me,' he whispered.

But he got no answer.

Rhun was woken by a gentle shake.

'What...?'

'Shh – keep quiet.'

Ysgyrran was crouched in the entrance to their little cave, silhouetted in the dim light of early dawn. Rhun extracted himself from the tangle of arms and legs that were Meical and the others.

'What is it?' he murmured.

'Someone's out there. Perhaps you spoke too soon.'

'Maybe. Christ, it's cold, though.' He shivered. 'At least it's stopped raining. Have you had any sleep?'

'Some.'

'Look, I'll wake the others – you keep watching.'

He woke each in turn, careful to keep them silent. 'Stay where you are but be ready,' he whispered.

'Can you see who it is? I mean is it a man – one of those men at the crossing?'

'I don't know – it was just a movement and I've not seen it again. But I'm certain it was human.'

They jumped as a low voice came out of the darkness, 'Human it was, but not one you need to fear, I'm thinking.'

'Who's there? Who are you?'

A dark shape resolved out of what seemed like nothing. The boys shrank back into a huddle. 'My name is no secret, I am Teifion – I live here. No need to fear me. But who are you? That was a perilous way to cross the river.'

'Teifion, is it? You must be the one we seek.' Rhun stood up and stepped out into the dawn glimmer. The voice moved out of the shadows to stand before him. A small man of middle years and dark countenance.

'Seek? You know me, then?'

'I do not, but Gethin said to look here for a man with your name. But we couldn't find your village in the dark.'

'Gethin – that'll be the wife's cousin, I'm thinking. So who might you be?'

'I am Rhun ap Cwyfan ap Erthig, of Lenteurde in the valley of the Lent, and these are my companions.'

'Ha! Well, I am the man you seek all right, but a simple Teifion is all I go by.'

'Rhun, I'm cold.'

'Shut up Tecwyn,' said Einion.

'But I am.'

Of course he is – we all are, Rhun thought. 'Look, is there any chance of a fire?'

'But of course, now I know who you are. Come, this way, it is not far. You are lucky you had my name – you seemed more to be in trouble than to be trouble yourselves, but one becomes wary of strangers in these times. Like that lot down at the crossing.'

'You saw them? D'you know who they are?'

'I do not, but they'll be up to no good, I'd wager.'

They followed Teifion through the scrubby waste beside the river. The path, such as it was, crossed lawns of coarse turf, sewn with the droppings of sheep and rabbits, and interspersed with patches of gravel where the river in flood had washed away the thin peaty soil. As the early light grew in strength they could make out larger trees ahead and a cluster of low-roofed huts sheltering in their lee, hazy with the drift of early morning smoke.

There was no wall, no palisade, just nets strung from poles set up for the purpose, and other gear of the fisherfolk. The place was strong with the reek of sheep and fish.

'Come in, come in. Warm yourselves. Wife – here are Rhun ap – er, someone – and his companions. They say they are sent by your kinsman Gethin. They are wet, they are cold and I daresay they are hungry.'

'Friends of cousin Gethin, is it? And how is he? – It's been many a moon since we saw him!'

'Oh, he is well, mother,' said Rhun.

'You must tell him, when you see him again that my own mother died at last – his aunt, you know. It was her time, she was very old, but he would want to know.'

'Now then, wife, they'll die of cold while you prattle! Come – get to the fire.'

They stripped off their clothes and stood naked to the flames. Teifion and his wife wrapped them in coarse blankets and set their wet stuff to dry. They sat in a loose circle and ate a porridge of hot oatmeal with rough barley bread. Slowly the life returned to their frozen bodies.

'So, you didn't come here to bring us a message from my wife's cousin. What brings you on such a perilous journey, and to where, I wonder.'

Rhun glanced at his companions. 'We are seeking news of our fathers who went to war and have not returned.'

'The war in the north? We have heard tales, even down here – there is war and unrest everywhere. Even we have not escaped.'

'Who would trouble you here?'

'Well, the likes of them at the crossing for one thing. Oh, nothing too serious yet, but the whelps of Powys squabble eternally and these are disputed lands. With the king moved to Pengwern, as we hear, there is precious little peace hereabouts. Now I've heard talk that they have sought Saeson help in their quarrels – and nothing good ever came from that! They've been few enough so far, but maybe they will grow bolder still, if this war in the north goes on.'

'We have had some experience of that ourselves,' said Rhun. 'They have been raiding more and more into our country. We met one band led by an Ænglisc man. We could not work out why, but your words help explain the puzzle. Gethin advised us to keep well out of their way. But we thought they'd got us at the river.'

'They've been there a day or two. We wondered why. So is it you they are seeking, d'you think?'

'Not that we know of. Why would they? I don't see how they could even know about us.'

'Whether or no, it was as well to heed Gethin – you would not be welcomed as guests at their court.'

'Now you see why we took such care at the crossing.'

'And yet I saw you!' Teifion laughed. '*Na*, do not fret – my eyes are sharp and I know this place. You are safe enough. They do not cross the river. These remain the lands of Cadwallon ap Cadfan and his arm is long – or it used to be. *Na*, they'll get bored soon and be away back to their lair – downriver from here, a long day even on a horse. Look, while you're drying, I'll go and see how things are with them.' He rose, adding a touch grimly, 'Mind you, it was good there has been so little rain of late or you'd not have made it.'

Little rain, Rhun thought. *What must it be like when it's serious?*

In an hour or so their clothes were dry enough. Teifion returned.

'No fear of your friends seeing you – their eyes are fixed eastwards.'

The boys scrambled to their feet.

'That's good to hear. Well, thank you, Teifion,' Rhun said, 'and also for your hospitality. But we must go – if you could set us on our way?'

'You don't know it?'

'We don't – we were just told to take the pass west of a

place called Yr Wyddfa, a high mountain they said, but we don't know where it is.'

'It is our greatest mountain in these parts – the great snow mountain, for it is rarely free of it. Well, there is a road the red-crests made which goes north from here, but do not go that way – it is treacherous now and you will get lost. All the hills are haunted here but those are worse than most, it is said. Besides, that way will take you to the eastern pass and would keep you closer to the people you're tying to avoid. If you want the western pass, you must go west before you turn north. It is a darker road perhaps, but you will be safer. Fear not, the way is clear enough and I will tell you what to watch for. And once across the pass you will find others to help you, folk there are not like the men of Powys.'

The path took a line west and a little north, following the valley of a smaller river as it came out of the hills to join Hafren just above the crossing place. The way was faint. Amidst the tangle of hazel and alder, bracken and bramble, the valley seemed impassable. Without Teifion's instructions they might have missed it several times. With them, as he had promised, it was not so hard to follow. Indeed, here and there they could see hints that it followed a much older road now all but vanished under the tangle.

It had been a nightmare. They had almost failed at the first challenge. Now they were recharged. They were young, it was an adventure and they were entering country no one back at home had ever seen – properly on their way. The way, eventually, into the shadow of Yr Wyddfa, the great snow mountain. And then, who knew what?

Chapter 7

Tecwyn was worried. He had been worried, quietly and to himself, ever since they had left Teifion, three nights back. Within an hour of leaving they had climbed into a land of rolling hills, but their path had led them through narrow winding valleys, deep and gloomy, crowded with trees and seemingly bereft of human life. As Teifion had promised, the few people they did meet had welcomed them and helped them on their way. They had been passed on, from one to the next, like some sort of relay. And that had held good for the first two nights, but it had been hard going and had taken longer than they had hoped. By yesterday it seemed they had run out of friends. Last night had been spent in a wild and lonely place huddled round a small fire, for now the hills had grown higher and emptier of folk. Up here they knew of no one to aid them or give them shelter. Up here, for the first time, they were on their own. And Tecwyn's private worry had grown. Until now it had been a general sort of worry, the fear of the unknown perhaps, but today the feeling was strong, and felt somehow different. It was nothing he could put his finger on, but he was quite sure something was wrong. Something had changed. The country they had passed through had been new and unknown to them, but it had not felt alien, not threatening. Not like this did. He felt as if it, or something in it, was watching him. At last the feeling worried him enough to share it. He was walking with Cynrig, as had become their habit, being the two youngest.

'Do you feel anything strange?' he asked, quietly.

Cynrig had been looking at the ground as they walked, thinking about stones.

'What d'you mean?'

'I don't know – odd, unusual – with this place.'

Cynrig scanned the hillsides, his eyes following the screes upwards to the rocky cliffs which overhung the valley, crowned with scrubby trees clustered along the edge. The high hills above were still hidden in rags of brown cloud which hung damply over everything, killing sound. It was like walking through a long box in silence. No bird sang, no tree rattled, just their feet crunched on the stony path.

'I don't like it much but it doesn't look odd. Just wild.'

'*Na* – but can't you feel it? Eyes in your back? Brr – it gives me the shivers. I've got goose-bumps, look,' said Tecwyn, holding up his arm. The short hairs stood up, glistening in the damp air.

'Well, that's probably just the cold.' But as Cynrig said this, he knew he was lying – he had felt something himself, he just hadn't let it trouble him. 'It's just your imagination. Besides, who would be watching us?'

'Twylwth Teg,' Meical said, his voice low. 'They've been there this last hour. Keeping pace with us.'

They stopped and stood looking up, trying to pierce the mists above them and see into the tangled growth above.

Rhun glanced back. 'Come on you three, keep up!' But they showed no sign of moving. Then the stragglers caught up and everyone stopped.

'What's going on?'

'Gwyllian?' Tecwyn asked. Meical nodded.

'What are you talking about, Meical?' Rhun asked. He glanced around, sensing the tension. It had been hard walking and steep. Everyone was tired; everyone was cowed by these relentless, louring crags.

'Gwyllian,' said Meical.

'I don't see anyone. Are you sure?' said Rhun.

'His mother's people I expect – eh, Meical?' said Ysgyrran with a laugh. Slightly strained.

'You shut up about my mother!'

The others shuffled nervously.

Rhun laid a hand on Ysgyrran's arm. 'Leave it,' he said. 'Do they mean us harm, d'you think?' he said to Meical.

'I don't think so – they are the Watchers.'

'Watchers, is it? Doesn't sound too bad.'

Meical looked uncertain. 'I've not heard they're danger-ous, but I wouldn't promise you they aren't.'

The group closed up into a frightened huddle.

'You're sure – they just watch? Why would people just watch?' Rhun's voice dropped to a whisper. 'Come on, Meical, you're scaring the others.' *And me too if truth be told*, he thought as he glanced around, *but best keep that to myself – don't want a panic.*

'Not people – like I said, the Gwyllian are of the Twylwth Teg.'

Dead silence. They may not have come across the Gwyl-lian before but they all knew of the Twylwth Teg, and they knew them to be chancy at best.

'Brother Cledwyn says there's no such thing,' said Eryl into the ensuing silence, but no one took any notice. Panic was palpably close now.

'Good man, Eryl.' Rhun looked at the others. 'You hear that? Eryl says Brother Cledwyn reckons there's no such thing, and he believes him, don't you Eryl?'

'Well, I did, but I'm not so sure now.'

The silence was becoming oppressive. No one dared speak, as if speaking might precipitate something. The skin crawled on their backs. No amount of Christian upbringing could remove the fear of the Twylwth Teg, and they were not all Christians.

Panic edged closer.

'Come on – let's get out of here.'

But Ysgyrran stood, feet planted firmly, his arms folded, and looked up at the rocks. 'They just watch, do they?' he said. 'Well, good luck to them, I say!'

Rhun looked at him gratefully. He turned to the others. 'Look, if they are Twylwth Teg, if Meical is right, we have nothing to worry about. We aren't doing anything wrong, after all. They can't know what we are about,' he said, 'and if they just watch they'll do us no harm. Just try to ignore them. But come on, we have to keep going – I want to get over this mountain before dark. We'll find no place to stop up here and I'd prefer not to sleep out in the open any more than I have to. If you're worried, walk in front and the rest of us'll keep an eye on you.'

'What d'you think really?' asked Ithwalh quietly as they started out again, following the younger boys.

'I don't know,' said Rhun.

Ithwalh glanced nervously around, scanning the tree line. 'Nothing good ever came from færies. Let's hope Meical is right about this lot.'

'Hush,' Rhun murmured. 'Best not talk about it – try to be strong, if only for Cynrig's sake. To be honest, I'm more worried that they aren't Gwyllian at all. I'm worried they are men.' He looked up and caught an odd glance from Einion – a glance more troubled than scared. '*Na*, say nothing now, just keep a good lookout.'

They toiled on, looking up nervously when they could spare their eyes from the path. They trod carefully, anxious not to disturb the eerie quiet. Rhun recalled the look on Einion's face – he had seemed really quite shaken. *Well, you never know,* he thought. Bravery in arms is one thing, but this was something quite different.

And eyes in your back aren't easy to ignore.

The road never faltered. It followed an ancient route ever upwards. A road made in times long past by unknown feet, it took them high into the clouds to a wide saddle. The tops were bare of tall trees. All around was a tangle of rocks and stunted hawthorn, shifting and ghostlike amidst the low cloud. Perfect cover for any who chose not to be seen. As if by unspoken agreement they walked as quietly as they could, anxious not to disturb the silence, anxious not to alert anyone. Or awaken worse.

The road wound among rocks, many of them enormous and all strewn about as if in a giant's game of knucklebones, with the occasional muddy patch where a spring welled or a pocket of peaty soil stood rimmed with rushes. Suddenly the sound of hoofs hammering up the track behind them sent them scattering for cover. Out of the mist burst a rider, lashing his horse to a dangerous speed. Rhun caught a glimpse of a man in a dark cloak which streamed out from his shoulders, heard the laboured breath of a horse driven too hard.

And then it was gone. Silence returned as if it had never gone away, broken only by the dripping of water off the trees.

Slowly they crept out of hiding, and gathered in a frightened huddle.

'What was that?'

'Not færies, that's for sure.'

'Was he looking for us, d'you think?'

'Like those watchers?'

'Why would he be? You don't go that fast if you're looking for someone.'

'I'm scared.'

'Look, he's gone. Ysgyrran's right – he can't have seen us. But, whatever he was doing, we mustn't stop now.'

Rhun turned away from them, determined not to let the panic back in.

'Besides – we don't know there were any watchers. So come on,' he said without looking back.

But as they set out a new noise caught their ears. Ahead of them this time. Warily they topped the rise to the sounds of shouting and the scream of horses. Turning the shoulder of a monstrous boulder, they saw a man lying in an untidy heap beside the road. Another fought to control a small string of pack horses. There were only three animals but they were frightened and they stamped and bucked in the man's grip. Suddenly one tore free and headed back up the hill, its eyes staring and its ears flat against its head. The boys spread out to bar its way. Ysgyrran made a grab for the flying halter, caught it and was dragged through a patch of mud on his belly. But his weight acted as a brake and the frightened animal came to a halt. The others gathered round, petting and soothing until they got the runaway under control.

As Ysgyrran got to his feet, the traveller turned from his own battle and saw the boys for the first time. 'Ach – did you see that?' he shouted. 'Damned man nearly scattered my horses over the mountainside – I could have lost everything.' He glanced round. 'Qaseem,' he cried. 'Quick – hold these.' He thrust the halters into Rhun's hand and ran over to his companion.

'Dear friend, are you alive?'

The man stirred and sat up. 'I don't know.' He patted himself. 'Oww! – that's a bit sore, but – no, mostly I'm fine,' he said, 'just not used to being ridden over. Who in hell was that anyway?'

'*Na, na,* lie easy, let me look at you.' He busied himself with tending his companion, leaving Rhun to hold the beasts. Rhun looked them both over. An odd couple. One old, one young. Their clothing was solid but much worn by travel and hard use. The strangest thing was their skin – they were both very dark and not just from the sun. Apparently satisfied, the older man stood up and turned to Rhun.

'Ah, good boy, you have the horses safe. Help me – I fear my friend will not be walking for a while – do you know anywhere we might stay?'

'I'm afraid not,' said Rhun. 'Sorry, we're not from these parts.'

'Not from these parts, is it? No – nor are we,' he said. Then he laughed as if he had said something hugely funny. His accent was thick and strange and Rhun was barely able to make out the words. Then his face turned serious again.

'But where...? Ah – well, never mind that. We will just have to go on. Come though, a favour more – help me get my friend onto one of these animals.'

After considerable rearrangement, the younger man was duly bundled onto a horse.

'So – we are all travellers, is it?' As he spoke he wiped his face and set to cleaning the worst of the mud from his clothes. 'I am sorry – I have not given you my thanks for your most timely help. My name is Balthazar. This is my companion Qaseem. We travel north to see your king Cadwallon. Where are you bound?'

'I fear you may not find him. We are sent to seek news of him ourselves.'

'What evil tale is this? All is not well hereabouts, it seems. But – look, why not travel together? You can tell me your news as we go.'

Rhun looked at the others, uncertain what to do. Could they trust these people?

He sensed their hesitation. 'Have no fear,' he said, smiling broadly, 'you distrust our looks, perhaps wisely, but I will do you no harm.'

'Thank you – we would be glad of some company, as it happens.'

They travelled on in rising spirits. They felt no more eyes on their backs, as if their new friends had banished such frights. Indeed, Balthazar was lively company, full of tales of far-off and exotic places, some of which they knew from tales told at home, most of which they had never heard at all. Massalia in the land of the Franks, and Rome and further still to his homeland in the east. He spoke of the adventures and perils of his own life, but as it turned out he didn't ask them for their story, seemed careful not to enquire too close. As though he sensed their caution and respected it. By contrast, Qaseem said almost nothing, but he laughed in all the right places for, though Balthazar knew well how to spin a yarn, it seemed he had heard them a thousand times.

'How is it you speak our tongue so well?' asked Rhun during a rare lull.

'Ah, we talk fondly of our homes but it is many years since we saw them. We travel for trade – wherever it takes us and a man cannot do business without knowing the tongues of his customers.' He clapped Rhun on the back. 'Yours is not so difficult for all that your neighbours pretend otherwise.'

'You are right – but so few of the Saesneg even try.'

Balthazar's face grew solemn for a moment.

'You Cymru would do well to remember that, I'm thinking, it may bode ill for the future.'

At last their path brought them down to a new river, this time one which ran away to the setting sun. Ahead of them towered tier after tier of hills, mountains indeed, reaching at last to the very sky, seemingly impassable. The river brought them down into a flat land of water meadows and meanders, where another stream joined it. To the west they knew was the sea. As they emerged from the trees and topped a last low shoulder of rock, they saw a wide estuary still bright with the afterglow of the sun. But it seemed that was not their road. Here Balthazar turned north and led them into a wide vale, deep in shade, dotted with trees and edged by broken tumbles of rock beneath the enclosing hills, and where a smudge of smoke in the middle distance spoke at last of shelter. They had seen no sign of the rider. Perhaps he was nothing to do with them after all.

Nestling in the shadows where the path crossed the water, was a group of low, round houses, as was still the way in these remote places, squat, stone-walled and thatched with reed. All was silent, the only sign of life being the smoke rising through the roofs. But the sound of horses brought the people to their doors, and the place was transformed into a bustle as a small crowd gathered. They made Balthazar welcome, chattering and poking at the packs. Recovered now, Qaseem dismounted and stood quietly apart and the boys gathered round him. They were inspected closely, their weapons noted, but no one spoke to them. At last Balthazar lifted his hands in protest. 'In the morning, good people; now my friends and I are in need of rest.' One house stood apart from the rest, hard by the crossing, its door set wide allowing the warm glow of a forge to spill into the dusk. A man stood, silhouetted, watching their approach. 'Balthazar! It is a while since we saw you. Is it slaves you are trading now?'

'Slaves! *Na, gof*, these are friends.'

'Friends, is it?' The smith took another look. '*Na*, fair enough, slaves do not go armed.' He turned to face Rhun, one eyebrow raised in question.

Rhun felt he should say something. 'We find we travel the

same road for a while.' He glanced at Balthazar. 'Though we go north from here.'

'Well, if you mean to take that road you'd be wise not be doing it at nightfall.'

'We do so mean,' said Rhun, 'but we'll gladly take your advice – can you or anyone here give us a bed for the night?'

'We can and welcome. The more so since I see you are clearly 'n Prydeinig – no Ængel would go armed with Roman weapons as I have heard. Oh yes, I see them, though it is many a long year since I saw their like. But however that may be, it is seldom we have a chance for news and we would be glad to hear yours. Come in, come in.' The smith led them inside and they gathered round the forge to warm themselves.

'So, you've seen no one?'

'None but friends. Did you expect something else?'

'Na, it's no matter.' No need to frighten these people unnecessarily. Nor raise their suspicions.

Food and drink were brought, for travellers were sacred, the more so for the news they might bring. News was vital to these isolated folk. They sat wherever room could be found. Mostly on the floor. The furnishings Rhun was accustomed to at home were still scarcely known in this deep country. Travellers were sacred but so also was the smith. Here, as anywhere, he was the one person no one could do without, the settled and the wandering alike, the men of war and the men of peace. And besides, who knew from whence came that gift, that power? No man in his right mind would trouble a smith.

As they ate, the forge filled with people come to inspect these travellers and hear such tales as they might tell. They found places to sit or stand quietly while they waited, greeting each other in hushed voices so as not to disturb the guests. And they were not disappointed.

'So, my friends, what news?'

Balthazar turned to Rhun with a smile. 'You first, I reckon.'

Rhun set down his bowl. He introduced himself and told

his tale simply and with as much detail as he felt he could without being indiscreet. When it was told there was much muttering. One of the villagers seemed to consider himself spokesman, an old man with a shock of white hair and a long moustache in ancient style. He looked grave and cleared his throat. 'This is ill news indeed, but we are glad to have heard it. Better ill news than no news at all – no one has come from the north this last six-month. These Saesneg will be the ruin of us all, I'm thinking.'

There was another general muttering amongst them, as each agreed with this simple notion and sought to add his two pence worth.

'Edwin certainly,' said Rhun, 'though you should not judge them all by his standard.'

'Perhaps,' said the old man, 'and we will not if you say so. And your tale reminds me of a young Saesneg lad who came this way – oh many summers ago now – he would have been about your age I'm thinking, travelling with my lord Cadfan – our new king's father, you know. In truth he seemed like-able enough.'

Rhun's heart leaped. 'Do you remember his name?'

'I do. Penda, I think they called him. But it was a long time ago. Do you know him?' The old man glanced at Rhun sharply.

Of course, Rhun thought, *that's how Penda had known of the route through these mountains.* It made sense now. He looked up. The room had gone strangely quiet; clearly they were all keen to see how he replied to this.

'Yes,' he said guardedly, 'we have met. He is a good man, I find.'

'Well I liked the lad, so its likely he has turned out well! *Na*, but you are Cymro and we are glad that you passed this way.'

The muttering resumed, but it seemed that Rhun had passed the test, if test it was and not just his imagination.

'That we are,' broke in the smith, 'and, look, we will help you in any way we can.'

Rhun grabbed this chance for a less loaded conversation.

'As for that, your hospitality is already as much as we deserve – but perhaps a few words of guidance to see us on our road in the morning?'

'Well spoken, *bachgen*. It shall be so, but come, some music! Alaw – where's your pibgorm? Talwrthyn – fetch the harp!' *A pibgorm*, thought Rhun. It was ages since he had heard one but he had loved its thin reedy sound, especially now heard against the warmth of the harp. And the music was quite as good as anything they had heard at home.

The evening grew loud and cheerful. Under its cover Rhun took the opportunity to ask a question of his own.

'Tell me, old one, have there been other strangers here of late? Cymro perhaps, but not of these parts?'

The old man looked suddenly alert. '*Na*,' he said, 'just you. Why, have you seen others?'

'Not seen, no. But we thought that we were watched as we came over the pass.'

'And you think it was Gwyllian, I expect,' the old man said with a twinkle in his eye.

'*Na*, I fear that it was not.'

'What is it you are not telling me?'

'Oh, it's probably nothing. A man overtook us on the pass, riding like all the devils in hell were on his tail, but it was probably coincidence. Think no more of it – just my imagination, I expect.'

The old man looked long at him. 'We have seen no such rider. So, have it your way. But we will keep our eyes open. Not much passes here without our knowing,' he said at last.

In the morning there was clearly no getting away early. Balthazar and Qaseem were up at first light and had opened their bundles upon the grass. Word had spread to the outlying farms and the traders were doing good business well before the boys stirred. By the time they had eaten and made themselves ready the morning was well advanced. They gave their thanks to the smith and made their farewells to Balthazar and Qaseem.

'Perhaps we shall meet again?'

'Who can tell? But I hope so. Go well, my friends.'

'Well, Rhun,' said their host, 'if you would go north of the mountains, you must follow the river. But I warn you, it will not be an easy road.'

'We were told to take the western pass – shall it be easy to find at least?'

'Ah – you'll need no guide there – just follow the river straight up the valley. It will be joined by another flowing down from the west. Follow this second stream until you reach the pass and then keep going. That's not to say the mountains will diminish – oh no, I'm afraid they only keep growing, the gods know how high, but keep Yr Wyddfa on your dawn side and you won't go far wrong. But it'll be warm climb – this sunshine looks set to stay, today at least if I'm any judge. It shouldn't take you more than a day, though it'll be a long one and it may well be full dark before you're through. Specially now with you setting out so late.' Then his face grew dark and he lowered his voice. 'Just be sure not to pass the mountain on your dusk side, for that way leads to Llyn Peris and there dwells Canthrig Bwt!'

'Canthrig Bwt – who is that?'

'Why, you do not know? Shun her – avoid her at all costs! She is a foul ogre who preys on travellers.' He paused and then went on in a loud whisper, 'they say she eats people – very fond of children…' He stood back to observe the effect of his words. 'Ha! But you should be right enough, you big chaps. Though if she's hungry…' he tailed off, his eye on Tecwyn and the other youngsters.

The smith's wife came bustling out of the house. 'Husband, husband, what are you thinking – to set them off with such dark tales? For shame! Here, my lads, take this for your journey and good luck to you all.' She handed out loaves and hunks of yellow cheese and dried meat to all the boys. 'That should keep you going. You'll not be short of some-thing to drink where you're going,' she said with a chuckle, 'and there'll be blueberries enough for all higher up.'

'Thank you mother, thank you both – we won't forget your kindness,' Rhun said solemnly.

'Ah, get on with you, you've a long enough day ahead of you without wasting time on words.'

They stood and watched until the boys were out of earshot.

'And as for you, you great fool! Fancy filling their heads with all that stuff just as they're setting out on their own!'

He laughed. 'Just making sure they go the right way. They'll be fine.'

The morning passed uneventfully. The valley started wide and flat and the going was easy, but it narrowed gradually and the trees began to crowd in from east and west. Sudden cliffs of rock seemed to bar their way but they had been told what to watch for and they picked it out with relative ease. By noon they came to a place where their path entered a narrow gorge. There was a shallow place where they crossed the river and took the western side. To the east, the steep hills pushed rocky cliffs right to the water's edge. It was not easy on the west bank but the east was impassable. An hour's struggle brought them hot and dirty to a wider place where two streams joined. A low hut stood by the crossing place. But no smoke. The high sun beat down into this enclosed place. The fears of yesterday stirred. They crossed the water as quietly as they could and approached the hut with care. It stood in melancholy silence, made the more so by the drifts of dead leaves gathered round the door. Ysgyrran approached and peered into the dark interior.

'You're alright, there's no one here.' The place was abandoned, the people gone, but it was not ruined so they were not long gone. The boys collapsed onto the warm turf beside the stream and rested.

Ysgyrran sat next to Rhun. 'What d'you think? Where are they?'

'I don't know – I just hope it's got nothing to do with us.'

'What do you mean?'

'Well, look, Tecwyn thought we were being watched yesterday and I'm afraid he may have been right.'

The others gathered round.

'Oh, not Meical's Gwyllian things, but real people.'

'I don't know why you say it like that!' said Meical.

'Well, you know what I mean.'

'Hmph.'

'That rider, d'you mean?'

'I don't know, but whoever it is it's not someone who wishes us well, I'd say.'

'So why didn't they attack us yesterday? We were miles from anywhere.'

'I don't know that either – perhaps they weren't ready. And after, when we had Balthazar and Qaseem with us, maybe they thought us too strong.'

'Maybe it was just the one.'

'And you think these people, whoever they are, might be why this place is deserted.'

'It's a bit unlikely, isn't it?' Meical chipped in, still smarting.

'Look, I don't know. I'm just saying.'

Ysgyrran looked around. 'Well, my guess is there's been no one here for days. Perhaps longer. Besides, we've not seen anyone since that rider nearly had us.'

'No, nor had the villagers back there – I asked the old man.'

'It's much more likely to have nothing to do with us, don't you think?'

'I hope so.' Rhun scrambled to his feet. 'Come on – we've got to get through here by nightfall.'

The valley opened out and the slopes became a little less steep. If anyone was tailing them, they were very good at it for they showed no sign.

But as the day wore on and they toiled up the narrow track beside the river, their fears grew. In the morning the stream had tumbled noisily by them. Now, out in the open sun, it too had grown hushed. The lower slopes were thickly clad with trees giving out into bald hills above them. Each felt the eyes, but now they could also hear noises, a snapping twig, a sudden rustle, as of someone treading softly, keeping in cover. More than one. At no time during the morning could they quite be sure – perhaps it was just animals – but by late afternoon they were certain.

The heat had grown. There had been barely a breath of wind all day. Now the air was become thick and close, matching the mood, and it was growing hazy so that they could no longer see clearly.

Yet nothing had happened. No one had seen anything untoward, but none now doubted they were being stalked. They had kept to the western bank. Whoever, or whatever was tracking them was still high in the woods to the east. Keeping their distance.

At last they came to the place where the valley split. They splashed across the shallow rocky river where the smaller one joined it, and scrambled up the bank onto the northern side. Small these mountain rivers may have been, but the water was bitterly cold and thick with rocks and deep hidden pools, making it a dangerous crossing. And a wet one. Once across they stood dripping and shivering on the grass in vain hope that this uncanny autumn sun might soak in and replace the water.

'Have we lost them, d'you think?' asked Ysgyrran.

'I doubt it but I can't see anyone, and I don't think anyone followed us out of the woods lower down,' said Rhun. 'Whoever they were, they weren't your Gwyllian, Meical!'

But Meical showed no sign of agreeing with him. He made the sign against evil. 'I don't know what makes you so sure,' he said.

'We must hurry, if we can get out of sight before they know which road we have taken we may yet be safe.'

But which road shall we take? he thought. Now it was upon them, and with urgency, it was not such an easy choice. To turn west would be to cross half a mile of open land, whereas the eastern way offered good cover almost immediately. Penda had said to take the western road, and everything the smith said backed that up. He looked east, longing for the cover it offered. But no – it had to be west.

'Come on, it's not far.'

But as they turned to take the left hand path they heard a noise up ahead. Someone else was crossing, higher up, and would be right in their way.

'*Iesu mawr*! they've worked their way around ahead of us. Quick – back into the trees!'

'Are you sure it's them? We're not supposed to go that way.'

'Who else could it be? D'you want to risk it?'

As he said it he saw a movement among the trees up ahead. Someone was definitely coming their way, though he couldn't make out who or how many.

'That's it! Come on!'

'But what about that Canthrig Bwt?'

'Well, what about her? We'll just have to deal with her if we meet her. Anyway, I expect the smith was just trying to scare us – a bit of fun, probably. Now come on,' and he set off at a run.

'I don't want to get eaten,' said Tecwyn, his eyes wide.

Einion shoved him in the back.

'You? Who'd want to eat you, you're barely a mouthful and that mostly bones. Now run!'

They plunged into the woods and ran in a ragged line along the narrow strip between the river and the trees, their fear of the very real threat behind them much greater than some unknown horror ahead. *Maybe Meical was right*, Rhun thought in desperation; so far they had seen no one – just heard noises. How did he know they were 'real'?

The hills crowded in on either side, seeming to bar the way, but then again, quite suddenly, they opened out around a long flat valley. On their left rose a great rock. A squat hill of rock hanging over the river with the glint of a lake beyond it. Suddenly new noises broke out behind them. The sounds of men crashing through the undergrowth, careless now of stealth.

'Make for that hill!'

A thick skirt of oaks clad its lower slopes, broken here and there by great rocky shoulders. Above the trees it wore a loose mantle of scrubby thorn, bramble and hazel.

The side which faced them was less of a sudden slope than the others and they scrambled to the top sweating, and bloody where they had been stabbed by thorns; clothes and skin torn alike.

On the top was a maze of old walls, their stones tumbled about them in ruin, deep in moss. Baulks of timber lay rotting, returning gently to the soil. Men had been here, but long ago. The place was still and strangely quiet as if it resented this disturbance. Gasping for breath, Rhun tumbled over the nearest wall and lay with his chest heaving, his legs turned to water that had been on fire with the effort of the climb. He pulled himself up and peered over the lip of stones. He wiped the film of grimy sweat from his eyes. No one in sight, no movement at all. No sound. *It's impossible,* he thought, *they were right behind us – I'd swear it. How could they just vanish – what are these people?* His blood chilled.

A voice broke into his thoughts. 'Have we lost them?'

He turned and looked wildly at the boy lying next to him. Ysgyrran, looking sturdy and comfortingly real. Rhun swallowed hard and fought for breath.

'I don't see how we can have.'

'How many of them, d'you think?'

'Well, it can't be many, or why didn't they take us hours ago? Why be so cautious?'

'So who are they?'

There was a long silence.

'I have no idea.'

Chapter 8

Rhun looked around at the others. They were only eight. 'Where's Einion?'

'He was with Tecwyn.'

'Tecwyn, have you seen him?'

But Tecwyn lay transfixed. He was staring into the tumbled landscape of their refuge, mumbling over and over, 'I don't want to get eaten. I don't want…'

'Tecwyn! Snap out of it – no one's going to eat you. Have you seen Einion?'

The younger boy turned to him. His eyes wide. He seemed scarcely to know who spoke. Llif, lying beside him, gave him a sharp slap. 'Come on, Tecwyn – we're all scared!'

Tecwyn shuddered, his small body convulsed. 'I'm sorry,' he whispered.

'Where's Einion? Did you see him?' Rhun was close to screaming himself.

'I don't know, he – he was behind me – at least until we got to the bottom of this thing – he kept pushing me. After that, I – I don't know.'

'Well it's not this Canthrig Bwt, then!'

'How d'you know?'

'What the smith said – she'd have taken *you* first! Now shut up about her, will you?'

Rhun could not see it. Had Einion been caught? Had he run off? Neither thought was good. Surely they would have heard if he had been taken – he wouldn't go quietly. And he wouldn't run off, would he? Here – now? Why?

'I said we couldn't trust him and now he's gone – just when we could do with someone his size.'

'Thanks Ysgyrran, I hadn't thought of that!'

'Well, I did say.'

'I know – just shut up about it! Let me think.'

The stillness was broken by a fitful breeze which seemed to chime with his worries. Rhun shivered as its unexpected chill caught his over-heated body. He peered over the wall and strained to catch any movement, but he could see nothing and could hear nothing except the wind and the rasping breath of his companions.

Careful to keep his head down, he rolled over and had a good look at where they were. The hill rose above its skirt of trees. Its top was a chaos of broken walls and tumbled stones and grass, interspersed with lumps of naked rock lying like basking seals. A few stunted trees were dotted here and there. To right and left he could see where the hill plunged to the valley floor in a tangle of trees and rocks. Ahead, across a narrow saddle, the hills rose relentlessly beyond sight, their tops lost in cloud and mystery. The place offered shelter but precious little else. They had no water and scant food. By dawn they would have to quit this refuge if they were not driven out sooner.

Still angry with Einion for his betrayal, and with Ysgyrran for being right, Rhun turned and snapped out the beginnings of an idea. 'I want someone to watch each slope. Ysgyrran – you stay here. Ithwalh – string the bows and bring us all one. The rest of you come with me. Let's see what we can make of this place. And Ysgyrran – keep an eye out for Einion – we still don't know for sure he's run off – he may just have got held up. And no – I don't know what might have kept him.'

'This place is big.'

'I wonder why it was abandoned.'

'It gives me the creeps.'

It gave them all the creeps. There seemed a presence here of ancient and un-nice things. Rhun felt suddenly puny and futile. The others stood around him, peering into the ruins.

They were standing in what seemed to have been the entrance to a large building. If there had been a gate once it was gone now, but the walls still stood to a good height in many parts, well above the heads of the tallest of them. The bulk of the interior was still fairly clear and level, but where the walls had fallen, the piles of masonry rubble were now heavily overgrown.

'What was it, d'you think?'

'A tower of some sort by the look of it.'

'These were powerful walls.'

'It's so big – was it built by giants?'

'I don't like it.'

'What are we going to do?'

Meical looked at them all, and then at Rhun.

'Rhun? You've got to think of something, they need you,' Meical hissed.

'I'm thinking they may have got us exactly where they wanted us,' Rhun said, his voice hollow. 'We've been driven here. Here specifically. Why?'

'Well, obviously they want to trap us somewhere they can be sure to finish us off.'

Rhun grabbed Meical's shoulder.

'That's it! Thank you, Meical. Look, we've got to turn the trap around. Take the others and spread out – we need to find all the routes in and out. A place this size must have had other doors.'

Ithwalh came over, carrying the strung bows.

'Anything happening?' Rhun asked.

'Not a thing – no sign of anyone. It's weird, why don't they attack?'

'They've made sure we came here – this very place where they can pen us in. But, like you say, why don't they attack. I'm coming to think that, whoever they are, they want all the odds stacked on their side.'

'Maybe they are waiting for dark.'

'*Ie*, that's what I think. Well, two can play that game, I reckon we can turn this against them. Here's the plan – we'll light a big fire in the middle of the old tower and then hide our best shots outside – you of course, and Llif and young Cynrig. The rest of us will be the bait.'

'Cynrig – are you sure?'

'Look, he may have his head in the clouds half the time

but he's as good a shot as you. He'll be fine. Besides, we'll likely need our best swordsmen down here – and that means Ysgyrran and Eryl, and Meical of course – and, well, me.'

He looked around. At the ruined tower on the hilltop, out into the mountains, and beyond where clouds were building dark towers of their own, high into the sky.

Leaving Ithwalh and Eryl on guard, the others spent the last few hours of daylight arranging their defences. Towards the back of the site, a few yards down the slope in a boggy place of reeds and myrtle, they found a spring. That was one problem solved at least. As the day wore on the weather became closer. The heat went out of the day and now a clammy chill seemed to press in on them, drear and threatening, too close almost to breathe. Cold gusts rattled the trees, picking up the fallen leaves and making them spin and twist like little dancing devils.

'Right, let's get that fire going. I'm starving and I'm cold.'

'Come on, there's plenty of dry sticks under the trees.'

'Look, someone's had a fire here before, and they've left some fuel.'

'Not long since either, I'd say.'

'I don't like to say it but d'you reckon that lake yonder might be Llyn Peris – you know, like the smith said?'

'Canthrig Bwt! I knew it!' It was almost a squeak.

'What – you reckon she cooks her kids before she eats them? Very civilized ogre. Besides, he said it was the other side of that big mountain,' said Ysgyrran, pointing. 'This can't be it.'

Rhun cut in, 'Will you all shut up about Canthrig Bwt! Look, calm down everyone. Let's worry about what we do know – someone wants us to be here. We've been neatly herded. But not to eat us – these were men, not some monster. Though God knows they may be little better. We've got to get a fire going. I don't know when they will come but we've got to be ready for them when they do. So get on with it!'

They scattered into the woods. While they were gone, Rhun and Meical set about making the fire.

By the time the wooding party got back, they had a good blaze going. Someone had cut several hazel wands, and they set about toasting small chunks of dried meat over the flames, far too impatient to wait for the hotter embers, in the vain hope that a bit of heat might make them easier to eat.

By nightfall they were as ready as they could be. With enough wood to last until dawn, they had stacked up the fire, and Rhun and Meical sat shoulder to shoulder, with their backs to the firelight facing the main entrance, grateful for the heat. Behind them sat Ysgyrran, Eryl and Tecwyn keeping a watch on the back door. Nothing would induce Tecwyn to leave the firelight. Ithwalh and Llif lay hidden amongst the deep shadows below the tumbled walls, and Cynrig perched in the only large tree, concealed amongst the last few leaves but able to command a view of the whole interior.

And they waited.

The time crawled by. Rhun fed the fire, easing his tired body when it stiffened. He could hear the others shifting now and then to avoid cramps of their own and to keep alert. Meical had drawn his sword and was gently honing the edge, the whetstone making a small hissing noise just audible above the crackling of the fire. Rhun glanced at his friend. Suddenly he realized how glad he was to have him here; how much he valued his steady, loyal company. Their trust was implicit, complete. Without his noticing, they had become like brothers. Meical looked up and caught his eye. They grinned rather foolishly at each other.

A movement by the gate made him turn his head, and the moment was gone. He stared out into the dark to the place where the main gate had once stood. What had before been an empty space now held a figure, standing feet apart, sword in hand. The bright bits on his clothing glinted in the light from the flames.

'Well, that's no ogre,' said Meical.

'Stay down, you lot,' Rhun hissed and scrambled to his feet. Out loud he said, 'Who are you and what do you want with us?'

Without warning an arrow thumped into the turf at his feet. He leaped back, though it was clearly meant to miss. It had come from straight ahead so at least one more must be hidden behind the man in the gate.

'There is your answer. We have taken one thing we sought. Now it is your turn. Surrender to us and we will spare your blood. But know this – you will not see freedom again.'

'What's he talking about?' hissed Meical. 'What has he taken?'

'Einion. It must be Einion.'

'Why?'

'Damn slave boy – I knew he'd be trouble!'

Rhun's face set in a hard stare.

'Surrender, is it? Not likely. We are only a few, why do you wait? Why not come and take us all?'

The man took a step forward. Two more appeared out of the darkness beside him. 'Oh we will, if that's the way you want to play it.'

'There's more behind us!' Tecwyn was on his feet pointing to two more who had appeared in another gap in the wall.

'Get down, you fool!' Ysgyrran grabbed him by his sleeve and hauled him to the ground. But too late. An arrow hissed out of the dark and Tecwyn fell. He cried out and as if it had been a signal, the attack came. The three from the gate ran at Rhun and Meical, swords drawn. One pitched headlong as if tripped, an arrow in his neck, killed instantly, but it did not stop the others. Now Rhun's hidden archers could not shoot for fear of hitting their own.

Swords met in a shower of sparks. The men were both full grown, experienced in battle and hardened by war. Even a few months ago they would have beaten down Rhun and Meical's defence with absurd ease, but not now. Rhun and Meical were young and agile. They had not wasted the hours of relentless training with Ecgrig. With their short swords, they were able to get under their opponents' guard, making their longer blades an unexpected disadvantage. Fighting as with one mind they went on the attack, each moving and striking and moving again as if in a dance, each supporting the other, each using the other in equal measure. Their attackers were caught in a storm of seemingly co-ordinated moves, strike and counter-strike, parry and feint, and they found themselves unaccountably beaten back. But not for long. Leaping backwards out of reach they paused and stood shifting from foot to foot, poised. Their eyes darted here and there, seeking weakness, weighing chances. When it came, the second attack was slow and deliberate. They had lost a comrade but they were determined, and now were nicely aware of who they fought.

Rhun and Meical crouched, swords ready, and stood their ground. The fighting was hard and bitter. Rhun drew on everything he had been taught, every trick and ruse, every scrap of his small experience, but as they fought he realized that he was being drawn away from Meical. On his own he was finding it more difficult to counter his opponent. And he was getting tired. Both boys lacked the strength and stamina of the older men. Rhun's sword began to feel heavy in his hand. He fought on, unaware now of anything but the other man's sword and the growing look of triumph in his eyes. Rhun was being forced back, forced to feel his way as he went. Suddenly his foot hit an obstacle and in a flash he realized he had backed into the dead man. He lost balance, dropping his guard. His attacker's sword snaked in, heading straight for his heart. By an absurd chance it caught in a fold of Rhun's shirt as he wrenched his body round to avoid the blade. The man was at full stretch and before he could recover another sword flew in and smashed his blade to the ground. Ysgyrran had joined them. And now it was three against two.

Ysgyrran had done no actual damage but the surprise was enough to allow Rhun and Meical to rally. But any relief was short-lived.

Behind him Rhun heard Eryl screaming defiance as he faced his own attackers over Tecwyn's inert body. 'Get away from him, you bloody filth!' his voice shrill with fear and rage. The two men at the rear entrance had hung back as if waiting for a signal. Now, with Eryl left alone, they had taken their chance. They leaped forward, narrowly avoiding the arrows. Eryl was good with a sword, he had a love for the weapon greater than all of them. But he was young, and small even for his thirteen years. His attackers closed in, laughing at this puny boy. Suddenly one cried out and stumbled groping for an arrow which had appeared in his leg. A wild shot and perilous but, oh, so lucky. They paused. He pulled at the shaft and it came away easily. He threw it aside but fell the moment he put his weight upon it. The other paused to look but then came on with renewed vigour, driving his attack into Eryl with the force of a wild animal. But the delay had helped, brief though it was, for Eryl found he was no longer alone. Out of the dark had leaped a new figure, sword drawn, and beside him two more – Ithwalh and Llif, useless now as bowmen, wielding their own swords. Together they engaged in a whirl of flashing steel.

Desperate to finish this – fearful of what was happening behind him, Rhun changed tactic. He leaned sideways and swung his sword back-hand up through a low arc, closing in to get under his opponent's guard. It was a risky move but with his short sword again he would have the advantage. At the last minute their swords came together in a screech of tortured metal. Rhun recovered immediately, he swung his sword down and over and drove its point up into his attacker's shoulder. Stabbing – that's what these old Roman weapons were made for. The man staggered back, clutching his arm, his sword hanging limply in his hand.

All at once there was a searing flash of lightning, followed instantly by an almighty clap of thunder. For a the briefest moment the whole scene was bathed in blinding blue light. Before anyone had a chance to recover, a huge voice boomed out over the enclosed space.

'This is a forbidden place. Why do you defile it?'

Man and boy stood rooted.

Directionless, the voice seemed to come from all around. Its sound floated on the air, at once coarse and silky. A monstrous, deafening voice. A voice from hell, splitting the night with sound as it had been split before by light.

In their blindness, the boys clutched at each other in their terror, exposed and defenceless, scared of the one as much as the other. But as their eyes readjusted, they saw that their attackers had gone. Gasping for breath, Rhun stood with his back to Meical and Ysgyrran, trying to maintain their tight defensive knot, but, apart from the dead man at their feet, there was no one in sight.

And then, into the firelight stepped a tall figure shrouded in cloak and hood, as if materialized from the very shadows themselves, a tall staff of dark wood in his hand.

'I say again – why do you violate this sacred place?' But now in the voice of a human.

Rhun croaked, 'We came here to escape pursuit. We didn't know it was forbidden. It's just a ruin.'

'It is now, but it was not always so. Once it was a place of mighty deeds and undertakings.'

'If we have done wrong, we are sorry. We meant no disrespect,' said Rhun, quite certain, as they all were, that this man could destroy them with a glance. 'What will you do now?' If they were to be punished for this violation, better to learn the worst.

There was a long pause. At last the man threw back his hood and approached the fire. 'Well, I'll get warm for a start,' he said. 'And you should join me. I doubt we will be disturbed again tonight.'

Confused, they stood about stupidly. All Rhun could think of to say was, 'You don't think they'll come back?'

'Not tonight, I'd say.'

Suddenly Rhun stiffened. 'Tecwyn!' Desperately he turned, terrified of what he might see, expecting the worst. A figure was squatting over Tecwyn's slight body. The others stood by messily, uncertain what to do to help, too stunned by events to think clearly.

'Is he dead?'

The squatting figure stood up. 'Not dead, but he is hurt bad.'

'Einion!'

'You! Get away from him,' yelled Ysgyrran. He launched

himself onto Einion and together they crashed to the ground, fists flying. They were evenly matched in size and weight but Ysgyrran had taken Einion by surprise. He rained blows onto Einion anywhere that he could reach. But Einion was tough and resilient. Ten years of casual knocks and more determined beatings had hardened him, and soon he was giving better than he got.

'Hold,' shouted Rhun, grabbing bits of clothing at random in an effort to pull them apart. Others joined him but it took their combined efforts to manage it.

Held down, Ysgyrran sat on the ground glaring at Einion. Einion wiped a trickle of blood from his mouth and inspected it, as if to check it was real. Rhun could see no anger in his face. He looked sad and tired, but nothing else that Rhun could read. Einion turned to face him.

'Yes, it is me. In the end I couldn't do it,' he said.

'Do what? What are you talking about?'

Einion got to his feet and stood awkwardly. His big figure seem to sag and he looked at the ground. 'I'm sorry – it was all my fault.'

'I don't understand, what's your fault? Couldn't do what?' said Rhun.

'He could not betray you,' the stranger said, gently. As he spoke, he stooped and gathered Tecwyn into his arms and carried him back to the fire. Passing Einion he said, 'Help me, there is a blanket in my bag.' The others stood in confusion, they understood none of this.

But Ysgyrran was far from pacified. 'I knew he'd betray us! I said he would! I see it all now – I'll bet he killed Peleg – and then claimed he'd revenged him! Liar!'

'I did not – never! I liked Peleg...'

'Shut up, Ysgyrran. You heard him – he said he couldn't do it. Just wait.'

Tecwyn lay quite still. The arrow stuck obscenely out of his chest. The stranger pulled out a knife and cut away Tecwyn's shirt to reveal the entry point, a dirty thing on such a fine surface. He examined the wound with minute care, gently opening the place where the arrow pierced the flesh.

'Pass me my bag.' Einion did so. The stranger rummaged inside and pulled out a small dark bottle stopped with a wooden plug held fast with wax. 'Here – open this. Carefully! Good – pour some on this rag.' He smoothed the soaking rag around the place and took hold of the arrow with one hand. 'Hold him. Make sure he does not move. Do not worry – he is far away. He will not feel it.' As Einion placed his hands on Tecwyn's chest, the man pulled suddenly and the arrow came out in a gush of blood. He smothered the flow with the rag and, holding his hand on the place, he sat back. 'Seems it jammed between two ribs – lucky it was not barbed. You may let go now.'

No one had moved. All but the two tending Tecwyn stood as if held by some spell, as if turned to stone. When the man had finished he sat back on his heels. Rhun found he could breath again. 'Will he be alright?'

'I think so.'

'So, will you tell us what's going on?' Rhun felt Ysgyrran straining under his hand. 'Wait!' he said.

'But he must have led them to us – I don't know – some sort of signal perhaps – can't you see? I'll bet it was them at the crossing on the Hafren too.'

'Will you wait! Well – will you? We can't be sitting on you all night.'

Ysgyrran nodded. His reluctance was clear but he held up his hands in a gesture of submission.

Rhun let him go and turned back to the tableau by the fire. 'So – will someone tell us what this is all about?' he said again.

For a long time he got no answer. The stranger finished Tecwyn's dressing. He murmured something to Einion that no one else could hear, and then seemed to take an age re-stopping the bottle, carefully re-melting the wax using his knife heated in the fire. No one dared speak again. The man did not have to say or do anything to make them any more aware of his power. He was not big physically but he managed to fill all the available space. His clothes were plain, drab even. Everything about him suggested humility, but it was a poor disguise. None of it could hide his authority: power flowed from him. He had never seen this man before but Rhun knew without doubt what he was. He had come across one the same not so very long ago.

'You are – *derwydd*?' he asked, uncertain of the right word, anxious to be respectful.

'That is a name we have accepted, yes. There are others but that will do. You may call me Afalach.'

'Won't you tell us what is happening? Have we done wrong?'

'You are Rhun ap Cwyfan ap Erthig. You and your companions seek answers to several questions, amongst which is the fate of your fathers. You have been pursued by a small band of men from the high country of Powys who sought to revenge an old hurt. And a more recent one as well for that matter. As for doing wrong – *Na*, none that I can think of.'

'How can you know all that?'

'How? Well, young man, you may feel you are a long way from home, but some of us have a wider view. We have ways to find things out over very much greater distances than that. You may not see us, or know us when you do, but we are everywhere. I am not the first of my brethren that you have met, I think.' He added casually.

'*Na*, you are not,' said Rhun who was ahead of him. Now, as if Afalach had painted a picture, they all saw again the strange fire and felt the mystery of that day on the hill above Lenteurde, when they had bid farewell to Peleg.

'So, who were those men?' Rhun asked.

'Why not ask your friend Einion here? He can tell you as much as I, and I believe he wants to in any case.' The druid turned away and busied himself with some small things of his own. As one, they turned to Einion.

'They were my people,' he said in a small voice.

Chapter 9

It was getting dark. The boy carried his burden across the yard to the midden. As he emptied it onto the heap, a low voice, just above a whisper, came to him out of the gloom.

'Are you Einion ap Ceol?'

Einion almost dropped the pot.

'Well, are you?'

'I am,' he said, uncertainly. 'Who wants to know?' It was just a voice; of the speaker he could see nothing.

'Never mind that for now, just know that I am a friend and that you and your father are not forgotten.'

Carefully Einion set the pot down, fearful of breaking it. Rough local ware, but still precious. Like as not he'd get a beating if he broke it. He looked around. No one in sight.

'What are you saying? My father is dead. How do you know us?'

'What! – But we saw him captured – you mean they killed him after?'

'They did not, but he died anyway. Not long since. He was old.'

'Ceol dead. That is ill news indeed. But look, you want to get out of here, don't you – to be free?'

'That's a stupid question – what do you think? But who are you to offer it?'

'I am someone who is interested in your fate.'

'Why now – after all these years?'

'Simple – I have only just found you. Look, you must trust me.'

'Why should I? Who you are?' He caught a noise from across the yard. 'I must go.'

'Einion – for now know that I am your kinsman – I shall return. Look for me at times like these.'

A big voice came from the hall. 'Come on, boy – what are you doing?' Einion picked up the pot. His heart was beating tenfold. Freedom! Could it be?

'Coming,' he called.

Freedom. It was all he had ever wanted – freedom for himself, more even for his father. He had hated the way his father had become small and mean during all those years of captivity, he who had been so large, so bright before. In the end his death had been a blessing. But freedom? Now he came to it, the idea scared him. How do you do 'free'? All his life he had heard tales of 'back home' where his father had been counted amongst important men, a warrior of Selyf ap Cynan king in Powys, in direct line from Gwrtheyrn himself. Since he was six Einion had only known captivity, and through all those years his father had promised him freedom. But he had never delivered it, and now he was dead and even the promise was gone. And Einion had become used to this life; ten long years, it was the only life he had truly known. He could scarcely remember the time before, and now these were as much his people as any. True he was a slave, true he hated it, but he had not been ill-treated – not really – and now he was even trusted – at least by Rhun. It would be much to betray that. And yet – freedom! There was magic in the very word.

A few evenings later the man came again. Einion spoke to him through the fence as before, though this time they had found a loophole and Einion could just make out the other's face in the gloom.

'They'll be watching, so don't just stand there – do something.'

Einion squatted and grabbed a handful of grass where it grew long against the palisade. He scrubbed idly at the dirty pot.

'So who are you?' he whispered. 'How do you know me?'

'My name is Cathan, I am your father's cousin. You won't remember but you very nearly killed me in the hills a month or so back – Na, do not shout. But it's true, I was the man your precious Rhun captured. But know this – I am no mere bandit! It is an ancient feud.'

'So how are you here?'

'I got away – those Saesneg are too cocky! It was easy. But I had to come back – I had seen the likeness of your father in you and when I heard your name I was sure of it. Now you tell me your father is dead – that is a sad loss. So how is it you fight for these people? – they're as good as Ænglisc themselves.'

'Would you rather I scrubbed floors and emptied piss-pots?'

'Na, fair enough. But it was a surprise.'

So Einion told him.

'This boy Rhun – you like him?'

'Not especially. He's the head-man's son so he thinks himself important. He's no worse than some, but he's just a kid.'

'Yet he gives you arms?'

'It's his way to atone.'

'But he trusts you?'

'I give him no reason not to.'

'That is good. Keep it that way.'

'I had meant to. You have a plan?'

'Na, not as yet.'

'Then I shall keep it that way in any case – if you have nothing to offer except false hope. And tell me this – why were you fighting for an Ænglisc man?'

'You knew that? Ie, of course you did – it's a long story, too long for telling now.'

Einion stared hard at him, but said nothing. Cathan's eyes slid away.

'I shall think of something,' he said, 'keep a look out for me – especially after dark.'

And he was gone.

For the next few nights when he had time to himself, Einion tried to conjure visions of life without bonds. There was a niggling question in the back of his mind about the Ænglisc man, but he thrust it aside. Why care about how? – Freedom was too alluring. But weeks went by and his secret visitor did not come again. Gradually the excitement died, killed by the everyday drudgery of routine. The visions blurred and their light went out. Cursing himself for a fool, Einion began to doubt he had ever come at all.

Then one night Cathan was there again.

'The word is that Rhun is to go into Gwynedd.'

'He is.'

'You're still part of this little army of his?'

'I am.'

'Good. Stay with him until you are well out of this country.'

'I had meant to – why do you ask it?'

'You can be our eyes. We need to know where he's going.'

'We know that – he's looking for his father – they all are.'

'That's what he says, no doubt. Look, Penda of Mercia has been here – he must have spoken to your Rhun – we need to be sure of what he's really up to – it needn't be for long, just 'til we know – then we can get you out.'

'Why wait? Why not now?'

'Na, we can't take you here – we need you on the inside. Besides, there's not enough of us. I've been in our own country seeking those who might help, but – look, the truth is there's not many left who remember your father, and we aren't getting any younger. D'you think you would have beaten us that day if we had all been in the prime of life?'

'Perhaps.'

'Huh! Anyway, it would be better to get Rhun away from here so we can take him without fuss – and the others. You get to be part of it. That should please you.'

Einion said nothing.

'Which way are you headed?'

'Up the Lent valley is all I know.'

'Expect to meet us on the road. But not 'til you're far away.'

And he was gone.

And they were far from home indeed before Einion saw him again.

It was getting dark. Einion lay behind the others. It was hard to see through the rain in the failing light and he could not be certain, but he was almost sure that one of the men camped down by the crossing was his kinsman Cathan. So this was it. This is where it all ended. He looked at his companions. How many would die? He wondered. How many survive and live their own lives in slavery? And he found that he cared. He didn't hate these people, it was not they who had enslaved him. So, should he tell them? Should he warn them of the danger? Not much point – they could see it for themselves. What was he thinking? Rather he should shout – attract attention – give them away. Wasn't that what he had always meant to do? It was what his kinsmen were expecting. He glanced at Tecwyn and the other younger boys. He had been asked to look after Tecwyn – he was a mouthy kid and a bit of a pain in the arse at times, but it was hard not to like him. Could he really bring himself to betray him, betray them all? Maybe it was not Cathan down there after all. It was hard to tell at that distance in this light. What if he was wrong? Then they might all be captured and he'd be no better off. Worse, probably. Perhaps he could just slip away in the dark – no one would notice until it was too late. Yes, that was an idea.

Then Einion heard his own name spoken. 'Me – sorry – do what?'

'Bring up the rear – make sure no one gets left behind. Now come on, let's go. Remember everyone, count to twenty – slowly – before you follow.'

And then it was too late. He couldn't say anything now. Nor could he stay behind.

'It seems they lost us after they missed us at the crossing. They were puzzled by that. They spoke to Teifion but he sent them by the north road – you remember, the way he told us to avoid. When they couldn't find us, they split up and it took 'til yesterday to pick up our trail. Well the day before by now I suppose. You remember – up in the hills when Tecwyn thought he saw Tywlwth Teg.'

'Was it only yesterday? It seems weeks ago now.'

'The one who saw us was alone and had to cast about

again to find the others. Then it took them until this afternoon to get back on the chase. They didn't waste any more time after that. I knew who it was alright. I was torn in two – I wanted to go to them – they are my kin and they came to rescue me and avenge my father! But I couldn't just walk away – I had to make sure Tecwyn was safe before I left.' He looked anxiously over to where the boy lay. 'I thought I had.'

'Fear not – he will not die yet.' Afalach had not turned, he seemed to have read Einion' thoughts.

It was Cynrig, Tecwyn's special friend, who asked the question no one else dared.

'So why did you come back, Einion?'

But Einion answered without hesitation.

'I thought they had killed Tecwyn,' he said simply. Then, 'Na, it was more than that.' He went quiet. Sitting there watching the fire as it burned low, he knew in that moment what he truly wanted. Freedom, yes, but not stolen in the dark. Rhun had declared him free but he wanted it earned and honoured, and he wanted to live it with the people he had come to love. Rhun had trusted him and he wanted to return that trust more than he had ever wanted anything. Rhun had believed himself a leader, and he had been right. 'They would have enslaved those they thought worth it and killed those they didn't. They expected me to betray you – but, well – I just couldn't do it. And now Tecwyn is near death and one of my kinsman lies dead yonder.'

The boys all turned to look at the corpse lying untouched on the edge of the light. As one, they turned to gauge Rhun's reaction, to take their lead from him, to be told how to respond to this shock. Rhun said nothing. He stepped forward and took Einion' shoulders. Einion no longer looked the older of the two. Now he appeared small and defenceless in contrast to Rhun. There had never been any question among the other boys as to who was leader. Now even a stranger would know at a glance.

Rhun and Einion stood face to face, their eyes locked. The air seemed to crackle along with the fire.

'So, are you with us again?'

'I am.'

Rhun put his arm around Einion's neck and hugged him to himself. 'If you ever doubted I was your friend, doubt it no longer,' he said. 'Will you sit with Tecwyn?'

'I will – it's my fault he was hurt.'

Ysgyrran could keep it in no longer. 'Look, that's a fine story – but how do we know the truth? I'm damn sure I'm not ready to trust him again that easily. And, by all the gods, he cut it fine before he came to our aid.'

'I believe him – why can't you?'

'What was he doing – seeing which way the wind blew before joining in?'

Einion looked up. 'I was,' he said simply. 'I couldn't go against them on my own. I couldn't run – where would I go? I was afraid. I own it. A life in slavery is not best for making you brave.'

Ysgyrran stood stock still, utterly disarmed. He turned away and walked off into the dark.

The others left him to it. They busied themselves with preparations for the night, in truth too embarrassed to be angry. Only Ithwalh stood in doubt.

'Look, Einion, I'm sorry – I killed your kinsman.'

'Don't be – he was not direct family. Besides, he asked for it. And I suppose he died as he'd have wanted.'

'You had best go after him,' said Afalach.

Rhun followed the direction Ysgyrran had taken. He didn't have to go far. He found him leaning against a wall, staring into the night.

'I think we have to give him the benefit of the doubt. We are too few to break up.'

Ysgyrran said nothing for a while. Then, 'I suppose you're right. But I was beginning to like him. That made it worse.'

'Me too. And I don't think either of us was wrong.'

'*Na*. Perhaps not. We shall see, eh?'

'Try to be easy. Come back to the fire now?'

Later, as they were eating, Rhun found himself sitting next

to Afalach. As he chewed his lump of meat, it came to him suddenly that the thunderstorm had never happened. There had been that one mighty clap and then nothing. He looked at the druid. 'I don't know how you did that,' he said.

'Did what?'

'You know – the thunder and the big voice.'

'You are right. You do not.'

Rhun grinned. 'And you won't tell me, I suppose.'

'You are right again. It is for me to know such things. It is for you to know that I do.'

'I see.'

'Do you? I wonder.'

He looked long and hard at Rhun, seeming to weigh him in some mental balance.

'Perhaps,' he said. 'But, instead, I will tell you the story of this place, since you seem not to know it. It is something you should know, for it is part of the story of all our people.'

As he began to speak his voice took on the familiar tones of a bard. They all caught the change and settled down. A man told a story, you listened. That is how it was.

'Know that this place is named Dinas Emrys, so called after a great seer and magician whose deeds were done many years ago when first the Ænglisc came to these islands. His name was Myrddyn Emrys, which in the Latin tongue is Merlinus Ambrosius, and this is where he first rose to fame.'

Cynrig leaned forward, his legs drawn up, his chin on his knees, his eyes shining.

'There was a time, at the end of the last age, when all the land was in dispute and turmoil, and great was the peril of the people. He who was Gwledig of all Prydein at that time was styled Gwrtheyrn by his own people, that was Vortigern in the Latin tongue, which was the tongue of his court, it is said. Your people, Einion, by direct descent I believe. What his true name was, is not told. Now, this Gwrtheyrn had been beset by enemies from the northern lands and had called upon certain Ænglisc princes for aid, but it had been an uneasy alliance and at last they had turned on Gwrtheyrn themselves in retribution for the many slights they had received from him, for he was not entirely a wise man. So now he had enemies on both hands – the men of the north and the wolves from the sea.

'He suffered heavy losses from both sides, and at length he retreated into the high country and came at last to these hills in the lands of Maelgwn Gwynedd. Here he sought to build a strong place, here upon this very rock. He had at his command many wise men and many men skilled in construction, and he set them to work. But it was to no avail. Each time they built the walls up, they came tumbling down again. For many days they laboured, each night going to bed satisfied with the day's work, each morning waking to find all in ruin. Great was their dread and Gwrtheyrn must needs drive them to their work everyday. So he turned to his wise men: "We are skilled in building, how is it that we can not build this place?" And the wise men consulted together. They cast runes and conducted rituals, calling upon arcane forces known only to themselves, and at last they spake thus: "Know, oh lord, that you must seek a boy, a boy born of no man, a boy of no more than nine summers. And know that you must bring him hither where you must slay him and cut up his body, and pour his blood upon the foundations. Only if you do this, will the walls stand."

'Great was the wonder of all assembled. Where might they find a boy born of no man – at any age? Yet, Gwrtheyrn sent fast riders out into the land to seek out such a boy and have him brought here. Far and wide they searched and found nothing. Days slipped into weeks, weeks into months, but with no success. Yet, at last, as the year was turning, one of their number found himself riding upon a distant strand, far away beyond the southern mountains. Drear it was, a wild and desert place. There, on a night when the full moon cast her baleful light upon the earth, he came upon a tower wherein dwelt a lady, and with her, her only son. "She is in great sadness, for the boy has no father," he was told: "none have lain with his mother save a demon who came out of the night and got her with child and was never seen again." And the man knew that he had found the boy he sought. So he gathered up the boy and took him to Gwrtheyrn. It is told that the journey was very hard, that they lost their way and were many days on the road, as if some other force was set upon preventing it. Great was the man's fear at this, but he dare not turn back. And at last he brought the boy before his lord.

'Now Gwrtheyrn was a hard man, given to fits of sudden rage, and all went in fear of his anger, but the boy was not daunted. "Why have you brought me here?" he demanded. And, with a black countenance, the king told him what must be done and why. When he heard these words, the boy laughed. "Your wise men are not wise men at all, but fools. I can tell you how this task may be done."

'The wise men protested. He is only a child. What can he know? And so on.

'"So, how can this be?" Gwrtheyrn asked in wonder. "They are right, you are but a child."

'"A child I may be, but am I not also my father's son?" replied the boy. "Follow my advice and you will succeed. If you fail, then you may take my blood. And good luck to you!"

'So they took him to the place – this place, here, where we sit amidst its later ruin.' Afalach held up his arm and pointed out into the flickering darkness. 'Beside the piles of tumbled stone, they had caused an altar to be built, and they had set upon it knives and axes ready for the ritual.' The boys shifted uncomfortably, not liking to look round, for the dark seemed to cling to their backs and crawl up their spines.

'"Dig here," said Myrddyn – for of course it was he – "and beneath this place you will find a great pool. This you must drain and in the bottom you will find a casket of stone, laid here by Lludd in ages long passed. Open it and you will find two dragons, a white and a red, locked in eternal combat. Release them and they will fight to the death. And when the victor is known, then may you build your strong place. But know this my lord, if the white dragon be slain by the red, so shall it be for you." And the people were in great wonder for the white dragon was the emblem of the people of Prydein in those days. But the red dragon they knew not at that time.

'So Gwrtheyrn caused the hole to be dug and all that Myrddyn had said was revealed to be true. There was the pool and there was the casket of stone. When they opened it, the two mighty dragons flew out. A great battle ensued between them, filling the sky with fire and rage for hours as it seemed, but at last the red dragon smote down the white and slew him amidst great ruin.

'In his dread at this evil omen, Gwrtheyrn cast out his wise men and would retain Myrddyn as his only advisor. And Myrddyn saw that the strong place was built and that it was good, but he would not stay. "Know, my lord, that the bearer of the red dragon will come and he shall mark your doom. And he shall also be Emrys!"

'And all that Myrddyn prophesied came to be. A great warrior Emrys, that is Ambrosius in the Latin, came into the land and challenged Gwrtheyrn, naming him the bane of Prydein. Alone and unadvised, Gwrtheyrn sought battle and was slain, for Emrys bore the banner of the red dragon, which now of course is the emblem of all the Cymry. But none could rid the lands of the Ænglisc and from that time they have been a constant presence in Prydein.'

He leaned forward and threw a couple of sticks onto the fire. 'But then, without them we would not have the company of such as Ithwalh – that was a fine shot in the dark, young man.'

The boys stirred. Several nervous glances were cast into the shadows, but then, with the tension broken they all grinned stupidly at Ithwalh who went scarlet.

'And was that really in this place?' asked Cynrig, filled with wonder.

'It was. And it is said that Myrddyn came back in later years and buried his gold here. But it is guarded and none have found it, though many have looked. The tower stood high and strong once, but now, as you see, all that was built has fallen once again. No men come here now, for it is sacred to the memory of Myrddyn Emrys.'

When they woke the sun was high in a sky blown clear of

any threat of rain or storm. Before they had slept, Afalach and Einion had attended to the corpse and together they had scratched a shallow grave and buried him where he fell. Then they had heaped stones upon the turfs to keep him there. Now the druid had gone, but in his place was a brace of rabbits, freshly caught. The companions set about reviving their fire and preparing themselves a late breakfast, grateful for some fresh meat to go with the dried stuff. No one felt in any hurry to leave. They reckoned they deserved a rest and felt safe here now. Even the Christians seemed to sense the protective hand of Myrddyn Emrys over the place. Even Canthrig Bwt was no match for that.

Tecwyn had woken in the early dawn and Einion had busied himself with tending him. The others had let him be, still not certain how to deal with the revelations of last night, leaving him to his own space.

'So – d'you still not trust him?'

'I suppose I must. But it's not going to be easy.'

'Just keep it to yourself, will you?'

Ysgyrran looked at Rhun. His leader.

'Very well – if you ask me, I will. For now.'

The sun had reached its zenith when the druid returned.

'I found them. They were hiding. I think I impressed them enough that they won't follow you further into Gwynedd. But do not rejoice too soon – I doubt you have seen the last of them. They are angry and bitter.' He turned. 'How is the young one?'

'Complaining he missed everything, the fool.'

Afalach walked across to where Einion was sitting by Tecwyn under Cynrig's tree.

'What's this I hear? Complaints, is it?'

'Well I missed the fight and they won't tell me what happened. Who are you? Are you a druid?'

'I am the man who is trying to mend you.'

'Oh, I'm fine. I want to get up.'

'Foolhardy, sudden, wilful you are, perhaps even brave, but fine you are not. You will lie there and you will not move until I tell you otherwise. Is that clear? Now be still, for the love of all things.'

Afalach knelt down and undid the dressing. The wound was still raw and red but he pressed around it gently with his fingers and leaned in and sniffed at it, and seemed satisfied. 'No vileness. That is good. You will do well.' He groped around in his bag and brought out another small bottle. 'Here drink this – it will help you recover.' He sat back on his heels and turned to Einion. 'He will sleep now – it is what he needs most. Come, there are things which need saying.'

'Sleep – I don't want to sleep!'

'Perhaps not, but you need to.'

Tecwyn looked stormy.

'Very well, we will bring you to the fire but you will not get up!'

They carried him with the utmost care and settled him by the fire. Afalach sat himself and Einion down alongside.

Afalach looked around the little crowd, examining them, holding each in turn with his eyes. 'We must mend this. There are things you should know before you continue your journey. Einion – why don't you start?'

Einion sat quietly and stared into the grey smouldering remains of the fire. He looked alone, surrounded though he was.

'You shouldn't see us all as bad,' he said, hesitantly, 'we're not all like those men and even they are not evil.'

'It's hard not to when they burn our farms and steal our livestock. Not to mention attacking us in the night.'

'And they killed Peleg.'

There was a general murmur among the boys. Einion looked wretched.

'I know. But it could have been any one of us that night – even me. One thing is for sure: it was not my kinsman Cathan who did it – I killed the man, you'll remember. I confess I know little of my own people, but my father was a good man – a great man once, I believe. I cannot be ashamed of him. And my kinsman Cathan – well, he thought so too.' He trailed off, not sure what to say, nor how to say it.

Afalach took up the tale.

'It was at Cær Legion, which the Romans called Deva – which is called Chester now among the Ænglisc. That was the beginning. Powys had been a great kingdom ruled by the descendants of that same Gwrtheyrn I spoke of last night. It stretched from Mersey in the east all the way to the sea in the far west. Wrœcensæte was a great town for many lives of men after the legions left. But in time the outer edges of the kingdom were nibbled away by hungry folk – by Ængels in the east and the sons of Meirion in the west. In the north were the sons of Maelgwn Gwynedd – your people, Rhun. All made uneasy neighbours. Yet Powys was still great. Then, before any of you came into this world, a king of the Ænglisc, Æthelfrith of evil fame, swept down from his kingdom by the great Wall, borne on a cold wind from the north, consuming all in his path, Britons and Ængels alike. A great alliance met him at Cær Legion and there gave him battle. Cadfan of Gwynedd was there, Cearl of Mercia was there, an Ængel himself mark you. Your father was there, Rhun. There also was Brochwell ap Cynan and Iago ap Beli. But the main force was led by Selyf ap Cynan, king of Powys. Great was he among our people and mighty was his army, and among his personal war band was your own father, Einion.'

Rhun looked up. 'My father told me about this battle – he said that Æthelfrith was looking for Edwin.'

'That is so. Edwin had been his neighbour and had fled from him many years earlier. He had been in exile with Cadfan of Gwynedd, and now he was grown, Æthelfrith was in fear of his return. Well, great was this battle and much slaughter was done on both sides. But the alliance faired the worse. Æthelfrith knew no mercy. It is said that no less than twelve hundreds of monks were slain in the first hour, who had been praying for victory. I fear their God of Peace was not with them that day. I can't say I approve of these Christian holy men – they are just Romans in different guise, and Rome was ever the enemy of my people – but that was a slaughter none could condone.'

He paused.

'When the day was done the might of Powys lay broken, Selyf lay slain upon the field. Elisedd ap Selyf retired into Pengwern for it is guarded by Hafren where that river makes a tight loop, and is easier to defend than Wrœcensæte or even Cær Legion. And he abandoned the upland country, and the people there were diminished. It has become a wild and perilous place.

In the years that followed, other Ængels stole their way up Hafren in ones and twos, and they whispered into willing ears words against the people of your own lands, Magonsæte and Ercyng, saying you were not true Cymro, naming you enemies, and stirring every opportunity to harass you and your kin. Thus it was, Einion, that your father and his cousins were led to their doom, for the one was enslaved and another slain here only last night.'

'But why, why should these Ængels wish to harry our people? Who were they?'

'Your friend Penda could tell you that better than I, I'm thinking. *Na*, it was done to unsettle the kingdom of Mercia and thwart Penda's ambitions for the crown. Without success I'm glad to be able to say, for Penda is a true friend to the Cymru. And he will be king, if he is not so already.'

'What will become of us – my people?' asked Einion quietly. 'Can you read it?'

'Oh, I think you may be sure they will rise again, and become strong again and, in time, do much honour to their forefathers.'

'And us?' asked Cynrig.

'Us?'

'Well, our people and – and you know,' he hesitated, 'will the Ængels win? In the end I mean?'

'Win? What a question! I don't know – I suppose they will, for a while at least. It depends on when you count the end to have come. And what you mean by win. For sure the Ængels will not go away like the Romans did, so you could say they will win.

'But remember, all of you, it is kings who conquer, not ordinary folk – the folk who grow things, and raise stock, and make things and tell tales. To win or to lose battles rarely means much to them – to us, indeed. All we want is peace to go about our business without interference and kings rarely give us that.

Oh, we may find ourselves fighting, as you do now, and sometimes on the side which wins – wins the battle at least. Kings may win a little power for a while, and much joy may it bring them, but win or lose, if we are not killed we still have to go back to work, back to tilling the fields and raising stock to feed those kings. Which king makes little difference. Some are good, some are wicked, but they are all much the same thing.'

He sighed.

'But perhaps we will win a little peace for a little while. Roman, Briton, Ængel – we rub along well enough as things go, and would probably go on doing so if it were not for kings. Oh, we change – nothing stands still, people come and go all the time. Take Rhun here. His mother's people were Franks, I believe, come from Germania to fight for Rome. Oh, do not look so surprised that I know of your mother – my knowledge is wide, though it is nothing you need fear.'

He looked around.

'And see, here is Ithwalh, a good friend and neighbour, whose father is of the Ængels, and there are many more like you two. Your home Lenteurde is ruled by a British king with an Ænglisc name! Many of our people live in places now ruled by Ænglisc kings, but are still the ordinary folk of those lands, no matter who rules them. Even if they no longer speak the same tongue, they are still our kin. Never forget that! But whatever tongue they speak, if they are still alive after the fighting, you could say, at least, that they have not lost.'

The company stirred. Tecwyn had fallen asleep. Afalach laid his hand against the boy's forehead.

'Now you should all rest. If only for his sake. He will do well but it will be a day or so before he can continue. You may rest here in safety for that long at least. But then you must carry on. Do as you were bid, take the path west of the mountain, and seek Elaeth in Lleyn. He alone still resists Edwin. From him, perhaps, you will learn the things you wish to know.' He glanced at Rhun and smiled, 'There are some things too recent for even the likes of me.'

So not all was lost, as Penda had hoped. That was news indeed. Their first news and a source of hope.

'What of you, Afalach?'

'Well, Rhun, I have my own wars to fight. I cannot help you beyond here. This place is mine to care for and I may not stray without great need. There are people in the valley still hiding in the woods for fear of yon Cathan and his friends, perhaps even of yourselves. I must see to their well-being.'

'We did wonder if it was our fault they had abandoned their house – if that's who you mean.'

'Do not blame yourselves – you have done nothing of which you need be ashamed. Not any of you.'

Chapter 10

As they emerged from the narrow valley west under Yr Wyddfa, the ragged little band came to a gap in the hills and found themselves looking down onto the glittering plain of the sea far away, embraced here in a vast bay. They were stunned by their first sight of it. They knew of the sea, of course, but now, when they saw it for themselves – so much water, how could it be so? The thin sun of autumn pierced the clouds here and there, painting the sea and the land below them with broad strokes of light. Ahead lay a land of hills marching away into the haze. Far away to their right lay a flat country with a long shore vanishing away northwards. The sun caught the flash of surf tumbling onto a sandy shore. They could see only a hint of the narrow strait which made it an island, but they knew that it was there, for this must be Ynys Môn.

Within a few hours the valley took them down out of the high country and into a broad swathe of low, rolling hills. They were relieved to be out of the mountains, relieved to be still alive. Tecwyn's wound was far from cured, but he considered it a small price to pay for not being eaten by Canthrig Bwt. He could face men, even men with swords, but the fear of her would stay with him for a long time. Their clothes were in rags, and despite their few days' rest, they were footsore and bone-weary of travelling. Seven nights on the road, struggling through rain and storm, stumbling through dense woods, up and down rocky gorges and across rivers, half-drowned and attacked in the night. But they had made it. Or nearly so.

The sun was at its peak as they stumbled out of the last shadow of the mountain. The ground levelled somewhat and the high hills drew back. A stream crossed their path, tumbling down from the hillside where, a little above the road, it fell noisily down a low broken cliff, throwing out fine drops which glittered as the sun caught them. The cleft, cut by the water of countless years, was lush with ferns and grasses, and overhung with rowan and stunted alder. It seemed to beckon.

'Come on,' said Rhun, 'Edwin's people might be anywhere – we must find shelter before we are noticed.'

They looked up the stream. 'Up there?'

'I don't know, but we're too exposed on the road – look, we have to find a safe place while we look for Elaeth – we don't know what is out there, and, well, this looks to be a good bet. I don't know – it's a feeling.'

Wearily they clambered up the rock. As they came out on the top they saw that it widened into a shallow grassy valley surrounded by low trees. Not wide, not long, but large enough to hold a house and keep it invisible from the road. It was in ruin but it still had part of its roof, and most of its circle of walling stood intact.

'I knew it! Here we are – sanctuary.'

They gathered in a group and inspected the place. 'We should be able to fix this up well enough,' said Ysgyrran, 'it's not that bad and there's water.'

'It's got a great view! You could see anything that moves from up here,' Tecwyn shouted from the top of the fall. He was mending, but it was slow. The wound was still livid and raw, and the day's effort crossing the final pass had taken its toll. He was exhausted so they had left him at the top of the fall. But this was Tecwyn – undeterred, he had climbed the rock to look out.

A great rock, split by its tumble from the mountain, made a perfect look-out point. Anyone lying there could command a wide view of the lands below stretching out westward into a grey distance, beyond where the land became water, to where the sea merged with the sky. A low smudge of cloud sat on the far horizon, making it possible to imagine you could see all the way to Erin. And, for all they knew, you could.

Rhun and Meical joined him.

'This is good. What do you think, Meical? Base camp?'

'Do you think it's near enough?'

'I do, for the time being. Until we know how things go, we'd be safer to keep our distance. It may not be easy to find this Elaeth and avoid Edwin at the same time. It'll be good to have a bolt-hole.'

They spent the rest of the short day settling into their new home. At once they set themselves to patching up the house as far as they could. There was plenty of wood, much of it dry, and as much water as they could ever need. Across the hill above was an abundance of heather for roof and bed. They sent out a couple to hunt for meat and green stuff and the rest set to work. As the day drew to a close they were ready. Dusk found them sitting round the fire, toasting gobbets of roughly butchered deer on sticks and well content. In the darkness no one would see the smoke and, hidden by the house and the screen of trees, there was little chance of their firelight being noticed.

They had left Tecwyn on his rock throughout the day to keep watch, but he had seen no sign of human life. No smoke, no noise of cattle, goose or sheep. No movement on the track or off it. It was uncanny.

'We must split up tomorrow. Three groups – you remember what Ecgrig said: if one gets hurt, that leaves one to help and one to carry the message. Ysgyrran, will you take Eryl and Ithwalh? Cynrig and Meical – you're with me. That should give us a fair spread of skills each. Tecwyn must stay here and rest – Einion will you stay here with him, and Llif you too so he may not be left alone for any reason?'

'Just a damn nuisance, that's you, young Tecwyn,' said Einion. But with a grin.

'I want us to fan out and discover what we can, but take no risks, we cannot afford to lose anyone.' In truth he was scared of doing so, they were so few. They had nearly lost Tecwyn, and, God knew, he had barely made it himself. How any of them had survived so far he did not care to ask. 'If we want to find anything useful, we may be gone more than a day. If we don't all make it back by tomorrow night, whoever's here must decide what's best to do.'

They set out at first light. Gone was the clear weather of yesterday; this dawn brought a day of low cloud and damp airs. But the poor visibility was perfect for covert activity. Rhun sent Ysgyrran's party north to see what he could find of Edwin's army. He took his own little band down into the low country which spread out beneath their camp. Behind them the high mountains rose into the murk. Far away ahead lay lower peaks silhouetted against the vast expanse of the sea. The land here was all hills, bald and rocky in places, cut by little rivers, their valleys clothed in dense woodland. They turned west and a little south following a line of lower hills which marched away into the distance. This was rich land, well populated, but they could find no one in it. No one alive, that is. They found plenty of dead. The farms were burned, the barns empty. Crops and livestock gone.

As they moved west, they came across a ghastly succession of broken farms and houses, one after the other, each with its harvest of death and its flock of squabbling carrion birds. Often, as they approached a house, they disturbed a cloud of flies, which rose to reveal a mass of maggots and bones, white and shiny in their new exposure, and the all-pervading stench of rotting flesh. They went warily, for some of the dead were still more or less intact, a sign of more recent violence. And there were so many. Mostly the very young and the very old. They buried such children as they could, solemnly and in silence. Three was not enough to do more.

Many of the farms were charred wrecks but not all. As they moved on they began to find places which, though deserted, had escaped the flames and which still contained a few things not looted by the Northumbrians. They scavenged for what little was left unspoiled. In particular they needed clothes. Their own were hanging off them, ripped and soiled by hard wear and battle, barely covering them. Besides, it would be winter all too soon and they needed warm stuff. They only took what was in the houses. They couldn't bring themselves to take stuff from the corpses, even those they could get near without throwing up. Poor Cynrig, the stink alone was bad enough, but his imagination fed his horror, he could feel the hurt, taste his own death, and his stomach heaved 'til he had nothing left but hot bile. Rhun and Meical took to going in without him. They managed to keep the contents of their stomachs by avoiding the worse bodies where they could. Even so, it was a foul task, taking the clothes of those they knew to be dead; but for sure, theirs was now the greater need.

Then came a change. They still found no one alive, and no dead either. The farms were still deserted, but they were whole. Clearly the people had fled, and Edwin's scavengers not yet come so far. It seemed they had reached the furthest extent of the destruction.

As the sun climbed to noon, they found themselves creeping down a twisting river valley. It was no more than a stream normally, but it was clear there had been much rain here recently which had filled it to abundance, and it had overflowed its banks in places, making the going difficult.

'We shouldn't go much further or we'll not be back by dark.'

'I can't believe we've seen no one – not even any Ænglisc.'

'It would be good to find a friendly face – someone to ask where we might find this Elaeth.'

And then they smelt smoke. Not the smoke of destruction but the smoke of a hearth.

'Perhaps we have,' said Rhun. 'Quietly now – this could be anything. Be ready to fight – or better still, run.'

The trees thinned and they came to the edge of a clear place where the stream ran through a boggy field thick with reeds and water plants. To one side, under a hill, was a low building, made square with stone, a house of sorts but not like any they had seen in this country. All seemed peaceful. As they hovered on the edge of the trees, uncertain, a man appeared. He was dressed in a long brown robe with a wide hood. It was very dirty and ragged, as was he. And he had seen them.

But when he spoke his voice was warm and welcoming.

'Come – come, do not be afraid.'

As they left the safety of the trees and walked out into the meadow, they could see a low wooden hut, partly hidden behind the strange stone one. Perhaps it had been well made once but now it was little more than a bundle of sticks and heather. A haze of smoke emerged aimlessly from its ragged thatch. Behind it was a cultivated patch, in which grew a few late pease and other vegetables.

He watched them as they came, hesitantly following the stream to the hut. 'Not looting, I hope?'

Rhun looked down at the bundle in his arms. He was unashamed. 'We were in great need, we only took what would no longer be wanted.' Outside his robe, the man had a crude wooden cross hung from his neck by a leather thong. 'You are a Christian, holy man?' he asked.

'I am Brynach. This is a sacred well and it is my task to tend it. God has set it here to offer its healing comfort to those in need. Are you in such need?'

'Not us, holy one – except of clothing – but one of our friends is, I think.'

Ysgyrran raised his head cautiously above the boulder. Not that the boulder was strictly necessary. Both he and his clothes were so tattered and dirty that he merged with the heather and whin bushes and was only visible when he moved.

'They've gone.'

Two other ragged lumps moved and resolved themselves into Eryl and Ithwalh.

'That was a bit close,' Eryl said. 'Didn't think they were so near.'

'Nor did I. We'd better keep off the road from here.'

'What if we got up to the ridge?' Eryl pointed up the low hill behind them.

'Good idea. Come on – run. We need to keep them in sight.'

Keeping low they scurried across the rough ground, leaping like hares as gullies and rocks crossed their way. When they got to the top they burrowed into the heather and looked out into the land ahead. It seemed flat, but only by comparison with the mountains behind. In fact, it was a tumble of little wooded hills and valleys criss-crossed by myriad paths which wove in and out of the folds. Here and there smoke rose to add to the dull haze of the day.

'There they are.'

'Look – there's more.'

The men they were following were not far ahead, and from this vantage point they could see little knots of them everywhere they looked. At last they had found what they sought. It had taken them the best part of the day, creeping about amongst the foothills, but now it seemed their efforts had been rewarded.

'Come on.'

They followed the line of the hill, careful to keep below the sky line. All too soon it ran out and they found themselves scrambling down into woodland. They found a path which took them through the trees down towards the main track. As they approached, they heard the sound of men. Voices.

But it was just noise. They could make out no words.

'What are they saying? Ithwalh – your lot are Ængels – can you make it out?'

'Why me? You all speak Ænglisc as well as I do!'

Ysgyrran caught a look from Eryl.

'What?' he said.

Eryl's face didn't change. He said, quietly, 'They're from the north, they'll speak differently up there I expect. I doubt if any of us'll understand them.'

Ysgyrran stared at him. Good thinking.

'Well, we'll have to get closer,' said Ithwalh.

Amongst the scrubby undergrowth a deep ditch ran alongside the road. It was full of murky green water but they crept down into it and made their way closer to the North-umbrians. They could hear the voices clearly but it made no sense. Not to Ysgyrran and Eryl. They turned to Ithwalh who held up his hand in a gesture of silence.

After a few moments they heard the men moving off. Ithwalh rolled onto his back. 'Not Ænglisc – they were speaking your tongue – but Eryl is right, they're not from anywhere I've been. I didn't get much of it,' he said.

'But not Ængels, you say?'

'*Na*, not Ængels. Northmen perhaps, but definitely Britons.'

'That is interesting. Come on let's get back – we'll not find much more now I'm thinking. We're running out of day.'

Sure enough, it was close to dark when they got back, but Llif spotted them as they made their way up from the road. He met them at the top.

'You're cutting it fine,' he said, 'but at least you're here. No sign of Rhun and the others yet.'

'*Duwiau*! Let's get to fire first. I'm frozen.'

Einion and Llif had had a quiet day. Tecwyn was comfortable, or showing no pain at least. They had a good fire going and some hot food ready.

Ysgyrran and the others fell on it: they had eaten nothing all day.

When they finished they sat around trying to dry what was left of their clothes. 'Well, he did say it might take more than a day. They'll not be back now, not now it's full dark.'

And nor were they. Nor all the next day. Rhun had said they should make their own decision but no one felt inclined to go anywhere. They just waited.

The next evening Rhun appeared alone. He staggered up the waterfall under the weight of a big bundle.

'Here you go,' he said, 'clothes!'

'Whose clothes?'

'Where's Meical and Cynrig?'

'Don't worry – they're safe. And the clothes are yours – be grateful, I've carried them a long way!'

The boys scrambled about among the bundle, sorting out clothes for each. Not much fitted very well but it was all good and it was all warm.

'Where did you get all this?'

'Ah well, we found them – the owners had no further need, being dead.'

'Dead!'

'Don't worry, we didn't get them off the corpses. But I have to tell you, there is scarcely anyone alive down there. Edwin's men have been very thorough.'

'We found the same. No one about but his men.'

'We didn't see any Ænglisc – just dead locals.'

'So where are Meical and Cynrig?'

'We found a holy man – a Christian – he looks after a spring. I left them with him. But look, he says it can heal folk. What d'you say, Tecwyn, fancy a Christian healing?'

'I'm fine.'

'Oh yes, of course!'

Later he took Einion on one side. 'What d'you think – how is Tecwyn?'

'Not good. We shouldn't have left Dinas Emrys so soon, I'm thinking.'

'We didn't have much choice.'

'I know – but it's undone much of Afalach's work.'

'Can he travel?'

'How far is it?'

'About half a day, maybe more if we have to carry him.'

'Half a day'd be alright I suppose – and he doesn't weigh anything. I can carry him easy.'

'If he'll let you.'

'Don't you worry about that, he won't be given the choice.'

As dawn broke they left the safety of their hidden place and carried Tecwyn off the mountain. He had argued, of course, but there was no chance of his winning.

'Don't think it's for your sake,' Einion had said, 'you'd only slow us down if you tried to walk.'

By noon they reached the holy well, and laid their invalid in the cot in the little square stone house.

Brynach examined the wound. 'This is not good. Whoever treated it first did well, but you have asked him to do too much since.'

'I was afraid of that. Can you do anything for him? We would give you everything we have only we have nothing.'

'Why, as for that, perhaps you do. For three generations now men have kept this well in Christian charity. Many years ago I completed the cure-house that was started by my predecessor, but now my own house is falling down and it has got beyond me. I am old and can no longer do such work. So, perhaps you could help after all.'

'We would and gladly, though we know nothing of building in stone – not properly.'

'*Na, na*, think nothing of stone – the repairs will do well in easier materials.'

Three days they stayed. The house was made sound, at least as sound as it had ever been, and slowly Tecwyn recovered. He recovered his spirit before his strength and protested bitterly when they would not let him up.

But all too soon Rhun knew they had to go. *He* had to go in particular. His purpose here was to learn as much as possible of Edwin and his army to take back to Penda and he still knew next to nothing. Besides, how much longer would they be safe here? It seemed that Edwin's army had not reached this far yet; certainly they had not found this place, but he feared they might any day. Edwin was at least a Christian, so alone Brynach might stand a chance, being a holy man, but with all of them there, none were safe.

But what to do with Tecwyn?

'We'll have to split up again. I must go at least, and I'd rather not take too many with me – it'll just add to the risk of being seen.'

'Tecwyn can't go anywhere yet,' said Einion.

'I know it. I would leave him here in any case – look, Einion, will you stay and look after him?'

'I will. I owe him that.'

Rhun looked at him gratefully. '*Na*,' he said, 'you have paid that debt, but he trusts you – as I do.'

He looked around. 'So, I propose to take you Ysgyrran – you know best where to find them, and Llif, will you come?'

'I will. Willingly.'

'So Meical, Ithwalh – will you look after this end? Seek out this Elaeth and get Tecwyn to safety if you can. I don't imagine he'll be hard to find. We'll join you as soon as we know what we need to know. Expect us within a se'night.'

Before they left, Meical sought Rhun out. 'You will be careful, won't you? We can't afford to lose you,' he said. But his eyes told a different tale. Rhun embraced him. 'I'll be safe enough with Ysgyrran and Llif.'

'Couldn't I come with you?'

Rhun looked him in the eye. 'Please stay with the others,' he said. 'They'll need people they can rely on and you may have to make decisions they aren't ready for. Einion will look out for Tecwyn but the others will need you.'

'Isn't Ithwalh enough?'

'He would be in the ordinary way, but he is Ænglisc and I think it would be better if we kept that quiet after all we've seen. The people round here – they may not gladly welcome an Ængel. Now let's see if Brynach knows where to find this Elaeth.'

Chapter 11

It was dark. Not so dark he couldn't see: the sky was luminous with the last of the sunset, but around him the trees were dense, and down here everything was just different shades of darkness. And the air was still. Unnaturally so. The clearing ahead was filled with a silence too loud to bode well. Where were the usual rustlings of the night-time hunters, the last chatterings of roosting birds? Cautiously Rhun raised his head above the bracken. Cautiously he stood up, poised. He had pushed forward towards the edge of the woods, leaving the others to catch up when he gave the signal. Well, he had given it, but there was no sign of them. 'Come on,' he called softly. 'Where are you?' He cursed. 'Ysgyrran, Llif – where are you?' He stepped out onto the cropped turf of the road and straight into a rabbit hole. He fell heavily, biting off a cry as soon as it was made. *Stupid! Stupid! You're not hurt!*

But too late.

A shout went up: 'Hold and make yourself known! Quick – over there! Don't let him get away!' A crashing of under-growth, the swift pounding of feet on dry turf and, as if by some sorcery, before he could unlock his muscles he was surrounded by swords. Swords in the grip of strangers.

'My lord, we found this in the woods.'

Rhun stood, his arms bound tightly behind him, a firm hand on his shoulder. He was battered and near exhaustion. They had brought him across the water onto Ynys Môn and to a strong place standing on the very edge of the island. It was old and it seemed that the Ænglisc, or someone, had made it out of something built for some other purpose, for this hall, at least, was made of stone.

He had tried to keep his wits about him, but it had been

dark. He had no idea how big the island might be, but he felt sure they had not gone far from the strait. But with the water on his right, he knew it was the wrong end. He was a long way from his friends.

The place was big and cold, and empty except for Rhun and his captors, and a man in an ornate chair set before a large fire, which burned within a ring of rough stones. His iron-grey beard and hair glowed with a golden tint lent them by the firelight. A hard man, once bright and fair perhaps, now stone-faced and cold, but with just the hint of fire smouldering in his eyes that was not got from the flames. Something about the man made Rhun's blood run cold. He took care not to struggle; his bonds were tight enough to draw blood but he would not let these men see how desperate he was. At all costs he must pretend to have been alone, they must not find the others. But this Ænglisc lord seemed much too interested in him to care about any who might have got away.

'A Wealas boy with golden hair – what does that remind me of?'

'We took him to be a warrior so we thought we'd better bring him along. He had this sword.'

The cold lord took it and held it in his hands seeming to inspect it closely. He set it down across his lap and stared down at it, stroked it as if he loved it.

'This is an ancient thing. Not the plaything of a peasant. So who is he?' he said softly. 'Well – who are you boy? Are you trouble, I wonder?'

Rhun squared his shoulders as best he could. 'I am Rhun ap Cwyfan ap Erthig of Magonsæte.'

The man's head jerked up. He stared at Rhun as if he were something distasteful left by a dog, but the strange glow in his eyes became brighter.

'Yes – you are! Of course – Cwyfan's boy. I remember you. Oh yes, I remember you. The snivelling brat who wept when his filthy little cat was killed. Oh, I've not forgotten you or that wild thing you called a pet! Damn thing bit me – nearly took my hand off.' He laughed and looked round as one offering a share in the joke. If he cared that he got no takers, he did not show it.

'So, what are you doing lurking in these lands, boy?'

Rhun knew absolutely that he must not mention Penda. 'I am in search of my father,' was all he said.

The man burst out laughing again. 'So, first the father now the son, how tidy. How complete. Oh no, not together, no, too late for that. I'm afraid your father has gone, preceded you, you might say. Ha, ha. No – if it is him you seek, don't think to find him here.' So here was Edwin, king of Northumbria, much changed of face but otherwise just as Rhun remembered him. Gallant and debonair in public, mean and vicious in private.

'Where is my father?' he shouted, 'what have you done with him?'

Heavy hands crushed him down, forcing him to his knees. 'Quiet!'

Pain shot up his arms, filling his eyes with tears that he could not dash away. Straining against the grip of his guard, Rhun looked up into the fiery stare he remembered so well. 'Where is my father?' he said again, levelly this time.

'Oh, your father is dead. You may be sure of that. He came against me with that usurper Cadwallon. But I am still here – they are not!' His voice changed from light to dark in those few words. He stood and walked to the window. He clutched the sill, knuckles white, leaning against his hands to look out into the night, failing to contain his rising anger. 'They thought I would not come. And when I did they thought they could drive me back into the sea. Me, with the might of Northumbria at my back and them a ragtag of you... you Wealas!' He spat the word out as if it were a bad taste. Now his voice rose, gathering fury as it went. 'It should have been me who was made Gwledig, not him! I offered him friendship, oh yes I did – but he spurned me. He spurned me! He could have been my ally but he would not. Not he, with his airs and his pride. Pah! Now I will take his lands and all in them!' He stood, clenching his fists, looking round as if to find something to crush and sate his frustrated rage.

'All who have come against me I have swept away – beaten down like straws before a mighty wind. I am invincible! And your father? I beat him too! I smote him down and smashed him and he is no more!' He jabbed a finger at Rhun, and then stopped, suddenly, as if frozen. His eyes seemed to swim and his voice changed again, becoming all silk and quietness. 'And now his only son walks into my hands. I cannot tell you how happy that makes me.' To Rhun's astonishment, he giggled.

This man is mad, thought Rhun. *Truly mad.* The cold chill of real fear ran up his spine. But through his fear he felt his own anger rise. 'I know you, Ængel! You are no great warrior – you are just a coward with a big mouth and a lot of fools to do your bidding!'

The very air froze. Absolute silence. Edwin stood as if stunned, not believing what he had just heard. Without warning his foot lashed out, catching Rhun under the chin as you might kick a ball to lift it skyward. Rhun's neck cracked. He spun back into the mess of rushes on the floor, his bound arms crushed under his own weight. The pain was huge. Blood trickled from the corner of his mouth.

But Edwin was not finished. 'You dare to speak so to me? Wealas filth!' He leaped down from the dais. His foot smashed into Rhun's ribs and stomach, again and again. He shrunk away, desperate to escape the blows, but Edwin's foot hit home, over and over. Soon he was a mass of blood and bruises. *He's going to kill me!*

Then it stopped, as suddenly it had started. Rhun lay in a tightly clenched ball tensed for more, but nothing came. 'You think I might kill you? Well, scum, I might, but not today. Ha! Not today, slave boy – yes, you heard me – slave boy! Take him away and chain him close. Somewhere private. And do not speak of him – let us not trouble our people with his presence. Take care not to kill him; I plan to enjoy this one. But know this, Wealas boy – you are dead to the world!'

They dragged him outside to a rough wooden lean-to, one of several which clung to the back of the hall like fungus, and threw him onto a bed of filthy straw. They chained his leg to a post and left him. He lay panting, every inch of him one immense pain.

The stars wheeled in their eternal dance, but Rhun saw none of it. If he had feared Edwin before, now he hated him as well. With venom. But there was no more room in his mind for thought than there was for stars – it was fully occupied dealing with the pain and the cramps and the cold. At dawn a man came. He brought a coarse blanket and a bowl of thin stew. Enough to keep him alive, not enough for the slightest comfort. And he released Rhun's arms so that he could feed himself. Edwin's word was absolute – they would not starve him.

In the weeks that followed he came to wish they had.

It started well enough. They put him to work as they might any slave. But always the dirtiest. Cleaning out the stables was a favourite. Yet he was accustomed to hard work and his pride would not let him fail. He would not let these people see him weak. No one spoke to him other than to offer a curse, so he had plenty of time to think. Would his friends risk a rescue? He hoped not – it would only get them killed, and he wanted no more friends dead on account of his stupidity. *Iesu Crist*! – a rabbit hole! To cry out at such a little thing. He could not believe how stupid that had been. Just thank God he had been alone.

And all the while his mind was bent on escape. For escape he must – beyond that hope lay only despair.

It had taken a while for the enormity of his father's death to sink in. But, once it had, the knowledge spurred him to thoughts of revenge – his early misery turned to anger. He just hoped his father had died a warrior's death. He thought often of his friends in those first days. *They don't know where I am or even if I'm still alive,* he thought. *What will they do? Go home, I suppose.* He thought of home, of his mother, of Gethin. *They don't know either – my poor mother – she was right. She has lost us both. No, it must not be so. I swear it on my father's memory. I shall escape!*

He could see the mountains on the mainland, rising

out of the sea like a great rampart, and longed to be there. And he did not despair. He was fed, the work was useful if unpleasant, and he had shelter enough. He set his mind to captivity and sought only to survive and to learn as much as he possibly could of Edwin and his army. And then to find a way out of here and take that knowledge to Penda.

But a more unpleasant mind was at work than he in his innocence could conceive. Gradually the work became dirtier and with less purpose. It seemed that tasks were invented just to humiliate him. The fouler the better. Always in filth, much of it his own, never able to clean himself. And always out of the public gaze, not secret perhaps but always discreet, and always spent in silence bar the occasional curse or order. And all the while watched by the silent figure of Edwin. He never approached, never spoke, just made Rhun fully aware of his presence. Yet, even now, not without respite. On days when visitors came, and there were many, Rhun was hidden away so that Edwin's glittering reputation might not be tarnished.

But they wore him down. It took a while, chipping away at him, bit by bit, 'til he stopped thinking of home, which only made matters worse. Better that his friends never saw him like this. The very idea of escape now seemed beyond him. His only strength came from his daily refusal to give Edwin the satisfaction of seeing him defeated. He would not allow that man to gloat over him again, not at the cost of any amount of pain and degradation.

And then one day Edwin stopped coming. His punishments went on, never ending, but now, without Edwin as witness, they seemed utterly without purpose. Rhun began to lose his grip on hope, on defiance, even on sanity. Only death without honour, he thought numbly, could be worse than this.

But he was wrong.

The nights were starting to turn cold when they came to him, unfastened his chain and took him into the hall. There was Edwin, dressed in all his finery as if for a great feast, but the place was otherwise empty again – without witness. Rhun stumbled, half-blinded by the smoke and light and was struck to his knees once more in front of the King.

'I have something to tell you, boy. News from home. Oh, I'm afraid it is not good news. No, but I thought you should know that I have had business in the east that took me to your part of the world. Perhaps you have missed me?' He laughed. 'No? Well, no matter. While I was there, I thought I should visit your charming mother – such a handsome woman, such a shame. And all your pitiful people. They put up a struggle of course, but I am afraid it was not enough. No, you are alone now.' He paused, staring down at the boy huddled at his feet. 'Alone. All you have left is me!' He burst into an insane laugh, which stopped as suddenly as it had started. 'Now take him away, he stinks!' And they dragged him back outside, threw him down and left him.

He lay on his damp straw.

So, that's it, he thought. His father dead, his mother dead, his home destroyed, truly there was nothing now left to avenge – nothing even to live for and it was no consolation to find out why Edwin had been missing his daily entertainment. That was it. The end. The end of all things good and decent. The end of light and of love and of hope. The end of life. He was as good as dead. His friends had left him and gone home and now they were dead. With his last shred of hope lost, he gave himself up to his fate.

'Let Edwin win,' he said to the night, 'it doesn't matter now. Nothing matters any more.'

The days passed in endless, numbing similarity. The leaves turned and began to fall. The sad, humourless game started again, played out over and over, in dull, leaden repetition. Always some excuse for grinding Rhun into the filth, determined to crush every last hint of spirit and self-respect, though in truth there were none left of either. Every task more degrading than the last. His days and nights spent amidst the filth of men and animals alike, his thinning body coated more in grime and dried blood than the scant rags that were all that was left of his clothing. His hair was a thatch of muck and straw, crawling with lice. If Edwin was watching, Rhun was beyond caring, beyond even noticing. His guards had ceased to take any real interest. So long as he did not die or give them trouble they scarcely noticed him. He had truly become nothing.

The days crept by. It had been raining for the better part of a week. Rhun was so wet he would have felt a part of the rain itself, had he been able to feel anything. He had become one with the drab misery and he felt nothing. Everything was sodden. They came to him in the rain and took him out into it. They told him the drain was blocked which took the waste out of the strong place and down the short distance to the sea. Now it was overflowing. Who better to get into it and clear it out than the Wealas slave boy, more muck than human as he was. They dragged him to the edge and slid him in, careful to avoid slipping in themselves. At the lower end of the drain was the place where it should pass under the wall. It was guarded below water level by an iron grille which must have caught something too big to pass and then become choked with the leaf-fall. He waded gingerly down the slope until he was waist-deep in the mire, facing the rough stone. In the summer the place was lush with life, plants which thrived on the nutrients in this midden. They were over now, but the ivy was still green and the dead growth still thick.

Clearing away the foliage, with one hand leaning against the stone facing, he bent to the task. In front of his nose was a short piece of rope, its end jammed into the wall with a rock, so mired as to be invisible from any distance. He pulled at it and its frayed end came out of the muck. He could make nothing of it and let it go. He dipped his hand into the thick stuff. He moved it around trying to find anything hard, or at least dense, that might be blocking the flow. He found nothing at a hand's depth so, leaning down, he pushed in deeper. Still he found nothing. Deeper. At last his fingers touched something soft that was not muck. By now he was in up to his armpit, his cheek pressing into the filth. *Please*

God let this thing be the problem. It was hard to breathe even without his nose being half-blocked. The stench would have been unbearable if he had not been so used to it, but he still choked in the foul air.

Slowly, with his fingers at full stretch, he started to tease the thing loose. Gently, gently. Slowly it came free and he was able to grip it more firmly and pull it up through the ooze. It came out with a long sucking plop, and he stood up, cradling this doubtful treasure in his arms. A bundle of cloth concealing something hard within its folds. It was held by a piece of frayed rope. He looked again at the piece still fastened to the wall and it was the same. Numbly he was aware that this was important, that he had discovered something significant, but his tired mind could not grasp it. Yet, whatever the thing was that he had found, it was not just an accumulation of muck. It was something solid.

'Bring it to me,' shouted his guard.

A curse came from behind the wall. And then, 'It's free – he's got it.'

Sure enough the level of the pool was dropping fast. He waded back to the edge of the drain. As he stumbled up the slope of the bank, he made to offer up the bundle, his eyes focused carefully on the ground. A stinging blow sent him sprawling back into the muck. 'Don't bring it to me like that! Get down to the water and wash the filth off it, then bring it to the Hall. My lord Edwin must see this. And clean yourself up before you come, you stink.'

The sea was ice-cold, even in these shallows close into shore, but it felt so good to be able to clean himself, to watch the muck float away after so long. He squatted in the shallow water like a small dark frog hung with weeds. And as his body became clean, so his mind strayed to the thing he had found. He was sure that it meant something, something which eluded him. And then it came to him – whatever he had found, it had been hidden. Hidden in a midden. He giggled like a simpleton. Hidden in a midden. *Oh, that's good.* And then another thought came creeping in. No one hid things in a midden unless they were important. Really important. But what? Who? It couldn't have been these people. He tried hard but his mind could not grasp it, and at last his thoughts wandered off again. He scrubbed at himself not caring how long he took, oblivious of the man watching over him. This was a rare thing, the opportunity to get clean, a small joy, but oh – so intense for that brief moment. For the first time in weeks he raised his eyes to the horizon. There, across the expanse of dull water made flat by the rain, the mountains rose grey upon grey with the occasional flash of dull brown revealed as the clouds chased each other across the sky. He stood looking as at a dream, dumbly, and he could not read it. The vision faded and drifted away. The man grew impatient. Rhun felt the tug of his chain.

In the hall the air was filled with the smoke from the eternal fire. Being kept outside day and night, Rhun was unused to it now. He stood hunched and shivering, as the acrid smoke filled his eyes and started tears.

Edwin looked down at him.

'So, you weep do you? Weep for what? Eh, boy – weep for what?'

Rhun coughed, 'Nothing, my Lord,' he croaked.

'Speak up, filth!'

'Nothing, my lord.'

'No, nothing. You have nothing to weep for, do you boy? No father, no mother, no home, no friends. No hope.' He leaned forward. 'No thing!' And he laughed, pleased with the feeble joke, for all there was no one to hear it.

Even a few weeks ago Rhun would have protested, denied any such weakness, insisted that it was the smoke only. Now he no longer had the strength, no longer cared. Vaguely, his tired mind acknowledged the truth. Edwin was right – he had become nothing. He had nothing left to care about, not even his own life. Especially not his own life. Perhaps Edwin knew this, perhaps not, it made no difference. In his secret cruelty, he knew only the pleasure he got from having this boy to taunt. To hurt. This small defenceless thing that had dared to defy him. Dared to bite his hand.

'So what is this you found in the drain? Here – bring it to me.'

Dazedly, Rhun shuffled forward and placed the bundle on the floor, careful to avoid touching Edwin or his clothing. Edwin stirred it with his foot. The cloth, once blue, and rich with golden thread, clung wetly to its contents. Edwin kicked it and it rolled off the dais onto the floor of the hall. As it rolled the cloth unwound, and set its contents free.

It travelled, as slowly as time, across the floor and fell among the ashes, to lie glittering in the firelight.

A golden crown.

Edwin leapt down from the dais and gathered up the precious thing. He held it up and examined it. A simple design, ancient and unadorned. To Rhun's surprise Edwin spoke his thoughts out loud. 'What wonder is this? What is the royal crown of Gwynedd doing in my drain?' He climbed back onto the dais. 'Well, of course, it was Cadwallon's drain when this was put there. His crown. Perhaps he hid it hoping it would be safer there than on his head. Hah! He was wrong! It was safe in neither place! And now truly shall I be Gwledig.' But he was speaking to himself. But then he turned to Rhun standing below him. 'D'you see, boy? Your father's friend Cadwallon had hopes of recovering this, though how he thought he would do it from Ireland I cannot tell.'

Rhun's looked up at him blankly. This seemed to irritate Edwin further, if that were possible.

'Why boy, your father's friend – Cadwallon – ran away to Ireland at the sight of my army. Well it seems he planned to return. See – here is his crown. Much good may it do him.' He smiled at Rhun. Almost friendly. But it was a lie. Suddenly his face changed. He kicked Rhun hard in the stomach. 'Get him out of here, he offends my eye.'

After that he was left alone. They still fed him but he was no longer dragged to work. He spent his days as the animals do – eating when fed, staring into nothing between times. Reduced to a mere physical being, content just to eat and sleep. A small thought still nagged at the edge of his mind, but he could not bring it into focus so he let it drift away.

The winter snows came and wrapped his little world in silence and calm. One of his guards came and gave him blankets and a mass of straw to keep out the biting wind.

'Got to keep you alive,' he said, 'my lord's orders.' As if he needed to justify his action, to dispel any idea that he had been generous. Rhun barely noticed the man or the blankets.

Somewhere folk celebrated the turn of the year. Here the Ænglisc observed the passing of mid-winter in ways of their own. But Rhun knew none of it. It was enough that he was fed. The passage of the seasons meant nothing.

Then, when the days began to lengthen, there came another shock.

The snows had gone and the thaw had at last washed away their grubby remains. He had been lying on the dirty straw with his head outside to catch some of the thin sunshine of a rare calm day. He often did that now the days were warming. Idly he would watch the small birds pecking about in the mud and grass, squabbling over territories and seeking sites to build the new year. He wondered what they could find to eat in such a barren place. They were most of what little life he saw in those days. But he had made a friend. There were a few domestic hens which wandered freely. One had made her nest in a corner of his den. She had seemed to know that he was harmless and had become a companion in his loneliness. If she resented his eating her eggs she made no complaint, though he was careful not to take them all. He spoke to her. His voice had come to reflect hers, a mere croak through cold and lack of use. He spoke to her often and she had become used to his voice.

This morning she came clucking in as if with news. 'Good day to you, mother. It's a fine day, *Na*?' She stared at him. Her head jerked in the way of all chickens, as she voiced her view. He took her cluck as response enough and lay staring up into the sky, quite content to watch the clouds. The chicken settled onto her nest, making small crooning noises.

A sudden movement caught the corner of his eye and he

craned his head back to see what it might be. Two figures had come into view. Nothing unusual in that perhaps, but these two awoke a distant memory, even seen upside down. Light-headed, he was unprepared for what he saw. He twisted his body in sudden panic. In one convulsive movement he turned and struggled onto his elbows. The chicken fled in a panic of her own, squawking with a futile flapping of wings. The noise and movement caught the attention of the two passers-by.

Rhun was struck truly dumb. Could it be? How? He scrambled awkwardly to his feet. The pair stopped and then cautiously approached the lean-to.

'Ysgyrran,' he croaked, 'can it be you?'

They came closer and examined the filthy, semi-naked apparition. 'Who are you to know my name?'

Rhun held out his arms to touch them. Could they be real? Please God, make them real. But – no! no make this a dream, they cannot be here. Must not be here.

'Go – go hide – run away – you'll be caught.' He pushed them away.

Llif jerked back, disgusted by the touch of this foul thing. And then Ysgyrran froze.

'Rhun – Rhun, is it you?'

Rhun stared wildly. He tried to speak. Then he seemed suddenly to collapse. His chest heaved with a huge sob and a rush of tears. Half-blinded he reached out and clutched at Ysgyrran's clothing, patting him, pawing at him.

At last he found his voice. 'It is you. You're real – really you.'

'Rhun! What is this? What have they done to you!'

But Rhun had crumpled.

'Llif – stir yourself – help me!' Ysgyrran caught hold of Rhun and settled him gently onto his filthy bed. He was thinking at lightning speed. 'Go, keep a look out – we mustn't be seen here.'

Llif reacted as if stung. He ran to the corner of the hall and cautiously peered round it. No one had noticed. They had a moment at least. No one had said they shouldn't walk this way but somehow it had always been tacitly discouraged. Now he knew why.

Ysgyrran joined him. 'I've settled him down – at least he believes we're real now.' He paused. 'I've never seen anything like it. That anyone should be treated so.' He spat as if to rid himself of a foul taste. 'Come on – we mustn't be seen.'

'Can't we help him?'

'Not now – and say nothing. They must know who he is – if they've kept him hidden all this time they'll not want to reveal him now. Not to us, for sure.'

Rhun lay stunned. It had been Ysgyrran and – and – Llif. That's it, Llif – good with a bow. They had been real. He hadn't dreamt them. Suddenly he felt sick. His heart seemed to have become too big for his chest and his eyes blurred. He wept. Deep convulsive sobs. Tears of joy, tears of relief. Tears of shame.

It was several days before Rhun saw his friends again. Days spent in a torment of disbelief. His mood swung wildly between hope and despair. But in the moments of hope a small persistent thought was born. It nagged at him, but he couldn't grasp it. A surly slave brought him food each day as usual, but he saw no one else. Then at last they came again. This time in the dark.

'Thank the gods you are alive. No one said anything about you being here – we had no idea. They got me and Llif together. We didn't know where you'd gone or what had happened to you.'

'He never told me of you either. He said you were all dead. My mother too.' He stopped. Staring blankly. That small thought again – just flitting beyond consciousness – what was it?

The moment passed. 'But, Ysgyrran, how is it you are free to walk about?'

'There's nowhere to go. This place is closed up like a clam.'

Llif butted in, 'They don't think much of us. They've not

treated us badly but that's as far as it goes. We've got no idea why they're keeping us at all.'

'Bargaining chips?'

'I don't believe they need any – more likely for ransom. Unless they mean to sell us as slaves.'

Rhun watched them, still scarcely believing they were real.

'And yet they keep you, and you are safe,' he said.

'They do and we are. But you – how come you're here chained up – worse than a dog?'

Rhun looked at him vacantly for a moment. He struggled to remember, to clear his mind.

'I defied Edwin. He didn't like what I said. It seems he has always hated me – since I was a just a child.'

'Why – why on earth should he hate you?'

'It was my kitten,' he said. 'How foolish that sounds now. Edwin killed it. He had no need – it was only a kitten. But he knows I saw him do it. He likes to be seen as kind and generous. He is truly mad, you know.'

'To hate you for such a small thing. The coward!'

'Why hasn't he killed you?'

'I don't know – he seems to enjoy having me alive. He couldn't hurt me if I was dead.'

Ysgyrran and Llif absorbed this. They could recognise the truth of it, despite their own treatment having been so much better. They knew of Edwin's wild mood-swings. Who did not, that had ever been close to him?

'Well you're alive and that's the main thing. Look – I hate to do this but we must go. If we are caught here, all our lives are at risk.'

'You will come back?' Rhun sounded like a child again. Pleading. Not believing, not daring to trust.

'Oh yes – never fear,' said Ysgyrran.

But Rhun did fear. He sat and tried to puzzle it through. Edwin had ignored him for – oh, days, it must be. *Na*, it must be more than that – weeks perhaps. As the seasons, time itself meant nothing any more. But now here were Ysgyrran

and Llif alive and well. Could that mean escape? *Na, na* –
not that – not now, it was too frightening. Confronted by
the possibility, the enormity of it terrified him. Even if he
believed it possible, he dared not believe it might happen.
He felt tiny, defenceless, exposed and vulnerable. He
cowered back into his straw sanctuary. 'Don't worry, chicken
– I won't leave you,' he whispered.

A week went by. With each day his fear grew. Perhaps they
wouldn't come. Perhaps he had dreamt it. At last he decided
it must have been a dream, he wouldn't have to leave after
all, he could stay here safe with his friend. At least she didn't
scare him. But then, again as dusk fell, they were at his door.

Ysgyrran got straight down to it. 'Look – things are
moving out there. And I think I've found a way out.'

'Good – but *na, na* – you go – you can get away safely, but
leave me. I'm alright here.'

'What are you babbling about?' Ysgyrran was astounded.

Rhun seemed to have shrunk – into himself as much as
into his hovel. Now he peered out, through haunted, staring
eyes. 'Go away!' he said. 'Please – leave me alone. Go – get
away, but leave me here.' He shook his chain. 'See, I'm safe
here. With chicken,' he added in a whisper.

Ysgyrran reached in and grabbed the chain. To his astonishment the leg iron which held it to Rhun's ankle fell open.
'Look – it's not locked! It's not locked!'

Rhun looked abject.

'I know,' he croaked.

'You know! Then...' he stopped, searching to make sense
of this. 'Why are you still here?'

Rhun collapsed. His voice scarcely audible, choked with
tears.

'It came open. I didn't want them to know – they might
have said I'd broken it.'

'But why didn't you try to run?'

'Run?' He sounded astonished. 'I can't,' he said. 'I don't
dare – they'd punish me.' He paused. 'And I couldn't leave
chicken – I promised.' He looked up, his voice utterly bleak.

'I'm safe here. If I stay here and don't tell them, they won't hurt me.'

Ysgyrran simply could not believe it – these were the words of some craven, broken thing, yet this was Rhun – Rhun their leader, Rhun ap Cwyfan ap Erthig – who had never been timid in his life. What had these bastards done to him?

'Well, you'd better dare now – we're not going without you! Look, Edwin has gone – marched out with most of his army. There's nobody much left here. The place is scarcely guarded and we're ignored most of the time. I guess they won't let us go or they would've done it already. But I've found a place where we could get past the palisade unseen – where it comes down to the water. I reckon we could just walk away if we chose our moment.'

'Na, na – you go. Leave me, I can't go with you. I must stay here or they'll be angry.'

Llif broke in, 'Well, we've got to go right now, someone's coming.'

'We'll be back tomorrow at dusk – you can go and you will go – be ready. And say goodbye to chicken!'

The following night they stood by the palisade, cleaving to such shadow as it afforded. Cloud hung heavy and low, and darkness had fallen early. A bleak wind blew just hard enough to rattle the trees and cover any noise they might make. The water lapped clammily at their feet. 'I'm sorry, I hadn't reckoned on the tide. We'll have to swim for it. Get your clothes off, we daren't risk a soaking – come on.' Ysgyrran stripped and added his clothes to a bundle he had under his arm. He grabbed Rhun and tore the last of his rags off him. 'You won't be needing these anymore in any case,' he said grimly. He dropped them onto the mud and trod them in as they waded carefully into the channel.

At first Rhun had resisted this rescue. In terror of the outside, the unknown, he had struggled feebly to stay in his shed. Ysgyrran had had to drag him out.

'Come on, I'm not leaving you here whether you like it or not. So get used to it, and stop whimpering – they'll hear us.'

Now he was like a puppet, dumbly doing what he was told. After a few steps they were up to their waists, pale ghosts half submerged, slipping silently out of the compound.

And then they were out again. Standing on the beach. They were dripping wet, they were freezing cold, but they were free. It had been easy.

'Quick – mustn't stop. Follow that line of trees.'

They headed out into the night, Llif leading, Ysgyrran half carrying Rhun. It was a dream. It was a nightmare. Rhun stumbled along, numb with cold and shock, his pale emaciated body struggling with the effort. Their path took them through a rocky landscape filled with gorse and scrubby trees: hazel, and thorn which cut them as they passed. After some ten minutes or so they came to a low stone wall and Llif clambered over.

'Sheep pen, is my guess,' he hissed, 'we'll be safe here for a bit.'

Ysgyrran hoisted Rhun over the wall and sat him on the grass. He weighed nothing. The rescuers climbed back into their clothes, a bit warmer now from their exertion, and took in their surroundings. They were in a shallow bowl, surrounded by the wall except in one place where there was a narrow gap once closed off with a hurdle which now lay broken and cast aside.

'Good – you keep watch while I get Rhun into some clothes.' For Rhun was still naked. The mad scramble to cover had warmed them all but that would not last without at least some cover.

'Come on Rhun, here are clothes. Stolen, I'm afraid, but don't let that bother you – their owner can freeze to death for all I care. But I don't want *you* to.' He scrubbed at Rhun's body with a handful of grass in an effort to clean off some of the grime, and get some blood flowing. He tried to get the shirt over Rhun's head, but Rhun was quite unable to function, standing stiff with cold and fear.

'Gods! Rhun, help a bit, can't you?'

'Ysgyrran – is it really you?'

'What d'you mean, is it me?'

'You're not some devil, sent to get me into trouble?'

'I am not – it's me, sure enough. It's you who's become a stranger. What did they do to you in there?'

Rhun looked at him, as if still uncertain.

'I don't think I can tell you yet. I don't want to think at all. Do you mind very much?'

'It's all right, you take your time. We've got to get safe before anything else and find out what's happened to the others. At least that. It's been months – anything could have happened.' He finished dressing Rhun in the stolen clothes. 'There,' he said, 'that's better. You'll do well now – if we can get off this damned island,' he added quietly to himself.

For that was easier said than done. Oddly, there had been no alarm, no hue and cry. It was as if the Northumbrians did not care that they had gone or more likely had not noticed. Yet that made it no easier. There was only one crossing off the island that they knew of. When they reached it they saw that it was well used and well guarded. Hopeless. There was no escape this way. Yet they watched it for a long time before accepting that they could never use it.

For two days they ranged up and down the coast, moving at a crawl to avoid patrols. They crept through the naked woodlands of the southern shore, approaching the water where the land would let them, ever searching for a way across the strait that was not guarded, and might not kill them. All the while they could see the other side. In places the strait was so narrow they felt they could almost touch it. But they could find no way over, for it was a deep and dangerous water. And icy cold.

Yet even in this place, ravaged and blasted as it had been by Edwin's conquering army, they managed to find a few folk to lend them aid, food and drink and brief shelter. But naught else. None dared keep them for more than a night, and they were forced always to move on. 'Make for the marshes,' they were told, so that is what they did.

And all the while Rhun said nothing and the others

didn't press him. He was stick-thin and he seemed for ever stiff with fright. He would start and cower at the slightest thing, the rustle of an animal moving through the undergrowth; the crack of a branch in the wind. At night they slept with him lying between them, to lend him their warmth and some shelter from his terrors. As they moved they made sure that one of them had hold of him at all times. He walked as if blind. And still he said nothing.

On the third day, as night was falling, they came to a place where the rocks gave way to a muddy shore.

Though the island was nowhere high, the strait was rocky and deep for most of its length. But on this western end both banks drew back and it became a wide estuarine place, lined, on either side, with a maze of reed beds and grassy salt flats, giving at last onto sand dunes which stretched away northwards beyond sight. Bleak, and cold from the bitter winds which came from behind the sunset and blew onto this desert shore. They had expected it to be easier here, but the mainland was further away than it had ever been. Unreachable.

'Ynys Môn! – sacred it may be but I've had enough of it! How do we get off this damned island?'

'Would a boat be any help?' said a new voice.

Chapter 12

It had been a quiet winter – quiet, that is, apart from the worry. The day after Rhun and the others had left, Einion had bundled Tecwyn up onto his back once more and Brynach had led them through the hills deep into Lleyn.

The country was not so hilly here and their destination loomed on the northern horizon, becoming more grim and inhospitable as they approached.

And then the challenge came. A sudden cry of alarm from a blackbird alerted them, followed at once by the voice of a man.

'Hold! – lay down your weapons.' A big voice, its owner hidden.

Brynach spoke quietly, 'Do as he says – you will come to no harm if you obey. Not sure what might happen if you do not. And say nothing – I will do the talking.'

They made a small heap of their bows and swords and stood back.

A small dark man emerged from behind the shelter of a tree. He was wild and unkempt and no match for the size of his voice. But they were in no doubt – he was not someone to be taken lightly. Before they knew it they found themselves surrounded by a dozen others, each with bows half-drawn, and serious faces.

'Who are you to be wandering the lands of Lleyn uninvited?'

'We come in peace, brother. I am Brynach – I keep the Holy Well south of here. These are my friends who come in search of y brenin Elaeth.'

The leader peered at him. '*Ie*, I know you now – you cured my sister's little girl when she was sick. But who are these others? They are naught but boys!'

He caught a glare from Einion, stooped under his burden.

'Most of them, at least,' he added with a grin. Meical took heart. *They can smile at least,* he thought.

'They have travelled far and are in need of council.'

The dark man conferred with his companions.

'We are agreed. We will take you to him, but we will also take your weapons – for the time being – boys or no boys.'

They stood in a huddle while their weapons were gathered up, no point in arguing, and allowed themselves to be herded up the track into the hills. The land became ever more steep and barren. More rock than turf, the tops of all these hills stood grey and forbidding. Their path was leading them in a wide westward curve towards the highest. On a shoulder, just below the highest point, yet standing on its own, stood a strong place, a great wall seeming to grow out of the mountain. All the way, no one had said a word, the only sounds being their feet on the rough path, the wind, and the chatter of small birds, the croak of ravens.

The place was massive. The boys had never seen anything like it; there was a place of similar antiquity not far from home but this was on a quite a different scale. It was built of stone, a material in abundance in these hills, and very ancient. The walls stood to a height easily twice their own, made of huge rocks, interlocked with precision, one upon the other. The gate, when they got round to it, was every bit as formidable as the rest. They were led up a deep, winding, narrow passage, and at last through a low tunnel, roofed in stone, and out into a wide windswept place rising to a low dome, and dotted with low round houses also built of stone.

'Maybe it was made by giants,' said Cynrig in a hushed voice.

'Very small ones unless ordinary folk added the walkway,' said Einion dryly, pointing at the walls. All around the inside, the tops of the walls were flat, forming a walkway inside the final outer parapet, at a height to allow a man to see over. It was like nothing they had ever seen before. Today it was deserted except for a few lookouts, but it was easy to see that many men could stand there if the need arose. And, indeed, many of them were busy about the place. The walls commanded a wide horizon. Apart from to the north where the mountain rose even higher, they had a view of all the lands around, the coast on three sides, and a long way out to sea. To the east they thought they could glimpse the snow-laden heights of Yr Wyddfa. To the west the land narrowed to a point, many miles away, leading out to an island on the far horizon, and they thought they might surely see Erin from here on a clear day. Much of the place lay neglected, had done for long ages by the look of it, but plenty still stood and it seemed that Elaeth had rebuilt enough to make sure he could defend his lands against the Northumbrians. This place was still very powerful.

'I still think it was giants,' said Cynrig, not prepared to let go of the idea.

'Suit yourself.'

Amongst the ancient stone houses were a few new ones of wood. They were taken to a large, imposing structure built rectangular in the new style, much like their own at home but on a single storey only. Inside was fire and warmth and food, and soon a crowd of men gathered, come to inspect the new arrivals. Yet the board was not laden; this was no feast of welcome.

Elaeth turned out to be an imposing man in his prime, strong and hard, just like his landscape.

'I am sorry if we are wary – these are the worst of times to be finding strangers in your lands. So tell me, what brings you here? You are too young to be warriors, surely. Yet you are armed and have a wounded man, it seems. I'm thinking there is a long tale here.'

Meical spoke for them all. It seemed natural, and none of the others seemed willing to do it, yet at this moment he felt Rhun's absence keenly.

'My lord, I am Meical ap Talhaiarn. These are my companions. What remains of them. We have come from the east – far across the great mountains – from Magonsæte. We have not had an easy journey and have been attacked. We are in search of our fathers who came here to help Cadwallon and were not heard of again.' He chose his words with care and told of their adventures as best he could without revealing more than he had to. *Better not mention Penda,* he thought. The search for their fathers was cause enough, surely? If Elaeth noticed the odd gap in the narrative, he did not say so.

'You think to find your fathers here?'

'We do not my lord, not here. Rhun ap Cwyfan, who is our leader, has gone with two others to seek news from Ynys Môn, or from as close as he can get. We were charged to seek for you and beg shelter for our wounded until he returns.'

'And how long might that be?'

'He promised a se'night, my lord.'

Elaeth pondered this for a brief while, as if choosing his own words with equal care. 'Know this – you are so many more mouths to feed so far as I am concerned. But we can manage a se'night, so I will do for you such as I can, but I fear it cannot be much in this time of war. Nor can I give you good news, if my guess is right.'

'We supposed as much, my lord, from what we have seen. And we have already heard of a great defeat. We do not wish to be a burden.'

Elaeth sighed. He stared into the distance, as if seeing something only visible in his mind's eye.

'It was Edwin, indeed, who had the victory. Now he seeks to destroy that which he cannot command. He is a proud and vicious enemy. That you are all here says much for your courage, or your luck. Perhaps you are warriors after all. Well, I can tell you the tale of the battle, though it is not a happy one, but I fear I know nothing of your fathers. Still, you mustn't starve while you are guests. We have not come to such a pass yet.' He raised his voice. 'Come! Food and drink for our guests. They have some hard listening to do.'

As they ate they settled to listen, each guarding his private anxiety. How many still had fathers to search for?

'Edwin came in the spring. He landed in the north on Ynys Môn in the great bay up by the Holy Island. For a while all was quiet. We waited, and for a long time he did nothing.

Then he came to Cadwallon under a flag of truce. It seemed that what he wanted was to be acknowledged Gwledig – he seemed to think it was his right. There was talk of reuniting the old kingdom of Cunedda, from here way up to the Wall. But how could we give him that even if it had been in our power? It is a sacred title, not to be taken lightly – none hold it by right. It is the gift of Council and had he been the chosen one, well, then we would have followed him. Not gladly – no one could love that man. But he was not. They had chosen Cadwallon; they could not change their minds because some overbearing Saesneg demanded it. So it ended. Well, then we saw Edwin for his true self – he flew into a towering rage and stormed out. He went back to his army and within no time they had swept across the length and breadth of Ynys Môn, burning and killing as they went. None were safe – women, children, none. At length they penned Cadwallon at Trwyn Du that is in the east.'

He glanced over to Brynach. 'I fear for your patron's monastery, there is much that was damaged in the fighting. And it seems Edwin has taken it and used it as a strong place. I am sorry for it, though I am no great follower of the Christ.

The struggle was bloody and Cadwallon was not defeated. Yet neither could he win. So he withdrew onto Ynys Lannog, and was besieged. It was no gain for him to be stuck there, so he took ship to Erin with such men as were still with him, swearing to return with a great force and drive Edwin into the sea.' He fell silent for a moment. 'We don't know when we might see him again. But Edwin has not been idle, as you have seen.'

'Do you know who went with him? Our fathers were there – we have had no word.'

'Alas, I cannot tell you. Many did get away, but names – *na*, I know not.'

The boys absorbed this, each in his own way, and kept their thoughts to themselves.

But Elaeth was not finished. He went on, relating the tale of this war against the Ænglisc, as if ordering it in his mind, making the tale as he went along. They must be the first to whom it had been told, and Elaeth seemed pleased to have an audience.

'Edwin was furious that Cadwallon had escaped him – it is said that no one was safe from his wrath – not even his own people. And he soon spread his rage further afield. It all went quiet during the winter of course, but as soon as the weather improved, he set about it with a vengeance. Once he had secured the island, he crossed the strait and ravaged up and down the coast. Oh, you can be sure he preserved the farms on Ynys Môn – he wouldn't go hungry, but over here he burned everything he found that was not immediately useful. Or as much as he could. Some have survived, I'm told. Many have fled to us, but no one was strong enough to resist him – I have heard he has got as far as Deganwy, so any aid is denied us from the east. He can hold the passes in those hills with the fewest of men.'

'And yet you are still here? You fight on.'

'We fight on. *Na*, in truth we have one or two advantages. These mountains for one thing, and we are a strong and proud people, not to be taken on lightly. We can defend this place with – oh, a couple of hundreds of men. And to be fair, our heartland is south and west of here so, once he had destroyed everything that lay between us, we were the better supplied. It is in easy reach but safe from any without ships. And – if you can believe this – he burned the ships he came in so that his army could not retreat! A man such as that makes a hard enemy.

'But he found us a more difficult nut to crack than he imagined. He came, of course – and we met him on the slopes below Bwlch Mawr. It was a long day and long will our people remember it. They came at dusk and made a camp. Vast it seemed – watch fires everywhere, glowing like orange stars. At dawn they assembled below us, thousands of them all well armed with pikes and swords – and their damned Saes knives – all with mailed shirt and helm. And banners – banners everywhere. As the sun broke over Yr Wyddfa it caught their metal work and they blazed with fire themselves. We could hear their murmuring, it was a beating, like the waves on the shore. Then a great shout went up – a great pæan of war. And they started up the hill.'

He paused and took a swig from his cup. His audience sat enthralled.

'We are warriors. Some of you are the sons of warriors, even warriors yourselves now – you will understand – to be a warrior is not what you are, it is who you are. To fight, to defend your own – your people, your lands, to wage war against your foes, against those who would threaten you. To win honour and glory! This is the very purpose and meaning of our lives. But these – these Saesneg – they are men of blood! Blood! They fight for the pleasure of killing, for the joy of blood spilled – they would fill the rivers with blood, drown the land in it. They grow drunk with the smell of blood, with the taste of blood. Oh, yes – I have seen them drink the blood of their foes – of the dead and of the dying. This is not honour – this is madness. And these men had it! Death, death, death. Blood and death.' He stopped as if choked off by the memory. He sat silent for a moment.

Meical glanced over to Ithwalh. His face was expression-less but he must have been in agony with this. What now, if he revealed himself? By contrast Cynrig sat, chin in hands, spell-bound. He lived for tales such as these. He was happy, at least.

'They came up the hill led by their wildest men – stripped to the waist, madness in their eyes. A great roaring seething mass of men and steel. A great wave of hate. But it broke against our walls. Oh yes, it broke like the sea yonder breaks against the rocks. For rock is stronger than all of them, stronger than the sea, stronger than hate, while it endures. And rock endures long. We had had time, d'you see? We had built canny defences on all those slopes. Long walls of rock stacked against the Ænglisc, like these you see about us here in this place. Our forefathers knew well how to build strong places of stone and we have not forgotten. They tried again and again to break down our walls but, as long as we have men to defend them, they shall not fall. Many were killed on that day. Many on both sides, though more of them than of us, I'm glad to say. Well, Edwin is no fool, for all he may be mad. What advantage to him to lose his best fighting men against so hard a foe as these mountains for so little gain? So he withdrew. I weep for the people who were not behind our walls – you have seen the results of his vengeance, I'm thinking. I doubt if many are left alive out there.'

Meical stirred. His leg had gone numb and he stretched it out to ease it.

'I fear you are right,' he said. 'We have seen it. Every farm we came to was destroyed. Not all burned, but all destroyed. We found no one alive. We buried the children – well, those that were worth the burial.'

'You did that? Well, we are grateful to you for your efforts. They mark you as men of honour.'

They fell silent. The memory of that day was still dark.

'It was like the hell that Brother Cledwyn describes,' said Cynrig.

'Brother Cledwyn? Who is he?'

Cynrig stared at him – had he said that aloud? '*Na*, my Lord, he is priest in our village,' he said, pink with embarrassment.

'Ah, yes – your village. I know of Magonsæte – it is a long way, is it not? How is it your fathers are fighting in Gwynedd?'

'Our people acknowledge Cadwallon Gwledig, as yours do,' said Meical, and choosing his words with great care he added, 'Even among the Saes of those lands.'

There was a pause.

Elaeth appeared not to have noticed this remark.

'So, you I know, Meical ap Talhaiarn; will you not introduce me to your friends? You have lost some, you say.'

'We have my lord. Two went with Rhun, Ysgyrran and Llif; we are who remain. This is Cynrig, the wounded one is Tecwyn, and this is Eryl, and Einion.' Then Meical fell silent. He had been dreading this moment more and more as Elaeth's tale had unfolded, now there was no way to avoid it. But Ithwalh took the matter into his own hands. As Meical paused, he stood up and faced Elaeth and the company.

'I am Ithwalh son of Hrethgar. I am Ænglisc,' he said.

Instantly the atmosphere turned to ice. An angry hubbub arose from the company.

'Silence!' roared Elaeth. 'He is a guest!'

He turned to Meical. 'But he cannot stay. My people have suffered too much at the hands of the Ænglisc.'

'Then we must all go, my lord. We thank you for your tale; it is a pity your hospitality is not so fine.'

Elaeth exploded. 'You speak to me so in my own house!' he roared. ' You are either very brave or very stupid!'

Meical flinched, but from somewhere he conjured enough strength to go on. He raised his voice against the angry cries from the hall.

'I am sorry, my lord. I do not seek to anger you. But Ithwalh is our brother. We have fought side by side against our own enemies – and they were Prydeiniwyr. My lord, you must know that not all those out there at your gate are Ænglisc – Edwin has many of our own people in his army.'

'What are you saying?'

'My lord, we heard men talking. They spoke our tongue though not with our accent. Nor your own. We guessed they were from the north but they were still Britons.'

He remembered what Afalach had told them on Dinas Emrys. He had no idea where he found the courage to say the words, he just spoke them as they came to him.

'My lord, Ithwalh is from our home – we have all grown up together. Edwin is as much his enemy as ours. He threatens us all.'

The air crackled. There was a loud silence for what seemed eternity. Then Elaeth shrank as if he had been an over-filled bladder suddenly pricked.

'You are right, Meical ap Talhaiarn. We are not in our right minds over this. Ithwalh son of Hrethgar, please accept my apology – you are welcome here.'

Meical knew it wouldn't satisfy them all but it would do for the moment.

'But we cannot carry guests for long. We know nothing of your fathers; tell me now why you wish to stay.'

'My lord, I would not leave until Tecwyn has recovered or there is no longer any hope that he will, and in that time I hope to have news of Rhun ap Cwyfan. But you must tell us when we are no longer welcome and we will leave this place and seek him ourselves.'

Rhun's promised seven nights were long gone. Days dragged by and they heard nothing. As each day passed, Meical's anxiety grew. But there was no sign of Rhun and the others.

Ithwalh sought out Meical and took him on one side. 'Tecwyn is mended now. We must think what to do. Elaeth has not yet asked us to leave, but you know we can't stay here much longer.'

'*Na*, you're right. But what can we do?'

'We've got to earn our keep. God knows we need the practice. We must be able to do something.'

So they offered their help to Elaeth and it was accepted, and they took their turns guarding the walls of Lleyn. The fighting was spasmodic – Edwin's men seemed content to harry the defenders without launching another full-scale attack, yet the fighting was real enough, and hard enough when it came. It was the boys' first taste of real war. It was grim and it was relentless. There was little time to go soft. They could all do something useful, but when Elaeth discovered Ithwalh's skill as a fletcher they put him to work at once. And no one mentioned leaving.

The year moved around. The gales of autumn were come and gone. On a rare day of late sunshine, Ithwalh and Meical found themselves on duty, sitting in a nook in the outer wall, looking ever north into the haze.

'They have been taken – or killed. They must have been, or why have they not come? They can't still be out there, free.'

Meical looked wretched. '*Na*, I don't know either. But he is not dead – I can feel it.' He stared out sightlessly and shivered.

Ithwalh looked at him, curiosity in his eyes. 'You get this

from your mother perhaps – the sight?' He knew the stories, as they all did.

'I don't know, but I'm as certain as I sit here. He is not dead.' Grim, determined.

'Well I hope you're right – and the others?'

Meical stared out into the distance as if searching for some sign, and not finding it. 'I cannot feel the others,' he said quietly. 'They are not so close.'

Ithwalh studied him. *Yes*, he thought, *it is clear now – though I fear it may be in vain, even if Rhun returns.* But he drew some comfort from Meical's words.

They sat together in silence, each with his own thoughts. Their eyes looked out over the land but their minds wandered far away.

'I know what you're thinking,' said Meical after a moment, 'I'm thinking it too. I know we should be going, but – I don't know – it feels like betrayal, that's all.'

'But shouldn't we be getting our news to Penda? It's not much, I suppose, but isn't that what Rhun would have wanted?'

Meical turned and looked at Ithwalh, his eyes glittering. 'You are right,' he said. 'I expect we should, but I cannot go, not until I know Rhun is safe, or that he is dead and beyond my help.'

But winter came and shut down the land, and no one could go. Snow fell heavily and they were locked in and could do nothing, fret though they might. The fires were lit at midwinter and again at Imbolc, for there were many here who were not Christian, and slowly the year turned. When the nights began to shorten, Meical would wait no longer.

He went to Elaeth. 'My lord, we must go – Rhun has not found us, so we must try to find him. Will you help us?'

They went by night, following the coast, led by a guide given to them by Elaeth. They were not all there. Meical had thought it best to split up again and Einion had agreed to keep Cynrig and Tecwyn with him and stay with Elaeth, safe behind stone walls. Though not without protest.

'We're always being left behind! It's not fair – just because we're the youngest!'

'*Na*, just the least cautious! Look, Tecwyn – both of you – the reason is the same as Rhun's – too many of us and we risk being seen. We're supposed to be rescuing him, not getting caught ourselves. I'm not going to argue – Rhun's not here to tell you – I'm asking you instead. Besides, someone has to carry the news home if we fail.'

And Tecwyn had had to console himself with that.

Now, as dawn broke, their guide brought them to a low marshy place, sheltered from the open sea by a low spit of land, made mostly of sand and wind-blown grasses. On the landward side lay a wide pool of brackish water where they found a small cluster of houses huddled close by the shore, nets hung from poles, sheltered from the west by a belt of low stunted trees which bent their backs to the wind as if they would prefer to be anywhere but this gloomy place and might set out at any moment. North, beyond the pool and across the strait, they could see the low shoreline of Ynys Môn showing ghostlike above a thin blanket of mist, which stubbornly resisted the wind. The air was loud with the cries of the shore-line birds.

Their guide pointed eastwards.

'Edwin's men patrol all along this coast. You must be wary.'

A villager came out to meet them. 'Well met, Garn. What brings you here and who is this with you?'

'Well met, Morfryn,' said their guide. These are guests of my lord Elaeth. They are in search of some of their friends who have been taken by Edwin, curse him. Or so they hope. They're most likely dead either way.' He spat as if to express thoughts unspoken, if of their faint chance of success or at the Northumbrians, was unclear.

'There has been so much death around here – one or two more corpses wouldn't be noticed. But best get you out of sight. The patrols are never far away. We are only safe here ourselves because we are useful, so I wouldn't want to annoy them.'

The hut was small, barely enough to hold them all. They crammed in somehow.

'So, you want to get onto the island, eh? Well, you might manage it I suppose. I hope it's worth the risk – don't want you getting us into trouble.'

Meical looked at the others. 'We do,' he said. 'We have to know if our friends are dead or if any of them still live. I can think of no other way than to go and look. Can you?' *What is wrong with these people,* he thought, *can they not see how urgent this is?*

The man was surprised by the anger in this young voice. Or was it fear?

'I suppose not,' he said, deciding not to take offence.

'So – can you tell us the way?'

'You'll not use the crossing place, they have that well guarded – *Na*, boat is the only way. And down here – well away from their garrisons. I will not take you, but I have a small craft you could use, if any of you are able.'

Meical and Ithwalh looked at each other, nonplussed. It was Eryl who spoke. 'You will not need to take us – I know small boats.' Morfryn looked at him. Undaunted, he said again, 'I know small boats; just let me study the ways of these waters.'

'Well, I hope you do – I can't afford to lose it. I'll show you the tides. But know – there is no easy crossing.'

They lay low all that day, while Eryl studied the tides. He knew about tides but had never experienced them. He knew that they came and went regularly, but here they seemed wildly complex. Morfryn told him what words could tell, and he stayed and watched the eccentric ebb and flow all day. They seemed at first to be without rhyme or reason, but, with Morfryn's help, by evening he reckoned he had the measure of them.

And then he had to resolve the more tricky problem. He went in search of the others.

'Look, we can't all go – the boat is tiny – it'll barely carry the four of us. If they are all still alive, there'll be no room for another. And don't think I'm going to row back and forth for your pleasure. *Na* – I'll go alone. I'll not be needing to fight I'm thinking, stealth's my best hope. Besides we're going to need someone here to make sure we don't land amongst enemies.'

'The fisherfolk can do that, surely?'

'Why should they? Morfryn said he wouldn't risk any trouble – I reckon he thinks he's risking enough just lending us this boat. And what difference would it make? We can't all fit in the boat. Look – I've done this sort of thing all my life. It can't be that much different from a river – how many of you know how to handle oars?' Eryl looked at them defiantly. 'I thought so,' he said. 'Far better I go alone.'

'But you're...'

'Too young?' Eryl cut in. 'Too small? Good that I am – I can hide places you can't and move a whole lot more quietly than any of you.'

Meical gave in. In truth he knew it. 'Just you be careful,' he said. He said it for himself. The words were meaningless.

They let darkness fall. The moon rose into a clear sky, so there would be ample light. Perhaps too much, but better that than none.

They pushed Eryl off and he rowed strongly across the black, oily water. He had not wasted the waiting time. The low tide left yards of exposed mud over which he would be unable to reach hard ground and he had no idea how long he might have to wait. The slack of high water was the only time possible. The moon lacked a couple of nights 'til full and he thanked God for it. He wouldn't be totally blind even if it clouded over. To those left behind, the crossing was agonisingly slow and exposed, but at last they saw his boat push its nose in among the reed beds on the far side and vanish from sight.

There was a tree amidst the reeds, standing on a muddy little island of its own; too large for its place, the roots grew out over the water like legs. Eryl made the boat fast to it and scrambled up the bank. A water fowl started from its roost and flapped away across the water, shouting its distress. Eryl froze, his heart in his mouth. He stood quite still, as if a part of the tree, his ears straining for the slightest sound. Nothing. No shout. No splash. No tell-tale crack of a stick under a careless foot. At last he breathed again and relaxed. He wrapped himself in his cloak and curled up under the tree for the night. Dawn would be the time to start looking.

As day broke, Eryl crept out of his hiding place. The land here offered plenty of cover but he needed to get to higher ground. He could see nothing from water level.

What he had taken to be an island turned out to be a spit of mud standing out into the channel, fully exposed now at low water. He looked about himself, careful to mark the place in his mind, and made his way to the edge of the reed beds, moving gently like a small breeze. A lifetime of hunting the rivers at home with his father had made him an adept at this work, and he didn't want any more alarms like last night.

The ground ahead sloped gently up to a low ridge. Once away from the water, the ground turned to sand which soon gave way to richer soils amidst rocky outcrops. He could see no signs of habitation but he kept his head down as he crept, spider-like, up to the crest. Staying crouched on all fours, he carefully raised his head above the scrubby vegetation. Scattered around were stunted trees, leaning away from the wind and leading up towards the low horizon a mile or so away where larger trees just showed their heads above the skyline. He looked eastward along the coast. There the trees grew more densely, forming a froth of woodland which overhung the rocky northern shore of the strait.

That would be the way to go, he thought. Not much point in going inland from here: Môna may have been an island but it was still a huge place, impossible for one person to search alone. If he wanted to find the strong place that Elæth had spoken of, he would have to find someone to ask. He dared not waste time blundering about. Much of the country along this coast was woodland, but there must be farms – or woodmen, someone to tell him what he needed to know. This place had been the heartland of the Kingdom of Gwynedd for time out of mind – there must be someone he could trust.

Sure enough, farms did appear, set in little clearings among the trees, but in ruin with no sign of life, human or otherwise. So Elaeth had been wrong – Edwin's army had wreaked destruction here as well.

There was plenty of activity, none of it reassuring; much movement of armed men foraging. Late into the morning he came across a small herd of leggy piglings, last year's brood he guessed, for he could hear their mother snuffling in the undergrowth. *That's better,* he thought, *perhaps not all is destroyed.* He crept forward. The trees thinned and he came to a farm that was not in ruin. Moving like a ghost, he found himself a spot where he could see and hear, and lay in watch. There was the usual buzz of life, nothing untoward, just farmers going about their usual work. And they were not Ænglisc. Their accent was strange, yet they were speaking his own tongue. But whose side were they on? They had survived so far – were they now enemies? The people chatted amongst themselves, seemingly at ease. But as he listened it became apparent that they were very far from content – quite the reverse, they were angry, but wary of saying so out loud. He had to risk it. He stepped out into view and called, quietly.

'Hello there, can you help me?'

The farm people reacted as if stung. Suddenly the tools they were holding became weapons. But it was in defence, as soon as they saw that he was alone, they relaxed.

'Calm, calm, it is just a boy – who are you, boy?'

Eryl had been ready to run, but now he walked into the yard. 'I am Eryl ap Arofan and I am seeking a friend,' he said. 'Will you help me?'

His words were met with silence. They were not actively hostile but they were very wary. *I'll have to take a risk,* he thought, *there's only one way to find out whose side they are on.* 'I think he may have been captured by the Northumbrian invaders.'

That worked. Looking swiftly around, as if in fear of discovery, they gathered him into the house.

'Stay here,' the farmer said to one of the hands, 'keep watch – tell us at once if someone comes.' Once safely out of sight, they gave him food and drink and set him before the fire, and he told them his tale. When they had heard him out, they all had something to say.

'You are in the right of it. Trwyn Du is where our king held out for a while. Now the Northumbrians have driven the monks from there and made it a place for their wickedness. It is desecrated now; I do not see the holy men returning. I weep for our land.'

'Your best plan would be to stick to the coast and follow the strait. You can't miss it that way.'

'He speaks truly: if your friends are alive, then you should seek them there. But if you do find them, I don't know how you will get them away – it is a strong place and you'd still have to get them off the island even if you got them out. They guard the only crossing.'

'The same way I got here, I hope. My boat is hidden among the reeds, back along the coast. It's big enough for four – at least four of my size. I'm more concerned about getting them out in the first place.'

'I think all you can do is go and see. You can make no plan until you have. Should you like one of us to guide you?'

Suddenly Eryl thought he would be glad of some stalwart company, but he knew it was not sensible.

'Better not – the more of us there are, the more likely we are to be seen. But I wouldn't mind some directions.'

For what remained of that day and much of the next, he crept eastwards along the coast. At last the mainland shore fell away to the south and the channel opened out into a vast expanse of mud. Now he could see the southern horizon was wholly filled by a rampart of snow-capped mountains, marching eastwards into the distance where they fell abruptly into the sea. On the island, the high ground which had followed the strait turned once again into low tumbled country. Eryl guessed the tide was on the turn, for he could see nothing moving out on the mud-flats, but where the crossing came ashore it was still well guarded.

He was forced to take a wide sweep inland to avoid capture. But his luck was in and before the sun was set he came at last to Trwyn Du. He could not have missed it. It was as the farmer's son had described. The place had been built strongly in any case, much of it in stone, but Edwin had made it stronger, by digging a deep ditch and topping the resulting rampart with a strong palisade.

In another thing Eryl was in luck: the land here was more broken than he had dared hope and it offered him plenty of good cover. He lay up until night fell, and then, well before the moon rose, he crept out of hiding and made his way, dodging between tumbled rocks and small trees, to within fifty paces or so of the dyke. From here on he would be totally exposed. He waited poised, all senses alert to the least alarm, and then with his heart in his mouth he crossed the gap at a low loping run and dropped into the ditch. He held his breath, straining to catch any sound from within the strong place, but he could hear nothing. Cautiously he scrambled up the raw bank and crouched hard up against the palisade. Now he could hear noise inside, not loud but definitely the noise of alarm – much running about and subdued calling. And then he heard two voices clearly.

'They've gone, I tell you – got away somehow. Don't ask me how.'

'Gods! Don't let it be me who has to tell the king.'

'Keep your voice down! Listen – only you and I know – best say nothing. The army's gone and we'll follow soon enough – no one'll miss them except himself and he's miles away. Besides, he's got too much on his hands to care about losing a couple of Wealas brats, I reckon.'

Eryl's heart leapt. Wealas brats! Surely it must be Rhun and the others – too big a coincidence not to be. Surely? That meant at least two of them were alive. Didn't it? Surely it must. Far from safe, by the sound of it, but alive and away from here. But if not all three, then what of the third? Was he still captive? Was he dead? But then, had all three ever been here? Perhaps one of them had been dead for ages. But which one?

Think, Eryl, think! What exactly did he know? Three of his friends had vanished, and, thank the stars, it seemed that at least two of them had not been killed but been captured. And they were still alive. But who and what of the third?

Then he heard the answer.

'Did they take the fair-haired brat with them?'

'How should I know? Perhaps – he's gone too is all I know.'

'But if the others took him, how did they find him?'

'How should I know?' he said again. 'We should have killed him straight away like the king said.'

'What d'you mean, we? It was your job – don't bring me into it.'

'Oh, come on – you know how it was – there was too much going on. Besides – the kid was half-dead already.'

'Yeah, well – let's hope the king never finds out. He was special, that one, though the gods know why.'

'Look, what're the chances? He was off his head anyway – most likely he's dead – wandered into a swamp or fallen off a cliff or something.'

'You'd better hope so!'

The fair-haired brat – they must mean Rhun! So all three of them had been here after all. And if these two hadn't killed him, it seemed likely that he was still alive as well; so far at least.

He crept back into hiding. So – what to do? Two had got away and one had vanished. Surely they must be together – big coincidence otherwise. *Na*, it must be so. Well, if they had got away he could find them. And if he was going to find them, he'd better do it quickly in case others noticed the absence and went in chase.

But where to start? He hadn't passed them on the way, so they must have struck inland. He sat in an agony of indecision. He could cast north and west and see if he could pick up the trail. It was too dark now – would be even when the moon rose, but perhaps he would spot it in the morning.

What to do, what to do? He stared into the darkness, trying to see his way. *Na*, to try and follow them would be madness – the island was too big to be hunting around on the off-chance, even in daylight. Ysgyrran and Llif had got away in any case, so the chances were they only needed his help to get off the island. But Rhun might not be with them – he might be wandering around at random – the man had said he was off his head, whatever that meant. If so he could be in terrible danger. All in all, better to get back to the coast. And quickly before Rhun could blunder into the crossing guards or some patrol. As like as not Ysgyrran and Llif would search about until they also found that the low coast in the west offered the only really crossable place that was unguarded. Could any of them swim? Would they try? He realized he had no idea. So he'd better be there to meet them and with luck he might find Rhun on the way.

The moon rose as he set out. It was a clear night and the moon was full and it lit up the land like a huge silver lantern. The terrain still offered plenty of good cover but in this light he should easily be able to spot someone just wandering about. But he saw no one. No Ængels, no Rhun, no one. Apart from the crossing guard, the land seemed empty.

By the following night he was back where he had started, hunger gnawing at his belly. He found the boat and fell upon the food that he had left in store. He had not found the others but he had discovered they were free and was fairly certain he had made the only reasonable decision. Come daylight he would start looking for them again. Now he curled up and slept.

All next day he roamed up and down hoping to get on their scent. But again he saw no one, at least no one he wanted to see. Back at the boat, he spent another night on his little island.

He was woken by the rain. It was dark and cold and wet. Suddenly doubt filled his mind. He was fooling himself, wasn't he? They might have escaped but he had not found them, and he doubted now that he ever would. They might be anywhere – dead, re-taken. He might even have passed them in the woods – how would he have known? Even if they were safe, what were the chances he would find them?

A cold dawn broke and found him hunched, hugging his knees, waiting. The clouds had gone and taken the rain with them and the sunrise brought new courage; yet throughout the day he fretted, waiting for the tide, and the darkness to cover his retreat. He had failed. As the day passed he had finally accepted the truth but, though he got up several times to get the boat ready, he simply couldn't bring himself to leave. Not yet. They had agreed a se'night and he still had three left. Miserably he watched the day pass until the light began to fade. 'Come on,' he said, out loud as if to convince himself, 'one last look.'

He followed the shoreline this time. Keeping low at water level where the reed beds grew thick and tall. Suddenly he stopped, one foot in the air. Voices. Not loud, just on the edge of hearing. If he had been making more noise himself he would have missed the sound. With infinite care he set his foot down and crouched low.

Voices. Two voices. One young, the other less so. He parted the reeds in front of his face and peered out. The shadows were deep, but there was still enough light to see clearly. Nothing. He had heard them but could not make out where they were. Then one of them spoke again. *Crist*! they were right beside him!

'Ynys Môn! – sacred it may be, but I've had enough of it! How do we get off this damned island?'

Ysgyrran! That was Ysgyrran's voice. And unless he had been talking to himself, he was not alone. Eryl stood up and stepped clear of cover.

'Would a boat be any help?'

Chapter 13

It was Tecwyn who saw them first. Fully recovered now, and never one to sit idle, he had taken to joining the watch on the northern rampart – partly, in truth, to get away from Einion who took his responsibility far too seriously in Tecwyn's opinion. So it was his young eyes which caught the movement; saw the tiny figures moving amongst the scrub and scattered boulders away down at the foot of the slope.

'It's them! I'm sure it is – look, can you see?'

The guard joined him. 'Hard to tell. Could be.' He called out to his companions, 'Looks like we've got company – the lad here reckons it's his mates. Too early to be sure, I'd say, but we'd better be ready.'

This caused a sudden flurry of activity. In no time the rampart bristled with men armed with bow and slingshot. In silence they watched the indistinct blur of movement resolve itself into a small knot of people, and then into Tecwyn's friends.

'False alarm – the boy is right.'

Einion and Cynrig had joined him. 'Can you see – are they all there?'

It was the question uppermost in their minds. It would be a huge relief to get just the search party back in one piece. But had they found the others?

'I can see five at least – no, wait there's six – they are all there!' And the relief was huge. After half a year or more of anxiety they would at last be together again.

'Are they pursued?' asked the lookout.

Tecwyn studied the country below. 'I don't think so – I can't see anyone behind them. Wait! They've stopped.'

He strained his eyes.

'Saesneg – Saesneg!' he cried, 'they are attacked! There's men there! Look – coming in from the right!'

'Where?'

'Look, oh look – there, coming through those trees!' Tecwyn was hopping up and down in rage – why couldn't they see? He leaped up and threw himself off the wall.

'What's he doing, the mad fool?'

'Quick, get down there – take some men and get him back!'

Tecwyn was hurling himself down the slope, screaming at the top of his voice to warn the rescue party. The others pounded after him. He slowed, seeking a target. One swing and a flick and a man dropped.

'Come on you lot, hurry!' His high treble scream carried like a bird's. Ysgyrran had turned. He was fumbling for the sword he no longer had. Tecwyn took careful aim and downed another of the Northumbrians, giving the friends time to react. Llif grabbed Rhun and drove him up the slope. The others turned to face their peril. In awe of Tecwyn's skill with a slingshot, the Northumbrians held back. Too long.

Ysgyrran grabbed Ithwalh. 'Quick – give me your sword. Cover us. Come on, Meical!' And they dashed forward, slashing away wildly in their outrage. Reinforcements thundered down the hill and threw themselves into the mêlée. This was enough for the Northumbrians. This hadn't been meant as a full-scale battle, they were just on patrol, and these men weren't Edwin's crack troops. With two already down, they fled.

The rescue party came stumbling in, amidst a storm of cheers.

The garrison was out in full now, lining the walls and gathered around the entrance. They stood and watched the new arrivals.

Einion pushed his way through. 'Are we glad to see you! We thought you were all dead.'

'Don't rejoice too soon,' said Meical grimly, 'he's in a bad way.'

The crowd parted to make a corridor. They stared, gawped – was this ragged scarecrow really Rhun? Rhun ap Cwyfan, the bright leader about whom they had heard so much? It was barely credible. They watched Meical help him across the wide compound, guiding him like a dumb animal as rescued and rescuers alike were taken to the house set aside for the tending of the sick and wounded. Tecwyn looked at the others, standing uncertainly in mute wonder by the gate. *If that is Rhun, who will lead us now?*

It became the one question no one dared to ask.

A man came to take Ysgyrran and Llif to the hall.

They found Elaeth with a gathering of his war leaders. Strong men, hard men for the most part, but Elaeth produced a smile.

'Ysgyrran, is it? Llif? I am glad to find you still living. Come, sit. A drink for these two – you'll have a drink?' He seemed unsure how to start. Finally he just did. 'So – what can you tell me of Edwin?'

'He has gone, my lord,' said Ysgyrran, 'that seems certain. At least he has gone from Ynys Môn.'

'Tell me.'

Ysgyrran took the lead.

'They spent the winter quietly enough, but come the spring people started arriving. Envoys, we guessed. We couldn't get close but it's hard to keep secrets in a place like that – it was pretty clear that it wasn't good news. I'm afraid we couldn't find out any details but it did seem that Edwin has trouble elsewhere. And far from here, is my guess.'

'Back in Northumbria, do you think?'

'Perhaps – no one said anything about Northumbria. I'm sorry, my lord, I don't know.'

Elaeth smiled. 'It is a pity, I am thinking, that young Tecwyn is so handy with a sling. We might have learned something from those two he downed earlier if they had lived.' He turned to his own men.

'Your thoughts?'

A general murmur arose. The men all had views and several spoke at once.

'If that man has been making war against his own kind as well as us, it would be no surprise if someone had taken the chance to fight back while he was away. Rheged perhaps – or even Strathclyde?'

'*Na*, Rheged is a spent force. Strathclyde, though – that is not a land he could take on easily.'

'He would be king of all in Prydein, Ænglisc and us alike.'

'It would be good to learn just how many men he has left here to keep us entertained.'

Elaeth turned back to Ysgyrran. 'Can you tell us?'

'Alas, I can't, my lord – not for sure, but I have an idea it may not be many. We came along the coast, expecting the worst but we saw almost no one – just the ones who attacked us. And it was pretty clear they were far from his best people.'

Elaeth nodded.

'Perhaps it is as you say. Well, we must send men to find out. I'll not sit here if I don't have to.'

Eryl chipped in, 'One thing we do know, my lord – only the leaders are Ænglisc.' He dropped it in quietly but it had the same effect as a hornet in a small room.

'So – we fight our own people! Well, we've done that often enough,' he said grimly, 'but never before in an Ænglisc army.'

They took Rhun off the mountain the next day. He needed help that he could not get in that austere place. If he was to recover he needed better care than fighting men could give. They had talked about some staying behind to help with the defences, but Elaeth would not hear of it. They should stick together now, the better to face the big question when it arose. As it surely would if things with Rhun did not improve, and quickly.

The contrast could scarcely have been greater. Down here, out of the stone country, winter seemed already to have passed. The hedges and trees were still bare but their feet were bright with the flowers of a new year. In the fields early crops were already showing green above the plough. There were folk aplenty working out among the fields, but word of their approach had gone ahead and they were met by a small crowd of villagers, women for the most part, several with small children clutching at their skirts. Amongst them was a tall graceful woman in middle years.

'You are welcome here,' she said, her voice sweet and warm, beguiling, as if she were all their mothers in one. 'I am Aelwen, wife to Elaeth. Do not feel you must stand on ceremony – you should get your friend to rest as soon as possible. Gwenifer,' she called, 'take them to the sick house.' A young girl appeared. 'My daughter. She will see your patient settled. After, come to me here in my house.'

The girl was about thirteen, just coming into the first bloom of womanhood. She looked strikingly like her father. A softer version, gentler, and yet somehow just as strong. And not in the least shy of these boys.

She bustled them into a house which stood a little apart from the village, its feet at one end standing on stumpy legs in a stream where the water dashed down from the mountains. Meical and Ithwalh helped Rhun inside leaving the others clustered round the door. Rhun had been co-operative as usual but he was not really there. Left to himself, he would have just stood where he was put.

'Lay him there,' she said, pointing to a low bed set against the wall, under the only window. It looked south, giving a view out over the sea and into a wide sky. The room had a board floor, unusual in these parts, strewn with dried herbs and grasses. It was sparsely furnished. Apart from the bed, there was a chair, a low lampstand with a single wick holder, and a simple table, scrubbed to a pale honey colour. A brazier stood in one corner, laid ready for lighting, a wooden bucket of charcoals stood at its side. On shelves above the table, were crowded many bottles and jars of all shapes and sizes. Bunches of dried stuff hung from every beam, giving the place a sweet smell, a healing smell. At both door and window, thick leather curtains were set ready to be drawn against the weather. This was a far cry from the spartan conditions on the mountain. It reminded them of Brynach's healing well, though here there was no holy man to tend it. Rhun would find peace here if he could find it anywhere.

Gwenifer stood looking at her patient. His eyes were closed, but she had seen them open and she tried to conjure their colour as it would look in this face when it was in health. His skin would be warm gold, darker perhaps than his hair. Now it was pale, stretched thin and tight over the fine bones. So fragile. She wondered if she would ever learn what he had been through to so mar his beauty.

Meical made to sit down, but Gwenifer stopped him. 'We must clean him up, but not now,' she said. 'See, he is asleep, he will do well for a while. Now you must speak with my mother.' Reluctantly Meical let her draw him away.

As she led them back, Ithwalh sneaked a sideways glance at Meical. *This is going to be tough for him,* he thought.

The village was larger than their own, though here the houses were not square but round with conical roofs of reed, the way that all men had made houses until the Romans came. It looked prosperous, the people busy in the fields or down along the strand where they could see long lines of nets hung to dry and several dozen boats pulled up onto the strand. The only sign of war was the shortage of men: except the old and the very young, so many were away defending their lands from the Northumbrians. Gwenifer led the little troop to the largest house, which stood alone with the usual cluster of little sheds and lean-tos clinging to its skirts.

Aelwen welcomed them again, this time with food and drink. She asked after the state of the war and for news from beyond Lleyn. She seemed most interested in hearing of their own adventures and of their homes and people, and she plied them with questions as they ate. Though she made them all feel welcome and at ease, they could feel her assessing their worth, not judging them but weighing them up against some unspoken measure of her own. At last she looked at Meical.

'Do not worry overmuch for your friend. You may rely on my daughter: she is wise in herb lore and has the gift for it.

Better even than I who taught her. Together we will see him through this dark time.'

'Thank you, my lady. Please tell us how we can repay you?'

'Do not think it, young one – I require no payment. It is not for payment that I have been taught my craft. Nor my daughter. But you may make yourselves useful – with so many of our menfolk away fighting, it is hard to keep up. There will be work enough to keep you all busy.' *Besides*, she thought to herself, *it would not do for you to lose your edge while helping your friend to regain his.*

The boys were boarded among the villagers and soon learned the truth of Aelwen's words. There would be no time for games here, no time for boredom. Little time for worry either.

Meanwhile, Rhun lay staring and wordless. Every day the same. They had scrubbed him raw and shaved his head to deprive the lice of a home. It made him look better and worse at the same time. They salved his sores and gave him drinks made from the herbs of healing which grew all around the sick house. They did all that could be done to treat his body and it responded well, as if grateful for the attention after so much neglect. Daily his health and strength improved. But still his mind was absent. At night he would toss and turn in troubled sleep until he would waken tired and drawn, or lie staring up into the darkness when sleep eluded him. His body would respond to the warmth of another, but his mind seemed unaware. Indifferent. His days were similar. Wherever they set him he would stay, but he would sit and stare into nothing. When they gave him food he would eat, when they gave him drink he would drink, but he seemed to notice neither. Day after day Meical sat with him, to help if he could, to fetch and carry, to help feed and bathe and dress – just to be there, should any change occur. He would not leave even when they made it plain that he should, until they stopped asking. He would stay in vigil, waiting for that moment.

Meical never learned what it was they gave to Rhun, but

gradually his strength returned. He slept, really slept, long and undisturbed. Proper rest, and it seemed that rest was what he needed most. The change was slow but it was sure. Yet, despite all the gains he made, his mind seemed as far from cure as ever.

'You must get him to talk,' Aelwen said to Meical. 'Whatever troubles him, he must bring it out and face it. Without that, I cannot promise he will ever fully recover.'

But Meical knew of no way to do that. He had talked to Rhun, largely at random having no point to start from. He spoke of themselves and their friends and of times remembered, but Rhun had responded to nothing; he seemed unaware of Meical's very presence. All Meical could do was sit patiently, just making sure that he would be there if – *na*, when – Rhun returned from whatever dark place he was in. He would not give up hope.

The year waxed and the days grew longer, and with the spring came the storms. The boys were no strangers to storms, living as they did in the skirts of hill country, but storms here played out on a larger stage than at home. Terrifying storms they were. Storms which pushed great seas into the bay amidst driving rain and thunder. Huge waves crashed onto the shore, sending walls of spray and spume to unimaginable heights, threatening to wash away the houses and drown them all. None of the boys had any experience of the sea. They were amazed. For two long weeks, storm after storm raged into their little world, driving any private worries far from their minds.

And it was one such which brought the change. The last and greatest of them all.

The day had grown dark before its time as mountains of cloud built up, towering into the sky. The air had been thick and hot, but now the wind tore through everything, heedless of house or clothing. They were sat huddled around a smoky fire when the cry went up.

'The boats – see to the boats!'

They scrambled to their feet and stood in the doorway

looking out into the dark afternoon. Of them all, only Eryl had helped on the boats. The others had done what they could in the fields, but Eryl had taken to the sea and the hard business of wresting a harvest from it. He had been keen to learn. And now he had learned a lot more about tides.

'It's a high spring – the boats – we've got to save the boats! Come on, they'll need all the help they can get!'

Men, women, even the children, slave and freeman alike, all were out on the foreshore struggling to pull the boats up out of harm's way. The horizon had vanished. To the east the sky was still clear, but in the west the rain had mixed with the sea and flying spume and they had become as one. As the storm hit, the boys threw themselves into the task, grabbing ropes where they could and straining to make a difference. As each boat was saved they turned to another. More ropes were passed to them and they pulled again. And again. All their minds focused on the sheer physical effort. The day wore on. Darkness fell, though no one noticed the time passing. It stretched on endlessly, wild and mad, as the storm lashed them with rain and sea, mixed with sand whipped up off the dunes. It was like being flayed alive; any piece of exposed flesh was rubbed raw. Their minds were numbed, yet though it was bitterly cold, they felt nothing except the cracking of their muscles as they hauled on, hour after hour.

'Hold on – we're getting there!' a voice shouted, its owner unknown. And they held on, they held on heedless of anything else.

Many times they came close to disaster as the wind and the pounding sea swept them off their feet, plunging them into the boiling surf, survival as much a matter of luck as anything. Then, as exhaustion came close to claiming them, a monstrous sea hurled itself onto the beach, the greatest of all that day it seemed. It crashed down like a savage beast and caught Ysgyrran as he turned to lay hold of yet another hull. It caught him full on his side and beat him to the ground. Its strength was enormous. Arms flailing, he fell. Blindly he clutched at anything to save himself. His hand found Llif's sleeve, as so often now by his side, and caught hold, and they were both bowled over by the force of the water. The rope they were hauling was wrenched from their grip. Ysgyrran scrambled desperately to dig his feet into the sand and keep a hold of the younger boy, horrified that his instinctive action had dragged his friend into such peril. Wave after wave crashed over them, pulling back only to leave them choking for breath and blinded by water.

'Rhun!' The shout was wrenched from Meical. 'Rhun – get back!' A pale figure was standing at the top of the beach. Dressed in a long white shirt, sodden and plastered to his body by the gale, he looked spectral, a thing of nightmare. But Meical knew at once who it was. Leaving the others, he staggered up the beach to Rhun's side. 'Come on – you can't be out here – it'll kill you. Come on, won't you?' But he had to fight his friend. Rhun seemed determined not to be taken. He had been woken by the sheer noise of the storm and had heard voices crying in it. An innate desire to help had gripped him, the sound of people in distress was all he had needed.

'We must help them!' he shouted.

Meical was amazed at the power in Rhun's voice. These were his first words since he had arrived. But there was no time for wonder now.

'Don't be stupid – there's nothing you can do, you're not strong enough!' yelled Meical, but Rhun didn't see him, didn't hear him, didn't know who he was. He plunged into the boiling surf and joined such strength as he had to the others grabbing for Ysgyrran and Llif, and at last they were dragged to safety.

There had been no time to think, no time to do anything except suffer the crashing of the waves on their backs and hope to come through, their whole beings focused on reaching safety. Once there they collapsed in exhaustion. Meical shook the water out of his hair and wiped his face in the crook of his elbow. He looked around for Rhun and could not see him. With his heart in his mouth he scanned the shore line. His eye was caught by a ragged patch of white on the edge of the surf, but which was not surf. It was Rhun, lying face down on the streaming sand.

'Rhun!' he screamed, running back for him. Without thought for himself he grabbed at Rhun, lifting him into his arms. Another wave hit them both and Meical struggled to keep his grip. Fighting the surf, which sucked the sand out from under his feet and made him stumble, he half carried, half dragged his friend to safety and laid him gently on the sandy grass. His eye were closed and he lay limply as if dead. But he was not dead – Meical could see his chest moving, oh so slightly – he was alive, if barely. The others gathered round in wonder that Rhun was there at all.

Meical struggled to his feet. 'Help me, someone,' shouting to make himself heard above the din of wind and sea, 'I must get him back to the sick house.'

Suddenly Gwenifer was there. 'Here, let me. You get back to the boats.'

Meical stared madly at her. Then her words sank in.

'Yes of course,' he shouted. 'Can you take him?'

She nodded.

'He's not yet so heavy.'

And then it was over. All but two of the boats saved and much of the gear. As soon as it was clear that there was no more to be done, they staggered away from the danger. Now they sat steaming by a fire, lit in the lee of the houses, while the last of the storm blew itself away towards the dawn.

'That was close,' said Llif. 'I thought we'd had it that time!'

And suddenly Ysgyrran knew. He must not stay here and wait for some chance event to destroy them all. He must go. He knew all there was to know about Edwin. Rhun would no longer lead them. He had awoken, yes, but as some sort of weird version of himself, nervy, even craven – how could he ever lead them again? Not soon enough in any case. Their fathers were dead or were not dead; either way, they were not here and no one knew where they might be found. No point in hanging around in lost hope. Now it was clear to Ysgyrran what he had to do. Penda must be given such news as they had and there was no more time to waste. He just hoped it would not come too late.

The next day he was gone. At first Meical had protested, calling him disloyal.

'How can you leave him – now, just as he has recovered?'

'Recovered, you say – you call that recovery? You saw him last night – he is mazed – he'll not lead us again.'

'What are you saying – you will make yourself leader? Is that it?'

'You think I can't?'

'But Rhun is our leader – we're his war band. You cannot think to desert him? He's not dead. Besides – is it for you to decide?'

'Meical, you are a fool. You'd follow him like a dog, no matter where he led you – the gods know, I would too – but even you must see his brain's gone – he'll not come back from wherever he is – not now.'

'You don't know that – he's not had time enough.'

'And neither do we. We can wait no longer. You stay here if you must, but we have to go.'

'We? Who's we?' Meical looked desperately round at the others. 'All of you? Would you all run away and leave him!'

The others shuffled their feet and looked awkward.

Ysgyrran locked gazes with Meical. 'I'll lead any who will come,' he said grimly.

No one moved. As if they still had not made up their minds, might still be swayed.

'But what about loyalty?'

'It's not about loyalty – it's about what we have to do. Penda needs news, someone has to give it to him. And it's not going to be Rhun, no matter how loyal we are. Look, Meical – we're still Rhun's war band, that's not changed. If he ever recovers we'll be behind him to a man, but don't you see? – Now we have to go.'

Meical looked at them in turn. And it became clear that they were not on his side in this. No one looked happy but they all looked determined. No – surely not. How could they just run off and leave him here with Rhun? He could not believe they would just abandon him. He fought back tears – tears of anger and frustration, and, he realized coldly, of fear. He could put up no better argument than loyalty, and if that was no longer enough he was at a loss. Yet, to be left here, with just what was left of Rhun? That was a fear indeed. But he would not shirk it.

'Go then, but I cannot,' he muttered bitterly.

To his surprise, Einion stood up. 'And neither can I. Rhun gave me my freedom and I gave him my word. I will not leave him now.' And Cynrig too, though he said nothing and looked at the ground.

Ysgyrran looked triumphant. 'You are all fools – but stay if you will – I'll not lead the unwilling.'

Ithwalh looked sorrowfully at Meical. 'We should go – we have spoken of this before.'

'I know, I remember. No – you go – all of you if you must, but I'm sorry, I cannot.'

And they did, all save Einion and Cynrig.

In the absence of her lord, Aelwen had re-armed them and given them a guide, and they had set sail across the bay to a distant shore beneath the mountains in the south.

Meical had watched them go. Perhaps Ysgyrran was right. Perhaps Rhun would never be able to lead them again. But it felt like a bitter betrayal. He understood the need for haste, but this felt so final and he couldn't bring himself to accept it. Not yet. They had been given a task and they should carry it out as best they could, but they must do it without him. His task now lay with his friend; like Einion, he believed his debt was too great to be ignored. He turned away from the sea and made his way slowly back through the village to the sick house.

He went in dread of what he might find, imagining bad enough but fearing worse. How much added damage had been done by Rhun's insane efforts during the storm? Had he even been really aware of what was happening? Or was it just the trance-like state of the truly mad? He stood by the bed and looked long at the sleeping figure. His insides felt hollow and his tongue too big for his throat.

To his utter astonishment, as he sat down Rhun awoke and looked at him and knew him.

'Meical – have you been here all along?'

'I have, of course – where have you been?'

Rhun looked out of the window into the sunlight. 'Dark places,' he said. 'Where is this? Where is Brynach?'

'We are with Elaeth's people in Lleyn. Brynach is safe by his well, so far as I know. You were taken prisoner and we rescued you – at least Eryl and Ysgyrran and Llif did.'

Rhun shivered and relapsed into silence.

At last he answered, 'Yes,' he said quietly, and paused again. 'Ysgyrran and Llif – yes they found me. I thought they must be ghosts. Foolish. But Eryl? I didn't see him there.'

'*Na*, he wasn't with you. He went alone into Ynys Môn and found you there.'

'Alone?'

'Alone – he's turning out to be quite something. Ysgyrran and Llif had got you out but they wouldn't have got off the island without Eryl. He took a boat across by night.'

'A boat? I don't remember it.' He paused again as if to give this some consideration. 'A boat, by night – yes, he could do that.'

He looked around the room. 'How long have I been here?'

'You got here about a month ago. But it's been half a year since you were taken.'

'Half a year!' He struggled onto an elbow, found the effort too much and fell back. '*Ie*, perhaps it has been that long. I remember seeing Ysgyrran and Llif, though I was told they were dead – oh, but it was a dark place, full of monsters – I didn't dream it, then?'

'You did not – the monsters were real enough.'

Gwenifer came in with a pitcher. 'He has woken?' she said, her voice light, excited. Rhun glanced at her.

'Hello, I'm Gwenifer.'

'Hello,' said Rhun, suddenly shy. 'I'm Rhun.'

'Oh, I know who you are!' She laughed and the room seemed brighter. 'Welcome home. I will tell my mother.'

When she had gone, Rhun looked at Meical.

'She is Gwenifer, Elaeth's daughter. She and her mother have been nursing you,' he said.

'As have you,' said Rhun quietly. It was not a question but a realisation. An acceptance. He smiled. 'She is beautiful,' he said as he drifted back to sleep.

With the storms gone, spring had come in earnest, as if it had received a signal and was keen to be getting on with it. The land was sprinkled with swathes of daffodils. The hedges and smaller trees showed that green haze which you notice only out of the corner of your eye. Under them winked clumps of primroses and herb-robert, and the first infant spikes of the new year's wild garlic. The turn in the weather was immediate, bringing calm and warm spring sunshine. Dawn found Meical sitting alongside Rhun, hopeful as ever, but prepared for silence; content just to be there.

Rhun awoke suddenly and sat up, staring out into the new day.

'Meical? Hold me? I'm cold.'

Meical was so surprised he almost failed to respond. Cold? He slipped an arm around Rhun's shoulders and drew him close, nuzzling his hair, a great joy welling within.

Rhun leaned into Meical's body and stared out into the distance. Neither said anything. Meical held his breath.

At last Rhun spoke, his voice barely loud enough to hear, 'The crown – he has the crown.'

'What d'you mean? What crown?'

'The crown of Gwynedd – Edwin – he has it.'

'How?'

'I found it.'

'You found a crown! Where? When?'

'It had been hidden – in a drain. The drain was blocked and they made me go in to clear it. It was the crown – oh, it was all bundled up and I didn't know 'til later. I got it out and took it to him. Not that I would have had any choice. But I should have remembered – I couldn't make any sense out of it then, but I realise now it didn't get there by chance. It had been hidden! To keep it safe. And now he's got it. And he will be king for real. And it's all my fault!'

'Never think it! How could it be your fault?'

'But I should have done something – I just ran off and did nothing.' Rhun's eyes were over-bright, on the edge of tears. Meical searched for words to calm him down.

'Look – you couldn't have done anything. You were chained up – a prisoner – what could you have done? As for running off, don't you think he took it with him? Besides – Edwin can't be king just because he wants to be.'

'Who's to stop him?'

'It doesn't make any difference. He could be the most powerful man in the land, he could command great armies, have all the cattle and gold in – oh, the whole world, but none of that would make him king. You know that!'

Rhun was not to be consoled. The deep pool of emotion, kept suppressed for so long, at last boiled up and overflowed. Harsh sobs racked his body and the tears fell strong and hot, released at last, carrying with them all those months of fear and anger and guilt.

Meical held him closer, distraught himself. He could think of nothing better to do than to keep on talking.

'Oh – he can steal power but that won't make him king. Not in the minds of the people. It's like respect. It's something you have to earn. You can't command respect – it has to be given or it's just fear. It's like you and us. You were always our leader, from the start. And you still are – we all think so – that hasn't changed because you've been ill. And it's because we respect you – love you.'

Meical paused, as if scared by what he had just said yet wanting to say more and faltering.

'Why d'you think Einion is still here with us?' he said at last.

There was a long silence.

'I gave him freedom.'

'*Na*, you gave him respect – you trusted him when no one

else would, and you got it back tenfold. He could have run away with his freedom.'

Rhun said nothing for a while. He wiped his eyes with his sleeve. Then he whispered, 'You are wiser than I, Meical – thank you.' His voice grew stronger. 'But Cadwallon must be told and I must get word to Penda. Somehow. He must think we are all dead!'

'As to that, Ysgyrran has already gone.'

'What! When – why didn't you tell me?'

'How could I have done that – you were miles away? Anyway he wouldn't wait – he said Penda had to get the news and we had wasted enough time already. They left this morning.'

'They?'

'They – Llif , Tecwyn, Eryl, Ithwalh – they chose him as leader and they've gone. Well – he told them he was the new leader and no one argued. All except Einion and Cynrig.'

'Einion and Cynrig? Why did they not go?'

'Einion for the reason I just told you – he'd given you his word he said, and wouldn't leave you. I don't know about Cynrig – he just said he was staying, but he didn't say why.'

'So they are going to Penda. That's a relief – he'll get the message ,which is what matters most.'

'And so will our people – they mean to call in home on their way.'

Rhun looked blank. Then his face went ashen.

'Why didn't he wait? He might have told me,' he whispered.

'I don't think he thought you would care one way or the other – until right now neither did any of us.'

'Na, na – you don't understand – I could have warned him.'

'About what?'

'They are all dead.'

'Who? What d'you mean? Who's dead?'

'Everyone – the whole village – Edwin told me. He said he'd been there and killed everyone.'

There was a brief, horrified silence.

'They can't be.'

'It's what he said.'

'Why would he do that?'

'To taunt me, I suppose. He enjoyed doing that.'

'*Na*, I mean why would he go to all the trouble of going there and killing everyone? It makes no sense.'

Rhun was dumb. He had no answer for that. Why indeed? And then a new thought struck him.

'*Na*, wait!' he said. That was it – that thing which for ages had been niggling away on the edge of his mind, suddenly it came into focus. '*Na*, he was lying. Of course! He was lying. I knew something was wrong – I just couldn't see it.'

Meical stared at him.

'Listen – he told me that first day I was taken – he said that everyone was dead – Cadwallon, my father – everyone. He was boasting, as if he'd killed them with his own hand. And then – oh weeks later – I can't really remember – he told me he'd been to Lenteurde and that they were all dead too. He was all I had left, he said.' He paused. 'But then later he told me that Cadwallon had got away and gone to Erin. So – don't you see – he'd been lying! And if he'd lied about that, he may have been lying about everything else as well. You're right – it's a long way, Magonsæte; maybe he never went there at all.'

Meical looked pensive. 'That Edwin is even nastier than I thought,' he said.

To his surprise Rhun laughed. 'Be glad you don't know him any better.'

Rhun seemed filled with a new energy. An excitement, as if this revelation had blown away the last cobwebs of those bitter months.

'Well, they've gone – it's out of our hands, I suppose. So now we must find Cadwallon.'

'Cadwallon! But he's in Erin. You're certainly not going to Erin!'

Chapter 14

As it turned out, they did not have to go looking for Cadwallon, Cadwallon came to them.

With the coming of spring the sea roads had opened again, and only a few days after the storm, at first light, a sail was seen rounding the point far to the west. Once they saw it was alone it was watched with mounting excitement: a ship alone was not likely to be a threat. Word had been sent up the mountain and now, long before it could reach them, a small crowd gathered on the fore shore with Elaeth at its head.

Whoever was in this ship, whatever its purpose, it meant change and they longed for change. Now it was promised, the weight of the long winter's vigil seemed to be lifted. Rhun was recovered, or almost so, and now those who had stayed at his side were keen for something new – to do something, whatever that might be. Too long had they been cooped up, without a leader and without purpose. And for two of them at least there was a chance they might still find their fathers.

The ship had flown into the bay, its great sail belly-full with the strong westerly breeze, but then it seemed to take forever to reach them. At last the steersman turned the ship's high prow into the shore, the sail came down and the long oars brought her in the last few lengths.

None of them had seen so big a boat before. Their own little rivers were good only for small craft – this was huge. A proper ship, a good twenty paces long. Built for long voyages out of sight of land, it rode easily on the swell, its twin banks of oars keeping it steady. Six oars to a side, a single sail of fine-woven stuff: long strips of cloth stitched together in a pattern of red and ochre. The man on the steering oar peered over the side and brought the ship gently onto the sand. As they watched, the oars were lifted and men began to jump from the high prow. Several busied themselves securing the ship with long ropes, the rest advanced up the beach and stood in a tight arc facing Elaeth, one man to the fore.

Elaeth studied him. 'So, you have come back.'

'We have come back.'

'Just you?' The question almost implied a criticism, but not quite.

'Others will follow, we came to see how things are. Are we not welcome?'

'My lord – never think that. You are as welcome as the spring after a hard winter. More. Come, the people will want to see you; their winter has been hard indeed.'

From their vantage point, the boys watched in silence. So this was Cadwallon, y Brenin Gwynedd, perhaps the true Gwledig of all Prydein, at least in the north. Only Rhun, of all of them, had ever met this man. Only Rhun had ever been in a position to meet him; the rest were of far too lowly stock.

Yet his arrival turned the faint chance of seeing their fathers into a distinct possibility.

Einion sat next to Cynrig. 'Can you see your father?'

'I don't think so.'

'They'll not be with Cadwallon – except maybe yours, Rhun – and I don't see him.'

Rhun had said nothing. It was several moments before he did.

'He has not come. I think now he never will.'

No visitor could be allowed to arrive without a fuss. Guests were sacred. Food and drink was the least anyone could expect; even an enemy got that much so long as he was not come in active war. But the arrival of a king gave an excellent excuse for a feast. The big house was thrown open and long tables were laid out. Long cook-fires were built. Boar and deer were set to roast, fish were wrapped and set in the embers to bake, casks of beer and mead set up, there were loaves and butter and honey, such fare as was rarely seen. It is not every day one entertains such a guest. And even more rarely, one so longed for.

Abandoning their vantage point, the boys followed the crowd up to the village, keen to watch though careful to keep out of the way. In vain, as it turned out.

'Rhun!' A voice called across the compound. 'Rhun – will you come? Elaeth asks for your company.'

'Me? Why?'

'I have no idea – you'll find out soon enough, I'm sure.'

He hurried over to the big house where the preparations were in full swing and a crowd was gathering. Elaeth saw him and beckoned him to one side.

He put his hand on Rhun's shoulder and looked at him closely. 'You are recovered?'

'Very nearly, my lord.' He held his arms out as if they were strange to him; but his renewed strength was clear for all to see.

'I am heartily glad of it. You looked like a ghost last time I saw you.'

'I am sorry, my lord – I do not remember.'

'It is of no matter, yon Meical stood well in your place. But come, the feast will be some time yet. There is one who would meet you first.'

He took Rhun out and across to one of the guest houses. *What's this?* he thought. Had he missed his father in the crowd? Surely not, but his heart skipped a beat at the thought. As they entered the house the single occupant turned, one eyebrow raised in enquiry: 'So, have you learned circumspection?'

Rhun's faced cracked into a big smile. Not his father, but one as great in his mind.

'You remembered, my lord.'

Cadwallon did not laugh.

'I do. I remember all too clearly. So – your answer?'

Rhun looked into those cool grey eyes, suddenly nervous as if a child again.

'Perhaps, sir – but only just, I'm afraid.'

Cadwallon leaned back. He relaxed. Now he smiled and his face lost all trace of its former sternness.

'I am glad. We all grow old quickly enough.'

'I had not realized I was entertaining a friend of yours, my lord.'

'My apologies, Elaeth; young Rhun and I go back a few years. But Rhun, what brings you here? Elaeth tells me you have been through quite a bit since we last met. Why are you not in Magonsæte?'

'My lord, we came looking for news. News of you and of our fathers. We had heard nothing but rumour, and,' he hesitated, one eye on Elaeth, 'we were charged to report all we learned to Penda of Mercia.'

Elaeth's response was he feared. 'Penda!? Penda! You would report of our doings to the Saesneg? You are a spy after all!'

Cadwallon held up a hand.

'Peace, Elaeth. Penda is not our enemy. He is my ally.'

Elaeth looked somewhat mollified, but he was clearly not at peace.

Cadwallon turned back to Rhun.

'So, he is king then?'

'He was not so when we left – he should be by now if his plans have worked out. It was why he couldn't come himself.'

'I see. Yes, I see that.'

'My lord, we expected to find you dead. I rejoice that you are not.'

'Thank you – but I fear I do not have such good news for you – you in particular. Rhun, I have to tell you that your father is dead, slain at Trwyn Du when they trapped us there. You need not fear, he died bravely. I am truly sorry.'

Rhun sat in silence for a while. The two men watched him, loath to disturb.

'Edwin told me so,' he said at last. 'He said he had done it himself. He laughed about it.'

'Edwin? You have spoken with Edwin?' Cadwallon cried. He turned to Elaeth who held up his hands. 'It was his story, my lord. I thought he should tell it himself.'

'I was captured my lord. It was stupid, I deserved it. But, as you see, I got away at last – at least he didn't kill me. Please, my lord, can you tell me aught of the others?'

Cadwallon stared at him. 'It was that easy?' he asked.

'Not easy,' said Rhun quietly. 'But I survived.'

'I am sorry my troubles have taken you so close to that man. It is quite possible he did kill your father – he is no coward and was in the thick of the fighting. I'm afraid I don't know about the others – you should ask my people.'

'Thank you, my lord, I will.'

Cadwallon had a disturbing trick of pausing, leaving space which it was tempting to fill, often to your disadvantage. Rhun resisted.

The king smiled. He recognized a worthy adversary and filled his own gap. 'So, what of Penda?'

'He asked that we send him news of Edwin's strength and movements. He just wants to know what's going on; he was chafing with no news. He was unsure about his own future when we left him. That's why he had to send someone else. But if he is not dead he is king by now, I should think, and with the might of Mercia at his back.'

'Is it wise to send such details to an Ænglisc king, my lord?'

'As I say, Penda is not our enemy, Elaeth. Nor yours. So Rhun, have you sent him word? I recall you two getting on well when we visited your father's house.'

'Some of my people have gone. They will be there by now if they have not met with trouble.'

'Well, let us hope they have not. Will they return with a message from him, I wonder?'

'It is possible they have been sidetracked, my lord.' He fell silent. Cadwallon glanced at him, expecting more. But more was clearly not forthcoming. *There's a tale there*, he thought, *but there's another I want to hear more urgently*.

'So – Edwin. What can you tell me – his strength and his plans?'

'I am sorry, my lord,' he paused, wondering how much to say, 'I was not in a position to find things out. They kept me out of the way. As I understand it from my companions, what little we learned we have told.' He glanced towards Elaeth.

Cadwallon looked at him. 'If I am not mistaken, there is more to this than you are saying,' he said gently. 'It was not easy, you say. Will you not tell me?'

So Rhun did.

He left nothing out. None of the hurt, none of the humiliation, none of the degradation. He spared them no detail. Hesitant at first, trying clumsily to assemble his memories into some coherent order. But once he had started it came fluidly and it poured out nonstop. In the presence of this man he felt strong enough. And once he had confronted it, he found he could recount it without fear. That telling it would help. And it made a good story. He kept back only the tale of the crown. *Better not to tell that in public, not yet*, he thought.

Cadwallon and Elaeth were visibly shocked. Both were hard men, unsympathetic. They had both led hard lives, life itself was hard. They had both known sickness and hurt, cold and casual cruelty, they were no strangers to slavery and forced labour, certainly not to warfare and feud and death. Even torture. But this deliberate, secret viciousness out of spite alone was a shock to them both. That a man could derive pleasure from so hurting a harmless thing was abhorrent.

'I have heard stories of this man. I never believed them – I supposed they were just stories told against an enemy, no more. God knows, we have had to fight him hard enough to make me hate the man, but I find it hard to believe even now, in truth. His people in Northumbria think highly of him, I am told. He is a formidable opponent and ruthless, that is for sure. But that is war – not this dirty – I don't know – I cannot find a word for it!' Elaeth seemed really offended. 'He is a man without honour at the best of times, but this is perversion. That is the word – perversion. Ech!' and he spat as if to clear away a bad taste.

'There is one thing I haven't told you, my lord.' Rhun squared his shoulders. 'May we talk in private?'

Cadwallon would have allowed anything in that moment. He glanced at Elaeth who suddenly found he needed to be doing something else. He swept out of the hall, gathering his people with him.

Rhun sat in silence. *There's no easy way to say this,* he thought; *best just tell him.*

'My lord, he has your crown.'

Cadwallon gripped the arms of his chair and half-rose. He froze there, his knuckles white. Then he sat back and stared at Rhun. 'He has the crown of Maelgwn Gwynedd? But it was hidden. How?'

'I found it my lord – I'm sorry – I couldn't help it!'

He explained how it had come to be.

'And you gave it to Edwin!' he shouted, half-rising again. The air tingled. He studied Rhun as if he would eat him. Then he collapsed back into his seat. He dropped his head into his hands and held it there saying nothing. At last he breathed a deep sigh. He looked up, and was changed. '*Na, na,* do not upset yourself, I'm sure you are not to blame. After what he did to you, who could expect you to do otherwise? But I thought we had hidden it better than that.'

Rhun still hardy dared move, but he said quietly, 'It was the weather, my lord. Too much rain, and maybe the rope was not strong enough. The stone was rough.'

'I doubt the drain was built for such numbers to use,' said Cadwallon. 'The monks were not many.'

Then, as if in answer to an unspoken question, 'We hid it. We were hard pressed and in great peril. None of us could tell if we would survive. Better to hide the crown than lose it to the ocean, they said, and I agreed. Now I am not so sure.'

'At least it is not altogether lost, my lord.'

They thought about this as if it might make the facts less awful.

'He will have taken it to Northumbria, I suppose. He will see it as a lever with the councils – he will expect it to legitimise his claim. God knows, I have lost it: what makes me a worthy holder?'

Rhun looked at him, and Meical's words came back to him.

'You were chosen, my lord. Not him. No amount of crowns and warfare will change that.'

Cadwallon looked surprised. 'You underestimate the power of persuasion. And, in the end, he can take the land by force, with or without a crown – never forget that. But – well, your words encourage me – thank you.'

'They were not my words, my lord, but Meical's. He used similar to console me when I first remembered.'

'Well then, I shall thank Meical. One of your friends, I take it?'

Rhun didn't hesitate.

'He is, my lord. The best. I owe him my life.' He paused for a brief moment, 'My lord, I will fetch this thing back for you if it is the last thing I do. And if I can, I will kill Edwin, I swear it.'

Cadwallon stared hard at him. Then he lifted his goblet and drank off the contents in one swallow, and slammed it down onto the table.

'Well then, we have much work to do! Let us be about it.'

He shouted a name and a large man, heavily armed, came into the hall.

'My lord?'

'Come, Isaf, call Elaeth and join us: we must talk war at once, it seems.'

He paced up and down the long firepit while they waited.

'So – Elaeth – and you, Rhun. You should know that we have been the guests of Domnall mac Áedo who is Gwledig in Erin. When Edwin drove us off our rock, Erin seemed the best place. They were our enemies too once, but that was long ago and we had become friends – trade carries on, you'll find, despite the quarrels of kings. Alas, Domnall grows old and has his own troubles. He lends me ships and men to sail them, but I must find men amongst our own people to meet Edwin. We are still several hundred strong, not enough for war but enough to start. And you give me courage; perhaps we shall not be without aid.'

Both Elaeth and Rhun were quick to respond.

'There are men a-plenty in Lleyn and throughout the mountains. All would aid you in this.'

'My lord, we met with many in the south who would join you. I think they feel the lack of a leader – Powys has become an unruly place since Cær Legion. I can vouch for that myself.'

He has seen a lot since we last met, thought Cadwallon, *but that's another story which will have to wait.*

'We will send a fast boat to Erin and bid the others join us at Cær n'Arfon. We must follow the road to Deganwy and over the passes to the north. We have to chase these damn Northumbrians out of our land! Will you go, Rhun, find your friends and take your road the way you came? Find all the people you met on the way and bid them gather all the force they can. Make for Penda. I will send any who will go with you but you must lead – the people will know you. If your friends find their fathers that will be all to the good. They will follow you, you may be sure.' Rhun looked blank. 'What – you do not believe me?'

'My lord, will they? Why?'

'Why ever not? You are your father's son.'

'I don't think it's up to me, do you? I would not willingly follow a fool just because he was the son of a brave man.'

'I could order it so.'

'I would ask you not to, my lord. You see that, surely?'

'I do. And your answer does you credit. But listen, Rhun, you are no fool. You are your father's son in more than just birth. From what you have told me, all the people with you would follow you to the depths of Annwm if you asked it of them, and I don't doubt that applies to those who are not here. What makes you think your father's men would be any different once they know you?'

'But that's it, isn't it? They don't know me.'

'So – go find them.'

Rhun left the hall. Excitement – no, elation – pumped through his body. At last he saw clearly again. Felt truly himself again. The last shadows were blown away and he was free. This was more like it – haste! haste! he had wasted too much time already!

Rhun looked about for his three remaining friends among the gathering crowd and saw them down on the strand. The boys had been left kicking their heels, not important enough to be among the main guests, but keen not to miss anything. Neither did they want to be given jobs, so with nothing else to do, they had wandered back to the shore to watch the landing. Most of the men on board had been warriors, Cadwallon's own war band, or a part of it. Some thirty or so came ashore, bringing a mountain of gear with them, leaving the crew to settle the ship.

They looked tough and dangerous. And they were all well armed. Their gear was good and there was a lot of it. The boys watched as the crew sweated over landing such a cargo. But at last it was done and the men stood around taking in their new surroundings.

Suddenly one broke away and came running.

Cynrig leapt to his feet. 'Tad? Is it you?'

The man grabbed Cynrig and threw him into the air, caught him and hugged him to his chest.

'*Duw, bachgen*, what are you doing here!'

He stopped. His eyes had been shining, now they veiled over. He looked around at the others, noting faces, trying to place them. Slowly realisation dawned. 'I know you, don't I – from home? But how – why?'

Rhun stepped forward. 'Welcome Afaon, we came to find you. And all our fathers.'

'Rhun, is it? Man – you have changed – I barely recognized you.' And then he looked suddenly guilty, as if found out in an act of which he was ashamed. 'You will not find yours, I'm afraid...' He hesitated, wanting to say more but unable to find the words.

'*Na*, I know. Cadwallon has told me.'

'I am sorry for it, Rhun – I was not able to help him.'

'I understand that.' Rhun said. 'Please – don't trouble yourself.'

Cynrig squirmed in his father's grasp, 'You can put me down now, Tad.'

Afaon looked at the boy in his arms. Suddenly the truth of it hit him.

'You brought him with you? What were you thinking? He is only a child!'

'And I am glad I did. He has already saved my life once, and not only mine.'

Afaon looked at him as he had been struck. 'Are you mad!? You have been in battle?'

'I am old enough!'

'I was talking to Rhun.'

They had all got used to relying on their own resources, they were no longer a bunch of callow boys. They had grown. Afaon must be made to understand, now more than ever.

'As I said – some of us owe our lives to his skill with a bow.'

'But he's just a child!'

No, he is not, Rhun thought. Peleg had been a child – they had all been children on that awful day. But Cynrig was no boy, nor Tecwyn, nor any of them, not any longer. They had seen and done too much.

'He was when we set out, but you'll find him changed now, I think. Besides, I couldn't have left him – once he knew Tecwyn was coming he'd have followed anyway.'

Afaon stared at him hard. 'Tecwyn too,' he muttered. He looked around.

'Tecwyn – is he . . . .'

'*Na*, fear not – he is gone on an errand for me. There were more of us who set out – all still live, as far as I know. They have gone to take home such news as we had, but they were fine when we saw them last.'

Afaon stood rooted, as if in doubt and unable to move. Then he seemed to sag.

Carefully, as if he might break him, he set Cynrig on the ground. He set his hand on his son's head, his fingers gripping the hair lightly, in a gesture of protection. They looked at each other, father and son, and Afaon saw the truth of

Rhun's words. He let go. '*Ie*, he would do that.' He sighed. 'Perhaps it is for the best. But I am afraid we have been less lucky. We lost more than we could afford.' And he told off a list of names. Of the twenty who had gone with Cadfan, only fifteen remained.

So, Rhun thought, *Eryl has lost his father too and I can't tell him – well, that's ill news enough, but please God let me be able to tell it to him one day*. They had gone; they had left him and followed another, but still he could not help feeling responsible for them. Now though he was just relieved there were so few to be told.

'Afaon, you must know – Cadwallon has charged me to go home. I am to follow the route we took coming here, south about the mountains. I must gather as much force as I can on the way, and then seek out Penda of Mercia. He would send as many with me as will go and yet not slow us down. Will you come with me?'

Afaon stared at him. He looked around at the other two standing quietly by: they, Cynrig – none of them looked the least surprised by this news, though they can only now have heard it themselves. *He is a leader indeed*. 'Will I follow Cwyfan's son? By God I will, and so will any who knew him.'

The feasting was long and joyful. The king was returned. Spring was here, the sap was rising and their hearts brimmed with new hope. As darkness fell, and the eating was done, the tables were cleared away, a great fire was lit, and the people danced by the light of its flames.

The dances were stately at first, elegant, trodden with neat steps. The dancers formed a wide circle, hand-in-hand, which turned to the rhythm of the music. They split and moved in intricate patterns, only to return to their partners and form the circle anew. It split again, and each time the circle broke the patterns changed. Stately at first, but never sombre. The dancers laughed as they swung and spun each other in their tight measures. Their faces shone in the firelight, cheeks polished by joy and, perhaps, a bit by drink. As the night drew on, gradually the pace of the dances quickened and they became wilder, drums beating harder, louder, until they seemed to fill the sky.

One by one people began to drop out, walking or crawling away to the beer barrel to fortify themselves, or just to lie panting, their voices filled with laughter. And then the young folk, and some not so young, began to pair off. Sweethearts of long standing, newly formed couples, boys and girls, or otherwise as suited, wandering away from the light of the fire to carry on their celebrations in private.

Meical saw Rhun and Gwenifer move off, their arms entwined, their heads together and in that instant his world changed. His breath stopped as if he had been punched. His chest tightened as if suddenly bound up and he staggered and nearly tripped. The other dancers spun away and left him standing on his own, scarce able to breath.

He stared after Rhun and Gwenifer, trying to see through this riot, and suddenly he couldn't bear it. To be surrounded by all these happy people, laughing and dancing. He stumbled blindly from the firelight and turned away until he was swallowed up by the night.

Unseeing, he came to the shore. Brought up short, he stood at the water's edge and let the small waves lap over his feet. He looked up into the sky, thick with stars, and he felt that he would burst. It was stupid – stupid, but he just couldn't bear it. He sat heavily, down into the gentle surf. With his face buried in his hands he wept. Deep sobs of pain. His body shook as the hurt flowed up out of the depths of him. It was so unfair. How could he do this?

The night was calm. The sea lapped gently around him. At last he lifted his head and drew in a shuddering breath, feeling weak, almost sick. Meical looked up at the vast panoply of stars and was humbled. He cursed himself for a fool: *What am I doing? Rhun's my friend but I can't command him – and I can't hurt him. I mustn't mind. He deserves nothing less than such a fine girl.* Besides, he had to take a wife eventually – he must have children – it was bound to happen sooner or later. And that it should be Gwenifer should come as no surprise. She was pretty and clever and, most importantly she was here when Rhun needed someone bright and fresh and clean and Meical had been none of those things. But still – he had been there too and for so much longer. He was worn out by it. Yet, as hard as he tried to rationalise it, the less he found he could accept it. It should have been him! Instead, here he was alone and utterly wretched. Deep inside himself he felt abandoned, bereft. And broken, broken in a way that might never mend. He longed for something greater than himself and his petty life, something which would swallow him up or take him away and make him forget. But it was vain. He couldn't escape. And he was so tired. He had not been made to be so strong for so long. He gave himself up to his grief, a grief which racked his whole body.

Yet at last his tears lessened. He thought of their lives here, far from home in this strange place that was not their own. And he knew he was being a fool. What was he, after all? The son of a blacksmith, nothing more. They were both so much greater than he, and so suited – Rhun the heir to Cadfan and all the fathers of their people; she the daughter of a king. Who was he, a blacksmith's boy, to hope that there was a place for him in such lives? Oh yes, Rhun was his friend – they had fought together and laughed together, played together when they were young, but that was then, in other places at other times. Now they were here. Gwenifer and he had shared a closeness while they were both nursing Rhun, a closeness which had grown in their joint endeavour, and, without thinking, he had supposed that she understood. But it seemed she had not. And Rhun was recovered now and had no more need of sick-nurses. He needed joy now, and laughter and life. If he got that from Gwenifer, Meical should be the last person to begrudge it. He had been too tired to laugh. He still was.

He sat alone in the darkness. No one came. No one knew he was there. They were all far too busy to notice even that he had gone. He felt utterly wretched, the more so because he knew he had no good reason. But he couldn't go back and join in the revelries – it would be such a lie.

At last he stirred. He stood up and his clothes clung wetly to his body. It was cold now, and he shivered. He took a roundabout route and made his way to the house where he stayed. As he had hoped, no one noticed him. They were either asleep or drunk or otherwise occupied. He slipped inside unseen. He stripped off his wet clothes and fell into bed. Exhausted.

Something in the night disturbed his dreams. He woke but was unable to break the surface enough to know what it had been. Or care. And, once asleep again, it vanished from his mind.

It was the early sun, streaming in through a crack in the wattles, which woke him properly. He lay staring up into the darkness of the thatch, piecing together the night before, reassembling his misery, hating himself for doing it.

'Meical,' said a quiet voice, 'are you awake?'

He jumped as if bitten.

'Rhun!' He struggled to rise. 'Is it you?'

'It is – but don't get up. Lie easy.'

Meical lay back and closed his eyes. In shame as much as anything. His face wore a band of sunshine like an inverted mask.

'Have you been here long?' he said at last, 'where...'

'Everyone's still asleep. I've been here since first light. We missed you.'

Rhun sat stiffly on the edge of the bed. He had wanted to reach out and touch his friend, to reassure him somehow, but he had not wanted to wake him. And now, in this strange reversal, he found his tongue tied. Meical too stayed silent, staring at the wall to avoid the sunlight lest it reveal the perilous glitter at the edge of his eyes. His silence was a barrier almost too high to cross.

'She's not free, you know,' Rhun said at last, 'at least not for anything but to be a friend – she's promised to another – a king's son from somewhere away south of here.'

Still Meical said nothing.

'We missed you – where did you go?'

The glitter in Meical's eye became a tear, which rolled

fatly down his cheek. 'I'll be alright,' he said in a whisper, 'you don't have to stay.'

'Are you mad? After all you've done for me, d'you think I would leave you like this?'

Meical rolled his head over and looked up. Suddenly he sat up and threw his arms around Rhun's neck, thrusting his face into the warm fold of his shirt. He spoke, but through the tears and the thick cloth his voice was muffled, and Rhun couldn't make out the words. At last Meical heaved a huge sigh and said, clearly now, 'I'm sorry.'

Rhun hugged his friend, too surprised to move. He tried to offer comfort and found he didn't know how. He ran his hand up the bony knobs of Meical's spine and patted his shoulder. *He needs to put on some weight*, he thought absently.

They sat there in silence, clasped together, exchanging warmth, neither daring to say anything.

Meical pulled away. 'I'm sorry,' he said again, 'I'm being selfish. I've been a fool. I'm alright now.'

'*Na*, I've been the fool. I should have seen.'

Meical sniffed and wiped his nose on his arm, leaving a thin trail of mucus glistening on his skin. He didn't notice.

'I thought I'd lost you,' he said. 'I'm being selfish – but I've been so worried, for – oh, so long. I thought I'd lost you forever, and, and then when you recovered I was so happy and – *na* – she's so good, so fine, and you found such joy with her, and – I don't know, I couldn't bear it.' He knew he wasn't making much sense, but he couldn't find the right words – couldn't put into words what he felt and wanted so desperately to say.

Rhun stared at his friend. Meical's distress seared him. He cursed himself for his blindness. He had been too full of his own excitement, too elated by his return to strength and new purpose. And here was Meical, his true friend, and he had hurt him. And now he was beginning to understand how and just how deeply, and to know that to hurt Meical was the very last thing he wanted. Once he had thought his friend to be ordinary; now he knew how wrong he had been.

'Come on,' he said at last, 'let's find some breakfast and clear out of here before anyone wakes up.'

'My clothes are still wet.'

'Never mind – it's a fine day, they'll soon dry in this wind.'

They walked for hours in the warm spring sunshine, under a wide sky and high-flying clouds.

They didn't speak of anything more than the things they came across or saw in the distance. Instinctively they both knew that there were things it was too soon to say. Perhaps might always be. Perhaps didn't need to be said at all. They understood each other now in a way that they never had.

And then there was no more time for talking. Cadwallon would be away, and they must leave at once.

Chapter 15

They had landed on a lee shore in a freshening wind. Despite the boatman's skill, the surf had caught the boat and tossed them out onto the sands. It was not a good beginning. Soaked and battered, clutching their few belongings, they had made their way over the dunes and headed inland, leaving the boatman to wait out the weather.

The wind was strong but the day was fine. The sun chased small shadows ahead of them as puffs of cloud flew across the sky. Their way had taken them at once into familiar country – this was where they had parted from Balthazar and his silent friend all those months ago. Now it seemed like an age had gone by, as though they had been on *Tir-Na-n'Og* and were returning to find the world utterly changed.

They came to the village and halted by the forge.

'How is it with you, smith?' Ysgyrran called in through the open door.

'Who asks?' came a voice from inside.

'You'll not remember us I expect – we passed through – oh, half a year ago now, or thereabouts.'

The smith came to the door, wiping his hands on an old rag to no noticeable effect. He looked at the little group and nodded.

'Oh, I remember. Not many pass this way and you came with that Balthazar – I'll not be forgetting that one in a hurry. But there were more of you, surely – have you not fared well?'

'Ach, not so badly – we are all still alive, or were when we left the others.'

'Not eaten, then?' he said with a broad grin, glancing at Tecwyn. '*Na, na,* do not mind me. My wife scolds me for my little jokes.'

Ysgyrran said with an edge to his voice, 'Not eaten, but it was no easy journey.'

The smith looked at him, only slightly chastened. 'Well, you are welcome back, I'm sure.' Then he turned to their guide. 'And here's another old friend. So, Brioc, are they with you, or are you with them?'

'A little of both, I think. But I am charged to guide them to their own country, so we travel together.'

'Well, stop and eat at least, we would welcome some news – good news, if you have any; there has been little enough of that these past several moons.'

And they had stopped long enough to tell the little they knew. Cadwallon and his army destroyed, Elaeth still besieged in his own lands after long months of bitter fighting, and now Edwin gone at last, but leaving devastation in his wake.

'And so we travel east – our people must be told.'

Others had come in while they were talking. Amongst them the old man who had spoken with Rhun. He spoke quietly to Ysgyrran while the others were eating.

'What of your leader – Rhun, was it?' he asked.

'*Ie*, in truth he was our leader. But Edwin took him and broke him. We have him back now, but he is useless to us.'

'This is ill news, ill news.' He looked into the distance for a while. 'He was a lively one and you will take it hard, I'm thinking.'

Ysgyrran looked a little put out.

'Oh, his body is well enough – it is his mind – it wanders in distant places, places none can follow.'

'What strange thing is this – his wits are gone, you say?'

'He is in a dark dream. He awoke once but he scarcely knew us when he did. None of us know what happened to him while Edwin had him captive, but it was not good – you can be sure of that. And when he did not know us, I knew that others must take the news home. It was clear that he could not.'

'This will make a sad tale to carry home.'

'It will, but what else could I do? They must be warned. And perhaps they may even see for themselves one day.'

The old man didn't answer. He seemed troubled by the news.

'And what of the others? You are still only five – surely there were more? You say they are not dead,' he asked.

'*Na*, they are not dead, but they could not leave,' Ysgyrran tried to keep the bitterness from his voice – *they* would *not leave*, he thought savagely. He sighed inwardly. Better to keep that thought to himself. The war band was a thing of the past; talking now to this old man finally made that real. They had been young, excited, ignorant when Rhun had called them. But they had seen war and death and hardship since then and now Rhun was as good as dead, and the whole war band idea was dead with him. He, Ysgyrran, was now leader. He had only four to lead but it was up to him now. 'In truth, it may be better so – we will travel the more swiftly for being fewer – and perhaps more safely.'

Once across the pass where they had first met Balthazar and Qaseem on that strange day, they were among people they knew. No watchers from the crags on this journey, real or imagined. Dusk on the third day found them walking easily down the wooded valleys east of the mountains, down towards the crossing place which had been the scene of such a narrow escape all those months ago. For the while the weather had favoured them. It was grey and overcast but there had been little or no rain and the wind which had treated them so roughly on their arrival, had dropped to a gentle breeze. With luck the river would be low enough for an easy crossing. And this time by the proper route.

'This is the end of my writ,' said Brioc as they walked. 'In the morning you must go on alone – you know the way from here, is it not so?'

'I think so. It is no great distance east of here. And we should be among friends within a day or two.'

Llif had been walking ahead. Suddenly he stopped. Alert and poised, he held up a hand in warning.

'What is it?' Ysgyrran called quietly.

'Hush! I heard a horse. Fisher folk don't have horses.'

Instantly the mood changed. The trees clung close to the track; they were not thickly crowded but they obscured any view ahead. Without a word, the travellers melted into the woods, and, using them as cover, crept quietly forward. The understory thinned as they approached the river, the dense growth grazed clear where Teifion's people let their animals roam to feed. To keep in cover, they were forced to stray a good distance from the road. It was as well they did, for when they reached the small village it seemed that they had only just missed running into trouble. True, nothing looked to be out of the ordinary: smoke from the evening cook fires seeped from the roofs, and hung in wafts amidst the usual tangle of nets, apparently at peace. They could hear voices, not raised, not in fear or anger, just talking as normal, but they sensed that this peace had only just fallen. They could feel the residue of tension in the still air, as if some threat had come and only recently gone. Suddenly a curtain was drawn aside and golden firelight spilled out into the compound. A figure appeared, silhouetted against the brightness. It seemed familiar.

'Teifion – is that you?' Ysgyrran called in a soft voice.

'Who is there?'

They stepped into the light. Teifion gawped at them for a brief moment. 'Quick,' he hissed, 'get inside before you're seen!'

He bustled them into the house and stood alert outside, straining his ears to catch any disturbance. All was quiet.

'*Duw* – you gave me a fright! What are you doing appearing like ghosts out of the night?'

'I'm sorry, Teifion – you'll remember us perhaps – we were here some time ago from Magonsæte?'

'Of course I remember you – but what brings you here now? And where are the others?' He looked at the five of them wildly.

'We're on our way home. We left the others in Lleyn.'

'Well thank the stars you didn't come any sooner – they've only just left.'

'We heard horses – who?' Llif asked urgently.

'Men from Powys,' Teifion said darkly. 'They crossed the river this morning and have been casting about all day. You just missed them – they're back across the river now.' He slapped his forehead. 'But why am I surprised to see you? Fool that I am – of course you'd be close by or they'd not come here now. I should have expected you. We've seen nothing of them since we last met and now they turn up just as you do.'

'So, they guard the crossing again!'

'And they know we're here – don't you see what that means?' said Llif.

'I see it, but it makes no difference.' Ysgyrran turned to Teifion, 'How many of them?'

'Hard to say. Half a dozen maybe, not many more than yourselves, but they are warriors.'

'And we're just boys?'

'I'm sorry, forgive me, but two of you are, for sure,' he checked. 'Well, one maybe.'

Ysgyrran laughed. 'Don't underestimate the wasp! Others have done that to their cost. Still, you are right – we could do without the trouble just now.'

'Wasp, is it? Well you know best.'

'One of the most deadly with a sling I've ever seen,' said Brioc.

Teifion met Tecwyn's enormous grin. 'Well – as I say – you know best. But if you want to avoid trouble, you would be wise to go by another route – head north for a bit. Not too far – that is not a road you want to follow for long, but it would be preferable to going south – it might be many days by that road before you could easily cross the river, and by then you'd be in wild country. *Na*, best get into the hills north a bit and then make your way east as soon as you can in safety. You'll surely find another crossing further down river. Somewhere you are not expected.'

'I think Teifion is right,' said Brioc. 'If there are people who wish you ill and will not let you pass the river, or worse, you would do best to follow his advice – he has the measure of the situation better than any of us and I cannot help you here.'

Ysgyrran looked at him. 'Thank you for staying with us as far as you have, we have been glad of your company. You should get some rest in any case,' he said, 'stay 'til daybreak at least. But we will go now: it is us they are after, not you.'

'*Na*,' said Teifion, 'you need none of you leave in the dark. They are gone back across the river – have no fear of them tonight. Food and sleep is what you all need more. Wife – food for our guests! You should all eat and rest a while; dawn will be soon enough for you to go on.'

Ysgyrran hesitated a moment or two, but he saw the wisdom in Teifion's words. And they were all tired enough to welcome a quiet night under cover.

But he would not stay for long. As dawn approached they made their farewells. They left the village and crept north-wards through thin veils of an early morning mist. They picked up the old legionary road almost at once, and set out across the water meadows at good speed. The road was lined with old willows but the rest of valley floor had long since been cleared of trees to make grazing land, and they wouldn't feel safe until they reached the woodland on the far side.

But they were past half way before anyone thought to look back. As the dawn strengthened the mists melted away and now there was a clear view of the road behind them.

Sensing some danger, Eryl turned. 'Horsemen! See – there, coming out of the trees!'

Ysgyrran reacted at once. 'Run!' he cried and set off. The others pelted after him, running for all their worth, already feeling steel in their backs. A cry came up from behind. They had been seen. Now they heard the drumming of hooves on the hard road.

The distance shortened, the drumming grew lounder. Their hearts were pounding, their breath coming in harsh gulps. They could almost feel the hot breath of the horses on their necks as at last they reached the trees and plunged in amongst them where they grew the thickest. They were forced to duck under the dense low-hanging branches as they scrambled up the steep slope, sometimes on all fours. Cries of anger came from their pursuers as they realized the thicket was too much for their mounts.

The boys clambered on, sweating and panting from the effort. The trees thinned as they climbed, at last giving out to a swathe of short cropped grass rising to a rocky summit. Tecwyn could go no further. He collapsed on the ground, fighting for breath and they gathered round him. 'That's it,' he panted, 'they can kill me if they must but I can't do any more running.'

But now they had all stopped running they could hear – what? Nothing. No sound of pursuit. Silence.

'*Duw* – that was close! I wish we'd left last night like I wanted to.'

'Have they given up?'

'I don't know – we should be able to see from the top. Come on, Tecwyn – one last push.'

After a few hundred paces they came to a narrow bald ridge. Just short grass blowing below a rough spine of rock. They scrambled up and lay looking back.

'Any sign?'

'*Na*, nothing.'

Though their immediate view was blocked by trees, they could see clearly the line of the road and across it into the more open country beyond. Far away they could see the line of the river and, beyond that, the hills which led back into their own country. Home. The sun was just peeping over the distant ridge. It seemed to beckon.

There was no sign of their pursuers on the hillside, and no sign of movement as they cast their gaze wider. But as they watched, a lone figure passed across a gap in the trees far below them, making slow yet steady progress along the road northwards. He didn't ride like a warrior, but he was just too far away to be certain.

'Where are the others?'

Ysgyrran looked round wildly. 'Maybe they've fanned out. We'd better be going.'

'Where?'

'North – what else can we do? Teifion reckoned there were more than the half-dozen he saw. Who knows how wide a front they can cover? They could find us any minute. Come on – and try to keep quiet!'

Dragging Tecwyn to his feet, they set off northwards, following the line of the ridge. Using such scant cover as they could find, dropping to their hands and knees again in places to stay below the skyline, they followed the ridge until it dipped and at last they reached the safety of the trees. They came to a halt and stood clutching at each other as they struggled to draw breath. They looked back up the rocky hillside. They waited. Five beats – ten. Nothing. There was no sign that they had been followed. They could hear no sounds of pursuit.

'Come on,' said Ysgyrran, 'too soon to stop yet.'

They crept forward, senses alert to every sound. The woods rapidly grew denser, now with a tangle of under-growth. It concealed them well but it made progress slow and noisy as they were forced to push through clinging vines and brambles.

The morning wore on. The sun had climbed into the sky long since and now it sent fingers of light probing among the trees, peering in on them when they crossed a gap. The air grew warm and there was no breeze down here among the dense growth. Flies swarmed about their heads, thirsty for the sweat which stuck the dust to them. After an age of creeping along like thieves, half-blind, Eryl had had enough. 'Don't you think we'd do better if we could see?'

'What d'you mean?'

'Well, here we are scrambling along, but into what exactly? Where are we going?'

Ysgyrran stopped. 'We're not getting caught. That's the main thing.'

Eryl said nothing. The others gathered round.

Ysgyrran looked at Eryl. *Why is it always him?* 'Well? Do you have a better idea?'

'No, not really.'

'So, shut up then.'

Eryl stood still, saying nothing. Ysgyrran lost his temper.

'You always do that! If you've got something on your mind, then spit it out! Or shut up and let me think.'

'Well, it just seems to me we're going the wrong way. We need to be heading east.'

'I know that! But we're being chased – remember?'

'Well – are we?'

They all stood still. Of course they were. Weren't they? They had had to get away, somehow running had seemed the only thing to do.

'What d'you mean?'

'It's just that we haven't actually seen or heard anything for hours. Maybe we aren't being chased at all. And we'll never get across the road if we don't try.'

'All right, clever boy. What would you do?'

'I just think we ought to keep closer to the road – so we can get across as soon as we get a chance. We must be going miles out of our way.'

'I want to go home,' said Tecwyn. 'I'm fed up with this.'

'Not you as well – I wish I'd come alone! I should have left you all with Meical – he'd have been happy to have you!'

He looked at the others as they stood around. No one else said a word.

'All right, we'll head south and get back to the road. It can't be far away if it runs at all straight like it should.'

Dodging from tree to tree, they made their way down through the wood. Nothing else moved. No birds, no small creatures, as if all other life was in suspension. Now there was no sound at all except the rustling of their feet in the leaf-litter. They picked their way with infinite care through the uncanny silence, which, far from making it easier, merely added to the tension. Any incautious movement seemed to make noise enough to be heard miles away, and by the time the ground levelled they were so wound up the smallest thing would have tipped them into panic.

They stopped a few dozen paces from the road. From here they could see the line of the track snaking through the trees ahead.

'Come on, it seems quiet enough.' Ysgyrran stepped out of the trees towards the road. Just as he did so, a rider came into view around a bend. Ysgyrran froze. He swallowed hard and held his breath in case the slightest noise escaped him. He held a hand up in a frantic gesture to stop the others. With as little motion as possible he stole a quick look at the newcomer. Still a fair distance away, he seemed unaware of being watched. He wore a deep hood and seemed to be examining something in his hand. With his head tilted down the hood masked his view, blinding him momentarily to what was ahead. With his heart pounding, Ysgyrran retreated into cover.

'I don't think he saw me,' he hissed. 'He's going slowly enough, but – come on, we can't stay this close.'

They scrambled back up the slope a short way and eased themselves down into the undergrowth as quietly as they could.

The rider was closer now. He was slowing down. They willed him to carry on but just at the point where he was abreast of them he stopped and dismounted. He tethered his horse to a branch and sat down with his back to them and rummaged through a bag he carried slung around his neck. He was eating! They couldn't believe it. Why choose here of all places? Ysgyrran's inner voice was screaming – *Go on, go on, get on your horse and choose somewhere else!*

But there was no hope. The man sat there as if he had all the time in the world.

'Thanks very much, Eryl,' hissed Ysgyrran. 'Next time you have a bright idea, keep it to yourself!'

There was nothing to be done. Taking the utmost care not to make a sound, they crept back until they could no longer see him. Then they turned and ran.

But Ysgyrran knew that Eryl was right. They could not just

keep heading north, they had to try to get back somehow. Yet, it seemed the pattern was set for the day. Whenever they tried to cross the road something stopped them. And their flight was achingly slow. The country here was a mess of steep hills and little valleys, broken by the occasional small river and many deep defiles, cut by smaller streams which trickled across their way between steep muddy banks. The ground lay under ancient leaf mould and was strewn all around with moss-covered boulders. The trees pressed together as if meaning to hinder them out of malice, and every unknown sound was an alarm. They remembered Teifion's words the first time they met. He had said these hills were haunted. They began to believe it. The oppressive silence of earlier had gone, but now every sound had become a threat. A twig would crack, unaccountably. Or there would be a rustle in the undergrowth just far enough off to conceal its maker, but loud enough to feel imminent. And each time it happened they shrank into a frightened huddle. And each time they felt brave enough to try the road again, they were driven back once more by the sound of approaching horses or even, on one occasion, of marching feet.

The most unsettling thing was that they saw no one. Since they had escaped their hungry rider, they had just heard noises. Somehow that was worse than being able to see and size up who or whatever made them. They came to believe not just that these hills were haunted but that someone, or something, was determined to drive them out of their way. They were experienced hunters – they knew what that might mean.

So they gave up the road, and kept to the woods and hill-tops, and kept on northwards until the day grew dim and they were forced to stop. They dared not light a fire, but slept fitfully under the bole of a huge oak, pressed close together for warmth. Ysgyrran awoke to a low grey day of drifting rain, with feelings to match. Sleep had done little to restore him; waking to a damp dawn under a dripping tree did nothing to help.

Tecwyn and Llif were talking quietly. 'Not much chance of going home now.'

'Not much.'

'Where are we going to go, d'you suppose?'

'How should I know?'

Ysgyrran stared gloomily into the rain. He had made himself leader, now the others looked to him at every turn and setback, as if he had all the answers, and he found that he had none. He had been right to leave Lleyn, he knew he was, but he had led them into a maze and they were lost and without friends. Eryl had been right and that rankled.

He stirred himself. This would not do. Tecwyn's question was easy enough to answer in words, he just had no idea of how to turn that into a plan.

'We must go to Penda, of course. The gods only know where he is but we wouldn't have found him at Lenteurde in any case. Let's face it – it was always going to be a diversion.'

For three days they roamed the hills, trying to find a way out and eastwards into safety. They could only carry so much weight and their supplies were running low. They saw no more of the men who had been following them, yet the sense grew that they were being herded, forced to go in a direction that was not of their own choosing. And they were far from feeling safe even away from the road. Yet, despite his doubts, Ysgyrran did know vaguely where they were and roughly what would happen if they carried on. He knew that Hafren was still somewhere to their right, flowing north itself before it made the great loop eastwards around the high hills far to the north of Magonsæte. With luck they might find it and follow it. He had never seen it, had never been that far from home, but he had a vague idea they might reach Wrœcensæte and with luck get round any who might be their enemies and head south into Mercia and their own country at last.

Yet now they were hungry and they were tired and their spirits were sunk to their lowest. Even to hope seemed foolish. They just kept plodding on, trusting to Ysgyrran's lead, barely aware of the direction, just following the line of least resistance through the eternal trees. It had scarcely stopped raining for days, intermittent and not hard, but persistent, and they were wet through constantly, unable to light a fire to dry or even to warm themselves. This was not travelling as they had once thought it: through safe country where they might expect to meet only friends. Here they must move like shadows and leave no murmur of their passing, under constant threat of their lives.

At length they came to another sizeable river valley. Deep and narrow, the river at its bottom tumbled strong and wild. So even the way north was blocked. Tempers were beginning to fray. The smallest thing now earned a sharp word, and this was no small thing.

'Now what'll we do?' wailed Tecwyn.

Ysgyrran turned on him. 'I don't know – just shut up! Snivel and whine, snivel and whine – if you've got nothing useful to say then don't say anything. I've got to think.'

'Easy now, Ysgyrran – it's not his fault. Anyway, what's to think about? We have to find a crossing place or turn back.'

Ysgyrran clenched his fists.

'Thank you, Llif – I had thought of that!' he said though gritted teeth.

'Up or down?' asked Eryl.

Ysgyrran looked as if he might knock him down, but he controlled himself with effort. He looked around, eyeing each in turn. 'Go on then – what do you suggest?' he said at last.

'Well it might be easier upstream,' suggested someone.

'How far, though?' said Eryl. 'I think we should follow it down – we know there's a road somewhere; perhaps there'll be a crossing.'

'But we also know there might be enemies on it. One at least – we saw him, remember?'

'Well, we don't know for sure he was an enemy – he might just have been a traveller. Besides, that was days ago.'

'And what about since? Don't tell me you didn't hear the same things we all did.'

'Better risk it than stay here,' said Ithwalh.

'It's that or do nothing,' said Eryl. 'If we go any further into these hills, there's no knowing what we'll run into, and no knowing if we'll find Penda this way. And we've run out of food. I don't see we have a choice at all.'

It was a bitter pill, but Ysgyrran knew that Eryl was right again. There was nothing for it but to follow it downstream in the hope of finding somewhere to cross that might not kill them at once. The way would not be easy, but then no direction would be any easier.

After a hard scramble they did come to a road of sorts. More of a track than a road, and for sure not the one they had taken when they left Teifion, but still a road. They stared at it wearily. They had no idea where it led. They had no idea where they were. Ysgyrran could think of nothing to say. *Some leader I turned out to be,* he thought bitterly.

'You are not doing so well, are you?' came a voice, as if it had read his thoughts..

As one they spun round, drawing their swords.

'*Na,* put up your weapons, I am no enemy.'

The stranger stood against the back-drop of the trees. His drab clothing blended with the colours around him rendering him almost invisible until he moved. He did not appear particularly threatening, but that meant nothing. They knew without thought that this was not someone it would be wise to cross.

He smiled. 'I am Dyfnwal,' he said as if that explained everything. 'You will be cold, I am thinking – come.' He walked away. No one moved. All eyes turned to Ysgyrran.

'It's that man, isn't it? The one we saw last time,' murmured Ithwalh, reaching for his bow.

'Stay!' said Ysgyrran, urgently. 'I think so, he looks the same – but he doesn't behave like an enemy.'

'Should we go?'

Eryl said, 'We don't know he's an enemy – he's says he's not. And he gave us his name.'

'This time I agree,' said Ysgyrran. 'He turned his back to us – Ithwalh could have shot him easy.'

'I'm glad he didn't. I could do with a fire, I'm frozen,' said Tecwyn – and this time no one disagreed.

They hurried to catch up. The stranger led them into the trees. Reaching an open space, empty of anything but grass and a scattering of leaves, he stopped and squatted down. After some moments he rose again and stepped aside.

'Here, warm yourselves,' he said.

A small bright fire had sprung up, as if from nothing.

'Stand to it while I gather some bigger stuff.'

They did not move a muscle until he was gone.

'How did he do that?' whispered Llif.

'*Derwydd*,' said Ysgyrran, quietly. Cautiously they approached the flames, anxious for the heat. Anxious enough to overcome their fears.

'Can we trust him?'

'*Duwiau*! I don't know,' snapped Ysgyrran. 'But I don't see why not – the Derwyddon have only ever helped us before. Besides, Eryl's right – what choice do we have?'

The others squatted down, holding their hands out to the blaze. Tecwyn rubbed his together: 'Well, I don't care how he did it – I'm just glad he did.'

When the stranger came back, Ysgyrran confronted him. 'So, Dyfnwal or whatever your name is, what makes you think we're lost?'

'Oh, I have been behind you for some while now. And I confess I have seen you fail to get across the road on several occasions.'

'If you're not our enemy, why didn't you help us?'

Dyfnwal did not answer him.

'Now it seems that you have wandered away from the road you thought you were following,' he said. 'That would make you lost, to my mind. So here I am, helping you.'

'Are you following us? Why?'

'Following you, is it? *Na*, I go my way without your leave or lead. But be glad that I do – you seem unable to find your own.'

Ysgyrran looked stormy.

'What would you have had us do?' he snapped. 'We've

been trying to get away eastwards for days now. We wanted to cross Hafren by the old road but the way was guarded and we couldn't cross without being taken. We know those men of old.'

'Do you now? Well, I dare say you are right. It may even be so, but, for myself, I don't believe they were concerned about you – they have bigger game to catch.'

'But they chased us!'

'You do yourself overmuch credit. They would have stopped you of course in any case – they would want to know who is wandering in their lands. Yet greater things move here than you know. More is afoot than your small adventures.' He looked at them, his eyes hard and without expression. 'Come – warm yourselves.'

He dipped into his scrip and produced some bread. 'Here – eat while I answer your question.'

He fed the fire with some of his gatherings. 'You travel to take news to your people. And then, I believe, to Penda of Mercia? I would have you change that plan.'

Ysgyrran was determined not to let his surprise show. It was bad enough to be told by a complete stranger that he overvalued his own importance. He stood firmly, with his arms crossed. 'Change our plan, is it? Why should we do that – we don't know who you are. And how is it you think you know our business?'

The Druid held up a hand. 'I do not think I know it, I *do* know it.' He barked. Then he relented. 'Do not be alarmed – your friend Teifion told me, of course. We have been keeping an eye on you. More than one, in fact.'

'Teifion!'

'Hush, Tecwyn. Who's been spying on us?'

'I did not say spy – I said keeping an eye, quite a different thing. But my people, of course. You met one not so very long ago – by night on Dinas Emrys. He passed the word among us.'

They glanced nervously at each other. That was not a night any of them would forget. But the mention made them feel a little more secure – they had liked Afalach, so much as it had been possible.

'Afalach said he could not leave his people, yet you wander freely?'

'He is a guardian, I am a healer – it is necessary that we follow different paths.'

'He healed me!' said Tecwyn.

'Ah yes, well we all have some skills in that direction.'

Eryl looked up from the fire. 'We do know you, though, don't we? Somehow?'

Now it was Dyfnwal's turn to look surprised. But he smiled.

'One is much the same as another, you will find. Yet, it is so, we have met before. I helped your friend find his way a year or so back. Peleg, as I recall.'

'That was you? But that was an old man – you're not old.'

'Is that so? Well, I am sure you are right.'

Their skin prickled. Talking to these people was like wrestling smoke. But Eryl persevered.

'I always wondered about that. Brother Cledwyn had already seen to his burial. We were all there.'

'It was necessary, and good, to satisfy the lady Angharad. And your Brother Cledwyn, for that matter. But do you see, Peleg was not a follower of the White Christ. Am I not right?'

'*Na*, he wasn't,' said Ysgyrran.

'So he needed another way.'

Tecwyn cut in, 'But I saw him in the smoke! He was dead – yet he spoke to me!'

'You saw what you needed to see.'

They sat and thought about this.

At last Ysgyrran said, 'Rhun is Christian – most of us are – yet he arranged it, didn't he?'

'And the more respect to him for thinking of another's needs.'

'You make me feel we are in the wrong somehow.'

'Oh, you are not wrong. Each must follow where his heart takes him. And yet allow others to follow their own.'

'Rhun knows that – I think maybe Brother Cledwyn knows it too.'

'Many priests of the elder church – like your Cledwyn, they know how to keep the balance, even if their superiors do not. People approve of your god, they understand him. For myself, I like him too, but – well, I distrust priests in any frock. Especially these new ranting Romans and their fellows.'

'Are you not priests yourselves?'

'We are not. We are healers or teachers, helpers in general in our different ways. But we have no dogma.'

'But you held the ceremony for Peleg.'

'As I said, he needed another way. It was not enough for him merely to be laid in the ground, it was necessary to draw a line. A ceremony helps. That does not make me a priest.'

'But what about spells? – You can do spells. Are you not magicians either then?'

'You have seen us doing spells?'

'Well, I thought so – we saw Peleg in the magic smoke – at least a lot of us did. And Afalach – he made a storm and spoke with the voice of thunder. Besides – you didn't light this fire by any means I know.'

'Did he tell you that was a spell?'

Ysgyrran hesitated. '*Na*,' he said cautiously, 'But when we were sitting round the fire afterwards, Rhun said he didn't know how Afalach had done the storm thing, and Afalach just agreed with him. As if he didn't want to reveal a secret. Yet we all heard it. And saw the lightning.'

'Yes, he would do that. Some secrets are important – mystery itself is important.' He paused. He stirred the fire with a stick as if to make the point specific. 'But it need not be magic.'

'But you are powerful,' said Tecwyn quietly.

Dyfnwal looked at him, one eyebrow raised.

'You could say we have some influence – the Empire knew that. They tried to destroy us. You can see with how much success.'

He paused.

'Yet, because of that, these days we like to keep ourselves...' He paused again, as if in search of the right word. '... veiled. It is better for all that way.'

There was a silence while they assimilated this idea. Then Ysgyrran changed the subject to one he was just as anxious to know about.

'So, why d'you want us to change our plan?'

'Ah, well, things have changed while you have been wandering in the wilderness,' said Dyfnwal with something approaching a smile, 'it is no longer necessary to find Penda of Mercia, for he already has the news you bear.'

'He has? How?'

'Why, Cadwallon has told him. And your friend Rhun.'

The others were stunned. Cadwallon has come back and got ahead of them. Already? With Rhun?

'Rhun! How? He was barely alive when we saw him last.'

'Do you give up on him so easily? It seems he is made of sterner stuff than that.'

'But...'

'*Na*, there is much you do not know.'

The fire grew low more than once whilst Dyfnwal told the tale.

'So, you see the most important job you can be doing is to discover as much as you can of Edwin's present situation and get that information to your friend Rhun.'

'Why didn't you just tell us all that days ago?'

'Would you have believed me? You were in a different frame of mind then, I think.'

'You could have tried.'

'Could I? Believe this now – I did try to catch you up, but you just ran from me. In the end I thought it easiest to let you exhaust yourselves.' He seemed amused. 'Perhaps I helped a bit,' he said.

Ysgyrran half scrambled to his feet. But then he sank back and sighed. He even tried a lopsided smile. 'I've not done so well, have I?'

Dyfnwal looked at him, without expression.

'Do not distress yourself,' he said at last. 'Besides – it may well have been for the best. Now at least, you have some-thing immediate and useful to do.'

Ysgyrran flinched, as if he had been slapped. 'That's all very well, but the last we heard Edwin was in Northumbria.' He looked at the ground. 'God knows where he is now, 'cause I don't.'

'Well, *I* do. As it happens, you are heading in the right direction and it is no more than a day's march or so from here. And it also happens that an old friend is going that same way. Perhaps you could join him.'

'Who?'

But Dyfnwal seemed not to hear the question. He jumped to his feet. 'No more time for rest, you must be going,' he said as he packed away such things as he had got from his scrip and set about dismantling the fire. He dug in the soft loam of the woodland floor and buried such remains as there were deep into the damp earth. He scattered the place with dead leaves until satisfied, and took them back to the road. Which lay no more than a few hundred paces away.

'I must leave you here. Keep to cover, but follow this road to the next river crossing. It is not far. There is a good bridge there, built long ago. But remember, it may be important that you do not mention our meeting. And avoid being invited to explain yourselves to anyone you don't know. Apart from me,' he added with a laugh. 'Now go – you may have little time.'

Suddenly the world turned perilous again. This man, however strange, had sheltered them, just with his presence, and they felt naked without him. Yet he would not wait, and there was nothing for it but to go on.

Cautiously they set out following the line of the road but well above it to keep themselves out of sight.

When they looked back Dyfnwal was gone.

'How does he do that?' asked Tecwyn.

'*Derwydd!*' came the reply.

Chapter 16

Within no time, it seemed, they came to a huddle of buildings by a bridge, its timbers standing dark against the white of the rushing water. The bridge appeared to be unguarded, but that meant nothing. If this was Dyfnwal's idea of a safe crossing place they did not think much of it. They had been running in fear for so long they had grown wary of any stranger. How were they supposed to get across this in safety? Yet all was quiet – sombre; in keeping with the greyness of the day. They kept their distance and lay under the dripping trees, watching, trying to gauge their chances of crossing without being seen – or caught if these people were unfriendly. Perhaps later, when night fell, they might risk it.

For, quiet it as may have been, it was not devoid of life. As they watched people came and went, going about their daily tasks. Much of the activity seemed to take place around one building, a big rambling place; a survival, perhaps, from the time of the Empire, now falling gently into decay. It looked for all the world like a tavern, but who came this way that might use it? There was nothing like it in their own village – anyone could provide food if needs be, and any traveller wanting to pass the night would be expected to put up at the hall, and Lenteurde was on a busy enough route. This place was in the middle of nowhere, or so it seemed to them. Who would build a tavern here? But there was a road, and there was a bridge, so it must once have been more important than it now appeared. They lay in watch through the last of the day. More than once Ysgyrran wondered who Dyfnwal had meant by 'an old friend'.

As evening drew near they heard the rattle of horses coming up the road from the south. The same road that led back to Hafren and their enemies. Instantly alert, they lay poised for silent flight, back into the deep woods.

The road crept into the village between high banks. Below them they could see hooded heads, but no more. Nothing more until the small cavalcade had passed and stopped by the tavern. Two men, and three horses, each heavily laden. Too far away to make out clearly, but they didn't have the look of warriors. There were no weapons in sight, for a start – and, besides, this was not the way warriors went about their business. So, what were they? Merchants, perhaps. And that rang a bell. As Ysgyrran watched, the men gathered their horses together and one of them threw back his hood to speak to the innkeeper – and suddenly he knew them. He leapt to his feet.

'So that's who he meant! Come on, you lot!' He hurled himself down the short slope and tumbled into the road. The others scrambled after him.

'What are you doing!?' Llif said in a sort of rasping squeak.

'It's Balthazar – come on!'

The others just gawped.

'Balthazar?' they said as one.

'Yes, Balthazar – now come on.'

'Wait – conceal your weapons first,' said Eryl.

'What d'you mean? We haven't time for that!'

'At least make them less conspicuous – we don't know who we'll find down there.'

Ysgyrran fumed but he conceded. 'So do it – but hurry! Tecwyn – make yourself limp! Like you have a twisted ankle – Eryl, help him.'

They ran down into the village and then, making their way at the pace of Tecwyn's fake limp, they barged in amongst the small crowd that had started to gather around the new arrivals. Ysgyrran grabbed the halter of the leading pony, staring for all he was worth into Balthazar's face, willing him to recognise them and to understand. 'I'm so sorry, master,' he panted, 'Tecwyn tripped and we got left behind.' God knows it was weak enough, but it would have to do – he could think of nothing more clever in the moment.

More people joined the crowd, drawn by the commotion. Now one or two drawn blades appeared with them.

Time stood still. It seemed an eternity before Balthazar said anything. Ysgyrran could hear the blood pumping through his temples. *Come on, come on – they'll not hold off for ever.* Balthazar looked at each of them, his expression unreadable.

Then he put his hands on his hips and leant forward. 'So – what are you waiting for? You know what to do – get the packs off and see to the animals. Come along!'

He looked around. 'What can you do? Youngsters these days! But, well, a man must make do with such help as he can get in these times.'

It was touch and go. At first it seemed as if the locals would not swallow this. They shuffled and looked uncertain. One or two of the blades were lowered, but not all. Then a boy came out of the tavern and made to take the horses. The simple action seemed to break the spell. Balthazar made an imposing figure, standing calmly with his arms folded, and faced with that certainty, the crowd relaxed and began to disperse. Balthazar paused by the door and watched the boys as they followed the tavern lad around the corner of the building. 'I expect those animals to be looked after before you attend to yourselves – you know my rules!' he called after them. 'Come, Qaseem, supper and rest for you and me.'

It was much later that Balthazar himself came out, bringing a tray with bowls of thick broth and slabs of coarse bread. They fell on it like dogs.

'I'm sorry, I thought it better that I made you wait,' he said quietly. 'I have no idea what game you're playing – and I warn you, I will not be played with – but rest easy now, all tales must wait until morning. And until we are away from here, I'm thinking.'

Ysgyrran looked up from his food. Balthazar had never been easy to read – now his face was set, grim and stern.

Impossible to fathom. Best keep it simple, he thought. 'Thank you,' he said.

'Do not speak. Just eat and stay quiet.' He turned to leave. 'Try to attract no more attention.'

Ithwalh woke first. The sun had crept high enough to pierce the gloom of the stable and shine in his eyes. The air was clear and quiet, the sky blue for the first time since they had landed on the coast. The straw was warm and his body nestled into the unaccustomed luxury. He thought back over the last few days – the cold and the rain and the fear. Now it seemed like a bad dream. The tavern boy came in carrying a tray.

'Here's some breakfast,' he said. 'Your master says to stay here 'til he calls.'

So, while Balthazar conducted his business, they kept to the stable and took full advantage of their enforced idleness. In truth, none of them were eager to move out of its comfort until they had to.

Much talk the previous evening of the exotic wares he carried had made sure of a good crowd. Today the mood of the village was quite different from the evening before. Now they had been made welcome and Balthazar had done good trade, with people coming in from outlying farms to inspect his wares and acquire a few modest luxuries. But by noon they were all done, and within the hour they were on their way, waved off by those who the night before had drawn blades against them, if only in doubt. As they coaxed the horses over the rush and noise of the stream beneath the bridge, one figure stood apart from the crowd. Cloaked and booted for travel, shrouded by a deep hood, he followed them with his eyes until they disappeared down the track. But they were far too busy to notice, and too far away to see the look of satisfaction in those eyes, even if they had.

The early sun had promised better weather. Now it seemed set in for the day at least. The sun shone as if it understood that they were in need of a new mood, and it lifted their hearts. But no one spoke until they were well clear. Then Ysgyrran caught up with Balthazar who was striding ahead as usual.

'We cannot thank you enough for your help back there – I don't know what would have become of us else. I couldn't believe our luck when we saw it was you.'

'Luck, you think?' said Balthazar. 'I wonder – although my main wonder is what you ragamuffins are doing here at all. No – hold – I would hear the story from the start. When last we met you were heading into Gwynedd in search of your fathers. I take it you did not find them? And there were more of you surely? Where is the fair-headed one who led you before?'

Ysgyrran bit his tongue. Then he said, 'Rhun has stayed in Lleyn. It is a long tale.'

'So, let me hear it – we have all day.'

They walked alongside the tall man and told him their tale, each chipping in his part.

'We've been casting about in those woods for days trying to get across the road into the east without being seen. It was a risk but we were becoming desperate.'

'It was a risk indeed – reckless, even. But brave, I would say. You must be admired for that at least. It is a good thing you didn't have your swords on show – I think you would have lost any argument they may have prompted. So, I ask you, what brings you here? And why so determined that you should risk all for it?'

Ysgyrran looked at the others. They seemed to come to an agreement though nothing was said.

'Balthazar, you are not of our country; perhaps you will not care for our quarrels,' he began.

How to explain this?

'We were charged to take such news as we have to Penda of Mercia. But we just met another – friend – and we find that much has happened since we left Rhun in Lleyn and that errand is no longer needed. Now we are charged with a new task – it seems Edwin of Northumbria is come east and is in camp somewhere north of here. We need to find it and learn of his current strengths and situation and then find a safe road east – urgently.'

Balthazar stopped suddenly, causing them to stumble together around him.

'Edwin?' he said. 'Well as to that, his camp lies no more than a day from here. That is where I am going myself.'

That clinches it, Ysgyrran thought, *Dyfnwal must have known*. Subtle as snakes, these *Derwydd*. But he said, 'That is a bold thing – will you not be in danger?'

'Listen, boy – Ængel, Saxon, Briton – they are all one to me. I have my living to make, what do I care who gives it to me? Kings make good trade and I have nothing against your Edwin – he is no enemy of mine, nor I of his. Besides, the Ænglisc pay in coin.'

Ysgyrran looked thunderstruck. And then he wished he had said nothing. Better not to have placed any trust in this man. Who knew what peril he had brought upon them?

'Of course, you are right – I'm sorry.'

'No, no, be comforted. There is no need to be sorry. Look – to take sides is bad for business, but I understand how it is.' He sighed. 'And I do have my preferences. I will take you to where you may have a good look at this enemy of yours and then find you a good road east. If you must.'

Ysgyrran made no reply. They walked on in silence for a while.

'What d'you mean – if we must?'

'Well. . .' said Balthazar slowly, 'it is not my business to tell you yours, but it occurs to me that if you want to find out what Edwin is doing, you will need to do more than just look in from a distance. You will need to get in.'

'You mean go into Edwin's camp? What – as spies?'

'Spies!' squeaked Tecwyn. 'Great – we can find out what Edwin's up to and then find Rhun and tell him.'

'*Duw*, Tecwyn, will you ever shut up? You make it sound easy.'

'Well, it would be – not easy, great, I mean.'

'Tecwyn's right – much better if we can tell Penda what

Edwin plans to do next – and Rhun, if he is really well again,' said Eryl gently.

Balthazar gave them a long look, enigmatic as ever. At last he said, 'We are going to have to come up with a good story – how am I going to explain a gang of boys in my company? It is one thing to present you as some sort of guard to the simpletons back there in the hills, but Edwin and his people will be another matter.'

'We were almost mistaken for slaves once – you remember. Could we not play that game again?'

'Slaves – you want me to sell you?' He sounded quite shocked. 'How will that help?'

'*Na*, not sell us – could we not be slaves of your own?'

'Why would I need five slaves?'

'Well, perhaps some of us could be yours and the others, I don't know – stock?'

'And what if Edwin or one of his theigns wants to buy you?'

'Oh – I don't know – couldn't we be promised for some lord somewhere else?'

'Well I suppose so – some Frankish lord perhaps, they might believe that. But you do realise this would be a huge risk.'

'It was your idea!'

'Ha! And so it was. Well, yes – but look, you say you have been prisoners of this man – what if you are recognized?'

Ysgyrran thought about this. Not many of his decisions had been good ones so far; what if this was another bad one? Perhaps the worst. He might be condemning them all to death. If they were recognized, Edwin would not treat them as honoured guests: that was for certain. But it seemed unlikely – they had never actually been under guard as such, merely kept within the compound. The chance was worth it, he was sure.

'It's true we were prisoners but no one took much notice of us. I reckon we'd be safe enough. Besides no one ever looks at slaves.'

Balthazar pondered this in turn. *That is true*, he thought.

Slaves are nigh on invisible. He looked Ysgyrran in the eye. 'Right, you and your Ænglisc friend here can be my slave minders, and we'll chain the rest up. I hope neither of us will regret this.' Then he called, 'Qaseem – it seems we have slaves. Dig out those old slave irons. Get some suitable clothes for these two, but best leave the others in their own rags. And hide those swords.'

They came down out of the hills following the river downstream until it joined with a smaller stream meandering in from the west, where they found a ford and an easy crossing. High up on the hilltop to their left, and behind them now, they had passed under the shadow of a great stronghold. But nothing had emerged, no one had challenged their passing and they were now in a wide, flat-bottomed valley where the river wound in complicated curves through lush green meadows dotted with alder and willow, the road following its western bank as close as the meanders would allow. The hills were lower to the east but, though it was not so late in the day, the sun had already dipped below the high hills to the west when they came at last to Edwin's camp. They made a strange sight, Balthazar striding ahead in all his colourful finery, behind him a short line of ragged slaves driven by a couple of small drab figures folded into dark cloaks, and, bringing up the rear, the three pack-horses led, as usual, by Qaseem. The road ran along an old causeway, steep-sided above the flood plain. As they approached, armed men stepped out to bar their way.

'Stay!'

'Hail, friends,' called Balthazar, 'have you no welcome for an honest trader? I have all manner of wares to entice your king.'

He spoke in Ænglisc, though with such a thick accent that the boys barely understood him. And it took the leader of the guard a moment to work out what he had said.

He looked Balthazar up and down, inspecting him closely. He walked slowly down the line. He examined the horses and their packs. Finally he turned. As he passed, his hand shot out and grabbed Tecwyn by the neck, forcing him to look up.

'You deal in very small slaves, old man,' he said.

'But of course – special slaves for special customers.'

The man turned Tecwyn's face this way and that. 'What price for this one?' he asked casually.

'Alas, my lord, he and his companions are all promised to a customer in Gaul,' he gave a broad smile and winked, 'you know how those Franks like a boy.'

'Not just the Franks,' said the guard and looked about to argue. But then he shrugged and let go.

'You mangle our tongue old man, but you are not unwelcome. Ælfwulf – take these people to the king's lodgings, but see you set a good guard on them 'til we know them better.' As he waved them by, he paid not the least attention to any of the other boys.

They were in.

Tecwyn's heart was still beating so loudly he nearly missed the muttered remark from Balthazar as they moved on: 'Old man – who's he calling old...?'

The place was teeming. The encampment seemed to fill the whole valley this side of the river, hugging its banks, following its complex twists and turns. Set apart within an ancient earthwork stood an enormous tent, heavily guarded, surrounded by several smaller tents. The place stood in the knee of an ancient loop of the river. The main course had long ago abandoned this backwater, but it was still full of water which left Edwin's sanctum moated and accessible only across the narrow neck at each end.

'You will stay here,' said Ælfwulf. 'The king will send for you when he is ready.'

Under the alert gaze of a couple of heavily armed men, they settled the horses and unpacked. They had lost the sun, but there were still several hours left of daylight. Loth to miss the chance of a sale, Balthazar and Qaseem set out their wares as was their custom and waited.

'Tend to the animals and keep the others out of sight,'

he said, 'We don't want any one else looking for a bargain of that sort.'

Ysgyrran and Ithwalh busied themselves with the animals. They provided the perfect excuse to move about even if under strict guard. As soon as they had unpacked, they took the animals down to the river to drink and let them crop the rich riverside turf. They were careful not to draw attention to themselves, to blend in – just be parts of Balthazar's equipment like the packs and the saddles. Not nearly as interesting as the merchandise.

And they took it all in, eager to gather as much information as they could.

By the end of the second day they had become familiar figures. Not for who they were but for what they did. As well as the trips to the river with the horses, Balthazar had gone about the camp delivering items here and there, and had used the boys as carriers. The fear of recognition was always with them, but it was as Ysgyrran had said – no one who saw them thought of them as people, more as pack animals themselves. Now, after many such trips, they understood the defences, they had a fairly clear idea of numbers, and even roughly who was where. Enough to be of good use to an attacker, but they could learn nothing more. It was maddening. It was one thing to know the size and character of the force gathered here, but they could get no idea at all of what was planned. Edwin himself was not here. It seemed he was away, but they heard no word of where or why. But they could not believe that Edwin would sit here and do nothing, such an idea was far from anything they knew about the man. Rumour was everywhere, there were plenty of men coming and going, people arrived daily and Balthazar did brisk trade, but no hint was dropped of what was planned. Nor when.

As each day passed they feared they would be too late, that Edwin would move, or make a sudden attack; that their plan would fail and all their efforts would be wasted. It was particularly bad for those kept hidden away in the tent. Their frustration began to rub off on the others and they were all growing snappy and on edge. It was not until the evening of the third day that the summons came. Ælfwulf arrived as they were packing away the stall.

'Gather your choicest offerings – the king will see you now.'

Balthazar sprang to his feet. 'At last! He's back! Come, Qaseem, help me here.' He vanished into the tent and when they followed, they found him rummaging amongst the several bundles as yet unopened. 'I set these aside specially. They should please a royal eye.' Then he turned to the boys. 'You lot stay here. Yes, all of you – it's no good complaining, it was your plan.' He paused. 'No! Ithwalh – you come with me. You can help Qaseem carry this stuff, and keep your ears open – I still have trouble understanding these northern Ænglisc, you may hear things I miss. And for all our sakes, try to act like a slave. Whatever you do, don't draw attention to yourself, or let on you're Ænglisc yourself – is that clear?'

'Of course – I'm not stupid!'

Balthazar paused and looked at him. 'Let us hope not,' he said, tartly. 'The rest of you finish packing the stall away for the night. Stand guard but be prepared – we may have to move without warning.' He looked at their anxious faces. 'We will learn what we can, have no fear. It is good that we have been called for at this time – they will be sitting over their meat and should be all the more relaxed. With any luck they will all have drunk enough to loosen their purse-strings.'

It was late into the night when they returned. The boys were waiting: it had been impossible to sleep until they knew what had happened.

Balthazar bustled in cheerfully. 'Well, that was a strangely pleasant evening – and useful. Your enemy seems a decent, open-handed man.' He held up a bag which chinked with the sound of coins as he shook it. 'Generous, I would say. Not at all how you described him – I saw no sign that he is cruel or arbitrary.'

'Oh, he's good at that. But you have not been his prisoner for half a year.'

'True, true. Well, anyway, you'll be pleased to know that I have learned something which may be useful to you. It seems there is a strong place no more than an hour or so's march south of here. It is understood that Penda is there with Cadwallon of Gwynedd, and the two of them are gathering an army. What will interest you is that it seems Cadwallon's arrival has come as a surprise and it may have thrown out Edwin's immediate plans. Whatever is the truth of that, it appears that the place is too strong to take on so, for the time being at least, Edwin has resolved to stay here until Penda grows impatient. It appears that he hopes to tempt him out so he can fight him on his own terms. He is of the opinion that this will give him the advantage. I am not a warrior, I do not know if this might be true.' He waved his hand dismissively and gave a sort of shrug. 'But I may have missed something – Ithwalh, my friend, did you learn more?'

'Not much, but you're right – Edwin was not expecting Cadwallon. I heard a lot of talk about that. It seems Cadwallon travels faster than Edwin's spies – he had no more idea than we did that the king was back from Erin, and he certainly wasn't expecting as big an army as Penda and Cadwallon have between them.'

'He would be thinking Penda was his only problem, I expect,' said Eryl.

The others looked at him. 'What do you mean?' asked Ysgyrran.

'It's what Rhun told me – most of the other Ænglisc kings are on Edwin's side – and some of Penda's own people.'

'When did he tell you that?'

'I asked him when we left home. That's why Penda sent us – he didn't dare leave Mercia until he'd made sure of his own crown or, at least, found out which way the wind was blowing. But Rhun made me swear not to mention it – and then, well, I forgot all about it.'

Ysgyrran stared hard at him. He made as if to say something, but seemed to change his mind.

The next morning they expected to see a change in the

camp. Yet there was nothing to show that Edwin's return had made any difference. If they had hoped that it would, they were disappointed. There was nothing for it but to carry on as normal.

They had learned as much as they could about the forces assembled here, their size and likely capability, and they knew something at least of Edwin's plans. Now they needed urgently to get away. The knowledge would be useless if only they knew it. But as the day grew old, it began to dawn on them that they were as good as trapped, stuck here in Edwin's camp.

'Balthazar, I'm worried,' said Ysgyrran.

'I should think you might be – but, tell me?'

'It's this slavery business – it was such a good idea but we didn't think it through. Now we're stuck here 'til you go.'

'Why so?'

'Well, it wouldn't do for Edwin's people to spot that you had suddenly lost your slaves, even if we could get away unseen. Specially as they know we aren't for sale.'

'Ah yes, that might indeed prove a problem. But there is time, I think. The news of Cadwallon's arrival seems to have thrown them a bit, but nothing was said this evening to make me think anything is going to happen at once. Maybe the opposite.'

'That may be so, but we still have to go now – even another day may be too late.'

'Would you have me leave such a profitable place? That would be much to ask. I had not meant to be moving on for a while yet.'

They owed much to Balthazar, not the least for the clothes they all stood in. How could they ask him to leave now? And even if they could find a way to slip out of the camp unseen, what might these Northumbrians do when they saw Balthazar no longer had his slaves about him? It was true that no one took any direct notice of them, but that did not mean their presence had not been noted.

He cursed inwardly – why did everything have to be so complicated?

'That's what's worrying me. If you won't be leaving, we need to find a way out that won't bring suspicion on you.'

But then the decision was taken out of their hands.

Chapter 17

The days had passed in a blur. Cadwallon had left Lleyn within a few days of his arrival and marched east to the old Roman port at Cær n'Arfon, his numbers swelled now by several hundred of Elaeth's own people.

No one had resisted their advance: it was as if Edwin's forces had melted away with the last of the snow from the mountain tops. But the march through that devastated country had been grim. Everywhere they had passed burned-out ruins littered with corpses half-eaten and stinking. They had buried such as they could and burned the rest in great pyres.

But many people had come out of the hills, down from the remote places where they had been in refuge, and joined them on the march, and they now numbered thousands.

When they reached Cær n'Arfon, Cadwallon set up camp in the ruins of the old Roman fort set back on a hill overlooking the harbour, where the fleet of ships from Erin jostled to get close enough to the wharf to discharge their loads. The old Roman wharfs were crowded with people and goods. Few of the buildings were still good enough to use, so men simply sat where they had been landed, surrounded by their weapons and gear.

Rhun went amongst them as soon as he could get away from the fort, searching for those who had followed his father. Of all the men of Lenteurde who had gone to the war, only Afaon had been with Cadwallon's advance party. Rhun found the others gathered in a group. Now came the test. They saw Afaon first, greeting him as a comrade. Most saw the boy with him, none knew him.

'What news?'

Afaon turned to Rhun. 'Here is one who would speak

with you,' he said, and as he did so he laid his hand upon Rhun's shoulder, as if offering him for approval.

Rhun stood in silence.

Twenty men had set out from Lenteurde with his father. Fifteen men returned. Three had fallen at Trwyn Du alongside Rhun's father, two more had died of their wounds on the flight to Erin. But here were fifteen men glad to be back, still angry at their losses and keen to get back at Edwin in any way they could. Cadwallon had given Rhun renewed hope and purpose. Afaon had done much to reinforce that, but now he felt exposed and vulnerable. Could he really hope for acceptance by these men?

He stood before them and strove to appear confident at least. 'I am Rhun ap Cwyfan,' he said simply.

Immediately a hubbub broke out. Suddenly they knew him – or most of them at least. *Cwyfan's boy! Is it you? Of course it is! Do you not know him? But you have grown so – changed – you were but a child when we left. How is it you are here?* And so on, yet, when even those from the outlying farms who had not known Rhun well, at last understood that here was their dead chieftain's son, that one truth remained unspoken: no one seemed keen to say that one big thing.

And then they did not have to.

'My father is dead. I know this – Cadwallon has told me. Though I think I already knew it in my heart.'

There was a murmuring of acknowledgement and no little relief.

He looked around. 'I see that Ysgyrran and Llif and Eryl have lost their fathers too,' he said quietly. 'It is another thing to hold against Edwin.'

There was a long silence when no one spoke, as if to do so would disturb something best left alone. Rhun stood unmoving. He looked at each one, holding each gaze for a moment.

'Cadwallon has charged me to travel south about the mountains to find more people and meet with Penda of Mercia. Will you go with me?'

This was it. This was the moment at which Cadwallon

would be proven right or wrong. No matter how much respect Cwyfan had earned from these men, just being his son was no recommendation in itself. To the depths of Annwm is it? Why would these battle-hardened men follow him anywhere?

But he had not considered himself. How could he? And chance sometimes favours the moment: as the sun dipped below the horizon he was lit up in its last golden rays, and he seemed to shine, his hair aglow as a cloud of gold itself, and in that moment any doubts were blown away. A cheer broke out and was taken up by all and they crowded round him; they had come from Erin with a sense of doom, knowing that they must try but with little hope of success; now here was inspiration, a bright, fresh thing that could to turn that hope to glory.

They set out at dawn the following morning and headed south for the pass below Yr Wyddfa. The journey was in stark contrast to when Rhun had taken this same road the year before. Then he had been finding his way, with a bunch of half-terrified boys. Now he was returning at the king's command, leading a small army. No room now for fears of monsters and watchers from the shadows. The rumour of his coming flew before him and people came out to join him, emerging from the high valleys as if even the mists themselves had taken human form to help in the fight against the Northumbrian invader.

By the time they reached the Hafren crossing they numbered some two hundred. Two hundred take time to cross a river and Rhun grabbed the chance to seek out Teifion, who barely recognized him.

'You are much changed, my lord,' he said.

'I am not your lord,' said Rhun, gently, echoing the words of Penda all those eons ago. 'But, tell me, Ysgyrran, Llif – the others, I heard rumour of them a few days ago, so I believe they still live – have you seen them?'

'I have, my lord, they came through not long since. I had to send them north about for fear of capture, but they were in good spirits when they left me and hoped to be home within a couple of days.'

Rhun had had a dark moment then. Home – was it still there? Had Edwin really been lying? Well, he could not go to find out – now was not the time for personal worries, no matter how urgent. He had said nothing so far to any save Meical; he would say nothing now. But he was glad that Meical was by his side – Meical, grown so close now there was scarce need for words at all.

From there they followed the old road down the river, east and north towards Pengwern. This was country they might have feared to cross at any other time, but now with an army at his back Rhun half hoped he might meet with his old adversaries. But the land seemed deserted. Not the desolation he had seen in Lleyn, but as if everyone had gone or was hiding. Well they might, he thought grimly.

The road took them to an old legionary camp. There they were met by a small force bearing tokens of peace and were taken across the river northward into the hills. They passed strings of heavily laden pack-horses all heading in the same direction, and at last they had come to a vast strong place, and laboured up the steep slope to where it crowned the hill, dark against the horizon. Ring after ring of ditch and bank, each defended by newly erected palisades and the whole crowned with a huge open space, filled with tents and wagons and people. Cadwallon had chosen well. At the first gate they were greeted with cheers and cries as they made their way through a sea of camp followers crowding the outer defences. Small children ran alongside them shouting in their enthusiasm, dogs barking at their sides.

At this place were gathered all the fighting men who had rallied to Cadwallon's call. Penda of Mercia was greatest among them, perhaps, but here was also Elisedd from Pengwern, Elaeth out of Lleyn, their own king Merewalh and many other lesser leaders. The land around was bare of trees and Rhun could see clearly a host of men and arms gathered on the surrounding slopes.

As he entered the inner defences he was stopped by a shout.

'Rhun, my lord Rhun!'

'Gethin!'

They stood, staring at each other as though they had been strangers. Then they fell into each others arms.

'Gethin, man, how good it is to see you. But how is it you are here?'

Gethin did not answer at once. He stood looking Rhun up and down.

'It's your hair, of course,' he said at last.

'What d'you mean, my hair – what about my hair?'

'It's how I recognized you, my lord – you have changed much since last we met.'

'Is it so much?'

'You left me a boy. Now I find a man. *Duw*, you are taller even – I'd swear it.' He paused, and his voice went quiet. 'And there is that in your eyes which speaks of evil times.'

Rhun said nothing for a moment. A pain seemed to pass across his eyes. 'It is true, I have been in dark places,' and he rallied, 'but Gethin, that is no longer important. Tell me – how did you leave my mother, our people? Are they well?'

'They were fine when I left them. Did you expect otherwise? You mother is well – she is too strong to show her fears, but she has been much in the company of Peleg's mother – I think she finds comfort there.'

So, Edwin had indeed been lying. He ran that bitter thought across his memory. *Now I have the full measure of the man*, he thought. *As if I needed more*. Still, the relief was great.

'*Na, na*, it is of no consequence. So, how are you here – and where are you all camped?'

'We are not many, my lord: we joined Guthlac and came with king Merewalh. We're camped up at the northern rampart.'

'Did Ysgyrran reach you?'

'*Na*, I have not seen him – is he not with you?'

Rhun stiffened. He raised his head and looked out

over the surrounding hills as if they might suddenly reveal Ysgyrran and the others and return them to him. *Please God – let nothing bad have happened.* But he rallied – no need to worry Gethin. Not yet, at any rate.

'It's a long story. I'm sorry – look, he left us to seek Penda and perhaps to get home. If he didn't reach Lenteurde perhaps he went straight into Mercia.'

'Probably did – we've not seen him. But I have not seen him with Penda either.'

Rhun looked blank for a moment. *Na*, he thought, still best not to worry Gethin – nothing he could do but guess and there was no fruit in that. And nothing now was more important than finding Penda.

'I'm sure that'll be it. Look, can you guide my people to your camp? I will join you as soon as I can. I doubt we'll be allowed much rest.'

'For sure – it's this way. We pass the king's tent.'

Gethin fell in beside Rhun. As they walked he looked over his former charge. The difference was startling. Gone was the impetuous boy, gone was the conflict of self-doubt and reckless over-confidence. Now he saw balance and certainty and self-awareness in their place. But his shrewd eye also saw the worry.

At the place where the leaders were meeting they parted. The guard recognized him and made to announce his arrival, but Rhun brushed past him and walked in unbidden. He did not do it with any intent except to hurry, but he could not have made a more dramatic entry if he had tried.

Silhouetted against the sky outside he stood simply as the black shape of a man. The meeting went silent as those gathered turned to see who had interrupted their talk. It was Penda who recognized him first. He leapt to his feet, his chair falling with a crash, and he gathered Rhun into his arms. Then he held him out at arm's length as if to inspect him. 'Gods, man, where have you been? I've been hearing terrible things about you.'

Rhun grinned widely. 'It has been interesting,' he said. 'But I'm back now.'

'You were gone so long, I was sure I must have sent you to your death.'

'*Na*, not that. But still,' his face fell into a frown, 'I failed you and I am sorry for it.'

'Failed? Never think it – I sent you for news of my lord Cadwallon and instead you send me the man himself! I don't call that failure. Together we have an army that can truly face Edwin.'

'So, you are king then?'

'I am.'

'Then you are my lord now, I suppose.'

Penda barked a short laugh. 'I think Merewalh might have something to say about that! In any case, I would prefer to keep you as my friend. But come, we can talk later.'

He ushered Rhun to the table, rescuing his own chair and pulling up another. Rhun sat, acutely aware that everyone was looking at him.

Cadwallon, with typical dignity, had waited until they were settled. And when he spoke he revealed nothing of his inner thoughts.

'Welcome Rhun ap Cwyfan, you were successful on your travels?'

'My lord Cadwallon,' Rhun said simply, 'they are but two hundred; I had hoped for more.'

'But two hundred! That is greater than I expected, and I thank you indeed for them.'

Later, when the meeting closed, Penda wouldn't hear of Rhun's joining his men just yet. He insisted Rhun accompany him to his own tent. 'You'll be needing food and drink, and I'm needing to hear a story.'

They had walked together to where Penda was camped among his people. Too many for the strong place to hold, they were spread out along the slope below the western ramparts. Now they sat with wine beside a small brazier wherein burned a few logs giving off the pleasant smell of apple and cherry, keeping the chill of evening at bay.

'So – tell me all. I have heard nought but rumours and

few of them good. You have been a guest of Edwin's, I am told.'

Rhun held up a hand.

'Penda – tell me something first, I beg you. Have you seen any of my companions?'

Penda looked puzzled.

'No, should I have?'

Rhun's heart fell.

'Ysgyrran left us to seek you. All but four went with him. He wanted to give you such news as we had – it is a long story – did he not find you?'

'Not yet. How long ago did he leave you?'

'Half a moon – more by now. It seems he has failed you too. It seems the whole venture has been pointless.'

'I told you – you have not failed me. And I will not believe that he has until I have proof. Nor should you. Anything might have happened to him, and no reason to suppose it bad. And as for the venture being pointless – it is easy to be wise in hindsight; the plan was still good and the journey worth the undertaking. Who knows that Cadwallon would have hurried to our aid if you had not told him we stood in need of it?'

Rhun took some courage from Penda's words, but he only half believed in them. He sighed. 'Perhaps you are right. I hope so.' He took a pull from his cup. 'Edwin's guest, you say? I would not recommend his hospitality!'

It was late when Rhun returned to his own people. They had settled in and most were already asleep. He was about to turn in himself when a shout came up from the foot of the hill below him. It was too far to make out any words but a challenge had been issued and it seemed someone had answered.

For a while nothing more happened but then a torch was lit and a knot of men could be seen climbing the hill towards him. 'Where is Rhun ap Cwyfan?'

'Here!'

'Then here is one who claims to know you,' said the man

in the lead, and he thrust a ragged figure forwards. The figure fell headlong onto the ground.

Rhun stood as if stunned. 'Eryl! How? Where did you come from? Quick – bring food and wine.' He stooped and gathered up Eryl's limp figure. 'Are you hurt?'

Eryl drew breath and stood unsteadily.

'*Na* – I look a lot worse than I am – but Rhun, man, it is good to see you. We heard that you were come but…' He trailed off, unsure of what to say.

'Rest easy,' said Rhun, 'I'm sure I would have thought the same.'

Meical appeared and kicked the watch-fire into life. Together they sat Eryl by the flames and watched while he tore off great chunks of bread with his teeth. But even mouthfuls of bread and wine could not stop him trying to talk.

'Rhun, I come from Edwin's camp. I have news you must hear.'

Chapter 18

As evening fell on their fourth day in Edwin's camp, Ithwalh and Ysgyrran returned from the river leading the ponies home from their evening drink. It was late in the day but a crowd of men were gathered around the stall. It seemed they were newly arrived in camp and Balthazar had wasted no time. He was holding up choice items for their inspection and in the full flow of his usual pitch.

Keeping their backs turned, hoods pulled low over their faces, the boys tethered the horses and set to settling them for the night, easing their gear and unfolding blankets. A small wind blew a scrap of wrapping from the stall, spooking one of the horses. It reared its head, pulling at its tether. As ill luck would have it Ysgyrran's hood fell back as he struggled to calm the beast, and while the light was not strong, it was quite enough to expose his face.

'You there! Hold!' One of the newcomers reached over and grabbed Ysgyrran's arm. 'I know you.'

Ysgyrran squirmed, trying to loosen the man's grip, but it was too strong.

'No you don't. Hold still! Yes – I thought so – you are one of those Wealas brats we held on Mona. How are you here?'

He grabbed in turn at Ithwalh, ripping the hood from his head and staring into his face. But it meant nothing to him. He let Ithwalh drop and turned his attention back to Ysgyrran.

He called over his shoulder. 'You there, merchant – where did you find this one?'

'What business do you have with my servant? Let him be!'

'Be easy, friend – I want to thank you. This lad was our

captive on Mona. The brat escaped – how kind of you to have brought him back to us!'

Balthazar could find nothing to say.

Inside the tent, Eryl stood by the entry gap, bobbing and straining to get a view.

'What's happening?'

'I don't know – there's some excitement outside.'

'What is it?'

'Ssh! Keep your voice down.'

He peered out cautiously.

'*Duw*! Someone has recognized Ysgyrran.'

The crowd was growing. Balthazar was clearly trying his best, but the Ænglisc warrior was having none of it. His voice became harder, losing its bantering tone.

'*Na, na.* Stand aside, pedlar. This promises some sport. Come, boy. Where did you go in such a hurry – and what did you do with the other two – are they here as well perhaps?'

He straightened up and looked around. He glanced again at Ithwalh. 'He is not one of them, but are there not others...?'

He stopped talking abruptly. He grunted and pitched forward amidst the fabrics and exotic objects arrayed on Balthazar's stall, bringing the whole lot crashing down about him.

An arrow stuck obscenely out of his back like a flag. A challenge. Ysgyrran stood still and stared, rooted to the spot. Suddenly it was followed by a cloud of others.

'Attack! Attack!'

There was instant chaos. At first the crowd, like Ysgyrran, had stood as if in a trance; now they scattered for cover leaving several dead lying among the wreck of Balthazar's stall.

Eryl did not waste a second. 'Quick,' he hissed. 'Follow me.' He bundled his sword into his cloak and wriggled his way out under the tent wall. Once clear, he fled into the gathering darkness. He could hear the commotion behind him but in front all seemed calm. Keeping to the river, he scrambled along the bank, keeping below the crest until he had put a hundred paces or so behind him. A clump of scrubby alders grew down to the river and he slid in among their roots and lay catching his breath. He looked back. No one was behind him. The others had not followed. He was alone.

From his hiding place he could see much of what was happening. There was still enough light to see a line of archers on the far side of the river, pouring a steady stream of arrows into Edwin's camp. By contrast, the camp was in uproar. Men ran here and there, shouting and trying to rally some form of resistance. The river was too strong to cross easily, so the best they could do was return fire and hope to drive off their attackers. But by the time they had formed a line of their own their opponents had vanished.

Eryl did not move. He lay as still as he could and watched. Within moments the cry went up again, a little further away. And then again, and again, each time from somewhere slightly different, dodging back and forth, never giving the defenders time to rally.

Some subtle mind has planned this, he thought. A series of stinging attacks, but no major confrontation? The Ænglisc had thought themselves protected by the river. They were wrong, but still it seemed that the force against them was not large enough for a full attack.

Eryl was puzzled. Who were these people? Was this the start of some bigger plan? By Penda, perhaps, or Cadwallon? Or was it pure chance – a local warlord fighting his own ground? If the latter was true it would achieve little without support. Then Eryl saw it in a flash. If Penda was to attack now, he would have a huge advantage. And if this was not him, nor Cadwallon, then they needed to know that it was happening. If Balthazar's report was true, he should be able to find them simply by heading south for an hour or so. Their strong place hadn't sounded like something you could easily miss, even in the dark. And sky was clear and filled with stars.

At once he was on his feet. He dodged along the line of the river until it was turned east by the line of a hill, then he took to the shadows and headed into the night as fast as he could run.

Things had gone less well for Ysgyrran. When his captor had fallen, another, a stranger this time, had grabbed him and hurried him out of reach of the attack. Balthazar and the others scarcely noticed – they were fully occupied with saving their goods from being looted or trampled into ruin.

Ysgyrran was bundled into a neighbouring tent and secured.

'This one seems to be an escaped captive. Make sure he doesn't get away again. My lord Edwin will want to talk to him.' Left with but one guard, Ysgyrran he lay in a bundle of fury desperately straining at his bonds, but all that did was to make them tighter.

'Do not trouble yourself, boy,' said his guard. 'You will achieve nothing.'

Balthazar spent no time thinking. He rolled the dead man off his goods and called for Ithwalh, 'Quickly! Get the horses!' And he and Qaseem tore open the front of the tent and managed to get themselves under cover, standing aside as Ithwalh led in the horses, prancing and trembling in fright. The tent did not offer much by way of shelter, but the heavy fabric would stop an arrow from across the width of the river. Frantically, Qaseem and Ithwalh set about gathering up the goods from outside and packing them into their bundles. The others ran to help, relieved to be doing something at last after so many days cooped up and to have something positive to do amidst this chaos.

It seemed to take forever, as they fought to keep the stock safe. But at last it was done. Exhausted, they huddled in their flimsy refuge amidst the bales and bundles.

'We must rescue Ysgyrran,' said Llif.

'Not you – we don't want you caught as well.'

'But that man's dead. I'll be safe enough.'

Ithwalh had been looking around. 'Where's Eryl!'

'He's gone,' said Tecwyn.

'What d'you mean he's gone?'

'He got out in the first confusion. He slipped out the back of the tent and legged it across the field. He shouted for us to come but then you called us to help and it was too late. He'll be well away by now if he's not dead. It was ages ago.'

'Maybe we can all get away now.'

'Not before we rescue Ysgyrran.'

'And not I,' said Balthazar, 'I am far too old for running about, besides, I am safe enough here if I keep my head down, and I am not leaving all this behind! But this is your chance! You go – no one is going to ask me what happened to my slaves after all this excitement. I shall simply tell them the truth – you ran away,' and he beamed his huge smile.

'I'm not going anywhere without Ysgyrran,' said Llif, 'so – what're we going to do?'

Balthazar looked at Ithwalh in some amusement. 'You're in charge now, I suppose. What will you do?'

Ithwalh thought for a moment. He looked out. The fighting had moved on. No one had yet had time to think about the dead. Two were lying almost within arm's reach.

'Get the gear off one of those dead men.'

'But why?'

'Camouflage,' said Ithwalh. 'If I look like one of them I might be able to get Ysgyrran out of there. I'll say Edwin sent me or something. With luck no one will question it.'

'Shouldn't we all go?'

'*Na*, it'll be better if I'm alone – less chance of being seen.'

Quickly they stripped the war gear off the nearest warrior. It fitted Ithwalh well enough if no one looked too closely. They peered out. The place was still in uproar; the whole camp by now. Men were running to and fro following order and counter-order, unsure from where the next attack might come. Here, in Edwin's inner sanctum, it was marginally quieter. Arrows still fell among them, and the people still milled about in uncertainty, but the centre of activity seemed to have shifted, at least for now.

Balthazar stood in the open entrance to the tent.

'Go – quickly, while they are distracted.'

Brandishing his borrowed sword, Ithwalh ran out into

the melée. Edwin's tent was unguarded so it seemed likely he was not within, but Ysgyrran's prison was perilously close by. Ithwalh stopped outside. No one had paid him the slightest attention so far. Muttering prayers to all the gods he could think of, he dashed open the door flap.

'Quickly now,' he shouted in Ænglisc trying his best to sound like one of the northerners, 'where's the prisoner? He's wanted!'

By the light of the single torch he could just see a body bundled on the floor. To Ithwalh's surprise there was only one man guarding it. Without giving him a chance to react, he stooped over Ysgyrran, who lay face down as if dead, and shook him violently.

'Come on – quick. Stir yourself! You – give me a hand here!'

The man was on his feet. 'What's going on?'

Ithwalh stood up. 'We are attacked – the king wants to know by whom and he thinks this one may have the answer. He's in a foul mood – I wouldn't want to be the one to delay him. Quickly now, untie his legs.'

The guard was no longer a young man. He had seen many years in the king's service and knew the shortness of his temper as well as anyone. He did as he was bid and knelt to loosen the bonds which tied Ysgyrran's feet. As he did so Ithwalh brought the pommel of his sword smartly down on the back of his head. The old warrior collapsed.

'Come on, Ysgyrran – wake up!'

'Ithwalh – is that you?'

'It is – now come on – we've got to get out of here. And we've got to be long gone before they miss you.'

Sword drawn, and holding Ysgyrran's arm up behind his back, Ithwalh marched him back to Balthazar's tent and ducked inside.

'Well done!'

'Now what?'

Ithwalh's mind was clear at least. 'We have to go,' he said, 'we must follow Eryl, wherever he has gone. Where's my bow? I've laid it aside for too long.'

'He's right,' said Ysgyrran. 'Untie me, quick, and let's get out of here.' He stood and looked over to Balthazar. 'My friend, thank you for all you have done for us, but we must go.'

'So go!' said Balthazar, 'go now while you can. Let us hope to see you again in better times, but go now.'

With the coming of darkness a mist had risen, curling up from the river. Now it sent long tendrils in amongst the tents, and they slipped out, sliding through the shadows. They had got as far as the ox-bow when a shout went up.

'Quick – into the water,' Ysgyrran hissed.

They slid down the bank and landed with their feet in the water. Perhaps in summer the ditch was dry, but now it was knee-deep in stagnant ooze, old and foul, the remains of a winter's rain and snow melt. The mist and the dark closed over them. They heard the sound of men running above their heads. They held their breath, hearts beating hard, waiting for the shout which meant they had been seen, expecting to be discovered at any moment. Yet they could see nothing themselves through the murk and perhaps they were as invisible. At last all sound of movement stopped. They could hear distant shouting but nothing now close at hand.

Ysgyrran decided to risk it before they all froze. 'Keep quiet and get over to the other bank,' he whispered. 'There – where the shadows are deepest. Under those bushes, look. If we can get up without being seen, we should be able to make it to the woods.'

They reached the top and no reaction. No cry came. All was quiet this side of the water. Keeping low, they loped the last few paces to the edge of the wood and vanished into its shadow. They crept up through the trees until the hill levelled out, and stopped. Looking back they could make out movement among the small fires, and still hear shouting and sounds of alarm, but they could see little clearly and nothing that told them what was happening.

Ysgyrran shrugged. 'Too late to help Balthazar now

– come on – we can't stop here. Our news is probably useless by now, but we have to try.'

'What about Eryl?'

'Damn Eryl! If he must dash off!' He paused. '*Na*,' he said, 'he was right. Knowing him he's gone south to find Penda on his own, and I suppose we'd better follow. Still – keep your eyes open.' They pushed on over the low rise and found themselves among a confusion of dilapidated buildings. Once they had been byres and barns and even houses, all built rectangular in the Roman style, but they were ruins now and deserted. Dawn was not far off, and they were above the river mist and the night was bright with stars. They looked about them. What had this place been? More than a farm, it seemed: it was clear that the ruins carried on along the hillside as far as they could see in the dim light. It must have been a big place once. All ruined now, sad and empty, yet it held no sense of menace. No ghosts walked here.

Ysgyrran tested the wind with a finger. It was light, scarcely a wind at all but it was enough! Drifting up from the south east – blowing directly towards the camp. Beckoning to the others, he made his way into the nearest abandoned building. There was still a good deal of the roof left, covering what had been a stock barn or something similar. Under its cover, a lot of old stuff still lay around, the remains of food and bedding for beasts long gone now.

'Keep quiet and keep an eye out – I've got an idea,' he said, his voice scarcely audible.

'What?' hissed Llif.

'I'm going to set this lot on fire. That should cause a stir! You keep watch. Tecwyn – build me a load of dry stuff while I make a flame. With any luck it'll spread towards the camp – that'll keep them busy.'

Once they had pulled off the top layers, the straw and hay below were surprisingly dry. It took Ysgyrran a few moments to strike spark, but once he had, flame took well. They heaped more dry stuff onto the little flames, which grew quickly and started to catch the timbers themselves.

'Come on – before it gets too big. It's going up fast!

'Which way?'

'South – keep the fire between them and us. Look – just follow me and keep the noise down.'

They ran out. The fire was spreading quickly, leaping from timber to timber, even reaching into the lower branches of the trees, shrivelling the leaves and making them crackle in the heat. Soon the whole hillside might be ablaze. They didn't wait to see. They found themselves in a shallow valley. They dashed down the gentle slope ahead, across a ditch and scrambled up the other side to the next crest. At the top the wood ended. They ran out into clear ground and straight into a drawn sword.

Ysgyrran stumbled to a halt.

'Not so fast!' A rough voice barked, in their own tongue. 'Where d'you think you're going?' As he spoke the barn below exploded into a storm of fire and lit up the sky. 'Treacherous vermin! What have you done?'

Ysgyrran cursed himself for a fool. He should have expected outer pickets. But they were only two, and for the briefest moment he still had the advantage of surprise. At once he ploughed on. 'Get out of my way,' he roared, 'Ithwalh, Llif quick! Tecwyn –stay back!'

The others were right behind him. Swords drawn, they piled into the melée.

But the odds were against them. Their opponents were twice their size and heavily armed. The boys' wild charge was easily beaten off and then their attack was returned in earnest.

Ysgyrran took the brunt of it. He blocked the first man's stroke but it had been a huge blow and he staggered under the impact. The man swung his sword for a second attempt. As he did so, Llif came in from the side slashing viciously at the man's undefended shoulder and forcing the stroke wide. There was a screech of steel on steel. Llif's blade glanced off, tearing away the man's cloak, and Llif saw that he wore mail under it. Now the second guard had joined him and they were faced with two warriors armed and armoured and experienced in battle – they were no match for this. Within a split second the first man rallied: he beat down Ysgyrran's sword and with a vicious swing brought his own weapon round and smashed it into Ysgyrran's neck. With a great cry of rage Ysgyrran went down amid a spray of hot blood.

Tecwyn dashed in screaming. 'Get off him!' He lunged, trying to get under the man's guard, but he missed and was smashed to the ground by a mailed fist. The second man jumped in and stamped down on Tecwyn's arm, trampling his wrist and crushing it into the earth. Crouching astride their prone victims, they stood at bay glowering at Ithwalh and Llif.

'You little shits! What have you done? I'd kill you all now but you'll answer to the king for this.'

Then he felt the touch of steel on his neck and heard a quiet voice in his ear. 'Which king might that be?'

Chapter 19

Eryl's arrival had been like the first shifting pebble of a land-slide. Rhun hadn't wasted a moment with explanations, they could come later. He had roused Meical and together they had bundled Eryl up the hill and into the main camp.

'Meical, will you go and tell Penda? – It's that big tent over there. I'll take Eryl straight to Cadwallon – join us as soon as you can.'

Arriving at Cadwallon's tent, Rhun had spoken urgently to the guard, and had waited impatiently while their message was carried in. Cadwallon himself had come out clad in only his night attire. 'Come in, come in – tell me this tale. Bring light,' he had shouted and, glancing at Eryl, 'and wine and food!'

Eryl was settled on a chair and he had told his story in between bites of bread and gulps of wine. 'We were under attack – I took the chance and ran for it. My lord, if you could attack now yourself – at once – you couldn't choose a better moment.'

Penda and Meical had come in while Eryl was talking. 'He is right, my lord. We must go this moment,' said Penda.

'I would give much to know who else wishes to attack Edwin.'

'I think there may be many in these hills who do not love him. He is his own worst enemy, burning and destroying as he does. For sure he'd find few friends west of here,' said Rhun.

'*Ie*, it was the same in the northern mountains when we came through,' said Cadwallon.

Penda cut him short. 'My lord, we must not wait. We must go now.'

And go they had. Rhun had been astonished, and

impressed with the speed these men got things done. No sooner had the word gone out than it seemed all was ready and they were on their way. Well within two hours of Eryl's escape, the armies of Gwynedd and Mercia were on the march.

Rhun marched at the head of his own small force. Meical and Eryl at his side, followed by Einion and Cynrig. Behind them were Gethin with his people from Lenteurde, and all the men who had returned from Erin. Getting on for forty fighters in all.

As they walked, Eryl had given Rhun the whole story. 'So you see we didn't do very well, at least not until we met that *derwydd* and fell in with Balthazar again. Ysgyrran is worried for him – he got us into Edwin's camp and now he may be in danger himself.' He turned an anguished face to Rhun. 'Rhun – we have to make sure he gets out alive. And Qaseem.'

Rhun thought for a moment. 'You can remember the way you got out? Can we get back in that way?'

'I don't know – I remember the way all right, but who knows what may have happened since I escaped.'

As night drew towards its end, the order came to halt and with it a strict command of silence. The armies had arrived at the head of a long shallow valley. At its bottom, no more than half a mile away around the corner of a low ridge, lay the camp of Edwin of Northumberland. It was close but the faint sound of clamour could already be heard.

Keeping his voice low, Rhun whispered to Eryl. 'Well, let's go and look at your escape route, if we can find it. We'll take just our own people and see what can be done. If we can get in, so much the better. I'll square it with Penda – perhaps we can add to the confusion. You wait here, I'll be back in a moment.'

Rhun was true to his word. In no time he was back.

'Penda suggests we follow the line of this hill to the north. Does that square with your route?'

Eryl nodded. '*Ie*, that's fine.'

Rhun turned. 'Gethin, Afaon, when we get to the top of the ridge, will you all wait 'til I send word? We'll go ahead – too many of us might attract attention, but be ready – there may be need of haste.'

Neither man hesitated.

'Fear not, my lord, we will be ready.'

Within minutes, they had made it to the top of the hill. There they had left the bulk of their little force in reserve, and now, keeping below the skyline and taking advantage of such cover as they could find, the five of them made their way north along the low ridge. The sky was just beginning to show signs of dawn, but all was still dark on the ground.

'What's that light?'

'It looks like a fire.'

The light grew as they spoke.

'It is a fire – a big one. Come on.'

Towards the end of the ridge, the hill widened and became a bare patch of rough ground which ran to a denser line of trees set just below the brow. Against this dark line a sudden movement caught Rhun's eye. A little knot of figures, locked in furious combat, lit dimly by the light from the fire below. The fighters moved in an eerie silence, any noise they made was overwhelmed by the roar of flames and the screams of men and horses from the valley beyond.

Rhun held up a hand and the others gathered around him. Holding his finger to his lips he gestured to them to follow him.

They slipped through the shadows until they were close enough to hear the sounds of the fight itself. Then the fighting appeared to stop. Rhun heard a voice, 'You'll answer to the king for this.'

Two seemed to be taking a stand against another two half their size, frozen in the moment, as if in a tableau made for his entertainment. Suddenly he recognized the two smaller figures: Ithwalh, Llif! Facing two heavily armed strangers. He stepped forward silently and held the tip of his blade ready at the neck of the one who had spoken.

'Which king might that be?' he asked.

The tableau moved as one, turning at the sound of his voice.

'Rhun!'

'You!' cried the one with Rhun's sword at his neck. He stared wide-eyed as if he had seen a ghost, but they had recognized each other instantly. No, Rhun thought, he had been wrong – this man was no stranger. You don't fight one to one without remembering your opponent's face, and that night on Dinas Emrys stood out starkly in both their memories.

Bewildered, the man looked around, taking in the other, half remembered faces.

'How are you here!?'

He glanced at his companion, but they were surrounded and each with a naked blade at his throat.

'Drop your weapons and get on your knees.'

Fear and rage burned in equal measure in the man's eyes, but he did as he was told. His fingers opened and he and his sword dropped to the grass.

Then he saw Einion.

'You too, is it?' he spat, 'still a traitor to your own people.'

'These are my people, Cathan – besides, what can you teach me about loyalty?'

Rhun said, 'Tie their hands. Use their clothes if that's all you can find.'

With any movement inviting a cut throat, the sentries put up no more resistance. Einion ripped the man Morfryn's shirt off his back and tore it into ribbons. Then he used them to tie his captives' hands. But Cathan wouldn't stay quiet. He was down but he was unbowed.

'Is this how you treat your kin?'

Einion stopped. He sat back on his heels and looked at the man Carthan.

'You're no kin of mine – not any more. You've forfeited any right to plead with me.'

'But we rescued you. In honour of your father we chased you half across the country.'

'You did, and then you dishonoured me. God knows – I had little enough to start with. And my father the more so if you did it in his name.'

The man turned and glared at Rhun. 'And you – we should have killed you long ago,' he spat.

Rhun leaned on his sword. He looked at his old adversary in silence for a moment.

'You tried; if you remember – you ran away,' he said, the disdain clear in his voice. 'Now you will answer to Elisedd your king. He will want to know why a man of his people fights for the usurper Edwin. Not to mention why you took it upon yourself to prevent me reaching Cadwallon. Be glad you failed. Best gag him too,' he added as he turned away.

At last he could take stock. Ithwalh was crouched by a dark bundle lying awkwardly on the ground. The blood drained from Rhun's face. With a sudden sickness rising in his throat he knelt beside the prone figure.

'Ysgyrran, old friend,' he said, 'are you still with us?'

Gently, with Ithwalh's help, he slipped an arm under Ysgyrran's shoulder and turned his face towards his own. Ysgyrran stirred. With his voice barely audible he said, 'Rhun – is it you?'

They stared at each other for a beat.

Ysgyrran was amazed. *How can this be Rhun? I left him for dead, and now here he is, as if nothing had happened.* He had been so sure that Rhun was lost to them, that even if he recovered his wits he would be useless as a leader, irreparably damaged at least, and now, suddenly, he wasn't any of these things. Instead, Rhun was here rescuing them and taking charge without a moment's hesitation. A vision of the storm back in Lleyn swam into his mind: 'We must help them,' Rhun had said – even in that state his instinct had been to help those in need. His eyes wandered and found Meical standing at Rhun's shoulder – *As ever*, he thought. *He knew – I should have trusted him.*

He struggled to speak, but only managed a cough. A gout of blood gushed from his mouth and ran down his chin to soak into Rhun's sleeve. 'Rhun – gods, man! – where did you come from?' he said at last, his voice a harsh gurgling whisper.

And Rhun understood. 'Hush, don't talk,' he said, trying to keep the anguish out of his own voice.

'Rhun, I'm sorry – I've messed it all up,' Ysgyrran rasped, looking up at Rhun, trying to focus. 'I thought you were dead. Or as good as. But I messed it all up anyway.'

'Don't try to speak.' Rhun shifted his hold, trying to see the extent of Ysgyrran's wound, knowing in his heart that it was mortal yet clinging to a desperate hope. What he saw filled him with horror: a great gash across Ysgyrran's neck, pumping blood, slowly now, into the gathering pool in the grass. And all hope fled.

A voice came from behind them. 'Come on Tecwyn, wake up!' Llif was kneeling beside the other dark shape on the ground. He looked up. 'Rhun – I can't wake him.'

Ysgyrran let out a thin groan. 'Not him as well?' he murmured, 'please – not him as well.' He closed his eyes, as if he were trying to concentrate. 'Eryl, now Tecwyn...' he murmured. Then his eyes snapped open as if by one last effort of will, and he stared into Rhun's face. 'Forgive me?' he said. Then he let out a long sigh and his head fell to one side.

Rhun stared blankly at Ithwalh, unable to believe what had happened. Ysgyrran was dead. 'Forgive me,' he'd said. *Na*, it was he who should be seeking forgiveness. In this last moment he had failed him. His stomach seemed utterly void, as if the flesh of his belly clove directly to his spine.

He turned to look over his shoulder. There was Llif crouched over Tecwyn's inert figure.

'Is he dead too?' he said, almost wearily.

Llif leaned in. He licked his lips and held them close to Tecwyn's nose as if he might kiss him. After a moment, which seemed to last for ever, he sat back.

'Not dead, I can feel his breath, but he'll have a headache when he wakes up.'

Rhun turned back. He stared down at the figure in his arms. He was no stranger to death, but not Ysgyrran? Please God, not Ysgyrran. One moment he was fighting furiously and he is now dead? It seemed impossible, it was so quick.

Yet his hands were sticky with Ysgyrran's blood and he knew it for the truth no matter how hard it was to grasp.

At last Ithwalh stirred. 'He's gone,' he said.

Rhun seemed drawn into himself; sucked in as if without breath. Then 'Damn!' he cried. 'Damn! And there's no time!' He let loose a great sigh and laid Ysgyrran's head gently back to rest on the ground. He turned. 'Cynrig – get yourself back to our men. Tell them what's going on and ask them to join us. Soon as possible. Sooner. Go – run like the wind!'

He turned back to Ysgyrran's still figure. 'I'm sorry,' he said, 'we cannot look to you now. But we will be back – lie here 'til we come again; you deserve better than to be left to feed the crows.' He glanced up and caught Ithwalh's eye.

'Ithwalh, tell me – what did he mean – when he said "Eryl as well"?'

'Look, Rhun, we thought you were dead – as good as, anyway.'

Rhun didn't miss a beat. 'Well, and so I was – you did right, whatever has come of it.'

'Maybe, but we didn't do well – Ysgyrran didn't have the luck.'

'I know – Eryl has told us.'

'Eryl! He's with you?'

Eryl stepped into view. 'He is.'

Ithwalh's face cracked into a mad grin. 'Thank the gods, Ysgyrran was furious that you'd run out without a word. He was convinced you'd been caught and killed – I suppose he thought Tecwyn was dead too. If only he'd lived a moment longer.' He paused. 'Too late now.'

'So, what can you tell me that Eryl hasn't already?'

'I don't know – the attacks were still coming in from across the river when we got away. Eryl had only been gone an hour or so. We set fire to some old buildings below – cover our escape – cause more confusion, we thought. Then we ran into those two. I thought that was it – I can't tell you how glad I was to see you!'

Meical touched Rhun lightly on the shoulder. 'The others are here,' he said quietly. He had found himself confounded.

He had almost hated Ysgyrran and the others for abandoning Rhun and leaving them in Lleyn, but now he was at a loss. In his mind he had made Ysgyrran into some sort of monster, and now he was dead and it was too late to mend anything. And now Ithwalh looked up and caught his eye and grinned, though a little sheepishly.

'I'm sorry, Meical. You were right, it seems.' He held out his hand. 'Help me?' Meical grabbed the hand, and hauled him to his feet.

'And I was wrong as well – I had thought the worst of you – but now…' he tailed off.

'*Na*,' said Ithwalh, 'I understand.' Perhaps the only one who had.

Suddenly a shout went up, 'Stop him! Quick – he's getting away!'

Rhun spun round. The man Cathan had broken free and was running, hands still tied, stumbling full tilt across the uneven ground.

'Ithwalh – kill him!' Ithwalh reacted to the shouted order without a thought. In one fluid movement, he pulled his bow from his back, nocked an arrow and let it fly. The man staggered and plunged forward. Then he disappeared, hidden by a fold in the land.

Rhun stared at the place where he had been. It had been Einion's voice; Einion had shouted the order. He looked down at the figure, still squatting by Tecwyn. 'He was your kin,' he said.

Einion shrugged. 'Not any more. Besides, Tecwyn is more kin to me now than that one ever was.'

As he spoke, a new sound came. The clash of full-scale battle echoing up from the valley below. The sound of a whole army on the attack: the cries of men, the clatter of spears, and the harsh ring of blade against blade, the eerie boom of steel striking on wooden shields.

No more time now to worry about Ysgyrran, or Einion and his kin. Rhun looked around. His little force still numbered nigh on forty. He knew them all by now and they knew him. He raised his voice. 'I made an oath to Cadwallon that I would find Edwin and I would kill him. And I shall – if I can. Will you help me?'

A ragged cheer went up. They were cheering. For him. In that moment he felt that he could do anything, that with these people beside him nothing was impossible.

He called to Einion. 'How is he?'

'He'll live. Llif reckons he'll wake up with a headache, but he'll live.'

They looked at each other.

'Before you ask – yes, I will. It seems he's mine to worry about, the wretch.'

Rhun nodded. No need for more words. He turned to Ithwalh.

'Come on then – show us the way!'

As they came out of the trees at the bottom of the slope Rhun saw that the flames had done enormous damage. There was little left of the old buildings which had stood there, or the trees which had surrounded them, except blackened stumps and smoke. The fire still raged but it had moved, blown by the wind, consuming the old buildings one by one. Men were hard at work trying to fight it. It was clear they would not be able to extinguish a blaze like this but they might be able to guide it. Some were beating at the edges with cloaks and blankets, others had formed bucket lines, drawing water from the river and soaking the grass and bushes in a frantic effort to control the flames and drive them away from the camp.

The noise was tremendous, blaze and battle mixed. 'This way,' yelled Ithwalh. The fire-fighters took no notice of them. As they passed into Edwin's inner compound, Rhun suddenly grabbed a handful of Ithwalh's shirt to bring him to a halt.

'Slowly!' he hissed. 'Let's see what we're up against before we go charging in.'

Ahead was a small knot of Edwin's men gathered around the entrance to the tent. One man was shouting to someone Rhun could not see.

'My Lord, we are attacked!'

And then there stood Edwin, buckling on his sword.

'What?! That bastard Penda attacking us – how? This isn't right – this is our day to attack *him* – how did I not know about this?' He was raging. Almost incoherent.

'My lord, we have been surprised.'

'I can see that, you clod!' He lashed out with the back of his hand and sent the man staggering back a pace or two. 'Don't just stand there,' he roared, 'get back to it and fight them! And no prisoners – kill them all!'

The man stared at Edwin as if he was mad. 'My lord, we are overrun. We'll be lucky to escape with our own lives.'

Edwin stood stock-still. Futile rage and bewilderment chased each other across his face. He stood glaring into the gathering light. The whole camp was indeed overrun. The fighting was everywhere. He glared at the man in turn.

'Go – why are you still here?' he spluttered. Then he turned on his heel and strode back into his tent. Shrugging his shoulders, the warrior gathered his fellows and made off to join the struggle.

Edwin was not left unprotected; a small troop of his personal warriors still stood guard. Muffled orders were heard and a swarm of slaves emerged, running up with carts and started tearing down tents and bundling goods.

At that very moment a cry went up. Rhun and his force had been seen.

Too late for tactics now, Rhun thought, *best just to pile in and hope to overwhelm them.*

'Come on – with me!'

Rhun's force was the larger and he had surprise on his side. The Northumbrians had been on the alert, straining to see the massive struggle as it developed on the far side of the ox-bow lake, keyed up and ready to meet the attack when it came, but an attack from the wrong direction caught them off balance.

Rhun's mind was racing. *Don't let them rally.* 'To me! To me!' he cried.

The two small forces crashed together. Rhun turned a sword aside, and smashed its owner in the kidney with the pommel of his own as he stormed past. The man fell and Rhun was onto the next, leaping and hacking almost blindly at anyone who stood in his way. Meical fought beside him with every bit as much fury, and together they smashed through the thin line almost at once. They turned and rallied. 'Get round them!' Rhun shouted. 'Split them up!' Several were down on both sides, but now Rhun's force easily outnumbered the defenders, and though they were not all seasoned fighters, they had the rage of the offended. Wound up by their anger, they cared for nothing but to crush these northern invaders, these foreigners who had sought to take their land and slaughter their people.

At last Rhun stopped, catching his breath. One glance told him he had the upper hand. Knots of men stood here and there, locked in the fury of combat, indifferent to blood or hurt, but many more were lying crumpled, beyond fighting, perhaps for ever. *Must keep the initiative*, he thought. 'Secure any who still live, don't let anyone get away!' he yelled.

Eryl grabbed at Rhun's sleeve.

'Rhun – I've got to find Balthazar – he may be in danger!'

'Balthazar? Here?'

'He was when I left. His camp was just over yonder.'

'Go to it then! Take Ithwalh.' He clapped Eryl on the back. 'Well, go on!'

Then he turned back to the fight – no time now to worry about Eryl.

'Gethin,' he shouted, 'deal with this lot and see to our wounded! And, while you're about it, stop those people packing any more stuff.'

Gethin stared at him for a moment, then he grinned and waved a hand.

Rhun turned to Meical. He lowered his voice. 'Meical, Cynrig – help me – we've got to find the crown if it's still here.'

As he said the words a cry went up from across the ox-bow. He spun round. A small knot of Ænglisc warriors, bloodied and enraged, swarmed around the curve of the pool. 'Gethin!' he yelled, 'see there!' he shouted, pointing wildly at the newcomers.

Gethin took it all in with a glance. 'Go on – we'll deal with them! Look, there's help coming.' The light was full now, and they could see a wave of men crashing through the encampment no more than thirty paces or so behind the Ænglisc.

Rhun turned back to the tent. Meical caught his arm. 'Edwin's in there,' he said. 'Are you sure you're ready for this?' He held Rhun with his eyes, trying urgently to say something without words. But Rhun understood. Now, at last, he understood.

He threw an arm round Meical's shoulder and gripped him and leaned in, head to head, his mouth close to Meical's ear. 'You're with me,' he said quietly, 'that's all I need.'

He stood back. He grinned. He glanced at Cynrig. 'Come on, the pair of you.'

Rhun thrust aside the curtain and pushed inside. 'Where is he then? And where's that crown – look everywhere.'

As he held open the door flap, the low sun poured in and revealed Edwin standing at the back of the tent, bathing him in the early morning light. It made him look almost holy, bathed in this golden glow. But with the sun in his eyes, it took him a moment to realise these were not his own people. Suddenly he started, drawing in a sharp breath and swore and the illusion was broken. He stood as if transfixed and stared wildly at Rhun.

At last he spoke, his voice a hollow whisper. 'You! But you're dead! I had you killed when I left Mona. I left orders. How are you here now? Are you spirit?'

A tense silence followed, broken only by the small noises of slaves scurrying round pulling out boxes and stuffing them with Edwin's personal belongings, and the din of struggle from outside as Gethin engaged with the newcomers.

But then Edwin saw the sword. Nothing ghostly would glitter like that. That was real enough.

'It *is* you,' he hissed.

'Not fighting your own battles, then? King!' Rhun spat the word in scorn.

Edwin ignored the insult. He drew his own sword. 'I shall just have to kill you myself right now – in fact, I should have done it myself long ago, not left it to others!'

'That's twice I've heard that today – so perhaps you should, but you were having far too much fun.'

Edwin laughed, 'Yes – you are right – it was fun! But now it is over.'

He ran at Rhun.

'All of it!' Rhun cried. He slashed down onto Edwin's attack and beat it back at once. No longer a boy. No longer abject. No longer naked and defenceless. Now he was grown and he was filled with cold anger. He rained blows onto Edwin who could only retreat. The space was cramped. Edwin's foot caught a low stool and he sprawled sideways onto the floor. Rolling away he scrambled to his feet, his sword poised. He was panting but unhurt and far too experienced to let such a chance slip by. Ducking down, he grabbed the stool with his free hand and hurled it at Rhun's head. Rhun ducked in turn, but it distracted him for a split second, and Edwin took full advantage. He attacked with all his strength, a strength which had once been so much greater than that of his young opponent. He cannoned into Rhun who was half his weight and together they staggered back, their blades locked. Rhun strained every muscle and just managed to keep his feet.

Now they stood poised, staring into each other's eyes, every fibre of their beings at full tension. The hate in Edwin's gaze was fuelled by his outrage that he could not easily destroy this boy. But Rhun was no longer the puny, emaciated thing Edwin had left to die on Ynys Môn. He was strong and fit and agile. And quick. Rhun sidestepped, broke the lock, and in a flash he lunged at full force. Edwin parried wildly, sending Rhun's blade aside, but making no difference to the force. The tip of the blade missed Edwin's heart but it caught his left sleeve. It slashed through the material, raising a great welt of blood on the flesh below. Edwin leaped backwards out of reach. He glanced at his arm. The sleeve was soaked with blood. He turned back to face Rhun. He laughed – his sword arm was still as good as ever.

'So – you have learned to fight. I preferred your tears!'

'They were never for myself.'

'Well, they should have been. You may cry them now!' Edwin leaped in again. His sword smashed down onto Rhun's. Sparks flew as the blades met. Now it was Rhun's turn to stumble. His ankle caught against the corner of a chest sending an agonising pain shooting up his leg. He didn't fall, but his guard dropped, just long enough for Edwin to press home his advantage. Reacting by instinct more than experience, Rhun caught the blade on the guard of his own sword and their blades locked again.

'It is over – boy!' He spat the word into Rhun's face. As he spoke he punched Rhun in the stomach. But his arm was weakened by the deep cut it had received, his fist met tensed muscle and the blow fell lightly.

'May be it is – but not for me!' said Rhun through gritted teeth. As he spoke he smashed his knee into Edwin's groin. Two may play at that game. The King of Northumberland, the man who would be Gwledig of all the northern people, screamed and dropped his sword. He doubled up, collapsed into an agonized heap, and lay writhing on the floor, gasping for breath.

Rhun stood over, him panting. The tip of his sword pressed into the soft flesh of Edwin's neck.

'Go on then – what's stopping you?' Edwin spat, his voice strangled by pain.

Rhun stood poised for a long moment while his breathing settled. At last he withdrew his sword and stood back.

'*Na*, I will not kill you. You may live – to remember that how you treat people, so shall they treat you. And that in the end you were defeated by a boy – and one you thought of as no more than a piece of rubbish. I wish you joy of it.'

'You are cruel in the end, Rhun ap Cwyfan,' Edwin croaked.

'You are a Christian, I'm told, so you should know what

the Christians say – whatsoever a man soweth, that shall he also reap. And you have sown nought but tares.'

'Oh, come on! I'm no different from you or your precious Penda!'

'*Na*, he is a king – you are a bully. Which makes you also a coward. I've told you so before, I think.'

'Enough – you have defeated me. So – kill me or let me go. Keep your pious lectures for someone who cares.'

'Give me the crown and I will go.'

Edwin's eyes glittered.

'So that's it – you want the crown. Ha! I might have guessed.'

Once again, Rhun regarded him in silence, his face impassive. But this time his contempt was clear for all to hear.

'Do not think I am cast from the same mould as you, Edwin Two-Face – 'Blessed Friend', indeed – oh yes, I know the meaning of your name, and I spit on it! *Na*, I made a vow to Cadwallon that I would return the crown you stole and that I shall do. Whether you live or die matters less to me, but I shall not be the one to do it unless you force my hand.'

Edwin looked round wildly. Rhun followed his eyes.

'Ah, thank you,' he said.

He walked over to the chest which had been, so briefly, the centre of Edwin's attention. He lifted the lid and looked inside. He pulled out the upper layers and there, nestling among the various items of clothing, lay the crown of Maelgwn Gwynedd. He hooked it out along with a cloak. Wrapping it in the soft fabric, he turned.

'Watch out!' Meical yelled.

Edwin was on his feet. Recovered now, his eyes blazed with hot fury. Before Rhun could react, Edwin lunged at him, his blade snaking out, flashing in the lamp light. Rhun's shirt caught the tip but not enough to turn it fully. It tore into his flesh, scraping along his ribs, carving a bright shallow gash.

'Ha!' Edwin spat. 'That makes us even.'

Rhun staggered, holding his sword as best he could in guard against Edwin's renewed energies. It should have hurt like blazes, yet he felt nothing. Edwin's blade had not cut any vital muscle, but his bloody shirt clung to him, hanging in shreds and hampering his movement.

'Here! Catch!' Without turning, Rhun tossed the crown towards the entrance flap. Cynrig jumped, frantic to catch the precious thing. He caught it in mid-fight and rolled, crashing into a bunch of frightened slaves cowering against the tent wall.

With his left hand free, Rhun had ripped the sodden fabric from his body and flung it at Edwin's face. Meical ran in to join him. Now Edwin fought like an animal cornered in its lair. With the remnants of Rhun's shirt still clinging to him, Edwin swept his sword round in a wide arc, holding it with both hands. The long blade missed them both, but it caused them to arch backwards in defence. Edwin brought it round and down in a smashing blow which caught both their blades and locked all three in a knot. He twisted round and Meical's sword spun away, wrenched from his grip.

Meical scrambled after it, he rolled and regained his feet, and stood poised to renew the attack. Rhun jumped back, but as he did his legs caught against the chest once more and he sat down upon it heavily. Somehow he kept up his guard. Edwin stood between them, for a split second unsure which way to turn. All three paused, each gasping for breath, each watching the other, judging the moment. In that brief quiet they all heard the commotion outside for the first time. There was a noise from the door. The flap lifted and a giant of a man burst in. Stripped to the waist, without any sort of armour, he stood and cried out a challenge, a bloody sword in each hand.

'Face me!' he roared, and his voice was that of a wild beast.

Edwin's eyes glowed in triumph. He laughed out loud. 'See, boy – it is over. You lose. As always! Ha!'

But even as he said it, his expression changed to one of disbelief. The giant at the door stood stock still like a tree. Then his body lurched – once, twice, more. A small ooze of blood appeared at the corner of his mouth and trickled slowly down his chin. Then gently, as if blown by lightest of breezes, he toppled forward and crashed to the ground. No less than six arrows stuck deep into his back.

Time itself seemed to stop. Each man in the tent, slave and warrior alike, stood staring at the dead man as if he were some demon out of the underworld who might suddenly spring back to life. No one seemed able to move, they stood as if gripped by a dark magic. Then Rhun heard a new sound, the noise of ripping canvas. He spun round and caught a last glimpse of Edwin as he vanished through a raw gash in the tent wall.

Meical cried out, 'Rhun – quick – he's getting away!' But Rhun made no attempt to move. He held up his hand, and stood in silence. When, at last, he spoke, his voice was utterly without expression.

'I have what I came for. Let him go.'

And he turned on his heel and walked out.

Meical and Cynrig looked at each other, they looked at the slaves, they looked at the dead man. Then they turned and followed Rhun, bearing the crown of Maelgwn Gwynedd, out into the clean air of a new morning.

Chapter 20

The battle at Meigen was over. Cadwallon ap Cadfan, king of Gwynedd and now, with the exception of Penda, re-affirmed as Gwledig to all present, sat, his elbows on his knees, turning the crown of his fathers in his hands. He seemed reluctant to put it on, relieved just to have it back. He looked up.

'I thank you for this, Rhun ap Cwyfan: you put yourself at great risk to return it. I accepted your vow, though you had no need to make it, and now you have fulfilled this part. But the other? Is he dead?'

Rhun met his eyes steadily.

'My lord, I let him go,' he said.

'You let him go?' said the king, after a pause. But he did not sound angry, just curious.

'I did, my lord. At least, he got away and I did not pursue him. In the end I could not chase him just to kill him, for he would not have come with me as prisoner. I thought it better he live with the knowledge of his defeat.'

'Despite all he did to you?'

'Even so, my lord. To do otherwise would have been to become him. Was I wrong? I would not wish to be forsworn.'

Cadwallon glanced across the tent to where Penda was sitting in silence. As if he sought reassurance. Penda nodded. Apparently satisfied, Cadwallon returned his gaze to the young man standing stiffly before him.

'Not wrong,' he said slowly, 'but you were perhaps – generous.'

Rhun shrugged. Their eyes met.

'He said I was cruel, my lord. It may be so. I suppose he sought honour in death and perhaps he may find it. But I don't think he deserves it.' He paused and stood up to his full height, with just a slight wince of pain. 'Yet, I don't know – in the end he taught me lessons I could have learned no other way.'

There was a moment's quiet.

'Then it is not over,' Cadwallon said. He sighed. 'Well, it was nobly done, and I do not blame you for it. Though, another time, try to be a bit more ruthless?'

'*Na*, my lord. That is one lesson I hope I never learn.'

Epilogue

On high ground overlooking the river, two men sat wrapped in dark cloaks. One tended a small fire.

'Were we right to interfere?'

'I think we could not have done otherwise.'

'It was a risk.'

'Naturally; what is not in these times? But the boy was worthy of it – he trusted his people and took the chance when it was offered and they returned his trust a thousand-fold. We were right not to doubt him.'

'So, a victory for the king. Cadwallon has won.'

'The battle, yes. The war – well, that is still in the balance.'

There was silence between them for a moment or two.

'Yet, he will be Gwledig as was ordained?'

'I believe he already is – although perhaps it will not now mean what it once did.'

'Surely Cadwallon will pursue Edwin?'

'I think it is certain. He will seek to regain all the lands of Cunedda.'

'But he will not succeed?'

'That I cannot see, but I think that time is passed. For one thing I can see – whatever may become of Edwin, and Cadwallon, and young Penda, Prydein is lost as we have known it. It will now change and, perhaps, become merely a story. Those of us who stay here, in these mountains, we will become Cymru and persist only here, on the edge of things. Elsewhere we will become Ænglisc and learn to speak a different tongue and perhaps worship different gods, or at least, the same gods in different ways and by different names.' He paused. 'The land will change, but life will go on, and you and I my friend, and all our kind, we shall watch over it, as we have always done. Come – the next chapter is begun.'

Then they stood up and walked away – gone into the night.

And the fire was gone with them.

Acknowledgements

This would have been impossible to write without the help of several real people and many actual books. But my most deep and heartfelt thanks go to my test readers for their diligence and honesty.

Historical notes

This story is set at that pivotal period in our history when the places we know as Wales and England first became separate entities. Until then we had all been Britons or, at least, Romano-Britons, living in the remains of the province of Britannia. Indeed, many may still have considered ourselves to be Romans, especially the towns-folk. Latin was still the official language of court, law and religion, as it would continue to be.

The Roman name Britannia was derived from the earlier Celtic name Prydein, and from which we later got Britain. The term Great Britain came very much later and means something distinctly different.

The battles of Chester and Meigen are recorded and real, as were their outcomes, although we do not know where the latter was fought. Rhun's activities and those of his friends are fictions. The story of Merlin (Myrddyn Emrys) is myth, and my version is no worse, I hope, than anyone else's. Arthur is not mentioned because his myth would not emerge until several hundred years after the events in this story.

Most people still call these years the Dark Ages. Modern archæologists and historians now prefer to call them Sub-Roman: the time between the collapse of Britannia and the emergence of England, Wales and Scotland. But the Age may well have felt pretty dark to the Britons. We had been Roman for a very long time. Counting back four hundred years from now takes us to the reign of James I – in that time we have managed to have an all-out Civil War, been briefly a republic, experienced the Age of Enlightenment, made and lost an Empire, gone through both Industrial and Technological revolutions, suffered two World Wars, watched men walking on the moon, and entered the Information Age. By contrast, the pace of change in the early first millennium was glacially slow; suddenly to have no Rome must have been an appalling shock and left local power-vacuums in abundance.

But it would be wrong to think that all the Romans simply went away – by that time, we were all Romans, or Roman citizens at least – it was only the administration and the army who abandoned the province, and many of the wealthier citizens who emigrated into Armorica (still within the Empire), enough, indeed, for that place to become known as Brittany. But the majority stayed put, particularly the common folk.

We still had an understanding of law and order, just no centrally organized force to maintain them, and our external borders were under growing threat of invasion. So we reverted pretty quickly into our original tribal regions, and duly went back to fighting amongst ourselves. With the army gone, the people had had to relearn how to fight, particularly those in the south and south east, for they had not been allowed to bear arms since Boudicca's uprising nearly four hundred years earlier, and in some places, not since the Conquest.

We were not without fighting expertise; many retired soldiers had married local girls and had settled here, but when, in the early days, we needed more fighting men we hired mercenaries. This had been normal when we were still part of Rome: Rome had used mercenaries for hundreds of years, many of whom were from parts of northern Europe which they had never been fully conquered, if at all. So we had had Ængels and Saxons (and others) among us for a very long time, especially in the east. I have made Rhun's mother to be partly descended from a member of Rome's mercenaries, who had come as cavalry from what is now North West Gaul. She had a quantity of Roman gladii as an heirloom, which is slightly puzzling as the cavalry used a longer sword, the spatha. Indeed, the gladius had been abandoned in favour of the spatha thoughout much of the army by last years of the Empire. Perhaps Angharad's heirloom had survived merely by being obsolete.

Modern research makes it clear that the arrival of the Anglo-Saxons in large numbers after the fall of Rome was a much less violent and more gradual process than previously thought. There was fighting, of course, but there was no blood bath and certainly no genocide. So do not think of waves of axe-wielding Saxons suddenly invading these shores; it is very much more likely to have been a long and gradual process of assimilation.

Many of the people of the new kingdoms would have been bi-lingual, and possibly tri-lingual. Indeed, some of what we think of as Saxon kingdoms were ruled by men with British names. Wessex, for example, was founded by a man called Cerdic and many of its kings had similarly British names.

Merewalh was the first king of Magonsæte and his name, though Ænglish in form, translates as 'Illustrious Welshman'. He gave all his children English names, which indicates a desire to be modern and part of the new thing, at least among the aristocracy. I have used this mix in naming Rhun's friend Ithwalh.

Macsen Wledig was the British name for Magnus Maximus. He was a military commander in Britannia who in 383 rebelled against Rome, set himself up as Emperor, and conquered Gaul and Spain where he ruled until he was defeated in 388. The name Wledig derives from the word Gwledig, which literally means "of the country". As a title, it was roughly equivalent to Bretwalda – "wide ruler" in Old English, or High King. But these do not quite hold the additional sense of "leader of a kin-folk" which Gwledig does.

Cunedda was said to have been Gwledig from Hadrian's Wall to north Wales until the establishment of the Anglian kingdoms of Northumberland and Deira.

Maelgwn, Cunedda's grandson, established the kingdom of Gwynedd. The plague which killed him and many of his people was a real event, from which Rhun's people fled to find a new home. I have no idea if he had a crown, or what it might have looked like if he did, but I do know that the ornate, richly decorated thing that the word conjures now, is an invention of only recent centuries.

Wales and Cornwall emerged as discrete places when the Anglo-Saxon advance finally cut them off from each other. Cornwall became a recognizable unit with its own kings independent of England, but Wales, being so much larger, never became a unified independent nation for any great length of time. Each spoke a regional variety of 'British', each of which then developed independently. Cornish (largely) died out by the end of the nineteenth century. Welsh has survived as a living language, despite the best efforts of the English, and is growing in usage. Rheged (corresponding roughly to modern Cumbria) also survived for a while, though Cumbrian as an identifiable language is now extinct. No one knows what form the language of the Britons actually took at the time, but we do know that modern Welsh is directly descended from it.

The word Welsh, itself, comes from the Saxon word 'Wealas' which means foreigner or stranger and with an inferred sub-meaning of someone inferior or distasteful, in much the same way as did the word 'barbarian' to the Greeks. The word 'saesneg' meant exactly the same thing in British (with regional variations); nowadays it has a similarly pejorative sub-meaning, and is generally used to mean English or Englishman. About this time, the people who lived in what is roughly modern Wales adopted the word Cymru to differentiate themselves from the rest of the population – it can be interpreted roughly as 'those who live together in these lands'. So I have used the word 'Wealas' as a sort of insult. The words Wales and Welsh did not come into regular use until later, and then only among the English or those speaking that tongue.

And lastly, the very word Celtic is a relatively recent usage. But it remains a convenient label for those people who lived in these islands during the Iron Age; many of whom still do.

People

All the kings mentioned are real, and set in their correct times and places as far as we know them. I have made Edwin into a monster, and Penda into a nice guy. The histories which tell us of them have it the other way round, but one has to remember that they were written by people with political agendas of their own and often what they wrote was propaganda. And my action is not without reason – the Cymru really did refer to Edwin as 'Two-Face', although I have given him a nastier side than maybe he deserved. Penda, on the other hand, was one of Cadwallon's allies at Meigen and famous for his support of the Cymru. His ill reputation came largely from his later wars with his own people, which ultimately he lost, and history is always written by the victors.

Powys had indeed diminished since the Battle of Chester and its kings did adopt Shrewsbury as the capital of a new region they called Pengwern. It was later absorbed into Mercia, and Powys shrank to those lands in, and west of, the border uplands. It has grown again in recent centuries but that is a result of modern regional government organisation and reflects better the tiny population than its political influence. The sub-kingdoms of Wrœcensæte, Magonsæte and Ercyng were all 'clients' of Mercia. (The first derives from the Cornovian centre on the Wrekin, and the second from the Roman town of Magnis.) Yet they were all to some extent independent, and probably a mixed bunch, as they are to this day. Only Ercyng survives as a definable place, although the name is now modernized as

Archenfield. The suffix -*sæte* survives in the modern names of Somerset and Dorset. And, perhaps, in Wrekin-seate, or Wroxeter; though that may share its origin with the likes of Exeter, where the latter part refers to *Castris*: Roman Fort.

The Druids may have survived the Roman attempt to annihilate them; certainly, there are plenty of people who say they did. I don't know, but it seems likely. Likewise, it seems likely that pre-Christian beliefs persisted alongside the growth of what has become known as Celtic Christianity, particularly on the fringes of Britannia, until the arrival of the militant evangelicals such as Augustine, in 596, and the strenuous efforts by the Church in Rome to eradicate what they saw as heresies, which was only officially completed in the Roman coup at the Synod of Whitby. There are still plenty of survivals, such as well-dressing, now dismissed as mere 'folk' practices and superstitions, but which were once central to our pre-Christian belief system. And in many places the beliefs and practices held by the Celtic Christians are seeing a strong resurgence. But one man's religion is another man's superstition. Believe what you will.

Giraldus Cambriensis (Gerald of Wales), an historian of the period, tells us that the Welsh wore only light clothing at all times of the year, breeches and a shirt, often without shoes, and that they would happily go without food for days at a time. He adds that they had little or no furniture, usually sitting on the floor, and that the people would sleep jumbled together in a sleeping area rather than in individual beds. Hardy folk indeed. And I imagine true of all or many of the more remote Britons. I have assumed that the young were hungrier than the adults, as is ever true, and Rhun, though fifteen and thus "come of age", was still young.

Slavery existed everywhere. Most early civilizations were founded upon it. Christianity was technically against it, but in reality virtual slavery survived here (although it was called Serfdom by then) until the Black Death in the 14th century, when so many people died that there was an acute shortage of labour and it was no longer possible to enforce it. Naturally, the rulers found other ways to suppress the people; and of course slavery per se still exists in many forms to this day.

Names

A great many British and Saxon names had specific meanings, usually made from two elements. For examples, in direct translation, Cadwallon means "battle ruler", Talhaiarn means "iron brow" and Angharad contains the meaning "much loved". And you may have been wondering – "Blessed Friend" is Edwin and "Noble Peace" is Æthelfrith. Subjective, no doubt.

Places

Most of the places I describe are real and you can still visit them. In fact, if you are at all clever with a map, you should be able to trace Rhun's journey west fairly easily, athough I have condensed the landscape here and there for ease of narrative, and many of the specific locations are imaginary.

Lenteurde is a genuine archaic form of Leintwardine, a large village west of Ludlow, which really was built over the Roman military town of Bravonium. Archæology suggests Bravonium was burned down in the late 3rd century and not re-occupied for a couple of hundred years, a fact of which I have taken advantage. The road which runs through it is the western arm of Watling Street, the road from Wroxeter (Viroconum) near Shrewsbury to Kenchester (Magnis) near Hereford. Once these two places ceased to be Roman military centres, the road fell into disrepair. Lenteurde is a suitably border-like name, being a mix of both Celtic and Old English roots, and it means 'The fortified place by the river Lent', which, in turn, is an early name for the river Teme. Though a great many modern towns are based on Roman originals, the Anglo-Saxons often avoided all things Roman, often re-purposing their buildings or robbing their materials for re-use elsewhere, and many Roman roads vanished when there was no longer much need to travel between the places they connected.

While the Romans introduced the rectangular house, often with a second floor, they were only common in the more Romanized areas and the towns and villas. It is thought most likely that the pre-Roman round house did not go out of use amongst the Britons and especially in the more remote regions, until very much later. In Anglesey there are the remains of a village of the period, Din Lligwy, in which the houses were round and the workshops rectangular.

Hafren is still the Welsh name for the river Severn. Edwin really did take over a monastery at Trwyn Du and fortify it. Brynach's Holy Well is real, though he is not; it is now known as Ffynnon Gybi or St Cybi's Well. Both Elaeth and his stronghold at Tre'r Ceiri are real, though I invented his tribal centre where Rhun recovers.

I don't know if Cadwallon returned to Gwynedd via Lleyn, but he did go to Ireland. Domnall mac Áedo was indeed king there at the time. Cadwallon was said to have stayed there for seven years, which was far too long for my purposes, but that is the only liberty I have taken with such scant recorded history as we have, apart from inserting my own tale.

Annwm is the Celtic land of the dead. It is closer to the Greek idea of Hades than the Christian idea of Hell; you would find no devils with pitchforks there. It is the land of the dead, not a place to persecute the less-holy-than-thou.

No one knows where the battle of Meigen took place, but local folklore suggests that a big battle of the time did take place where I have set it on the eastern bank of The River Vyrnwy just south of Llansantffraid in north east Powys. There is an ancient earthwork there called Plas yn Dinas surrounded by the remains of an ox-bow lake, in which I have placed Edwin's inner compound. Folklore also says that before the battle Cadwallon had been camped by Hafren. I have made him take over the ancient hillfort Gær Fawr which you can still visit, though I know of no evidence to suggest that he did. There is also a farm near Plas yn Dinas called Hendreboeth which translates as Old Burnt Place, and folklore mentions the burning of an old town of the Romans which was said to have stretched nearly three miles, from there down the river to Bryn Mawr, another nearby Iron Age hill fort. This seems very unlikely and I have not heard of any evidence to support it, but I have taken these two ideas and made them into the range of old buildings which Ysgyrran sets on fire.

Swearing

Duw means God in Welsh, *duwiau* being the plural, and *Iesu Crist* is the Welsh spelling of Jesus Christ. Though no doubt considered blasphemous, both are still in common use as expletives.

Throughout my story the Christians swear by God, and the Pagans by the gods. I have made the folk from the borders use *Duw* or God, fairly randomly, as an indication that they were as comfortable in either language. As many of them still are, though, it must be said, sadly few among those of English stock. Ysgyrran usually swears by the gods, and also uses English and Welsh pretty much at random.

Folklore

The Twylwth Teg, the Gwyllian and Canthrig Bwt are all genuine folk characters. I cannot vouch that they were in currency at the time of this story, but the people would have had a strong belief in such things, Christian and Pagan alike. Magic and the supernatural were strongly held beliefs until very recently, and I am not convinced they have gone very far away even now.

The Pibgorm

The Welsh Pibgorm or 'horn-pipe' is one of the oldest Welsh instruments known.

It is a wooden pipe with six finger holes and one thumb hole, not unlike the recorder but with a reed. There is a horn bell at one end to project the sound, and a horn wind-cap at the other to collect and funnel the wind through a reed. The reed used is a split cane reed (single reed) like that found in the drone of a common bagpipe.

The laws of Hywel Dda (codified 940–50) specify that every master employing a pencerdd (chief musician) should give him the necessary harp, crwth (a sort of lyre) and pibgorm, but there is no reason to suppose that they were not also in widespread use.

My thanks to the Welsh/American band Moch Pryderi for this information.

Sources

Some of the sources consulted during the writing of this book:

Mercia: Sarah Zaluckyj, Logaston Press, 2001

The Age of Arthur: John Morris, Weidenfeld, 1993

Britain & The End of the Roman Empire: Ken Dark, Tempus, 2000

Flame-Bearers of Welsh History: Owen Rhoscomyl, Welsh Educational Publishing, 1905

The Romano-British Peasant: Mike McCarthy, Windgather Press, 2013

The Anglo-Saxon Chronicle: J M Dent & Sons, 1960

Wales and the Britons: T M Charles-Edwards, OUP, 2014

The Emergence of the English: Susan Oosthuizen, ARC Humanities Press, 2019